THE
UNLIKELY
GIFT OF
Treasure
BLUME

PRAISE FOR
Treasure Blume

"This book had me from the very beginning. A charming, romantic read with fun, engaging characters. Loved this one!"
—RACHAEL RENEE ANDERSON, author of *Minor Adjustments*

"Treasure Blume is an instantly endearing, easily relatable character who handles her problems with just the right amount of humor. This book is a perfect rainy-day read—preferably with a cat nearby."
—TRISTI PINKSTON, author of the *Secret Sisters Mysteries*

"Treasure Blume will capture your heart one hilarious misstep at a time!"
—KRISTEN CHANDLER, author of *Wolves, Boys, and Other Things that Might Kill Me* and *Girls Don't Fly*

"Everyone should know and love Lisa Harris. She is undeniably a Treasure!"
—ELSPETH YOUNG, religious artist and illustrator of *Women of the Old Testament*

THE UNLIKELY GIFT OF Treasure BLUME

LISA RUMSEY HARRIS

SWEETWATER BOOKS
AN IMPRINT OF CEDAR FORT, INC.
SPRINGVILLE, UTAH

ISBN 13: 978-1-4621-1026-1

Published by Sweetwater Books, an imprint of Cedar Fort, Inc.
2373 W. 700 S., Springville, UT, 84663
Distributed by Cedar Fort, Inc., www.cedarfort.com

LIBRARY OF CONGRESS CATALOGING-IN-PUBLICATION DATA

Harris, Lisa Rumsey, 1976-
  The unlikely gift of Treasure Blume / Lisa Rumsey Harris.
    p. cm.
  ISBN 978-1-4621-1026-1
  1. Elementary school teachers--Fiction. 2. Love stories. I. Title.
  PS3608.A78318U55 2012
  813'.6--dc23
                              2012033123

Front cover photography by Savannah Woods
Cover design by Rebecca J. Greenwood
Cover design © 2012 by Lyle Mortimer
Edited and typeset by Melissa J. Caldwell

Printed in the United States of America

10 9 8 7 6 5 4 3 2 1

PIED BEAUTY

Glory be to God for dappled things—
For skies of couple-colour as a brinded cow;
For rose-moles all in stipple upon trout that swim;
Fresh-firecoal chestnut-falls; finches' wings;
Landscape plotted and pieced—fold, fallow, and plough;
And all trades, their gear and tackle and trim.

All things counter, original, spare, strange;
Whatever is fickle, freckled (who knows how?)
With swift, slow; sweet, sour; adazzle, dim;
He fathers-forth whose beauty is past change:
Praise him.

—Gerard Manley Hopkins

Contents

Blind Date

WHEN THE DOORBELL RANG, TREASURE BLUME KNEW IT WAS HER blind date. And she also knew he would hate her. She ran into the bathroom to hide.

Her cat Howls had no such premonition. He stopped his tongue bath, ran to the door, and began caterwauling, eager to inspect and greet whomever was on the other side.

Treasure could hear him but couldn't bring herself to follow her cat's example. *Why am I doing this?* she thought. But she already knew; she still craved her older sister's approval—which was stupid. Treasure looked at her reflection in the mirror and made a fish face. The bell kept ringing. Howls kept singing. Treasure kept stalling. She wished Howls was human and could answer the door. But, she decided, if Howls were human, she would have married him and wouldn't be having to answer the door at all.

Mr. Blind Date started to pound. *That's not a good sign.* Treasure had to move. She sighed and willed herself toward the front door. She wrenched it open while the still unseen date was mid-knock. Instead of his face, she saw his raised middle knuckle, which he brought down on her forehead in a swift, spare motion. "OW!" Treasure yelped. She rubbed her head and stepped back. He didn't speak. Not even to apologize.

Treasure decided to pretend like it hadn't happened. "Hi, you must be Steve. Patience has told me so much about you," she said, rubbing her head. Patience had told her almost nothing about Steve except that he

1

worked at the zoo, but Treasure figured that was the kind of nice, generic, pleasant thing you say when you meet someone for the first time.

The guy looked at Treasure. He wore a white linen pantsuit. His nose jutted out from his face like George Washington on Mt. Rushmore. He took a piece of gum out of his pocket and put it in his mouth before he answered. "Then you must be Treasure. I thought you weren't home, since it took so long for you to answer the door."

"Oh, ah, sorry about that." Treasure scrambled in her head for an excuse. What could she say? That she was hiding in the bathroom? That she knew he would hate her? That she didn't want to go out with him and wished that her cat was human so she wouldn't be thrust into the dating world? None of these truths would lower the awkwardness of the moment.

At this point, Howls saved her by squeezing between her legs to meet Steve. He began to shine Steve's ankles.

"Is this your cat?" Steve asked, looking down at Howls. He had wrapped his tail around Steve's knee. Steve gave him a none-too-gentle shove with his foot.

"Well, it might be more accurate to say that I'm his person, but yes, that's Howls." Treasure bent down and picked up the cat.

She could almost understand his obvious distaste for Howls. After all, Howls was not conventionally attractive, as cats go. For one thing, he possessed a loud caterwaul that earned him his name—Howls was short for Howler Monkey. And then there was his appearance. Howls sported a black and white tuxedo coat past its prime, one that looked like it had been rented out too often. He also shed with wild abandon, losing entire quadrants of black and white fur. Right now, for instance, his chest was as bare as if he'd had it waxed. All he needed was a gold eagle medallion.

"Would you like to come in?" Treasure asked Steve as she turned back toward the front room. She felt his eyes rake over her from behind as he followed her into the apartment.

"You know, you don't seem much like your sister."

Treasure ignored his statement. "Take a seat. I need to grab my purse. It's in the other room."

Steve eyed the couch but made no move to sit down. "Looks like it's covered in cat hair. I'll just stand."

"What kind of a zookeeper is afraid of pet hair?" Treasure wondered aloud.

"Reptiles," he said. "I work with reptiles."

"Well, that explains it," commented Treasure, turning away.

Abandoning Steve to Howl's care, Treasure went into her bedroom and shut the door. She closed her eyes and leaned against the wall. What was Patience thinking? Well, that was an unanswerable question. Patience's motto was "strike while the iron's hot." Unfortunately, Treasure's iron had never been lukewarm. But Patience didn't seem to care. She lived and spoke in clichés. And, as a flight attendant, she believed that her travels had transformed her into a guru of knowledge. She had decided that Treasure needed to start dating.

During her last flyby visit, she had shown up at Treasure's door and presented her with a Ziploc full of dirt. Treasure held the bag. "Umm, thanks. I didn't even know dirt could be a gift," she said, holding the door open.

Patience brushed past her and plopped her carry-on bag on Treasure's table. "Oh, Treasure, don't you see? You're the dirt." Only Patience could present a gift and an insult simultaneously. "You see, this looks like ordinary dirt. But it's not. That's Egyptian clay. I bought it in the airport gift shop."

"Exotic dirt. Well, that's different," said Treasure, examining the bag.

Patience pounced on the object lesson. "See, people think you're dull as dirt too. But you could be as exotic as this dirt, if you just broadened your horizons and got out of your comfort zone."

Treasure turned the bag upside down. A trickle of dirt leaked out onto her finger. Either way, she was dirt. She swallowed hard and looked up at her sister. "Fine," she'd said. "You can set me up on a blind date."

And now said blind date was standing in her living room: the man who Patience handpicked to broaden her horizons. Treasure shook her head. Based on his white linen suit (straight out of 1987), and his carefully spread sparse hair, it was obvious that he was all into exteriors. And his reaction to Howls—that bothered Treasure too. Not that she was surprised. But it didn't bode well for her. People who couldn't see past Howls's quirks didn't usually make it past appetizers with her. Howls served as a sort of canary for her dating life. The thought made her snort. Had he been a real canary, he would have been dead.

Okay, Treasure thought. *So it's going to be one of those.* Treasure spotted a tiny piece of paper tucked behind her jewelry box. It was her latest fortune, courtesy of New Fong's Noodle House. "Approach all areas of your life with a bold enthusiasm!" it commanded her.

"Bold enthusiasm," she repeated through gritted teeth. She grabbed her purse and marched back into the front room, determined to make the best of what promised to be the worst blind date of her life.

Steve had drifted into her kitchen. He had picked up a bag of Cheetos on the counter and was looking at the nutritional information critically. "You eat these? They're horrible for you. You'll probably die young because of them."

Jeez, if only, thought Treasure. Instead, she laughed, "Oh, didn't you read about all the preservatives in them? I'll have a shelf life of over one hundred years."

He didn't laugh. Evidently, neither Steve nor his reptiles had a sense of humor. "They also make you gain weight," he added. "And that's something no one needs," he said, looking at her rear end. Somehow, her behind always managed to steal the spotlight from the rest of her body.

"I mean, first impressions count a lot," he said, obviously filled with distaste for the first impression Treasure was making. "Take me for example. I'm very meticulous about my body and appearance. What's the first thing you noticed about me?"

"That your hairline is receding," Treasure blurted out.

Steve didn't respond, although his left eyelid did start twitching. He just stared at Treasure. She'd seen that look before. He had to be mentally running through everything Patience had told him about her during the flight when he'd been transporting a pregnant Boa to Zurich. And really, Treasure knew that all the facts were accurate: 5'5", shoulder-length strawberry-blonde hair, golden-green eyes, slightly pear-shaped. But whatever extra something that Treasure had or was couldn't be pinned down to the facts.

Steve cocked his head to the side. Treasure knew he must be trying to figure out what it was about her that triggered instant dislike in him. He shuddered and made a decision. "Excuse me," he said, taking his phone out of his pocket and putting it to his ear. "Oh, that's terrible," he said. "I'll be there as soon as I can." He shoved his phone in his pocket and turned to Treasure. "There's been an emergency at the zoo. They need me to come in right away."

"That's understandable," said Treasure. "Reptiles have emergencies all the time." She paused. "But it's funny, I never heard your phone ring."

"It's on vibrate."

"Sure it is."

Steve stopped walking toward the door and scowled at her. "I was trying to be polite. I don't know what your deal is, but I'm not interested. Even for the approval of a hot blonde stewardess." He wrenched her door open and jogged down the steps.

Treasure had had enough. "I just pity those poor reptiles having to spend time with you!" she shouted as Steve got in his car and roared away. He didn't look back.

Treasure picked up Howls and scratched him on his mostly hairless chin. "Looks like we're spending the night together again, Howls. Let's put on a movie. You pick."

Treasure went to her room, tore off her first-date sweater set (embroidered with Noah's Ark), and pulled on her sweats. She wouldn't try to call Patience. She didn't really want to talk to her. Instead she texted her. *No go w/ Reptile Man. What were u thkg?* When she returned to the front room, Howls was busy rolling all over any place that Steve had touched. "That's right," said Treasure. "Erase every sign of Reptile Man." She turned on *Brigadoon,* the old musical starring Gene Kelly and Cyd Charisse. She would have married Gene instead of Howls if he'd been available. She loved this type of movie, where everyone not only knows just what to say, but they burst into eloquently worded songs supported by entire orchestras. She and Howls were singing along with Gene to "It's Almost Like Being In Love" when she received a rude phone call from her neighbor three doors down. She paused the movie. "No, Mrs. Johnson, I am not scalding Howls. I promise. I'll keep it down. Good night." She looked at Howls. Her vocal talents were similar to his, in both volume and quality. Her next-door neighbor, Mr. Fong, happened to be deaf. He was easily her favorite neighbor.

In her hand, her phone buzzed with a new text message. *How'd u scare him off? I'll call u.* Of course, Patience would assume that it had been her fault, even though Steve started the date off by knocking on her forehead. She could not deal with Patience now. If she called, she'd want to go through everything Treasure had said and show her each erroneous statement and misstep. Treasure couldn't handle dissection. She deleted the message. Clearly, it would take more than Gene Kelly and Howls to banish this disaster from her thoughts and keep Patience at bay. And she'd already been told not to sing anymore, and if you can't sing along, what's the point of watching a musical? She turned off the movie and looked at the clock. It was 8:30 here in Vegas, so it was only 5:30 in Honolulu. Her best friend, Roxy, would be awake, and she'd be amused by this. She picked up the phone and started to dial.

Roxy picked up on the second ring. Treasure could hear music and voices in the background. "Treas, is that you? What's going on?" Even married and pregnant, Roxy had a busy social life.

"Oh, the usual. Another disastrous blind date. Am I interrupting?"

"No, nothing important. A couple of Lani's friends from the college are over here. They were just leaving. I'll just go say good-bye, then I can talk."

Treasure listened to the mellow tones of luau voices from across the ocean via her phone. This was the first time in her life she hadn't seen Roxy every day. They had gone through twelve years of school (not counting preschool) and then four years of college together. But during their senior year, Roxy had married Lani, an island boy majoring in marine biology. He wanted to return home as soon as they graduated, and Roxy, as always, was up for the adventure. In fact, she'd begged Treasure to move out there with them. "Come find a job here, Treasure. There are lots of elementary schools on the island." But the housing prices and Lani's dislike of her kept Treasure's feet planted on the mainland.

"Even if I could find a job there, I couldn't afford to live there, Rox."

"Live with us."

"Yeah, that's exactly what Lani wants. I think that was the whole point of marrying you, so he doesn't have to share you with me anymore."

"Treasure, you know that's not completely true."

"Granted. I'm sure there were a few other reasons he wanted to marry you. Anyway, I've got interviews set up in Ogden, Elko, Tacoma, and Vegas. What could Hawaii possibly have that these glamorous locations don't?" Roxy hadn't pushed Treasure any further. She let her be. And Treasure loved her for it.

"Okay, Treas, I'm back. Was it another Patience train wreck?"

"Picky, balding zookeeper afraid of cat hair."

"Wow."

"I know."

"That's impressively bad, even for Patience. But I'm not sure it beats the rodeo clown who bought your dinner with food stamps at the truck stop."

"He wore a white linen suit."

"Like the Colonel at KFC?"

"Exactly, but greasier."

"Dish. I want the whole story."

Treasure proceeded to regale her with Howls's antics and Reptile Man's pithy words of wisdom. Roxy laughed until she started snorting. "I'm so glad you called, Treasure, really. The highlight of my day so far has been that I've only thrown up twice. I was throwing myself a pity party. Your story definitely beats that."

"I can help you hang streamers. I felt like throwing one myself."

"Treasure Rhonda Blume. Are you curled up with that wretched cat, watching some old movie?" Roxy hated Howls. It was one thing they couldn't agree on. Howls had arrived on the scene when Roxy and Treasure were roommates at college. Nightly, he climbed a tree and serenaded the entire apartment complex. Several neighbors (Roxy included) volunteered to hunt him down with a BB gun. Treasure had intervened and adopted Howls, bringing him into their apartment, much to Roxy's disgust. In the end, it was hard to tell who disliked who the most. Roxy's dislike for Howls never waned, even after his rehabilitation into a semi-respectable cat, just as Lani's dislike of Treasure never dissipated.

"Put the cat outside to torment others," Roxy said, "and let's get some perspective on this." She regarded Howls as the scapegoat for Treasure's dating life.

Treasure dumped the cat off her lap. He immediately jumped back up. She didn't move him. It was hard to argue with someone who so clearly wanted to be with her. She adjusted the phone. "Okay, perspective, you said."

"Yes, perspective. Think about it. Aren't you happier right now than you would be if you had been forced to endure two hours with this guy at a Benihana?"

"Well, yes. You know how I hate it when the chef pops shrimp in my mouth. I hate seafood."

"You have your talent to thank for this."

"You know I hate it when you call it that."

"Gift, power, blessing."

"Curse, blight, doom."

"Whatever. It saved you from hours of torture and left you with a mildly enjoyable tale to tell your nauseated and balloon-shaped best friend."

"That's true. But we can't give the curse all the credit. After all, my propensity to blurt when I'm nervous or angry should receive some snaps. Combined, they really are the secret to my immense success."

"An admirable talent and a valuable skill then. They both helped you deal appropriately with this narrow fellow in the grass."

Only Roxy would use a dorky allusion to an Emily Dickinson poem. Dickinson was one of Treasure's favorite poets—maybe because she understood about being nobody.

"There's very little grass in Vegas."

"A narrow fellow in a white linen suit, then. And as previously discussed, Gene Kelly is dead, Howls is a cat, and Dickinson cannot be your role model."

"What's wrong with being Emily Dickinson?"

"She never left her house and died a paranoid and reclusive spinster sewing her poems into elaborate books. Tonight's episode does not give you permission to turn yourself into a hermit."

"Look, Rox, I think you've got to give up on the idea of me in a relationship. I know I have. It's just not going to happen. And the sooner you and Patience get over it, the happier I'll be."

"Hey, I'm not setting you up on dates. Have I ever? Besides BriBo?"

Treasure's one and only date in high school was Junior Prom with Roxy and her boyfriend Jeff, and Brian, the boy who was desperately in love with Roxy and went with Treasure just to be near her. Roxy nicknamed him BriBo because all he ever talked about was martial arts and his bo staff skills and his dojo. He droned on all night about his matches and prowess in battle. After that night, Treasure made Roxy promise she'd never set her up on another date ever again, and Roxy (who thought the boy might get a clue about how funny and sincere Treasure was if he hung out with her) had kept the promise.

"No. You haven't. I admit. But still, you get this hopeful tone in your voice when I tell you I interacted with any male over the age of ten and under the age of sixty," Treasure said.

"Yes. Abandon all hope. That's a much better way to live."

"Hurts less. And anyway, I have a plan for my life. I'll be fine."

"Crazy cat lady is not a plan. And I want you to be happy, not just fine."

Treasure looked at Howls. Roxy could always see through her. "Fine. Happiness is plan A. But can I keep crazy cat lady as Plan B?'

"Okay deal. Happiness, plan A. Cat lady, plan Z."

Treasure smiled. She'd rung a concession from Roxanne. Crazy cat lady was on the table. She was halfway there. She already had Howls.

"Thanks for the pep talk, Rox. I feel better, honestly. It was just a tough week with school starting and then this torturous date topping it off. I better go. I have to drive to Mesquite tomorrow. Grammy Blume and the Steppers are performing at the CasaBlanca."

"Wish I could come. I hate being away from you. How can I protect you from stupid people from here?"

Treasure shook her head. "You can't. But talking to you helps. It really does."

"I just wish I could show all those jerks the real you: the you that left me funny notes in my chemistry book. The you that cleaned out the refrigerator in the teacher's lounge on appreciation day. The you that held my hair back while I barfed when I had the stomach flu in college."

"Well, I was the only one who didn't spray a ring of Lysol around you," said Treasure, laughing at the memories.

"Just don't forget that you are so much more than other people think of you. And someday, someone will appreciate you like I do," said Roxy, her voice nasal with emotion.

Treasure heard Roxy blow her nose. It was time to end the conversation before Roxy began to cry. That happened a lot lately. "Okay, now you're getting delusional," said Treasure. "I'm fine. Really. Love you. Go to sleep now."

Treasure pushed "end" on her phone and picked up Howls, who had been rolling around on her lap. "*You* appreciate me, right?"

Howls licked her nose.

Treasure laughed, "That's what I thought. And really, what man could compete with that?" She went to bed, all memories of her bad date erased by the good memories from her friend and the love of one reformed house cat.

2 · · · · · · · · · · · · · · · · · ·

Family Quilt

LOVE HIM, WANNA HAVE HIS BABIES. THE ONLY PROBLEM IS HE *HATES* me!" Treasure belted the song along with country singer Sarah Johns as she sped past the last rest area before Mesquite. It was around 6:00 a.m. And Treasure was hustling to get there in time to watch Ruby's Red Hot Chili Steppers practice. Grammy Blume had hinted that they were working on a new routine.

Up until this year, Treasure had been the Steppers' gopher, handing out water bottles and cueing the music. But now, since she lived a good two hours away from St. George, Utah (three hours with the time change), she had reluctantly resigned her post. Ruby, the choreographer and namesake of the team, begged her to stay. "Honey, no one can gopher like you. I swear you've never missed a practice or a performance, and I know that Beverly would have broken a hip if you hadn't managed to run out on the floor and catch her during that Irish step dance number." Treasure had to agree. What other twenty-four-year-old woman in her right mind would play nursemaid and water girl to a group of crotchety, geriatric dancing divas? Only Treasure. Any other twenty-four-year-old woman would expect to be in the spotlight—not on the sidelines. But not on this team. The Steppers were a semi-elite dance team composed of mature women over sixty-five years old. It used to be over seventy, but they had lowered the age limit when Birdie Thompson moved into the retirement community. She used to be a gymnast and could still do an aerial cartwheel. What a showstopper, Ruby had sighed. But, she told Treasure seriously, she just didn't think she could lower the limit low enough for Treasure to join. It was the age limit that gave the Steppers their edge. "I wish you were fifty years older, honey! What a stepper you'd be!" Ruby had said. Treasure had laughed. She'd often wished the same thing, but for different reasons.

But she loved the Steppers: the costumes, the camaraderie, and the dancing. Oh, the dancing. Treasure would learn every routine, ostensibly to help Grammy Blume (and Velva Lee Stewart, who had early Alzheimer's). But really, secretly, she just loved to dance. When she danced, she didn't think. She liked how each member did identical or complementary movements that contributed to a cohesive pattern. She also loved the sparkle of the costumes and the blare of the music. It was almost like she could be another person when she danced.

Of course, she didn't ever get to perform, but still, she felt completely at home with the Steppers. They even took her on tour. She ate dinner with them at 4:30 in order to get the early-bird specials. She talked with them about weather, crazy teenage drivers, and the shoddy quality of canned goods. Together they hunted down the best prices on hearing aids. She went shopping with them to the mature sections of department stores. Under the tutelage of these ladies, she had lost her loathing of polyester and now regarded it as a sensible fabric.

When Treasure got to the CasaBlanca in Mesquite, she could see the Steppers' old school bus parked out by the golf course. It was hard to miss, since Ruby's hubby, Gary, had painted red flames on the top half. Treasure hurried into the casino and found them practicing in one of the conference rooms.

"No, no, no," moaned Ruby, as they finished the number. "You're all off on that hip action on the chorus. When the music says, 'She hit the floo', next thing you know, sonny got low, low, low, low, low,' you've got to make each hip swivel lower. Like this." She demonstrated in front of the group.

"If I get any lower, I won't be able to get up. Then I'll have to use my medic alert bracelet," said Alice Allen. She had her finger poised over the button.

"Is that a threat, Alice?"

"Just a warning, Ruby."

"Well, you keep your fingers off. Those paramedics would ruin the number."

Just then, Ruby caught sight of Treasure, standing in the doorway. "Hello, sweetheart! Come on in. We've missed you. We've never been so hot and thirsty!"

"I thought you found someone else."

"Well, we did. But he isn't nearly so reliable." Ruby nodded toward the rear of the room. Treasure had been scanning for Grammy but was startled by who she saw instead.

"Randy? What are you doing here?" Her older brother didn't answer. Instead he tossed a water bottle to Ruby (which she nearly missed) and grabbed Treasure in a quick side hug. "Well, I knew that when you left, you didn't want to let the Steppers down. Plus it's a great way to meet women."

Ruby shook her water bottle at him. "Don't you be getting any ideas." She turned to the group. "Let's take five, ladies. You're free to head down to the breakfast buffet. Remember, we need to meet back here at eleven for hair and makeup, then we perform at noon."

As the hot and sweaty grandmas trickled out of the room, Treasure found herself face to face with her Grammy Blume. It was hard to reconcile this vital woman with the withered shell that she remembered from her childhood. This Grammy was dressed in a leopard print leotard with a pink sweatband around her pale blue hair. That Grammy had sat in a La-Z-Boy boy recliner, picking obsessively at an afghan on her lap.

"My girl," said Grammy Blume, kissing her on the forehead. No one ever kissed her but Grammy Blume. She left red smooch marks on Treasure's forehead, but the way she did it made Treasure feel like a princess receiving a token of honor from an ancient queen. There was no one on earth quite like Tabiona Blume.

"Would you like to change, Grammy, before we take you down to breakfast?" asked Randy.

"Take me down? Like I'm a helpless infant? Or a Labrador?" Grammy turned her sharp golden eyes on Randy. He immediately looked down.

"What I'm sure Randy meant was escort you down. He's such a gentleman," added Treasure.

"Humph. I suppose. At least he doesn't ogle us like some of those rowdies."

Randy switched his gaze to the ceiling, trying not to laugh.

Grammy inspected Randy before she continued speaking. "I

thought that might be why he took this job. That and that young Birdie Thompson."

"Grammy," Randy said, exasperated, "she's still old enough to be my grandma! I promise my intentions toward every member of the Steppers are completely honorable."

"Anyway, Grammy, would you like to change?" Treasure broke in, before Grammy could answer Randy.

Grammy sniffed her armpits. "I suppose I am a bit ripe. It could put Randy off his feed. I'll just nip up and change. I'll meet you down at the buffet."

Treasure shook her head as Grammy trotted out of the room and caught the elevator. "She seems perky," Treasure said.

"Really? You think? We've been worried about her since you left. She doesn't seem to be quite as with it without you."

"So that's why you took on the job. What's been happening?"

"Yeah, Dad and Mom bullied me into it. Anyway, Grammy's been having more of those forgetful moments, and a few more hallucinations. Some of the old vultures wanted her off, but of course, Ruby wouldn't hear of it."

"Ruby wouldn't do that to her. Not as long as she can still do the splits."

"Well, the splits might not save her if she has another episode."

"Another episode? Do I want to hear this?"

"Trust me, you do. You know that part in the Shakira song when they all get into a kick line? Grammy was next to Lorna Sims, and Lorna has that thick white hair . . . Grammy started screaming that Orville Redenbacher was trying to kill her. She kicked Lorna in the knee, and half the kick-line fell over."

"Ouch."

"No kidding. Lorna was ready to sue. You know her third ex-husband is an attorney. It took Dad a couple of hours to talk him out of it. Grammy's on probation."

"Jeez, she was doing so well when I left."

"Well, we think that's what triggered the change. She has always been the most lucid and active around you. Apparently I'm a lousy substitute, and she takes out her anger on me. She misses you."

"And I miss her." Treasure's eyes clouded at the thought of Grammy's recent struggles. How could she have left her grandmother? Would she recede back into the unhappy hermit that she had been before? Treasure couldn't bear that.

When Treasure was young, Grammy Blume was just a scary old lady that her father forced her to visit. It was well known that Grammy didn't like anyone much, and after her husband died, Grammy had gone into a ten-year delusional seclusion. She talked to the invisible people in her head and hardly ever went out. She hid from visitors and was likely to meet anyone who dared ring her doorbell with a cattle prod. But that didn't stop Treasure's father from making sure that each of his children spent quality time with her. He diagnosed her illness as clinical depression and prescribed medication, along with weekly visits with her grandchildren. She didn't like it any more than they did. Patience, always a one-woman show, used these visits to talk endlessly about herself to a captive audience. Grammy would usually feign sleep in her La-Z-Boy as a protective measure. Randy seemed to get off easy. He usually played board games with her and her invisible friends. As long as Randy treated her hallucinations with courtesy, the games went well. During Treasure's visits, her main goal was to escape Grammy's sharp eyes by hiding behind a large ficus in her living room. However, she soon realized an important truth: it is impossible to blend in when you are colored like a red gingham tablecloth.

Usually Treasure's dad took mercy on her as the youngest and stayed during the visits. He would talk to his mother, and Treasure would creep into the bedroom to watch television until it was time to go. But when she turned twelve, Dad said it was time for her to go by herself. Treasure remembered the day vividly. It had been, up to this point, the worst day of her life.

"This time, I'll go in with you, but then I'm going to leave and run some errands. She needs to get to know you. Your sister and brother have gone alone for years and she never ate them," her father had said to her.

"She wouldn't eat us. She always looks at us like we smell bad."

"That's just Grammy. She looks at everyone that way. It'll be okay. I promise." Her father couldn't have picked a worse day to institute this new policy. But Treasure was too miserable to argue. Anything would be better than thinking about what had happened at school that day. She surrendered without a fight.

"Well, Bud, I see you've brought your new mistress to meet me. It doesn't seem proper, but then what do I know? I'm just your mother," Grammy had greeted them.

Treasure shrank back, but her dad pushed her forward. "Mother, you know this isn't my mistress. It's your granddaughter, Treasure. And I don't have mistresses. You taught me better than that."

"What kind of a dumb-fool name is Treasure?"

"That's a good place for you two to start talking. I've got to go. Treasure, I'll be back in an hour."

The door closed with the finality of a prison gate. Treasure faced the door. The door was safe, solid, and quiet. It wouldn't say loony things to her. Treasure decided she liked the door. She could spend an hour staring at the door, like a Chihuahua waiting to be let out.

But it was not to be. "Turn around here, girl. You can't stare at that door forever."

"Why not?" Treasure asked the door.

"Well, I've spent a lifetime doing that. Not time well spent, in my opinion."

Treasure turned. "Dad says everyone is entitled to their own wrong opinion," she said.

Grammy cackled. "Does he now? He picked that up from me. I told him that when he was a boy."

Treasure couldn't imagine her father as a boy, forced to live and listen to this woman every day of his childhood. No wonder he became a therapist.

Grammy looked at her with a critical eye. "Well, you seem to be rounding up quite a bit. I hope your silly crazy-naming mother has managed to buy you a brassiere. You certainly need one, with that see-through blouse you're wearing."

Treasure couldn't take it. She crumpled like a used tissue in someone's hand and started to cry.

Compassion was foreign to Grammy. Instead she ordered Treasure to stop. "Turning on the tears is not going to turn back the clock on your bosom, miss."

Treasure ignored her and let out a wail. It was loud enough to frighten the both of them. Grammy feared the police storming her door for animal cruelty (the girl sounded like a deranged parrot). Treasure feared Grammy would try to comfort her.

And Grammy did try. She moved out of her favorite chair and descended on Treasure. Treasure had never seen that happen before. But right then, she didn't care. She was absorbed in the enormity of her sorrows. She hadn't been able to leave them at the door: abandoned with a crazy old lady, mocked and made fun of at school, and blossoming early on top of it all.

Grammy laid a bony hand on her shoulder. It was suddenly clear to her that this child was crying over more than she knew how to deal with. "Come over here, girl, and tell me all about it."

Treasure began, haltingly at first, to tell the story she was too embarrassed even to think about. It was something that she hadn't even put into words yet. She told Grammy how difficult life at Warner A. Higbee Middle School was for her, how hard it was for her to make friends with the kids from the other elementary schools, how everyone she met (teachers included) seemed to dislike her. Sure, she had Roxy, but Roxy was a girl. Since about the third grade, no boy had ever seemed interested in her. Until now. She told Grammy how Petie Peterson had started walking with her to algebra and hugging her whenever he saw her. Roxy started calling him Treasure's boyfriend. The thought made Treasure's cheeks burn. She should have stopped it. She should have realized that there had to be a catch. But it felt so nice for someone to notice her, in a good way, that she let it go on. Until today. Roxy's boyfriend Jeff was on the basketball team with Petie. He told Roxy that the guys were getting after Petie for going out with Treasure. "I've got my priorities in the right place," he'd said smugly, cupping his hands in front of his chest. "So far, she's got the biggest rack in the seventh grade. When that changes, I'll move on. I mean, it's obvious, isn't it? Why else would anyone be with her?" Those mean words had flown from his mouth out of the locker room and into the lunchroom and classrooms. How could Treasure go back tomorrow?

Grammy listened until the gush of words trickled off, then stopped abruptly. She had her arms around Treasure's narrow shoulders. "Wipe those tears. The good news is you won't be news for long. We Blumes blossom early on top, but then we stop. The next headline will be your rear. Blumes are blessed with ample booty. But on top, I doubt you'll get bigger than a B-cup."

Treasure didn't move. Her grammy had just sized her up. Every time she thought the day couldn't get any worse, it did.

"Let's hustle, girl. We've got less than an hour to find you a mini-mizer." Grammy scooted off the couch and trotted toward her room. Treasure was amazed. She'd never seen her grammy move that fast.

She hadn't moved at all by the time Grammy came back, toting the keys to her ancient El Camino, Mullet. She'd had that car since it rolled off the assembly line in 1978. Randy had named it Mullet because, like the hair cut, El Caminos are business in the front, but a party in the back. Treasure could not remember the last time her Grammy drove anywhere. It had to be at least five years.

Grammy jingled the keys in her hand. "It's been too long since I've been behind the wheel. Do you remember the time we put the kiddie pool in the back of my car and filled it with hot water so you kids could have a mobile hot tub party?"

Treasure shook her head, amazed. She couldn't imagine her scary, crazy, stay-at-home grammy doing something like that. She wiped her tears and followed Grammy down to the garage. Her father, she knew, would be horrified if he had been privy to the sequence of events that landed her in the passenger seat with Grammy at the wheel. Grammy looked even more formidable than before. When Tabiona Blume got an idea in her head, there was nobody who would dare to drive it out.

"The first thing we do is buy you a more supportive foundational gar-ment, and then we burn that no good shirt," said Grammy, backing out of the tight space. "But you know, don't you, that that Petie fellow is a snake, right? And what do we do with snakes? Chop their heads off with a hoe."

Treasure liked that image. If only she could fit a garden hoe into her backpack. But it would never get past the metal detectors.

"I'm not the violent type, Grammy."

"Too much of your mother in you, I say. But anyway, what you can't do is listen to him. I'll tell you what you can do. You cut him cold. Stick your nose in the air and act like he's something slimy beneath your shoe."

"But what if . . ."

"But what if what, girl?"

"What if he's right about me? What if there is no other reason for anyone to ever want to be with me. No one seems to like me."

"Gracious, girl, don't go looking for truth among your peers. They're just as stupid as you are," Grammy said as she peeled out of the parking lot and onto the highway.

· ·

That day stood out as one of the key memories of her childhood. How different would her teenage years have been if Grammy had remained a crabby recluse? Ever since that day, she and Grammy had shared a special bond that no one else really understood, and part of that bond revolved around dance. The whole family was mystified when Grammy started dancing. But Treasure wasn't. She'd confided in Grammy that she'd been laughed off the dance floor at the junior high sock hop. Grammy, who had loved dance as a girl, got riled. Soon Grammy and Treasure started classes together at the local rec center, where Grammy had caught Ruby's eye with her astounding flexibility. Ruby knew star material when she saw it. Treasure's memory faded.

Randy looked at his watch. "We better get down there. There won't be much food left after the Steppers go through. I want some bacon before it disappears."

Treasure refocused on her brother and the present. As they turned to walk, she caught sight of someone coming toward her down the hall. "Dad!" she exclaimed, running to hug her father. Her dad had the same narrow nose and sharp features as his mother, but the roundness of his cheeks and strength of his jawline made him look more balanced than Tabiona. He had his cowboy hat in his hand. He looked more farmer than therapist. His face, from the eyebrows down, was a deep sunburned red. But his forehead was fish-belly white. The farmer tan was a silent witness to the hours he still spent in the saddle overseeing the Blume family land. It was only seventy-five acres and about twenty head of horses, but he kept running it, as matter of pride. He returned the hug and smiled into her eyes. "I didn't expect you to be here so early! Did you see Grammy already?"

"We did. We're supposed to meet her down at the buffet for breakfast."

Treasure's dad could always sense when something was wrong with his youngest. "Sweetie, what's wrong?"

"Why didn't you tell me what was going on with Grammy?"

"Well, we figured you had a lot on your plate, what with starting school and all. And you don't need to worry about her. We're here, and we'll handle it."

Treasure rolled her eyes. That was his standard reply for everything. "Where have I heard that before?"

Treasure knew her response stung Bud Blume more than he let on. They both knew exactly where she'd heard it—from him. It was what he'd said to her after the day that Grammy revealed the family curse to the both of them. Treasure's memory of that day was the most vivid of her life.

When Treasure's father returned to pick her up, Treasure had begged to stay overnight. Grammy had just turned on *My Fair Lady*, and they were just getting to the part where Eliza Doolittle fantasizes about killing Henry Higgins.

"Are you sure?" Bud asked his daughter.

Treasure didn't even turn around. "Yep. Pick me up tomorrow."

Bud looked quizzically at his mother. "How do you feel about this?" he asked, his eyebrows arching up into his hairline.

Grammy tossed a few popcorn kernels in her mouth before she answered. Then she glanced over at her son. "Bud, are you all right? You look like did when you stepped on my pet porcupine."

"I'm just a bit surprised," he stuttered.

Grammy hopped up from her recliner and handed Treasure the remote. "Pause that. I need to talk to your dad in the kitchen."

Treasure paused the show, then watched her now nimble Grammy tug her frozen father to the kitchen. She waited until they closed the door, then scooted over to listen to the conversation.

"Mother, you seem lucid. But you're acting crazy. Since when did you care about Treasure?" she heard her father say.

Grammy took her time before she answered. "Bud, this one is special. Did you know?"

"Of course, Mother. All my children are special."

"No, you idiot. This one has the gift."

Treasure heard her dad take a deep breath. When he talked again, it was in the slow, patronizing tone that he reserved for Grammy. "Sure, Mom. What gift?"

"I can't explain it all now, but she must be told. When you come to pick her up tomorrow, bring the blanket."

"What blanket? The one in my office? Mom, are you all right? I haven't seen you this animated since you won the bingo pot at the senior center."

"Yes, your great-great-great-grandmother's blanket. Experience Man-killer's blanket. Your girl needs to know who she is."

"Sure, Mom," said Bud in his therapist tone.

Treasure knew that meant the conversation was over. She had two seconds to move out of the way of the swinging door before Grammy came bowling through. "Your dad is leaving." Grammy said. "Now unpause that movie."

Bud came through the door and looked questioningly at Treasure. "You sure?" he mouthed. She smiled and gave him a thumbs-up. Shaking his head, he walked away looking dazed. Treasure hoped he'd be able to drive home.

The next morning, when her father came back, tattered blanket in hand, Treasure answered the door before he even knocked. "She's in the back bedroom, but she wouldn't come out until you came," she said. The door opened, and there stood Grammy Blume, dressed in a gauzy black skirt and a silver shirt embroidered with rhinestones. Treasure hadn't seen her wear anything but a dingy polyester housedress in years. She recognized the turquoise bracelet Grammy wore as one her cowboy grandfather won in a bronc-riding contest years ago.

"My girl," Grammy said and then leaned down to kiss Treasure on the forehead. She ignored her son. Treasure was amazed. She had never seen her grandmother initiate physical contact with anyone. She swallowed her surprise and winked at her grandma, brazen as a showgirl.

"This can't be the kid that has cowered behind me on every visit," said Bud in disbelief.

"Well, she's a whole new girl now. And so am I," said Grammy. "Now let's head into the dining room."

In the dining room, the blinds were drawn. The only light came from four old candles flickering in the middle of the kitchen table. "Sit," ordered Grammy. Bud and Treasure complied.

"You okay, Dad?" Treasure whispered.

Bud nodded, "I was just calculating how many years of therapy we'll have to undergo as a result of what she's about to tell us."

Treasure shrugged. "Six or so?"

"Bud," Grammy said, interrupting their whispered conversation. "You may unfold the blanket."

The blanket in question was rather unattractive and odd. It was an old quilt, made up of big patches of scratchy brown wool and smaller mystery scraps in oranges, reds, and yellows. Four of the brown patches had been embroidered in a seemingly haphazard pattern. One square bore Xs, one showed a sun surrounded by rays, another outlined the figure of a Dutch girl with a yoke across her shoulders, and the last had lines that mimicked ocean waves. All in all, there were four scattered embroidered blocks on the brown background.

Treasure had always been drawn to the blanket. It was obviously old and had some backstory that Grammy had alluded to, something about the blanket being the record of the family power. She knew what it meant to her dad too. He had often told her the stories of how he and his brothers would wrap up in this quilt on cold nights at their old unheated farmhouse. It was scratchy and unattractive, but it still kept them warm. On days when the world felt too rough and fierce, Bud would curl up under that quilt until its scratchiness drove him back out again. He kept it in his office for metaphorical value.

"Put it up here on the table," Grammy said, moving the candles. Bud caught one end, and together they spread the quilt as gently and respectfully as soldiers handling a flag. Treasure looked at it eagerly. It had been on her parents' bed for ages, until her mother redecorated and mildly suggested that the quilt would be better off put away in the cedar-lined chest in her father's office. "We wouldn't want it to yellow and age because of the sunlight," she'd said. Treasure never bought her mother's polite excuse for banishing it. For one thing, the quilt was mostly brown and yellow, and it had been in the sunlight its whole life. The real reason, Randy had told her one day, was that Mom thought it was horrendously ugly. Everyone did—except Treasure and her father, and Grammy Blume.

"This square here," said Grammy, pointing to a square near the bottom right-hand corner. "This is Treasure's square."

"Treasure's square for what?" asked Bud.

"Hers. To record her life."

Bud looked at his mother as if she had just announced (as she had several years ago) that she had decided to go with the aliens if they came again. "But it's an heirloom," he said. "You don't go changing an heirloom."

"You do when you're the heir."

"I don't want her poking holes in my quilt. That will destroy the value. And this quilt means something to me."

"The value in this quilt lies in what it will mean to Treasure. That's the whole reason for its existence. It isn't really yours. I thought that you were the end of the line, when I gave it to you. Now I see you were just a custodian. "

"What about this square, Grammy?" asked Treasure. She pointed to a square that had noticeable punctures. It was obvious that stitching had been picked out. Treasure could almost make out a pattern, something like a star perhaps, but it had been abandoned.

Grammy's attention snapped back to her granddaughter. She swallowed hard. "Well," said Grammy, "that one is mine." She bowed her head and stroked the fabric. "The time has come for me to tell you the story. I never thought I would have to. I thought I tricked the gift. But here we are, so I'll start at the beginning." She pulled out a dining room chair and perched on the edge, her hands holding the seat steady, as if the chair might buckle beneath her. Then she closed her eyes and began to talk.

· · · · · · · · · · · · · · · · · · · ·

The Story of Experience Mankiller as told by Grammy Blume

This quilt was started by your great-great-great-grandmother, Experience Wheeler Mankiller. When she was twenty years old, she decided to leave England and strike out on her own in America. People tried to warn her about the difficulties she was facing as a single woman, but she disregarded them. She was strong. She survived smallpox as a child, even though her parents had died. She had no prospects in England. So she crossed the ocean, bought a team of horses, and joined a wagon train, bound for the promised land in the West. It was not an easy journey, especially without a husband. She frequently fell behind. Instead of helping her, the other families on the train began to resent her. There was just something about Experience that rubbed people the wrong way. The final straw came when the train entered hostile Indian Territory, and Experience's horses got sick.

Experience and the rest of the train waited for two days for them to get better. Each night, they could hear the drumbeats from the nearby Indian encampment. The drums seemed closer and louder each night. Finally, the captain had had enough. He threw down an ultimatum. Either Experience could leave the horses and get in another wagon, or she could stay here alone. The train would pull out at first light. Experience was a stubborn woman. Those horses were the only ones on the whole trip who had ever been kind to her, she argued. They were her best friends, she said. She dug in her heels and refused to come. The captain made good on his promise, and the train left.

Experience didn't have time to fret. She had her horses to nurse. She had just gotten them back on their feet when the neighboring Indians attacked, painted and whooping. That raised Experience's ire. She grabbed her gun and raised it above her head. "If you so much as scare my horses, I'll scalp you with my teeth," she yelled. She must have been a frightening sight, with her blotchy, pock-marked face all red with anger. The braves halted their attack. Their whooping stopped, and they turned around and hightailed it out of there. Experience was surprised but grateful. She fell to the ground and prayed in gratitude.

What she failed to notice was that one brave had stayed behind. He watched her from the bluff above her camp for the rest of the day. At sunset, he made his way down toward her. She drew her gun, but she was so intrigued by his appearance that she didn't shoot. His skin was as white as hers. He spoke to her in English; otherwise, she would have screamed. He looked at her and smiled. He was a medicine man, he explained. His light skin gave him strong medicine, and he could see that she had strong medicine in her skin too.

"I don't know about that," she said.

He got off his horse and approached her. He touched the scars on her face. "You lived through the pox once, and you lived today. These scars saved your life," he said.

Experience knew she shouldn't let strange Indian men touch her, but he seemed to have cast a spell on her. She didn't move. "So they thought I carried the pox?" she asked. "That's why they ran?"

The Indian didn't respond. Instead he placed a shaking hand on her head and told her that she was one of the gifted ones, blessed by the Gods. "These scars are the sign of the deeper gift," he said. "You trigger fear and dislike in all you meet."

"That's not a gift. That's a curse," she told him, lowering her gun.

"Not so," said the medicine man, for he knew better. "Not only will it save your life, it will also fill it with truth. For no one who gets close to you can deceive you. Your gift will drive the impure away. Those closest to entering life and leaving it will not feel this dislike at all." He went on to tell her that this power would wane after her sixty-fifth year. He also said that she must count how many times the gift blessed her life. Then the gift would continue through her descendants, from the third daughter to the third daughter. If she did not count, then it would prove to be a curse throughout the generations that followed her.

Experience snorted. "What descendants? No one has ever wanted to marry me."

The brave smiled again. "But I do."

Well, Experience fainted like her sick horses. But the brave wasn't worried. He just picked her up and took her to his camp. When she woke, he was tending her as patiently and kindly as she had tended the horses. She decided to marry him and experiment on his words. She began to count each time she felt blessed by this gift. Together, they built a new life. He left the tribe to be with her and built her a cabin. They ran a trading post for years, Mankiller's Landing.

· · · · · · · · · · · · · · · · · · · ·

"This is her square," said Grammy, pointing to the square with the Xs. "Each stitch represents a blessing."

"There are so many," said Treasure in wonder.

"Over a hundred and fifty. Now, Experience was the third daughter in her family. And she had three daughters. She named the youngest Thankful, as a reminder of this gift. When Thankful was born, Experience worried that she would bear the pockmarks that were the sign of the gift. But she was born with skin as fair as yours, Treasure. As she grew older, she did get freckles, but not too many since she wore a bonnet most of her life. The rest of us with the gift have always had freckles.

"Experience realized Thankful was not like her other children. She took an immediate dislike to certain people. And it wasn't based on attractiveness, either. Many handsome men were called ugly by Thankful. And the man she married definitely wasn't handsome to most. He was a pudgy middle-aged blacksmith. But Thankful was drawn to him, in spite of his appearance, and always spoke of him as the most handsome man she had ever known. Experience realized that Thankful bore the gift."

"But it wasn't the same gift," Bud protested. Both Grammy and Treasure had forgotten that he was there.

"Well, they aren't identical, the gifts. They're more like variations on a theme. And Thankful got a nice benign strain. She lived a happy and joyful life with her plump husband. Her square is the sun, because of the brightness that the gift brought to her."

"Even more stitches than on Experience's square," said Treasure.

"Well, yes. Like I said, Thankful's gift made her life happy and bright, without causing pain. That's rare. Not everyone deals with it as well as she did." Grammy looked over the head of her granddaughter and met her son's eyes.

Bud glared back his mother. "Why are you saying these things? It's crazy. And it lacks empirical evidence. I should grab Treasure and run for the door." He made a move to stand, but Treasure put her hand on his arm.

"Let's hear the rest of it," Treasure said. Grammy's topaz eyes bore into her. She felt a jolt of recognition. She knew her grandmother wasn't crazy. And she knew she wasn't lying.

Grammy turned her eyes back to the quilt. "And so it goes. The gift is passed from the third daughter to the third daughter. This square," she pointed to the Dutch girl, "is my grandmother Hope's square. And this one," she said, pointing to the square with the ocean waves, "is my mother's. The bright scraps are the children who are born without the gift. You see how by my square there are three bright scraps? One for each child I bore: Travis, Trevor, and your father, Bud."

Bud wrinkled his brow. "Then how . . . ?"

"How did Treasure wind up with it? I just don't know. I thought I'd tricked the gift, by having three boys. And then you had three children, but with Randy in the middle, I thought we were safe, since it's a third daughter thing. Do you see why I thought you were the end of the line? I really have no explanation for how Treasure wound up with it."

"Grammy, how come there is nothing on your square?" Treasure asked.

Grammy took her hand. "Well, girl, I told you how the gift wasn't always kind, right?"

Treasure and Bud both nodded.

Grammy sighed. "Well, my gift was like Thankful's variation, only not benign. I couldn't cope with it the way that she did. I took an immediate dislike to everyone I met. And it made my life miserable. I spent a lot of years as an unhappy hermit because of this gift. And so, I haven't finished mine."

Treasure looked at Grammy with new eyes. This explained so much: why she disliked Treasure's mom, Harmony, so much, why she shied away from interaction with anyone, why all Treasure's uncles had cut off all ties with her. Grammy had become a recluse, fearful of strangers, hidden away on the family ranch until Treasure's dad insisted that she move into town so he could keep an eye on her.

"Really, I blame this gift for your father's death, Bud." Grammy's voice cracked when she spoke.

"Dad died herding cattle in a storm. I don't think this quilt can generate freak lightning," said Bud.

"Well, no, but I'm the reason he went away so much. He had to live away from me because I never could completely get past my dislike. It seeped out in a thousand little mean ways that I regret so much now. I picked out my square on the night that he died. But I've paid for my meanness," she said, wiping her eyes. "Paid for it with a miserable and lonely life."

Treasure stared in horror at her Grandma. It was just starting to dawn on her. This wasn't just Grammy's story. It could be her story too. Was this her future? It seemed as grim and dour as Grammy's old housecoat. She couldn't sit still. She stood up and blurted out, "And now you're saying I have this gift? What a lousy, stinking gift. How can you even call this a gift?"

Bud rushed in to comfort his daughter. "It will be okay, Treasure. We'll handle this."

Grammy broke her gaze with her son and looked at her granddaughter. She sat up square. "You've got to see it as a gift," she said. "It can bless your life. My problem is that I never used it properly. I just got into the habit of disliking everyone and not seeing beyond it to sort the sheep from the goats. That's what you're supposed to do with it. That's how Experience and Thankful used it. The goats won't want anything to do with you."

Treasure searched her mind for the parable of the sheep and the goats. She remembered it vaguely: sheep good, goats bad. Then she saw the obvious flaw. "But neither will the sheep!"

"Sheep are stupid, anyhow. Trust me, girl. I did have blessings from it. I will embroider my square yet. " She patted Treasure's hand. Treasure fought the urge to kick her.

"And so what does this mean for Treasure?" asked Bud.

"Well, from what I can tell, after talking to her, she has an opposite gift from mine,"

"You mean she likes everyone she meets?"

"No. The other kind of opposite. Closer to Experience Blume's original gift. My guess is that everyone Treasure meets takes an initial dislike to her. Would you say that's the way it is, girl?"

Treasure nodded miserably. What Grammy said was true. She didn't want to kick her anymore. She felt panic and anger, yes, but she also felt some relief. This thing she had struggled with as long as she remembered was finally real. She'd felt it tugging on the fringes of her life every time she met a new adult in elementary school. But now, at junior high, she felt it face-to-face every day.

"But you didn't dislike everyone, did you? Aren't there parameters around this gift?" asked Bud. "Let's pin down the facts, whether this is true or not."

"Well, yes, as far as I can tell. It's not like this gift is a person that I can hold a conversation with. But I'm guessing her experience will be similar to mine. The dislike will be strong with adults, but more especially with teenagers. I could never abide teenagers. Babies, little children, and geezers won't feel it at all. They seem to be outside the boundaries. At least they were for me."

"Does this mean that Roxy won't like me anymore?" Treasure tried to ask the question, but her voice wavered. She wished she had a disease instead. People sympathized with diseased children.

"No. Your Roxy is safe, since she met you before she hit puberty. For some reason, this gift hinges on puberty. It all depends on what age people are when they meet you for the first time. So, generally speaking, anyone who meets you before they're twelve, or after they're sixty-five won't feel the dislike. Like the Shaman said: anyone close to entering or leaving this life—"

Treasure interrupted. She just wanted her grandmother to stop saying the word *puberty*. "So Roxy is fine, and so is Randy. But Patience was twelve when I was born. This explains Patience." Treasure thought for a moment, then turned to her father, "But what does that mean about you and Mom? You both met me after you hit pub . . . after you were twelve. Do you dislike me too?"

Bud looked at his daughter. "Of course not, honey. We love you. You know we do," he said automatically.

"But you haven't always," said Grammy Blume.

Bud put his head in his hands.

Treasure watched her dad's face, silently begging him to deny it. He never lied to her. Ever. For every second of silence that ticked by, Treasure felt like she was free falling, and there was no safe landing.

Finally, he spoke. "That's another five years of therapy right there," he said, glaring at Grammy.

Treasure's eyes welled up with tears. Her parents hadn't loved her at first. Wow.

Grammy started to talk. "You never liked babies much at all, did you, Bud? But you always got over it. It was Harmony's bad reaction that should have been our first clue."

Bud looked up into Treasure's eyes. "Don't cry, sweetheart. I always get along with kids better when they aren't babies. Babies are plenty of work, and sleepless nights. But as a dad, I never let myself dwell on it. And I learned to love you within a week. It was your hair that won me over, your soft strawberry blonde hair that waved like a sea anemone— and your solemn little unblinking eyes." He took Treasure's hand in his. She shook it off.

"What about Mom?" she said.

Grammy clucked her teeth and stood up.

Bud reached for Treasure's hand again. This time she didn't shake him off. "She had real bad postpartum depression. She was so sad. And we didn't know why. I took her into you and told her that she'd learn to love you. And of course, she did. Fast. You can ask her about it yourself, when we get home."

Bud turned to his mother, scowling. "'You'll learn to love her.' I wish I had a block on that quilt to count how many times I've told people that about you."

"Now, Bud, don't be spiteful," said Grammy.

"You've got some nerve," said Bud. "Calling me spiteful, after the bomb of hocus-pocus you just dropped on my youngest girl."

As her father lost his cool, and her grandmother began to screech,

Treasure zoned out. It was like she was looking at the scene from far away, through a telescope. From this safe distance, she thought about all she'd learned. Could this story be true? It was crazy. And yet . . . Yet, it had the ring of truth about it. Treasure just felt it. It was as true and as real as the earth rotating round the sun. Deep in her soul, she knew that it was true. Now she would have to live with it.

Grammy's voice jolted her. They had stopped arguing, and now Grammy was talking to her. "What you've got to remember, girl, is that although people may take an initial dislike to you, that doesn't mean they can't get over it, if they try. And if they're good people, they'll try. That was my mistake. I never got beyond dislike with many people, and after a while I just stopped trying. Talk about sheep and goats. I was a goat—the goatiest of goats—right up until yesterday when you came by and stared at my door. Good people, true people, like your mother and father, will get beyond it and love you. That's the reason that this is a gift. It makes it so only the true of heart can get close to you. Remember that. I say, take it for what it's worth and see the beauty that unfolds for you because of it. You may find that you have more stitches on your square than Thankful and Experience combined."

That night, as she and her father drove home, Treasure sat with the quilt on her lap, running over the embroidery lightly with her fingers. "Every stitch a blessing," she murmured.

Bud looked over at the vulnerable little figure. "You're not alone in this," he said.

She looked up at him with surprise. "I know. I've got you, and Mom, and Randy . . ." she said.

"Not just us," he said, reaching out to cover her hand with his. "You've got all these blessings here. The lives of all your grandmothers and great-grandmothers."

Treasure yawned and tried to picture the faces of the women behind the stitches. She tried to imagine their hands as they embroidered, wishing that they could reach up through the threads and offer her the hope and support that the stitches represented. She ran her fingers over the puncture marks on Grammy's square. "Dad," she asked. "Grammy said to see it as a blessing. But does Grammy really believe that herself? If she had, wouldn't there be stitches on her square?"

Bud didn't answer.

Twelve-year-old Treasure couldn't reason it all through. Instead, she wrapped the quilt around her.

Bud finally found words. He just kept repeating, "It will be all right. We'll handle it," as if saying it made it true.

Treasure fell asleep with her dad's words running through her head, her hands stroking the blessings of her great-grandmothers.

. . . .

After breakfast at the CasaBlanca, during which Grammy Blume complained loudly about the quality of the link sausages before going to squeeze herself into her uniform, Treasure and Randy went to find their mother before the performance started. Treasure recognized her mother, Harmony, from across the room. She was a short, round lady with chin length blonde hair, wide blue eyes, and deeply etched laugh lines around her mouth. As a girl, people were constantly mistaking her for a Swedish exchange student. She was edging toward a slot machine. "Mom!" Randy and Treasure yelled together. Harmony turned around, looking guilty. "Okay, you've caught me red-handed. Or should I say, empty-handed, since I just lost two dollars." She smiled as she embraced both of her children. "But I'm sure I'll have better luck now that you're both here." She turned back to the machine. Treasure pulled her around and twined her arm around her mother's waist. "No you don't. We're here for some family bonding. What would Grammy Blume say if she saw you gambling?"

"Probably that I was squandering the family fortune, and teaching you guys the devil's ways," she said, chuckling. There had been a time when what Grammy might say about her ruled her world. But the years had softened them both, and she spoke without malice.

After Bud and Treasure had shared the story of the gift with her, Harmony gained a new understanding about the two women she was sandwiched between. She didn't really pay much mind to the gift, though. If you asked her, she'd tell you that each of her children was gifted. And Harmony had always worked to see the good in everyone, even her mother-in-law. This idea was something she also tried to teach her children. Everyone has something good about them, she'd say. Even that Simon Cowell has beautiful teeth. She put her arm around Treasure's waist and gave her a squeeze.

Treasure smiled back. It was almost impossible not to feel good around her mother. For a lot of women, becoming like their mother was their biggest nightmare. But Treasure couldn't relate. How she wished that she was more like her mother! She'd quickly trade her special gift for her mother's easy confidence and ability to turn strangers into friends. Every time Harmony went to the grocery store, it took at least two hours, even if she just went to get milk. Inevitably, the clerk or the deli man, would start chatting with her about fresh lettuce, or the black forest ham, and she'd end up invited over to dinner or asked to a baby shower. It absolutely baffled Treasure, but her mother hardly thought about it. She just went through her life, scattering seeds of comfort wherever she went.

"Now, where is your father?"

"He's finishing up breakfast and talking to Grammy. He's urging her to take medication again."

"Well, that conversation is bound to go badly. Randy, will you go find him?"

As Randy walked off, Harmony's gaze settled on her youngest child. "Well, how was your first week of school? I've been dying to call you, but I knew you'd be busy, and I didn't want to bother you. I've saved up all my questions, knowing I would get to see you this weekend."

Harmony was an elementary school teacher, just like Treasure. Only Harmony had twenty years experience and had formerly been the teacher of the year for the state of Utah. In fact, Treasure had been a fifth grader in Harmony's class. That year was one of the bright spots in Treasure's education. It was one of the few times in her life that she knew that the teacher really liked her and cared about her. But it wasn't just because it was her mother. Harmony made every kid in her class feel that way. She genuinely loved each student, even the ones with ADD. They're the ones who need me the most, she'd say.

"Do you love it yet?" her mother asked.

"Ask me again in another month. But I survived."

"Well, that's a start. How's your classroom?"

"Out in the trailers."

"Well, I guess that's to be expected, since you're a first-year teacher. I know I didn't have a decent room my first year. But it has air conditioning, right? In Vegas, you'll need it."

"Oh, we're supposed to have it, but it's broken, and I don't think getting it fixed is a high priority for the secretary."

"Bring in fans, and take the kids to the library as much as you can. If I were you, I'd notify the parents. The secretary will hop to it if the parents get fired up."

"Well, so far, that's sort of the problem. The secretary doesn't hop. She commands, and we hop. And most of the parents don't seem willing to get involved. A lot of them work weird hours, and lots of them don't speak English. I'll send a note home, though."

"A note won't do it, Treasure. Face-to-face is so much better. If you can start a friendship with them, it's going to make your job so much easier."

Treasure looked at her mom, waiting for her to realize why face-to-face wouldn't start friendships for her.

Harmony stared back at her, daring her daughter to use her gift as an excuse. "Treasure, that old story doesn't have any power over you. I know you've got good people there. Talk with the parents. The more times you talk to them, the faster they'll support you. And if they understand that their kids can't learn in that environment, then they'll jump on your bandwagon."

Treasure pictured her bandwagon, hay in the back, her name stenciled on the sides. She stood alone on the top, beckoning for someone, anyone, to join her. No one did.

She nodded and smiled at her mother. The smile didn't mean anything, but it made her mother feel better. *Really*, she thought, *Mom is giving sound advice, advice that would work in any normal situation.* The parents at her mother's school (the school that Treasure had gone to and student-taught at) were more like a militia than a PTA. If there was a problem, those parents would saddle up and ride into conflict in defense of their kids. The entire community rallied around the children. Treasure had seen it happen. But Treasure knew it wouldn't happen in her case. Las Vegas was one of the fastest growing school districts in the nation, and she taught in one of the toughest schools. Boundary lines shifted each year to ease overcrowding. At least a third of the students didn't even have the same address from one year to the next.

Treasure didn't want to go through all this here and now with her mother. It would just reinforce Harmony's conviction that Treasure should have stayed in St. George. They all wanted her to stay—her mother, her father, her brother, and especially Grammy Blume. They couldn't understand why she was so gung ho to strike out on her own.

Her little band of family had always tried to break trail for her. Each had their assigned roles. Randy helped her buy a car since the dealer would probably rip her off. Roxy handled grocery shopping since the baggers always smashed her eggs. Dad took her out to dinner and charmed the waiters so they wouldn't spit in her food. But in the last year, her mother did the most of all, landing her a job as a student teacher at her own elementary school. Despite a bad interview, Harmony persuaded the principal to select Treasure as a student teacher as a personal favor. And every time Treasure had a difficulty last year, Harmony would sail in like a fresh breeze, soothing bruised egos and laughing away tension. Because of Harmony, Treasure's student teaching hadn't been the gruesome experience it might have been, given her unique talent.

Since the day that Treasure and her father had told their family about the quilt and the conversation with Grammy Blume, they had all worked to protect her, even her mother, who pooh-poohed the whole notion of the gift. Treasure had to give them credit, though. They moved like professional basketball players running a zone defense. *I guess that makes me the basket*, Treasure thought glumly. But she was tired of being the basket: always stationary and vulnerable. No more, she had decided. She wanted to try and see if she could do this whole living-on-her-own thing. What would it be like, she'd wondered, to live in a place where she wasn't automatically introduced as "Mrs. Blume's daughter" or "Patience's sister" or even "that quirky Blume girl." She didn't know, but she wanted to try, and that's what had led her to Vegas, two hours and a world away from St. George, Utah.

"Look," she said, pointing. "There's Dad and Randy. They want us to come down there. The show's about ready to start."

3 ....

Show and Tell

"WE WERE SAVING THAT SEAT," SAID THE TALL, SLEEK BRUNETTE AS Treasure sat down at her first early-morning faculty meeting.

Treasure looked at the other teachers at the table, a knot of glossy, no-nonsense women in their early thirties. She knew she was in the right place. In the middle of the table was a sign that read "First Grade." There was only one empty chair.

Treasure rolled her eyes and plopped down in the chair. "Yeah, I get that all the time," she said. She had ridden the bus to school since junior high. She refused to be intimidated by the whole saved seat saga.

The brunette's eyes widened. Her authority had just been challenged. She eyed Treasure like she was roadkill. The other teachers scooted closer to the brunette. "The librarian usually sits with us," she said.

Treasure craned her head. "Isn't he over there, sitting with the fourth-grade teachers?" she asked.

The brunette didn't answer directly. Instead she reached into her purse and got out some hand sanitizer. She rubbed it vigorously into her hands and up her arms, like a surgeon. Then she passed it to the other women at the table, who followed her lead and did the same. She did not offer any to Treasure.

Treasure was unsure what kind of ritual this was, but she definitely felt unclean. Would they make her carry a bell like lepers in New Testament times? *That might actually work*, Treasure thought. At least she wouldn't have to talk to people as much. But she didn't have long to muse.

The principal, a large black woman with hair that bristled, stood up to start the meeting. She gave Treasure a curt nod of acknowledgement before beginning.

Treasure swallowed hard. She knew she would be watched during this meeting. Getting this job hadn't been easy. After graduation, she had peppered the West with resumes, recommendations, and grammatically correct cover letters. And since she looked better on paper than in person, the results were overwhelming. Forty-three schools had asked her to interview. Forty-three schools had turned her down after those interviews, with little or no explanation. After number thirty-five, Harmony had begged Treasure to let her pull some strings in her own district. But Treasure was adamant. She wanted to get hired on her own. It all boiled down to one last chance, with Las Vegas.

A teacher crisis, that's what Brian Williams said on *Nightly News*. In some locations, Las Vegas was suffering from a teacher crisis. They were begging anyone with a college diploma to commit to teaching for a year. The government would forgive all student loans. The district would pay for certification. And if you happened to have a teaching degree, you were practically guaranteed a job. Most of their hiring could be done online, Brian said. The last two statements, that's what sold Treasure. Anything she could do before she had to meet someone face-to-face increased her odds of getting hired. And so, six weeks ago, Treasure went to her forty-fourth interview, wearing a Columbia blue polyester skirt with her Winnie the Pooh sweater set.

The entire episode had started badly. Treasure had assumed the principal was the secretary and asked her if he was usually late when conducting interviews. The bristle-cut woman stared at her. "I am the principal. I was just looking for a paper clip out here." She stuck her hand out. "I'm Anita Bower. Let's go into my office," she said, getting up and opening the door marked *Principal*.

Honestly, it was a marvel that the interview had continued and that Treasure had landed the job. She still couldn't believe it. She would make this work. She would show Anita that she had made the right choice in hiring her.

Anita clapped her hands together and began to speak. "We'd like to spend this time in our grade groups, making sure that we're achieving some coordination in our efforts. I'm asking our veteran teachers to take the lead on this, but remember that our newcomers have a lot to con-tribute too. By the end of the meeting, we're going to ask you to present one idea you plan to incorporate in each grade level. All I ask is that the teachers be unanimous in support. Bonnie and I will be around to check your progress."

Treasure hoped vehemently that Anita would be the one to check on the first-grade group. She feared Bonnie, the senior secretary, the way she feared applying for a car loan. Bonnie was the Queen Bee of the elemen-tary school hive. She made sure that everyone knew that her brother was the superintendent, and she used that knowledge to amass power beyond the scope of a traditional secretary. She'd let some bomb drop, like the fact that there would be a ten percent pay cut in teachers' salaries next year, then add smugly, "At least that was dinner-table talk last night with Bob."

As a mere drone, Treasure tried to steer clear of Bonnie. She kept her head down and did her work. She even ran her own copies at night, after Bonnie left. And she wasn't the only teacher who feared her. She'd over-heard a couple of sixth-grade teachers talking about it. "Stay away from her, that's my plan," one said. She waited until she could see Bonnie's garishly-dyed helmet of hair bobbing away from her before she faced the teachers at her table.

"Well, girls, isn't this just what we were talking about?" said the bru-nette. She was obviously a veteran. "Most of us are doing that anyway. I know that you and Cathy follow the same lesson plans that I do, Kristen."

"And so do I," chimed in the last teacher, sitting kitty-corner from Treasure.

"Aren't you loving the Shel Silverstein poems? Well, I guess that means that we're all on the same page, except for . . ." She pointed at Treasure. "I'm sorry. I don't know your name."

"Maybe because you never asked," Treasure blurted. She noticed that the woman's hair was braided so tightly it seemed to be trying to pull her eyes off her face. "But it's not a big deal. I'm Treasure. Treasure Blume." She waited for the teacher to introduce herself.

She did not. Instead, she hid a laugh behind her hand. "Well, I'm sure I would have remembered a name that . . ."

"Distinctive?" Treasure finished for her. Fine, if she wouldn't intro-duce herself, Treasure would just call her the General. It fit. All she needed were military epaulets on her shoulders.

"Yes. Well, of course I know who you are. We all do. Each of us have had several students transfer in from your class. We were just saying how funny that was. We've never had that much teacher swapping at the beginning of a year."

Treasure didn't respond.

The General continued. "Anyway, as I was saying, Kristen, Cathy, and Tiffany and I all follow the same year-long structure, so we're probably the most coordinated group in the school. Our students could probably attend an hour in each other's class and pick up right where they left off down the hall. I guess we should have let you in on our little planning meetings. But we just didn't think to." She sounded as believable as bubble gum. "But I'm about ready to start Dr. Seuss. Isn't that about where you guys are too?" The three other teachers nodded. "What about you, Treasure?"

"Well we read the Emperor's New Clothes and other Chinese folk tales. I hadn't planned on doing Dr. Seuss as a class. I thought I'd let the students discover him individually."

The General drew back. "No one teaches the Emperor until Chinese New Year. And you don't plan to do Seuss at all? Your students will miss out."

"I'm sure it seems that way to you, but with the language barriers we have in the class right now, I'm not sure my kids could handle Seuss," said Treasure.

The knot of women began to whisper and mutter, shaking their heads in disapproval. "Seuss is great for any level," said the General decidedly. "It's been a tradition to teach it at the beginning of the school year ever since I began working here eight years ago. And we want your students to get the full first-grade experience, even if . . ."

Treasure wondered what she was going to say, then she decided she was better off not knowing. She felt confident in her own lesson plans. After all, her mother had helped her with them. But maybe she was being stubborn here. She had vowed that she wouldn't let her gift sway her from good ideas. And really, she thought, the General and her little army had experience teaching here, and she didn't. She cleared her throat: "I'd be happy to teach Seuss along with you. Could I borrow your plans, just to get some ideas?" At her mother's school, everyone borrowed ideas from each other. Synergy. That's what her mother called it.

However, her request elicited a much different response here. The other teachers looked askance at her, as if she had just asked world famous chefs for their secret recipes. They looked to their General for guidance, but clearly she was waging her own internal battle. The General weighed the impropriety of brazenly asking for someone else's lesson plans ("Just like plagiarism," one of the privates hissed) against the children's need for unity and conformity in curriculum. It wasn't the children's fault that they were in this woman's class. The General decided in favor of the children.

"Sure, Kristen will get you those plans" she said, without bothering to look in Kristen's direction. "Anyway, now that we're all on the same page . . ."

Treasure fought down the urge to ask her what page that was. Was it a page from a self-help manual?

"I thought we'd add something special this year. What if we ask our students to dress as their favorite Dr. Seuss character this Friday? Then we can hold a joint Seuss party."

"What a great idea," exclaimed one of the privates.

"You always come up with the best ideas," chimed another.

"Won't the kids love it?" said the last one.

The General looked as self-satisfied as Howls after a tongue-bath. They all looked at Treasure expectantly.

Treasure's mind raced through the implications. There was no way that most of the parents of her students could create Dr. Seuss costumes in three days. They didn't have the time or the money. And Seuss costumes weren't easy, like princesses or power rangers. Who kept green Grinch fur on hand? She had to object.

"I'm worried that most of my students won't be able to come up with something, and then the kids without costumes will feel bad," said Treasure.

"And spoil it for the rest of them," added Tiffany or Kristen. Treasure wasn't sure which one.

"It's not like it's required," the General went on. "And the best students, the most dedicated, will come through. This will just be another way for us to tell who really is the cream of the crop."

Treasure decided the General must attend classes at the *How to Speak in Clichés* clinic with her sister Patience.

"We can give out prizes for the best costume!" said Cathy, clapping her hands. "That will inspire them."

"No," Treasure blurted, "it will only make the ones without costumes feel worse." She knew what it would feel like to those kids. About the same way she had felt when her mother forced her to wear Miss Piggy moon boots on the first snowy day of junior high school.

The General narrowed her eyes. Treasure was sure she was about to split her thinly applied veneer and say something really nasty to her. At that moment, Treasure caught sight of Bonnie walking toward them, stopwatch in hand. The General and Co. turned their heads and watched her approach.

"Time is nearly up. Is the first grade united yet?" asked Bonnie. She gripped a clipboard in her hands. The pens stuck in her hair reminded Treasure of antennae.

The General smiled at her. "Of course, Bonnie. You know we were mostly coordinated before we even sat down at the meeting. We've got an idea. We're just working through some of the kinks." She indicated Treasure with a flick of her finger.

Bonnie's eyes followed the General's flick. "Oh yes, I can understand that. Go ahead and run your idea past me. I told Anita that I'd handle the approval process on these. There's no need for her to hear all the bad ideas, when I can sort for her. Honestly, the fifth-grade teachers wanted to play Frisbee Freeze Tag. I ask you, how is that educational?" she sniffed.

"Well, I think our idea is better than that. Every first grade class except Treasure's was planning a Dr. Seuss unit anyway . . ."

Bonnie interrupted the General and looked at Treasure sharply, "You weren't planning on covering Seuss? At all?"

Treasure realized she wasn't just dealing with any bee. She was dealing with the Queen. She took a deep breath. "I hadn't planned on it initially, but I'm happy to adjust and make room for Seuss."

Bonnie didn't answer. She looked back to the General, who continued. "And so I thought it would be fun if the kids dressed up as their favorite Dr. Seuss character. At the end of the unit, we'd have a party that would focus on literacy and word games."

"Fabulous," said Bonnie. "I can always count on you, Lucinda, for solid ideas. I'll mark the first grade as approved. You're unanimous, I assume?"

"Well," the General said, rolling her eyes toward Treasure. "Treasure has some concerns."

"Like what?" asked Bonnie, still addressing herself to the General.

Treasure decided to speak for herself. "Like the probability that most of the students in my class won't have costumes because their parents don't have the money or the time to create them."

Bonnie straightened her glasses. "Well, it's optional, right? And we'll certainly be able to tell who the dedicated students and parents are. I say that's one of the most important things that we do in the first grade. If we can get their commitment level pegged down now, then I think it will only help us in the long run."

Treasure couldn't believe what she was hearing. What kind of weird form of Social Darwinism did this woman believe in? And the other teachers were nodding as she spoke. Could they really be so eager to pin labels on their students like bugs in a collection? Treasure felt sure that Dr. Seuss would disapprove. After all, this was the man who championed Whos and Sneetches.

"That's what I said," the General said.

Treasure couldn't fight the Queen Bee and the General at the same time. She had to figure out a compromise. What would Dr. Seuss do? *Sneetches*, she thought. *That's the answer.* She raised her hand, just like a student.

"Yes, Treasure," answered Bonnie the Queen Bee. If she was surprised by Treasure's arm waving in the air, she didn't show it.

"I didn't really think it through. I withdraw my objection. I think it will be great."

"Well, that's settled," said Bonnie, making a check mark decisively on her clipboard before walking off toward the second grade table. The General leaned back and smirked at Treasure. It was obvious that she had claimed this skirmish as a victory.

But Treasure didn't care. She had a plan now. She looked at the clock. The bell would ring in five minutes, and she wanted to get out to her classroom before the children did. She snuck out of her seat and headed for the door.

· · · · · · · · · · · · · · · · · · · ·

From across the room, Anita, the school principal noticed. She saw the self-satisfied look that passed between Bonnie and Lucinda, and she feared for Treasure. Between the two of them, they had shredded at least three other first-year teachers. Anita shook her head. She should have been watching better. She should have checked on the first grade herself. Anita hoped the girl wouldn't crumble immediately. It would be a huge pain to go through the entire hiring process again. Especially since desperation had forced her to go against her own instincts in hiring her. Just thinking about Treasure's interview made her wince.

Treasure had not made a positive first impression. After mistaking her for the secretary, Treasure had managed to trip over the threshold of the door and knock over a pile of books. When she finally sat down in the child-size orange plastic chair, Anita was already struggling to reconcile the glowing list of adjectives on the recommendation (written by Utah's teacher of the year) she was reading with the glowless girl sitting in front of her. She put the recommendation away and squinted at Treasure Blume, as if seeing her slightly fuzzy might make a difference. "Well, Miss Blume, your qualifications are excellent, but . . ."

"But you just don't think I'd work out here?" Treasure blurted, her bony knees sticking up like a mountain range. "Don't say that yet. I can do this! I'm a hard worker. I researched your school. I know that 70 percent of your students don't speak English as a primary language. And I've taken four years of Spanish in high school, plus four years in college, which means I can conjugate verbs at lightning speed, even if I can't speak it well."

Anita sat back. She brushed away the awkward blurting and tried to consider what the girl said. A teacher who did homework? A teacher that actually wanted to be at this school? That was a good sign. Most of the teachers couldn't wait to get out of here, on their way to private and merit schools (especially after they met Bonnie). In fact, many of the teachers Anita had interviewed suddenly started backtracking when she outlined the problems facing her student body. But really, could this speckly white girl really handle teaching here? Anita had her doubts. But frankly, it didn't matter. Time was running out and she was short on teachers, especially those willing to teach the lower grades. And the girl was qualified and positive. She'd just have to push past this feeling.

"So what makes you think you could be a successful teacher here?" Anita asked. "So you looked online. But do you know anything about the kinds of problems facing these kids? And how to combat them? Poverty? Disabilities? Abuse? Neglect?"

Treasure swallowed hard. "Do I know firsthand? No. But I know how to deal with setbacks. And I won't give up. And I'll care about them."

It was an honest answer, Anita decided. She could see the sincerity and earnestness in the girl's face. It was enough. She would hire this girl. After all, she'd just told the district that she'd fill her vacancies with warm bodies or die trying. And here was a warm body before her. She couldn't turn her away. And, Anita reasoned, this girl would probably just be a place-filler for a year, anyway. So she gritted her teeth and offered Treasure Blume a job.

She was unprepared for Treasure's response. Treasure squealed, jumped up, and tried to hug her across the desk, pushing over a mug of pencils in the process. Anita watched with apprehension as the girl apologized and then shoved all the pencils back in the mug, point side up. It looked like a cup of porcupine quills when she finished. Then she stuck out her hand and Anita grasped it, disliking the fishy feel of her sweaty palms. "I know you might be regretting this now," said Treasure, pumping her arm with enthusiasm. "But give me five months, and you'll learn to love me."

The bell for school rang, interrupting Anita's memory. She shook her head. "Not yet, Miss Blume. Not yet," she said, as she walked toward her office, where Bonnie waited to hand her today's agenda.

· · · · · · · · · · · · · · · · · · · ·

"I don't have anything to show, but I do have something to tell," said Rosita, twirling her long pigtails in her hands as she stood in front of Treasure Blume's first grade class. She bounced on the balls of her feet until the rest of the students started to squirm.

"Just tell us!" shouted Octavio, a skinny, bright-eyed boy who reminded Treasure of a spider monkey.

"Octavio," said Treasure. "It isn't your turn to talk. It's Rosita's."

Rosita smiled, milking this moment as much as she could. "My sister is going to have a baby! She told Mommy last night, and Mommy started to curse. Then she started to cry. But I don't know why. Because I like babies. And I thought Mommy did too."

Treasure wasn't sure how to respond. Her ancient aide, Mrs. Gutierrez, had crossed herself at Rosita's announcement and began to mumble in Spanish. "Do you know the family?" Treasure whispered to her.

Mrs. Gutierrez nodded. "Sí. Leila is fourteen," she whispered back.

Rosita was still standing in front of the class, grinning while the kids chattered.

"I wish my sister would have a baby," said one.

"My sister is a baby," said another. "And I don't like babies like Rosita does."

"I know a baby is in the mommy's tummy," said Rosita, "but I don't know how it gets there."

Treasure decided that she would have to assign specific themes for show and tell from now on. She put her arm around Rosita, quieting the students. "You're right, Rosie. Babies are wonderful." The little girl beamed.

"But," said Treasure, making eye contact, "there are some times when we need to make sure that our families want us to share their news. Did you ask if you could tell this story?"

Rosita looked at her shoes. "Well, Leila wouldn't come out of her room, so I couldn't ask. But she didn't say I couldn't tell it." She glanced sidelong at her teacher.

"Next time, ask," said Treasure. "Okay then. Let's have Preston go next." While Preston got up, Treasure crossed back over to Mrs. Gutierrez. "Should we call her mother and let her know about what happened in class today?"

Mrs. Gutierrez looked askance. "These are private matters. Best to leave it alone."

"Private matters?" Treasure exclaimed. "She just announced this pregnancy to the whole class. It's not private anymore."

Mrs. Gutierrez shrugged. "What does it matter?"

"It matters because Rosie needs her mother to help her understand what's happening."

Mrs. Gutierrez didn't look pleased. "Can you say anything to change this? What can you do, besides make people feel uncomfortable?"

Treasure shut her mouth. Clearly, she wasn't going to get any support from her aide on this. Yet she really felt like she needed to talk to Rosita's mother. She wasn't sure what she could say. But she knew she had to say something.

"I'd like to go visit Rosita's home tonight, maybe around seven or so. Would you like to come?" Treasure asked.

"Rosita's mother won't be home," said Mrs. Gutierrez. "She works nights."

"I forgot," said Treasure, feeling stupid. Almost all the parents worked on the strip, as dealers, waitresses, or dancers. Vegas seemed more like Venus than Earth to Treasure.

Treasure left it at that and switched her attention back to Preston, just as he finished showing everyone his new Bakugan.

"Thank you, Preston. Blaze, it's your turn," she said, turning toward the redhead's desk and motioning for him to come forward. Blaze grabbed his backpack and ran to the front of the room. He plopped the bag on Treasure's desk and commenced unzipping. He fished around inside until his hand emerged with a Ziploc bag. "This is Darth," said Blaze, shaking the bag. "He's my best friend and a salamander. I found him in my cousin's backyard."

Treasure could make out a dark limp shape inside. The shape was not moving. Treasure couldn't move either.

"Cool! Take him out," shouted Spencer. Several of the boys had jumped out of their desks and were starting to crowd around Blaze.

Blaze grinned and started to crack the seal.

For Treasure, everything went into slow motion as she processed what she had already witnessed and what was about to happen. Would it be worse if Darth suddenly came to and she had a live salamander loose in her classroom? Or would it be worse when Blaze discovered that Darth had died? Either scenario guaranteed aftermath. As always, her mouth began to work before her legs. "Blaze," she shouted. "Don't!"

But it was too late. Darth was dead. The little corpse lay on Treasure's tissue box cover (the one Velva Lee had crocheted with daisies). Blaze wasn't speaking.

Octavio unbent a paper clip and poked Darth's abdomen. "Why won't it move?" he said. "I think it's dead." Treasure had no doubt he'd use it to perform an autopsy.

"STOP!" said Treasure, "Everyone back to your desks!"

Blaze picked up the amphibian and cradled it against his shirt. He had his head bent forward, but his eyes were starting to scrunch and pucker. Treasure knew it was only a matter of time before someone called him a bawl baby.

Treasure put her hand on Blaze's shoulder. "How could he be dead? He was just alive," said Blaze, stroking the little creature's head.

Treasure fought back her dislike of amphibians. Couldn't you get salmonella from salamanders?

In the back Eduardo started to laugh. "You killed it. You're a killer."

Blaze's tears evaporated as his mood turned to rage. He inadvertently squeezed the lizard as he balled his fists. "Shut up!" he yelled, slamming the squished salamander into Treasure's hands as he launched himself at Eduardo.

Treasure dropped dead Darth onto her desk and jumped between the two boys. "That is enough!" she shouted as she separated them. "Back in your seats! Mrs. Gutierrez, please sit by Eduardo." If Mrs. Gutierrez was fazed, she didn't show it. She heaved herself out of her chair and made her way over to Eduardo. Blaze lurched back to his desk, limp as his dead pet.

"Everyone just settle down," Treasure said, trying to regain her composure. She wondered how she could have prepared for today's circle of life show and tell. Heck, she'd just dealt with birth. Why not tackle death today too?

Blaze dropped his head on his desk and started sobbing.

Spencer raised his hand. "Can we touch it?"

Treasure didn't dignify his answer with a response. Instead she borrowed one of her Grammy's dirty looks.

Spencer dropped his hand.

Gingerly, Treasure approached her desk and picked up Darth. His black skin felt smooth. "Blaze is not a killer," she said. "It was just Darth's time to go." She didn't mention that Blaze's choice of a Ziploc had perhaps accelerated the process.

Blaze didn't look up.

"Blaze, would you like to tell the class about Darth?" she asked.

Blaze wiped his nose on his sleeve and came up to the front. "Darth was a good friend. And one time, when I shut his tail in the door, he grew a new one," he said.

"Would you like to hold him now?" Treasure asked.

Blaze nodded and accepted the limp body. "Why does stuff got to die?" he asked, looking up into Treasure's eyes.

"My dog died," Sharonda volunteered.

"But you didn't put the dog in a plastic bag, did you?" Octavio asked.

"You be quiet," said Micaela, the little girl who sat in front of him. Treasure noticed that her eyes were red-rimmed.

"Everything does," said Treasure. "So I guess that dying is part of living."

"That doesn't make any sense," said Spencer.

"Besides, the creature has gone to a better place," Mrs. Gutierrez suddenly added.

"Like where?" Blaze asked.

Treasure put her hand on his shoulder. "Somewhere that he's happy."

Blaze looked pensive. "He really liked the bathroom. That always made him happy when I let him loose in there." He shook his head. "But how can he be somewhere else? Isn't he right here?" he said, running his finger lightly over Darth's body.

Treasure had not anticipated teaching ontological philosophy, but she went with it anyway. "See how his body doesn't move anymore? His spirit, the part of him that made him wiggle and eat and scurry, is gone. This is just his shell."

"I want to touch his shell!" yelled Spencer.

Treasure decided not to evade him. "Blaze, if you want to, you can walk down the aisle and let everyone see Darth. But no touching."

Blaze wended his way between the rows. After everyone had a chance to see him, he came and stood next to Treasure. "Can we have a funeral for him?" he asked, his voice cracking.

Treasure decided on the spot. "Yes. We can," she said. She didn't know how she would dispose of the remains, but she needed to do it soon, or else Darth would start to reek.

"I know what we should do," said Octavio, jumping out of his seat. "We should flush him down the toilet. We did that with one of my fish."

"That's stupid," said Sharonda. "Salamanders don't live in water."

Blaze looked up. "I think Darth would like it. He liked water, and he liked the bathroom." He looked hopefully at Treasure.

Treasure gazed at Darth. He was only a couple of inches long. She had no idea if a salamander would clog a toilet or not. But one look at Blaze's face and she decided that she was willing to find out.

Treasure nodded solemnly and checked the clock. Show and tell was beginning to bleed into phonics, but Treasure didn't care. "Are you ready to say good-bye to him?" Treasure asked Blaze, who nodded. "Okay then, everyone get in line." The kids scrambled to the door. Treasure escorted Blaze and Darth to the front of the line. "Follow me," she said.

Mrs. Gutierrez looked askance at Treasure. "What are you doing?" she asked.

"We're going to flush him," said Treasure.

At first, Mrs. Gutierrez didn't budge. "If I'm not part of this, I can't be held responsible," she said.

"Well, I don't plan on broadcasting this," said Treasure. Her eyes met Mrs. Gutierrez's eyes. They both knew how Bonnie would react to this turn of events, if she ever found out.

Blaze scrunched his face toward Mrs. Gutierrez, still showing tear tracks on his freckled cheeks. She sighed and heaved herself up. "I needed to talk to Bonnie about my vacation time anyway," she said. "I think I'll go do that right now." She walked out the door, placing a soft hand on Blaze's shoulder as she passed.

Treasure nodded. She didn't let herself smile at her aide's decision. But she did feel hope about their partnership.

As she led the way down the hall, Treasure was faced with a dilemma. She knew she couldn't take the girls into the boys' bathroom or vice versa. The faculty bathroom was the only option.

As she shepherded her students out of their trailer and into the main building, she thought about her weeks here as a first-grade teacher. She loved her job, and she loved her students. The children had accepted her, easily and naturally. Before the first day, she reminded herself that even though children didn't feel the effects of her gift, they wouldn't automatically love her. It would take time to build those bridges. She was prepared for that. What she wasn't prepared for was the difference between kid-time and adult-time. With many of the kids, the initial scaffolding of trust went up on the first day. By the end of class, she'd had her knees hugged twice. It caught Treasure completely off guard. These children took her at face value and didn't see anything amiss in who she was. In that way, teaching first grade was almost relaxing for Treasure. There was no need to hoist a façade in front of these kids. Treasure had always been horrible at façades anyway, since the gift would always manage to leak through. But there was no need here. Her classroom was safe. And the kids seemed to sense it. They were as eager to talk to her as she was to listen to them.

Sharonda told her about the horrible Green Thing that tried to destroy her baby dolls at home. Based on her artwork, Treasure pieced together that the Green Thing must have been Sharonda's older brother, DeShawn. But even talking about her fear had helped Sharonda. When Treasure suggested that perhaps the Green Thing was DeShawn wrapped in a blanket, Sharonda was genuinely mystified. But the next picture she drew didn't focus on the Green Thing. Instead, she and Miss Treasure (the students all called her by her first name) were riding on a rainbow that contained all the colors in the spectrum, except green.

Little by little, each kid had started to unlock their fears and hopes and selves to her. Preston told her about his secret fear of chickens. Micaela talked a lot about her dad, but never her mom. All she would say about her was that she liked sparkles. Kysa showed Treasure the hand jive that only the Twister Sisters knew about. It really didn't matter that Treasure didn't know who the Twister Sisters were.

But there were two glaring exceptions: Eduardo and Liwayway. Eduardo spent much of his day glaring at Treasure from one corner of his desk. He had yet to speak to her directly. Whenever he walked by her, he made it a point to stomp on her orthopedic flats. Treasure wasn't alarmed too much. Wasn't this the way that most people responded to her? In her own life, she was so grateful for people who hadn't given up on her at first glance, that she was determined to keep chipping away at the tough little nut.

Liwayway was more troubling. Her family had just come over from the Philippines, and it was clear that she was suffering from culture shock. Liwayway didn't speak much English, so Treasure was at a loss as to how to communicate with her. She floated through Treasure's class like a little ghost. At recess, she hovered just outside the periphery of the ring of children, drifting away if anyone got too close. She reminded Treasure of a picture she had once seen of a frozen poppy on a rocky mountainside. Treasure wished she could pick her up and hug her, but she was somehow afraid the little girl would slip through her arms, translucent and insubstantial.

Treasure checked the hallway and then led them into the bathroom. With her fingers on her lips, she motioned for them to gather around the toilet. "Would you like to say anything else, Blaze?" she asked. Blaze shook his head. His eyes were welling up again.

"I want to, Miss Treasure," said Octavio, his hand in the air.

"Go ahead," said Treasure, inclining her head.

"All drains go to the ocean," he said, "Like on *Finding Nemo.*"

Treasure nodded. "That's a beautiful thought. Thank you for sharing." She did not mention that Darth was not an ocean-dwelling creature.

The kids seemed to sense the solemnity of the moment. They stood, quiet as retirees, heads bowed, eyes on the bowl. Blaze squared his shoulders and stepped forward. He dropped Darth's dark body gently into the water. He didn't watch as it sank. Instead he quickly pumped the bright silver handle, and the sound of the flush filled the silence. The kids began to clap, and even Blaze joined in. Treasure held her breath until the bowl began filling. She did not want to explain a dead salamander in a toilet to Bonnie.

"Excuse me," said Mr. Tillotson, the librarian, suddenly appearing with a newspaper. "I thought this was a bathroom."

"It is. We'll get out of your hair," said Treasure.

Mr. Tillotson ran a hand over his bald head.

"Not that I meant anything about your hair," Treasure blurted. "See we were just having a funeral, and . . ." She slapped her hand over her mouth, wishing she hadn't said anything.

Mr. Tillotson held up a hand. "I just need to use the bathroom," he said.

After school, Mrs. Gutierrez approached Treasure's desk instead of bolting toward the door as usual. "So you want to talk with Rosy's mother still? If we go right now, we could probably catch her."

"Yes," said Treasure.

"I'll go with you. I know the family," said Mrs. Gutierrez. She seemed resigned to Treasure's plan. She hesitated. "And we can stop by Blaze's home too, if you want."

"Great! I'll drive!" exclaimed Treasure, digging her keys out of her pockets.

Blaze's father had obviously just woken up and didn't let them in. But Treasure did her best to explain the issue on the porch.

"He had a salamander?" asked his dad. He did not look pleased.

"Well, he doesn't anymore," said Treasure.

"Good," said the dad, slamming the door shut. Treasure was about to knock again, but Mrs. Gutierrez tugged her back out to the car.

At Rosita's tiny two-bedroom apartment, Treasure let Mrs. Gutierrez take the lead. After introductions, the entire conversation was almost entirely in rapid-fire Spanish. Treasure could only smile and nod. She understood the gist and recognized words and phrases: *lo siento, los jovenes, embarassada, quincenera,* and even *ojala que.* Treasure assumed Rosita's mother was the only one home, until she saw a dark pigtail whipping around the corner. Then Rosita hurled herself at her teacher. She nearly knocked Treasure into their TV. Her mother, who had been clutching her chest and moaning, now clucked her tongue and motioned for Rosita to leave the room.

Rosita shook her head, and clung tighter to Treasure. *"Mami, esta mujer es mi Tesoro."* Treasure looked at Mrs. Gutierrez. "Tell her how much we love Rosy, her honesty and her bright imagination. Thank her for allowing us to teach her. Tell her how blessed we are to have her in our classroom." Mrs. Gutierrez shook her head. "Say it yourself," she said. So Treasure took a deep breath and began to speak in badly mangled Spanish. Rosita's mother's face softened. She stopped trying to pull Rosy off Treasure. Instead, she looked Treasure full in the face for the first time in the entire interview. She inclined her head and said, *"Gracias."* Rosy unclasped herself from Treasure and slipped her hand into her mother's. Mrs. Gutierrez smiled.

· · · · · · · · · · · · · · · · · · ·

When Treasure finally pulled into the parking lot outside her building, she felt drained. She didn't know if she could manage to get herself up the stairs to her apartment. And she still had to figure out how to make her Sneetch plan work. Her head was still at school when she spotted her next-door neighbor wandering around the parking lot in his bathrobe and slippers.

"Mr. Fong," Treasure shouted, even though she knew he was deaf. Of course, there was no response. She hustled across the lot, eager to get to him before he reached the street, and grabbed him by his elbow. "What are you doing out here, Mr. Fong?" she said, enunciating clearly. He could read lips if she went slow enough.

He smiled at her and pointed across the road toward the mailboxes.

"So because I was late, you were going to get your mail yourself?" she asked.

Mr. Fong nodded, making his big thick glasses bounce on his nose.

"Did you think I would forget?" asked Treasure, steering him back to the sidewalk.

Mr. Fong shrugged.

"You wait here. I'll get the mail." Treasure waited for a gap and then crossed, hoping that Mr. Fong wouldn't follow her. "You stay!" she yelled as a garbage truck blasted by her. She ran back across the road and handed Mr. Fong his mail.

"I didn't realize it was Reader's Digest day," she said as they climbed back up the stairs. "And tomorrow is grocery day. I know. Just knock on my door when you're ready for me to drive you."

After Treasure helped Mr. Fong in, greeted Howls, and ordered egg rolls and hot and sour soup from New Fongs (owned and operated by Mr. Fong's son), Treasure called her brother.

"Randy, I need a favor."

"Sure, Treas. What do you need? Is your car making that noise again?"

"No, it's not the car. Randy, can you get me thirty T-shirts, sizes 6 or 6x by Friday?"

"What color?" Randy asked. "I don't know if we have any in stock right now. I can check tomorrow."

"Yellow would be perfect, but white will do. Call me back when you find out. I'll pay for them. It's important. "

"Is it for a school thing? Because if it was, Costco'd probably donate them."

"No, I need them to make outfits for Howls. Of course it's a school thing."

"You can turn off the sarcasm, Miss I-Just-Called-My-Brother-up-for-a-Random-Rush-Request. Well, if we have them, I'll Fed Ex them to you tomorrow."

"Randy, you're a peach. I'm sorry I snapped at you. I'm just tired. Hey, did you ever read Dr. Seuss in the first grade?"

"I don't remember."

"But if you hadn't read it in the first grade, would your intellectual development have been scarred? What if you hadn't read it until second, or even third grade?"

"I think that mean Mrs. Hall scarred me more than any books I can remember. She used to haul me out of class by my ear. Who does that to a little kid?"

Treasure could not say, and so she bade a hasty good night to her older brother. There was another call she had to make before she could relax.

Roxy worked as a graphic designer. She answered on the first ring. "Treasure, I knew it was you."

"What gave it away? Caller ID?" she teased.

"Oh, I didn't check it. I just knew it would be you."

"Roxy, I need to ask you a big favor. Can you come up with a graphic design based on Dr. Seuss characters?"

Roxy took it in stride. "I suppose so, but why would I want to?"

Treasure explained the faculty meeting, and the Dr. Seuss costume party that her first graders would be participating in. "I didn't want my students to be the only ones without costumes. And I don't want to do anything elaborate like the Grinch."

"Or Horton," Roxy chimed.

"Or Horton. I just thought we could do Sneetch T-shirts pretty easily. You remember the book, right?"

"Sure I do. Do you want plain or star-bellied?" Roxy had always been the one who could hop on Treasure's train of thought the fastest.

"Probably fifteen of each."

"Right. I'm guessing you already called Randy to see if he could get you shirts."

"Yes, right before I called you."

"I'll start working right now. I think iron-on transfers will work the best. I'll ship them to you tomorrow."

"Roxy, I don't expect you to work on this right now."

"Let me do it now while it's fresh. Your kids will have the hippest Sneetch shirts in Sin City. Sneetches. Think the other teachers will catch the irony?"

"They don't strike me as the irony-catching kind of people. And anyway, that's not why I'm doing it."

"Whatever you say. Look, my fingers are practically crawling toward my computer on their own. Let me work. I'll call you and let you know what comes from this creative frenzy." Roxy hung up the phone without saying good-bye, just as the delivery boy rang the door bell.

Treasure tipped Yon big. He always delivered her orders personally, so he could check on his grandfather and then report to his father. So far, the Fongs were the closest thing she had to family in this town. Shortly after Treasure moved in and started helping Mr. Fong next door, his son had arrived at Treasure's door, with takeout menus in hand. New Fong had pledged his eternal gratitude to Treasure, along with free pot stickers every time she ordered. She had told him that it wasn't necessary. He'd shaken his head. "Not everyone would help an old man like you have."

"I love old men," Treasure had said, without thinking about how it would sound. New Fong had looked at her strangely but stopped her when she tried to explain. "I promise you will have good fortunes in every one of my cookies," he said. Then he'd bowed and left. For her part, Treasure was amazed that he had noticed. She felt gratitude to him for the dumplings and for his kindness. Food from Fongs was almost as reassuring to Treasure as Grammy Blume's chicken pie. It meant that not everyone hated her. She sat back to eat and turned on *Seven Brides for Seven Brothers*. She ate egg rolls as Howard Keel belted out "Bless Your Beautiful Hide," and Howls began to sing.

4

School Lunch

THE SNOTTY FIFTH-GRADER EYED THE WIENER TOT THAT DENNIS Cameron held in his gloved hand. "Do those have meat in them?" she asked. "I don't eat the bodies of dead barnyard animals."

Dennis considered a tot. Nuggets of hot dog deep fat fried in a corn meal crust. They horrified him. "Trust me, I doubt any of these animals ever saw a barnyard," he answered, slamming them down on her tray.

"Whatever," she mouthed. He watched her dump them in the trash can near the end of the line, then he turned to dump more wiener tots on more trays. He looked up at the ceiling in despair. Was this really his life? Was he, Dennis Cameron, ex-executive sous-chef at a four-star restaurant on the strip, really a lunch lady? "Just serve the food," he muttered to himself. "Don't make eye contact." He mumbled his new mantra, designed to help him survive the first month.

Really, there had been no way around it. The combination of two events had altered his life plan. First, he won full custody of Micaela after the divorce. And second, his mother was diagnosed with cancer. So he gave up his sleek condo and moved into his mom's little three-bedroom house. It was surreal to return to his childhood home as an adult. His old bedroom (which was now Micaela's) still had bunk beds and monkey wallpaper.

His life was changing, and he had vowed to change with it. Being a chef was too chaotic. He needed something more steady and stable, so he decided to work on an accounting degree. Nothing says steady and stable like accounting. Never mind that he hated it. He hated food right now too. But to be honest, this lunch lady gig was as ideal as it was embarrassing. It allowed him to be close to Micaela, who had just started first grade, and left his afternoons free for his classes and for taking his mom to the doctor. And taking care of them was his top priority.

The custody battle hadn't been much of a battle at all. Sheila hadn't even shown up at the hearing. She worked nights as a dancer at Bally's, so she'd become as nocturnal as a vampire. Dennis had been relieved. He'd had nightmares about what would happen to Micaela if her mother had fought to keep her: Micaela scavenging for food, living on a diet of coffee and lemon wedges, like her mother; Micaela awaking in the night alone, only to discover that her mother had decided to go clubbing. Both of these scenarios were entirely likely with Sheila, who now went by the stage name of Sparkle Plenty.

Dennis and Sheila had met at a cocktail party hosted by E! News Network profiling the hottest jobs in Vegas. Dennis's profile (hottest up-and-coming chefs you've never heard of) landed him at #66 on the list. Sheila's dancing gig pushed her to number #33. Personally, Dennis found her much hotter than that. She reminded him of the old movie sirens, like a Hispanic Julie Newmar.

He'd approached her and told her that if he were doing the ranking, she'd be much more than twice as hot as him. She didn't get it. "You're number thirty-three, I'm number sixty-six; you do the math," he'd said.

She was getting bored. "I don't do math," she answered.

He'd started to explain it to her. It gave him an excuse to keep ogling her.

She'd rolled her eyes and started to walk toward the ladies room when the food critic from *The Sun* approached him and congratulated him on his apple crab quiches. Sheila stopped mid-stride, turned around, and slipped her hand into Dennis's.

"Yes," she'd said. "My Dennis is a rising star." At the time he was delighted to be her Dennis. Looking back, he realized he should have recognized this moment as the second sign of trouble. The first—her inability to do math.

After they got married, Sheila decided she needed a baby the same way that she decided she needed a Pomeranian. All the hippest celebs were baby crazy, buying accessories like Gucci strollers and Burberry carriers, she said. She thought she'd look cute with a baby bump. It turns out she didn't look so cute after the baby was born. For months, she spent the majority of her time staring morosely at her belly. She refused to care for Micaela, tossing her into Dennis's arms so that she could work out with her personal trainer. She also refused to breast-feed since she claimed that her girls were merely decorative. She walked out for good when Micaela turned five, leaving her Pomeranian, Puff, and $100,000 worth of credit card debt for Dennis to remember her by.

Since that time, Dennis had back-burnered his career, juggling shifts and sliding down the restaurant food chain, taking less-demanding jobs in order to be with his daughter. And now that his mom was sick, he had to have more flexibility. She used to watch Micaela, but since she started chemo, she just didn't have the energy. Her skin looked translucent and papery. He had been afraid the corners of her mouth would tear when she forced a smile. Since then, his life had steadily spiraled downward, like a dizzy moth after a light burns out, until he wound up moving into his mom's house and working as a lunch lady at his daughter's elementary school.

Really, he was grateful that he was so close to Micaela, especially since she had landed in that new Blume woman's classroom. After meeting his daughter's new teacher at back-to-school night, he had done what almost every invested and caring parent had done: tried to move his kid to a different section. He wasn't sure what had triggered this response in him. Maybe it was her embroidered cat cardigan. He just knew that when he left that night after listening to her presentation and shaking her limp hand, he was determined to take action. He followed another couple exiting the classroom ahead of him.

"We'll have to come up with a more solid reason, Harry," the wife was saying. "The principal won't let us move Courtney just because we think her teacher is a fruit loop." Just then, she caught sight of Dennis and looked embarrassed.

She started to speak but Dennis interrupted her. "Hey, don't worry. I'm with you guys."

He'd hoped that his job at the school might help him sway the principal into making the change. No dice. Anita wouldn't listen. When he tried to talk to her about it, she looked harried. "Look, Dennis, I sympathize, but you've got to understand that I've already had fifteen requests to move kids out of Treasure's classroom, and heaven knows I'd like to help, but I am not shifting your girl out of that class. Some kids have got to stay. What do you think? That Treasure has a disease that's catching? Do you think I'd hire just anyone to teach these kids?"

Dennis decided that his wisest course was not to answer. Personally he thought Anita might hire a grizzly bear in a tutu if she had teaching credentials. He tried another tack. "Of course not, Anita. I know the kind of care you take, but Micaela's had it rough since Sheila left and Mom was diagnosed . . ."

Anita rolled her eyes. "Name a kid here that hasn't had it tough. Look, you've got nothing to worry about. You'll be right here to keep an eye on Micaela. You're better off than most."

Dennis snorted. Better off than most what? Certainly not better off than most of the students who attended culinary school with him. He saw their recipes on the Food Network and their faces in cooking magazines. What about him? So far it was a mystery that no one cared about. He read an interview with a guy who used to be a commis chef under him at his last restaurant. At the time, Dennis had barely trusted him to dice tomatoes. And now here he was, Mr. Big Shot, talking to the press about his career. He mentioned Dennis, a careless throwaway reference, something about how Dennis never allowed him to filet with his now signature move. The interviewer asked about him. The kid had laughed and said, "I don't know. It's kind of like he's fallen off the face of the earth. But wherever he is, I hope he's kicking himself." Well, Dennis kicked himself often, but not for failing to recognize this kid's talent. What talent? He used a vegetable grater to massacre beef. Big whoop. *But*, Dennis thought sadly, *a man who slings nuggets cannot critique.* And it really was like he fell off the earth and landed here, making minimum wage, slaving among the processed and pasteurized.

But Micaela. It was all worth it for Micaela. She was why he could stand this job in this place, and the way that simple honest food was defiled within its bowels. She was young enough that she didn't realize how distinctly uncool it was to have her father work in the cafeteria. When she went through his line, she grinned at him and said to her friends, "That's my lunch daddy." As long as he was her lunch daddy, he could keep working, even if he couldn't be pleasant about it.

Apparently his antagonism showed. He got bawled out by the head lunch lady, Thelma, for the wiener tot incident. Well, maybe not bawled out. He didn't think she was angry that he was antagonistic, just that he had tried to feed animal by-product to the offspring of a rather prominent vegetarian faith healer. She'd received a call on it right after the episode.

Having a bad attitude seemed to be a job requirement. Thelma was certainly capable of frightening small children. She spoke with a gruff manly voice that she used to bark at both the workers and the children. During his first five minutes on the job, Dennis decided that Gordon Ramsay had nothing on this lady. She had wispy, thinning black hair on her head and on her chin, and eyes like raisins, shriveled and dead. But one-on-one, Dennis found her to be quite different. She was understanding, thoughtful, and articulate, all of which seemed out of place issuing forth in a military style baritone.

"Dennis, I don't want to beat the spirit out of you. It's good that you have some fight. You need it for this job. Otherwise, you won't survive."

"Jeez, did I join the military by mistake?"

Thelma refused to respond to his wise crack. "I think it's something in your own head that's holding you back." She alone of the lunch bunch crew knew about his past.

He looked down at his hands, all the bravado gone.

"It's worth it to you to stay here, so please don't do anything that makes me have to fire you. I get that it's not the kids so much."

"No," he'd answered, "it's the food."

"Well, I'm open to ideas. You figure out a way to change it and meet budget, and I'll let you get creative. Would that help to ease all this angst you're carrying around?"

He nodded but didn't answer verbally. He was afraid it wasn't just the food. Maybe everything inside him that cared about food was dying, and his repugnance for cafeteria fare was just the last sputtering ember of his passion. He took off his hair net and went out the back door.

Poor Thelma. She was just trying to give him hope. She didn't know what she was up against. He didn't think he could deal with hope. It was much easier without it.

He left the lunchroom and sat in his van outside Micaela's classroom. After an hour, he checked his watch again. Micaela's class always seemed to get out five minutes later than any other class. What was that woman making the kids do? Didn't she realize that he didn't have the time to wait for his kid all day? He was about to storm in and drag her out when the door opened. He spotted Micaela skipping toward him, singing *American Idol* style. He jumped out of the car and started walking toward her. Because of her wild vibrato, he couldn't catch the words at first. She grabbed his hand and interlaced their fingers.

"Daddy, I learned a new song today in school. Want to hear it? Dial seven-oh-two, then five-five-three oh-three-one-two, and that will bring your dad to you."

"That's my cell phone number. Why would your class be singing a song about my cell phone number?" Dennis felt his sweat glands start to activate. An entire chorus of six-year-olds chanting his phone number? His subconscious could easily build a nightmare out of that.

Micaela shook her head. "No, Daddy. That's just my song. Miss Treasure made up a different one for each of us."

"Oh," he said, mollified. "But why would you want to have that memorized?"

"In case of an emergency," said Micaela, obviously parroting back what she'd been taught.

Grudgingly, Dennis had to admit it was a decent idea. He wasn't always sure that Micaela knew her last name, let alone his phone number. "But what if I change cell phone numbers?" he asked, pleased to point out a flaw in the teacher's plan.

"Miss Treasure says that if you notify her, she'll write a new song. It's on this note," she said, thrusting a pink sheet into his other hand.

> *Dear Parents,*
> *As a class, we are learning about emergency phone numbers. In addition to teaching them about 911, I am also teaching them their own home phone number, or the number you provided in the emergency sheet you filled out prior to school starting. If this number is not correct, or if you change the number at any time during the upcoming year, please fill out the bottom portion of this note, and return it to me. I will help your child learn a new song.*
> *Sincerely, Miss Treasure Blume*

Dennis folded the note. It was obvious to him that this woman lacked a life. Seriously, who had the kind of time it would take to make sure every kid knew their own phone number? But he had to admit that he felt better knowing that Micaela knew his, even if it meant that her teacher knew it too.

"As a class, we all learned Teacher's number too," said Micaela, swinging his hand. "Hers is 'If you're sad or have the flu, call Miss Treasure at eight-oh-five three-two-two-two.'"

Dennis sincerely hoped this limerick would not wind up written on any bathroom walls. Miss Treasure, he was sure, would field some strange calls. He picked up Micaela. "What should we make for Grandma tonight for dinner?" he asked, opening the van door.

Micaela smiled as she hopped up. "How about risotto? With duck livers? It's her favorite."

"Will you help me stir?"

"Yes, Daddy, I'm your sous chef," she said.

"Well, then, let's go buy some duck," he replied, helping her with her seat belt.

· · · · · · · · · · · · · · · · · · · ·

At 7:25 the following morning, Dennis was stationed outside the lunchroom at the computer terminal ready to receive lunch money. Usually the ladies took turns, but, thanks to his tot explosion, Dennis was now riding the desk permanently. He just had to take the money and input it into the kids' accounts. It wasn't so bad, and it saved him from witnessing the carnage of the lunch prep. Today was rib-e-que on a bun day. So far it had been very slow, a trickle of students interspersed with long silent stretches. He tried to catch up on the reading for his accounting class, but it was so boring he couldn't keep his mind on it. His thoughts kept wandering to last night's dinner with his mother.

While he and Micaela cooked, his mother sat by them on a little stool. She had finished the last round of chemo and was feeling much better. It felt like they could keep the cancer at bay, just with good smells. His mother actually seemed hungry. Then they sat down to dinner. When she began to eat, she couldn't swallow fast enough. "Delicious!" she exclaimed with a full mouth. Micaela grinned at her dad. It was so good to see his mom eat, even if she was behaving like a recently exiled *Survivor* cast member. He began to relax, and Micaela began to whine. "Grandma, don't you think Daddy should let me take dance lessons? All the girls in my class go to dance." Dennis scowled. They had been through this. He didn't have any rational reason for keeping his daughter away from dance other than that it reminded him of Sheila.

He opened his mouth to answer Micaela, and his mother bolted from the table and stumbled to the bathroom. He could hear her retching. He sent Micaela outside to pet Fishstick (his mom's Corgi, named for his shape and color), and then he knocked on the bathroom door. She didn't want him to come in, but he did anyway, kneeling beside her on the floor and cradling her head against him as she heaved. She apologized to him, apologized for not holding down the most flavorful food she had tasted since the chemo began. "Mom, don't apologize to me. Please," he begged. She stayed curled against his chest, the same way that Micaela did after a nightmare. He reached over to flush the toilet. There was something about seeing the grains of his recycled risotto swirling away. It was his best. But it didn't matter. Food, even good food, doesn't have the power to save someone.

Dennis shook his head, trying to shake away memories of last night, and looked up into the brown eyes of a chubby fourth grader. Based on the slabs of flesh that hung down from the kid's waist like saddle bags, Dennis surmised that this kid *did* believe in the power of food.

"My mom forgot to send me lunch money," he said glumly. Obviously the thought of missing a meal was devastating to him.

"Well," Dennis answered, "it looks like you could miss a few, buddy."

The kid started to sob.

"Okay, okay, don't cry. Today, you can have milk and a roll, and then we'll send home a note to remind your mom."

"Won't matter," said the kid, scuffing his shoes against the floor. "She won't get her welfare check for another week, and she told me that she isn't going to spend money to make me fatter."

Dennis asked the kid's name and looked him up on the system. Not only was there no money in his account, the records showed that he had already charged a week's worth of lunches. Thelma hated that. "This isn't a bar," she'd say. "You can't run a tab here." Dennis looked into the boy's pained and drawn eyes. He received a flash of insight. "Norman, how long has it been since you ate?" Norman lowered his head. "Tell me, Norman," Dennis added.

"Well, she lets me eat watermelon and iceberg lettuce. But that's it. She says it helped her lose weight too."

Dennis was forcefully reminded of his ex-wife's obscene eating habits. "But how long since you had some protein or dairy?" Dennis pressed.

"About a week."

Dennis stood up from his chair. He must have looked angry because the kid cowered, afraid that Dennis might hit him. Instead, he put his hand on the back of the boy's neck. "Come with me," he said, steering him into the lunchroom. Together they found Thelma hacking frozen rib-e-ques apart with the claw end of a hammer. If the kid had been scared before, he was terrified now, his legs pressed together tightly so he wouldn't wet himself. Dennis kept his hand on his neck and explained the situation. Thelma, her hammer dripping bits of melting meat, didn't look fazed. "Well, just put him on the secret account," she said, returning to her work.

"There's a secret account?" asked Dennis.

"Sure," said Thelma, aiming another swing. "It's on the desktop of the computer in the right hand corner. The icon's a dandelion. Open it and you'll see what to do."

Dennis and Norman jogged toward the computer together, eager to see if this mythical dandelion existed. They hunched over the computer. "Look, there it is!" said Norman, squealing. Dennis clicked. It opened a spreadsheet that began with this statement: "Use of this account is at the complete discretion of the Head Lunch Lady. It can be used for students at this school who the lunch ladies deem deserving of a free lunch, whether for a day, a week, or a month. All the donor asks is that the recipients keep this account a secret and that no one seeks to discover his or her identity." Below this statement ran a list of names and dates. Dennis scrolled to the end, added Norman, and typed the date. "How long, do you think?" Dennis asked.

"Until I lose at least ten pounds," said Norman, glumly.

Dennis nodded and added the stipulation. He turned back toward Norman. "It shouldn't be too long," he said, "but if you can, come through my line. I'll help you pick things that are your best bet for feeling full and still losing weight."

Norman crushed into Dennis. It was Dennis's turn to be alarmed. Then he realized that Norman was hugging him.

"Thank you for feeding me," Norman said.

Dennis patted the boy's curly head. "You're welcome," he said, choking up. "You're welcome."

Later, after lunch, Dennis cornered Thelma. "So what's the story on that account? I never saw an amount on it anywhere."

Thelma glared. She looked angry even when she didn't mean to. "I'm the only one who has access, besides Anita. The account usually has about a couple hundred dollars in it. We get a new deposit into it every two weeks. I don't know for sure, since it's the first year we've had it."

"Well, I'm glad it was there today. But really, how often does it get used? I mean, we have reduced lunches and free lunches."

"You saw the list of names, and we're only a couple weeks into the school year. And as for free and reduced, there are requirements for those. Some parents won't do it if they are here illegally, just because they're scared. Plus you have to be able to read and write to fill the forms out. And some parents won't just because of pride."

Dennis nodded, taking that in. "So who's the donor?" he asked, not expecting an answer. He didn't get one.

Thelma turned and hefted a stack of dirty trays. "Even I don't know that. All I know is that I'm mighty grateful for that account. Thanks to it, I haven't had to turn anyone away this year." She shook her head. "You know, for some of these kids, lunch is the only meal they'll eat today. Some parents can't or won't feed them. "

As Thelma walked back toward the dishwashers, Dennis felt like he'd just caught a dodge ball in the stomach. The only meal they'd eat? This slop would be the only food some kids would eat? He examined a rib-e-que, bending it back and forth. He tossed it at the wall. It slid down, leaving a trail of grease. It wasn't right. It just wasn't right.

He slid down against the freezers he had been leaning against, not caring that the seat of his pants might get glued to the sticky floor. He took a deep breath. Okay. The only food they'd get. He couldn't change that. But he could change the food. Thelma had given him the okay. And now he had a reason to care. Maybe he couldn't save the kids with food, but he could give them a gift, like the anonymous donor. He took a pencil out of his shirt pocket and began to plan new menus.

5 ·················

The Sneetch Party

TREASURE LEANED OVER HER IRONING BOARD FOR THE THIRTEENTH time, her hair curling from the steam. She blew a ringlet out of her eyes and tackled another shirt: only seventeen more to go. Both Randy and Roxy had come through for her. Randy lucked into a box of shirts that had been run over by a forklift. There were a few black marks here and there, but Treasure didn't mind. No one was going to examine them closely. And Roxy had managed to capture the essence of Seussism with a few graphic lines and a distinctive font. Treasure shook her head. She should never doubt Roxy. She always came through. The design was simple, only the words "Plain-bellied Sneetch" or "Star-bellied Sneetch" across the back, and an outline that suggested the neck and torso of a Sneetch complete with a star (or not) on the front. For Treasure, Roxy had gone over the top and thrown in a Sylvester McMonkey McBean iron-on for her. Treasure would have much preferred a Sneetch shirt. She didn't want to be cast as the filthy huckster who capitalized on the Sneetches' snobbery.

Howls was desperate to climb on the ironing board, since it had Treasure's undivided attention. She'd given up trying to grade papers with him around, since he would inevitably jump up and sprawl on whatever she was grading, leaving all kinds of hairs, tears, and smudges. "Don't Howls," said Treasure. "You'll knock it over and iron yourself." She nudged him with her foot. He jumped up on the table beside her, so that he could gaze at her eye-to-eye. She ignored him and kept ironing.

She really wanted to go to bed. Gathering supplies for the party

64

tomorrow had exhausted her. She wasn't sure how she ended up with the job. A week ago, she hadn't fathomed that she would find herself desperately combing dollar stores for orange oven, scrubbing pads and hauling around six-foot lengths of PVC Pipe. The lunchroom, she was sure, would be completely unrecognizable. But would the kids like the shirts? On Monday, she'd sent home a note inviting parents to help create a costume if they could. She had assured them that if they were unable, she would provide a costume. But what if the kids hated these? Maybe it was a stupid idea. Maybe she should have let the parents handle it completely, like the other first-grade teachers were doing. But, she reminded herself, she wasn't like the other first-grade teachers.

However, she had to admit it: this Seuss week had been fun. She was so glad she'd acquiesced and added it to her lesson plans. She renewed her vow not to dismiss suggestions just because the suggester hated her. The kids had mooed with Mr. Brown and scowled with the Grinch. A few, like Spencer and Micaela, could read all of *Hop on Pop* on their own. Even her beginning readers, like Liwayway, chanted along with *Red Fish, Blue Fish*. Kysa, who disliked disorder, did throw a tantrum because the kids wouldn't listen to the fish when he suggested tossing the Cat in the Hat out on his smug smiling face. She calmed down when Treasure allowed her to reorganize the homework cubbies. But one thing was sure, the Seuss discussions had sparked their interest in reading. Treasure brought out three big spinning book holders and built a book nook, with a lava lamp and bean bag chairs in the corner of the room. Time in the book nook was the most coveted of all classroom prizes. And the Seuss books were in the highest circulation. It thrilled her to see them embrace reading. In her own life, her love of reading was one of the salvageable elements from her dismal teenage years. Her ability to plunge into a book and shut out the world had given her a place to go in her head when the nasty things that people said intruded. The memory reminded her of the General's snide comments. But Treasure had to hand it to her. Seuss sold the kids on reading, even the stubborn ones. She made a mental note to thank her tomorrow at the party.

Treasure had learned in the unit along with the kids. The more time she spent, the more invested in them she became. They weren't just her students anymore. They were her friends. She remembered her maniacal high school P.E. teacher, who, during her sophomore year, loaded the whole class on a bus and dropped them off in the middle of the desert. "Now run back," he'd said. When the kids started chanting, "We hate you, we hate you," he had laughed and said, "I don't need any fifteen-year-old friends." But Treasure had no such pretenses. She knew she needed friends, even six-year-old friends. They were the best kind of friends to have (short of sixty-six-year-old friends). They brought her dandelions after recess. They jumped up and down when she announced they'd play Math Bingo. A few regularly told her that they loved her. Sometimes, they even accidentally called her "Mom." She would always answer and not correct them.

She had even made headway with Eduardo. It had been his birthday last Tuesday. According to the unwritten code of elementary schools, he was expected to bring a treat (store-bought) to share. Everyone did. Sharonda had brought root beer barrels. Octavio's grandma had lugged a cooler full of otter pops up the splintery stairs to their trailer. Even Spencer, the class entrepreneur who sold whatever he could get his hands on, shared a bag of M&Ms. But Eduardo sat stony-faced while Treasure and the class serenaded him with the birthday song. Treasure noticed but didn't push it. During the last five minutes of the day, when everyone was absorbed in an art project, she pulled him aside.

"Eduardo, would you like to share a treat with everyone for your birthday?" she asked him.

He put his hands in his pockets. "I don't got anything to share," he said, angry that she had made him say it out loud.

Treasure regretted her phrasing. How did she manage to seem so insensitive, even when her sensitivity prompted her to act? She brushed off her idiocy and pushed ahead with her idea. "You can pick something from my treat closet," she said, beckoning him toward the back of the room. He looked like he wasn't going to budge, but when she opened the closet, he edged nearer to her. "Let's see, I've got hot tamales, pretzels, graham crackers . . ." She looked down at him. Physically he was nearer, but his eyes hadn't changed. "But those aren't special enough for a birthday," she concluded.

"What's in those?" he asked, pointing to two boxes at the bottom. Treasure pulled them out. She had forgotten she even had them. Pez dispensers. When she got them, she'd had a vague idea that she would do a math game with them. But the details had yet to materialize, and

Eduardo needed them now. His eyes lost the guarded look. "Open them and let's see," she said, wondering if this was as close as he would get to opening a present this day. He tore into the box like a clawed animal. For a minute, Treasure feared for the Pez. But when he saw Spider-Man's head, he stopped. He lifted one up, fingering it gently, like a jeweler examining a stone. He didn't say anything and sat mesmerized.

"I think this box has Hello Kitty ones, for the girls," Treasure said, ripping into the other box and exposing the contents to him. His eyes flicked over to the other box, then back to Spider-man.

"Would you like to pass these out?" she asked. He nodded, still holding Spidey's gaze. "Well, then, we better get a move on," she remarked, standing up from where she had knelt beside him.

"Friends, Eduardo has a birthday treat for each of you," Treasure announced. He scrambled to his feet and began to pass out Pez dispensers, as Rosita squealed and Blaze declared that it was the most awesome birthday treat ever. After the bell rang, Eduardo approached her desk, instead of bolting for the door like usual.

"Can I have some for my sisters?" he asked. Treasure tried to act casual but could hardly contain the leap her heart took. This was the first time he'd ever initiated a conversation with her. She tried hard to keep her eyebrows from shooting up off her forehead.

"Sure," she replied. "And make sure you get one for yourself."

He unclenched his hand and showed her the sweaty Spider-Man in his palm. He dipped his hand into the Hello Kitty box, then walked to the door.

"Thank you," he said, turning back briefly, with a shadow of a smile on his face.

"You are welcome," Treasure had said, meaning every word.

The iron started to smoke, signaling to Treasure that she better quit thinking about Pez and focus on creating Sneetch shirts. Sneetch solidarity. That's what she'd learned in her first month. And so, she'd have to be a Sneetch herself (*to heck with Sylvester McMonty McBean*, she thought.) That was clear. Definitely plain-bellied. Roxy had thrown in some extra transfers, so she had enough, even though the child-sized drawing might look silly on her. She decided she didn't care. She'd be odd, if someone needed to be odd. She went into her bedroom and found two old white T-shirts that she could use (one for her, one for Mrs. Gutierrez). The iron hissed as it pressed down on the last transfer. She folded them neatly and tucked them into her school bag.

The students had been so keyed up about the afternoon Dr. Seuss party that Treasure had failed to capture their imaginations with her explanation of photosynthesis. *Plants use light and water to make the air we breathe!* She quit trying. She'd save her lima bean–planting exercise for another day. Mentally they were in Whoville, beating whangdangers and riding snarfgoodles. And to tell the truth, so was she. It was time. She read the story of the Sneetches, which she had been saving until this very moment.

"Those Sneetches are stupid!" yelled Octavio.

Treasure nodded but asked him why.

That stumped Octavio, who wouldn't budge from his original assertion. Sharonda piped up, "Because they think something on their belly makes them better."

"And does it?" asked Treasure.

"No. That's why it's stupid."

"That's not why I think they're stupid," said Blaze. "They're stupid because they keep paying that McBean guy."

"I wish I was that McBean guy. I'd make bank!" yelled Spencer, whose money-loving heart prompted him to charge unethical prices for his black-market candy on the playground.

"Well," said Treasure, "I think you're both right. But did the Sneetches stay stupid?" The kids shook their heads in unison with her. "When did they get smarter?"

Micaela raised her hand. "When they forgot about stars."

"That's right. When they decided that it didn't matter if they had a star or not. They decided that Sneetches are Sneetches. When they accepted everyone and quit trying to make people feel bad, they were all happier. And so, I have a present for you. We are going over to the lunchroom in just a minute for our party. But first, I have something for everyone in our classroom." She opened her bag and shook out a Sneetch shirt.

"Ta-da" she said. "We're going to be Sneetches."

"Do we have to?" asked Preston, the only kid in her class to dress up on his own. He wore a brilliant blue wig and a bright red shirt that said THING ONE in bold letters.

Treasure debated. On the one hand, forcing uniformity never had positive results, and it reminded her of Nazi Germany. Never a good sign. It seemed positively unSneetch. But on the other, what about Sneetch solidarity? "You don't have to if you don't want to," she said, digging through the bag until she found hers. Putting it on, she said, "Look, I have one too."

"Do we get to keep them?" asked Rosy.

"Absolutely," said Treasure. That was the clincher. The kids began to talk excitedly as she passed them out, pulling them over their clothes. The 6x nearly drowned Liwayway but threatened to rip under Manuel's arm pits. *Note to self: Next time, get a variety of sizes*, thought Treasure.

"Hey, I wanted a star-bellied one," whined Preston, as he took off his wig. Sharonda rolled her eyes at him. "You just don't get it, do you?"

"It's like we're on a team or something," Octavio shouted.

"That's right!" said Treasure. She led the way out of their trailer, down the stairs, through the doors, and into the main hall. She paused by the lunchroom door and waited until each of her little friends filed past her. Since lunchtime, Mrs. Gutierrez and all the other first-grade aides had transformed the lunchroom into Seussville, complete with towering orange fuzzy trees with striped trunks made of pipe cleaners wrapped around PVC pipe. In the corners, each teacher had set up a game based on one of the books. At one station, the kids listened for clues to help Horton. Another group had set up a rainy day booth with a goldfish in a bowl. There was a counting game based on *Red Fish, Blue Fish*, and a rhyming game with *Hop on Pop*. For their contribution, Treasure and Mrs. Gutierrez had set up Sneetch-on-a-Beach tag. Whoever had the star was it.

Treasure was about to join her class, clustered around the Hop on Pop booth, when she caught sight of the General. The General wore a long pink nighty and a blonde wig that stood straight up and then curled at the ends like a fountain. Gradually, Treasure realized that she was staring at a six-foot-tall Cindy Lou Who. Her eyes must have boggled, because the General started toward her. Treasure plastered a smile on her face and tried not to look at the tower of hair.

"Well, we're glad your class could make it," she said. "We'd about decided that you weren't coming after all."

Treasure looked at her watch. They were three minutes late. "It's a long walk from the trailers," she said.

The General looked her up and down. "A T-shirt . . . well, that's interesting. I try to inspire my students with my own costume. I don't choose the easy road."

"I can imagine," said Treasure. "How did you get your hair to defy gravity?"

"Oh, that's a secret," said the General, smiling.

Treasure swallowed hard but looked up at the General. "Anyway, I just wanted to thank you for all your hard work on this party, and for including my students in this experience. You were right. They would have missed out."

The General beamed. Treasure had just uttered her two most favorite phrases: *Thank you* and *you were right*. The only thing better would have been *I was wrong*. In a burst of generosity, she leaned over and whispered in Treasure's ear. "I use a cup."

Treasure looked bewildered "For what?"

"My hair," said the General. "I put a Dixie cup on the top of my head, then I rat the hair around it, and spray it all up with Big Sexy."

Treasure, who, thanks to the Steppers, was familiar with the aerosol hairspray, was impressed. "It's a marvel of engineering," said Treasure.

"Thank you," said the General gravely. "Well, I must get over to finish the cupcakes."

Treasure let her eyes float over the crowd, looking at costumes. She stopped cold. Her students were not the only ones wearing matching outfits. Woven through Hortons, Grinches, and her own little Sneetches, at least twenty students sported red and white striped construction paper hats with big red construction paper bow ties. Whose class was that? She had to find out. She approached Mrs. Gutierrez and handed her a Sneetch shirt. But before she could question her aide, she felt a hand on her back. It was Kristen, the omega member of the first grade teacher pack.

"Love your Sneetch shirts. Very clever," she said.

Treasure looked her over and smiled back. "I think the hats and bow ties are just as cute and probably a lot easier to make."

"Well," said Kristen, straightening her own construction paper hat. "What you said at our faculty meeting, it really stuck with me. I couldn't stop thinking about how some of the kids would feel without a costume, so I came up with this." She paused. "I'm really glad you spoke up at the meeting, and I'm sorry that I wasn't nicer to you. It's just when Lucinda get's talking, I feel if I object, then I'll be the odd one out."

Treasure made a mental note of the General's real name. "I've been the odd one my whole life, so it doesn't really bother me." There she went, blurting again. Her last statement had obviously made Kristen uncomfortable. She tugged at her paper bow tie.

"I hope this stuff doesn't stain my shirt," she said, trying to peer beneath her collar.

"Just don't get it wet," Treasure said.

"Looks like you better go referee Sneetch tag," said Kristen, nodding toward the far corner. Mrs. Gutierrez was seated on a chair fanning herself. The game had erupted into a brawl, and two boys were climbing one of the trees. Treasure hustled over and halted the mayhem. The rest of the party, she monitored her corner and vowed never to choose a game with so much physical contact again.

At the end, the General (Lucinda, Treasure reminded herself) walked up to the stage, her stiff hair swaying. "We will now present the awards for best costume. Each class has voted. Our individual winner is . . . Andrew Williams for the Grinch." The little boy waddled to the stage, swathed in copious amounts of green fur. Treasure thought he even had in yellow contact lenses, just like Jim Carey.

"And the teacher prize goes to . . ." Lucinda feigned uninterest as she opened the envelope. "Well what a surprise! It goes to yours truly! I am honored indeed to represent Cindy Lou Who." She took some time as she picked over the prizes, finally selecting a bag of Hershey's dark kisses before continuing.

"Our next awards are group awards. And well, it's a tie. The award goes to Kristen McKellar's class as the Cat in the Hat and Treasure Blume's Sneetches." Applause ricocheted off the linoleum flooring. "We won! We won! We won!" shouted Octavio, jumping up and down. From across a sea of striped hats, Kristen caught her eye and smiled. Even Lucinda didn't look offended. Did it feel any better to win an academy award? Or a Pulitzer Prize? Treasure doubted it, as she watched Sharonda and Octavio climb the stairs to claim their bag of Smarties. Together they held the bag over their heads as the rest of the Sneetches, Treasure included, cheered below them.

· · · · · · · · · · · · · · · · · · ·

Dennis Cameron watched through a crack in the accordion door that separated the kitchen from the dining area. Micaela won second place in the Hop on Pop rhyming contest. Her teacher stuck her award sticker on the middle of her forehead. Dennis thought she might peel it off; she hated to have anything on her skin. But instead, she wore it like an Indian princess. He felt warmth rise inside him like yeast as he watched her. The happiness of the kids even seemed to penetrate the fog of stale odors that clouded his lunchroom domain. And he needed it today. His plan to save school lunch wasn't going well.

Thelma decided to balance Dennis's experiments with traditional lunchroom cuisine. There would be two options for lunch each day. Dennis scoffed at the challenge. Who would purposely choose slop?

On Monday, he created a delicate angel-hair pasta garnished with a fresh tomato and basil sauce. Every lunch lady had been impressed. Thelma even told him, "If I knew school lunch could taste like this, I'd dare eat it myself."

But the kids had not. "Hey, there aren't any meatballs in my spaghetti!" one bespectacled boy accused him, after he'd dug through his capellini with a fork.

"Meatballs will clog your arteries," he snapped. He should have realized then that it would take time to educate their palates. But realizations always dawned on him slowly.

On Tuesday, the kids had a choice between his tandoori chicken salad and dinosaur chicken nuggets. The dinosaurs annihilated his salad. "You had no chance against nuggets. They're always a heavyweight favorite," Thelma consoled him. He tried not to get discouraged. *So kids don't like turmeric*, he thought. *I get it.*

But even he had to admit that the Vietnamese crab puffs had been a disaster. They got soggy sitting in the steamers. He simply wasn't used to preparing his food in mass quantity. He couldn't blame the kids for not choosing those. A few intrepid souls did come through his line. But later, as he saw his creations whizzing between tables, he realized that he had created flying saucers.

On Thursday, his turkey shepherd's pie fared only marginally better. At least he hadn't had to pry it off the ceiling tiles.

For today, he decided to scale back his ambitions and do something more simple, something they were more familiar with. Enchiladas. How could he go wrong with shredded pork enchiladas? He could cook entire pans of them at a time! And he was up against wiener tots in the other line, his old arch nemesis. This would be a slam dunk. And at first, it seemed to be. Almost every kid opted for his enchiladas. He piled them high with cilantro, lettuce, and fresh tomatoes. But the line backed up. He couldn't plate fast enough. When he was serving his own food, he found he could not just slap it down on the tray. It had to be pleasing to the eye as well as pleasing to the palate. "Oh come on!" he heard one sixth grader say "We're not going to have time to eat if we go through this line. I'm getting the tots instead." But the faster he worked, the faster his line seemed to dwindle. When he looked up, the tot line had swelled to the size of a river. He shook his head. At least the kids who chose the enchiladas would be rewarded. And that was when he heard someone start hacking. At first, he ignored it, and continued serving. But then it started to crescendo.

Suddenly, he heard a shout. "Help! The enchiladas are killing Lydia!" yelled a shaggy-haired boy. Dennis dropped his spatula and went through the door out to the dining room. A teacher got there first and started whacking the little girl on the back. The spasms seemed to gain violence. The little girl shook and writhed, like she was possessed. Dennis crossed the room in long strides. "Here," he said, handing her a glass of water, "try this." She drank, sputtered, and then started to calm down. It took several minutes before she could speak, and the drama had muted the entire lunchroom. When she finally opened her mouth, it was not to thank Dennis. "Too spicy," she rasped. It was all she said.

Dennis returned to the lunch line in shame and defeat. Too spicy? Half the kids here were Hispanic. Maybe it was the fresh wasabi he added. Doubt washed over him, threatening to drown him and suck him under.

After the kids left and the first grade aides were decorating for the party, Thelma pulled him aside. "Dennis, let's be honest. You know this isn't going well. We can't foot the bill on this much longer. The amount of food we're wasting . . ."

"I know, I know," he said morosely.

"I'll give you a week more, but I'm pulling the plug on this little experiment if we don't see some positive results."

"Positive results like what? Like Norman dropping ten pounds?"

Thelma eyeballed him. "How about us not having to throw out tubs of food? How about the kids eating at least half of what you've prepared. I swear, I've never seen so much gourmet garbage in my life." The words stung, but he knew she spoke the truth. Really, he was afraid. A week was such a short time. He didn't know if he could turn this train wreck around. But he had the weekend to let his ideas stew.

At the tail end of the Sneetch party, Micaela spied him and ran toward him. "Daddy, Daddy!" Look what I won!" she shouted, pointing to her forehead. "I'm the second-best rhymer in the whole first grade!" He swept her up into his arms in a big hug. "I can rhyme big and I can rhyme small. Rhyming for me is not hard at all," she chanted.

"And you can rhyme in winter, and you can rhyme in fall," Dennis continued.

"Yes, it's true. It's easy, I find. But now I have to go. My class is leaving me behind," she said, climbing down and running toward her teacher, who was bent over her crowd of kids counting heads. She whipped around, obviously scanning for Micaela, who ran over and hugged her leg. As he watched, Dennis realized that if he would have been at his old restaurant, he would have missed this moment. Suddenly, he was very grateful for his job as a lunch lady.

· ·

That night, Treasure called Randy, excited to tell him about the success of the Sneetch shirts. He didn't answer, so she left a message. It made Treasure wonder. This wasn't like him. Randy always had his phone on him. She dialed her mother instead. The phone rang six times before she heard her mother's out-of-breath, "Hello"

"Mom, are you okay? It sounds like your asthma is acting up again."

"Oh, Treasure, I'm fine," wheezed her mother.

"No, you're not. You're panting, and Randy's missing. What's going on?"

"Oh, we're just having some issues with Grammy Blume. Nothing you need to worry about. How was your Sneetch party?"

"Oh, no you don't. You only wheeze when you're under stress. What's up with Grammy?"

"Well, we've had a bit of a Gram-ergency. Your dad and Randy went to pick her up down at the precinct."

"Precinct? Grammy's been arrested?"

"Well, I suppose so. Technically, I think they are just holding her because she's a danger to herself and others. We don't know yet if LuNae will press charges or not.

"LuNae from the Steppers? LuNae, who-does-my-hair LuNae? Okay, tell me the whole story," said Treasure, perching on the edge of her sofa.

Her mother took as deep a breath as she could manage and launched into the tale. "Well, you know how the Steppers host the 'Sweat With Your Sweetheart' dance every year at the Retirement Village, down at the clubhouse, as a fund-raiser? Well, LuNae has a new boyfriend—Moyle, I think is his name."

"I thought a moyle performed ritual circumcisions on Jewish babies," said Treasure.

"That's a mohel. This is Varden Moyle. His son Dale was a big rodeo star. Remember him?"

Treasure didn't but agreed anyway. Her mother had a horrible habit of sidetracking, and if she allowed it, they'd be reliving Dale's glory days.

"Well anyway, Vard's wife passed on a couple of years ago, and he recently moved into the community. He just started dating LuNae. I guess it's the first time he's been out on a date at all. But apparently, at the dance, your grandmother found him quite attractive."

Treasure was shocked. "You're kidding. She hasn't found anyone attractive for fifty years or more."

"Well, Vard was wearing his cowboy boots, and she always has liked a man in boots," Harmony reflected, sighing. "Anyway, so Grammy was up at the front desk, and she shouted from across the room, 'Well, there is a man worth talking to.' And she started toward Vard where he was dancing with LuNae. Velva Lee tried to stop Grammy, but she wouldn't be stopped. Grammy walked up to LuNae and hip-bumped her across the room, saying 'Cut out, honey. I'm cutting in!'"

"She didn't!" said Treasure, squeezing her eyes shut to blot out the mental pictures.

"She did," her mother continued. "Then LuNae pushed Grammy back, saying that Vard was her date. And that raised Grammy's dander. And so she asked LuNae if she was Vard's wife, and LuNae said, 'Not yet.' And Grammy said, 'Well, what you need is a good punch in the nose.' And that's when she started swinging. Apparently she didn't hit LuNae, but she did hit Vard. They think she may have broken his nose.

But by then, the staff jumped in and was trying to restrain her. And that's when Velva Lee called us. Grammy was biting and kicking at everyone and shouting for Vard to save her. And all poor Vard could do was cup his nose to keep from bleeding on the new carpet. But LuNae was furious. She's the one that got the police involved."

Treasure groaned. How could this be happening? She knew her grandmother was cantankerous, but she'd never gotten into a brawl over a man before. She'd never liked a man well enough to approach him, as far as Treasure could recall. And now here she was, cantankerous and amorous. Now *that* was a deadly combination. Obviously, Grammy had become more unbalanced since Treasure moved. Why hadn't she taken Randy's report at the CasaBlanca more seriously?

"Oh, Treasure, your dad just got home. I'm handing the phone to him. I'll go get on the cordless."

"Dad, I'm so sorry. Is Grammy okay?"

Bud sounded deflated. "Hi, sweetie. I think so. I was going to give her a Valium to settle her nerves, but by the time that we got there, she seemed quite docile. None of the officers had the guts to put her in the holding cell. Apparently she just looked the chief square in the eye and said, 'Now see here. You're just a sprout. And locking me up is not respectful.' And so she was sitting in the chief's chair when I got there. All the officers were afraid to make eye contact with her."

"Bud, did LuNae press charges?" Treasure's mom wanted to know.

"Well, she doesn't have grounds, since none of Mom's punches ever connected with her. Only Vard got hit hard. And he's not interested in suing anyone. He said it was the most entertaining date he'd ever been on. I apologized to him, but he just laughed. He said, 'Son, I've had my nose broken three times, and this was the most fun. I knew I was a good-looking cuss, but I've never had the girls fighting over me before.'"

"Are you sure he didn't have a concussion?" Treasure asked.

"I didn't ask. I was just so happy he wasn't going to press charges that I didn't stick around. LuNae was working every angle she had to get him to sue. But eventually she simmered down, until we brought Mom out. She winked at Vard, and that launched LuNae all over again. She's the one who needed to be locked up."

Treasure thought about her next appointment with LuNae and knew that none of this boded well for her hair.

"Well, all's well that ends well," soothed her mother.

"Oh, it's not ended. Not by a long shot. The manager of the retirement village is madder than hops about the blood on the carpet they just had installed. The president was actually in the clubhouse. They want Mom out."

"No!" Treasure and her mother exclaimed together.

"Oh yes. In fact, I've got to get down there right now. I only dropped by to pick up your mom. They're holding an emergency hearing, and we need every character witness we can get."

"Honey, do you really think I'm the right one to testify, regarding Tabiona's character, I mean?" Harmony asked gently.

"All you've got to do is say that she isn't normally violent."

"I don't think I can honestly say that, honey. What about the Orville Redenbacher incident?"

"Well, the alternative is that she'll have to come live with us."

"Now that I think about it, I only heard about that from Randy. I wasn't actually there," backtracked Treasure's mom.

"I'll testify, if you need me," said Treasure. "I can get in a car and be there in three hours."

"It'll be over in three hours. You're sweet, but I don't think you can help," her father said gently.

"Well, there's one thing I can do," Treasure said. "If they kick Grammy out, she can come and live with me."

"Do you know what you're saying?" asked her mother in awed tone.

"It just makes sense. She's the most lucid around me, right? All these problems started cropping up since I left."

"Treasure, we appreciate the offer, but you have your own life to live."

"No, really, I don't."

The phone went silent on the other end.

"Well, just let me know what happens," said Treasure, and they hung up.

· · · · · · · · · · · · · · · · · · · ·

The phone didn't ring again until 2:15 a.m, sending Howls squalling. Treasure checked the caller ID before answering. "Hello, Grammy," Treasure answered, trying to settle Howls back down.

"Hello, my girl! I hear we're going to be roomies!"

6

The Accident

A T THE EARLY-MORNING FACULTY INSERVICE, TREASURE'S EYES FELT gooey. She looked at the clock: only fifteen minutes left. Installing her grandmother as her roommate in her tiny apartment over the weekend had proved to be labor intensive. Tabiona demanded a major overhaul. Treasure had to rearrange the front room and then switch out the guest room mattresses for Grammy's own king-sized Intellibed. The latest rearrangement had lasted until 1:30 a.m. when Grammy had relented. "I am satisfied," she had sniffed, "but I'm not yet pleased." At 1:30, with a 6:00 a.m. meeting the next day, Treasure was satisfied with satisfied.

When she'd dragged herself out to the car this morning, Grammy was still sawing logs in the guest room. Treasure wrote a note that listed emergency numbers and urged Grammy to start up an afghan. She had been reluctant to leave this morning, and not just because she felt as energetic as a mud puddle. Grammy alone in her apartment? Or worse yet, Grammy out on the strip? Either scenario prompted her to pray:

"Dear Lord, please prevent Grammy Blume from wreaking havoc like Godzilla. If it be thy will, please prevent her from figuring out how to undo the dead bolt."

The thought of Grammy terrorizing the city, or vice versa, monopolized the entire awake section of her brain. "Also, please bless Howls to have the good sense to hide from her." Clearly, Grammy could cow Howls. Her mere presence rendered him mute. Her stare sent him hunting for refuge. He spent most of the previous night lurking behind the toilet bowl.

From beneath the muddle of her thoughts, Treasure registered that someone was saying her name. What were they talking about? Something about purchase orders. But that couldn't have anything to do with her. She swam up toward consciousness to respond, pushing away her Grammy-related fears to listen.

Dressed in gravel-colored gaucho pants, Bonnie B. Baumgartner, the secretary, was speaking: "I'd like to remind everyone that private expenditures must be approved by me. We aren't animals! We have a process in place. And while I don't want to point a finger," she said, pointing her finger, "Miss Blume did not clear the Sneetch shirts with me, nor has she submitted any receipts." Every eye followed the Queen's bright red nail to Treasure's face.

Treasure roused her mental faculties and stepped into the now. "I'm sorry," she stammered. "I didn't know about the protocol."

"It's in the handbook," Bonnie said, dropping her finger. "Did you fail to read the handbook in its entirety?"

Treasure felt herself shrink. Bonnie had the talent of making people feel small—not physically (Treasure wouldn't mind that) but mentally.

"Well, since the shirts were donated, I didn't think I had to get them approved or reimbursed."

Bonnie pursed her lips. "For charitable contributions, you need to use a form in order for us to square up with the IRS. And don't even get me started on the topic of copyright infringement. I doubt you checked with the Theodore Gessel estate."

At this point Anita, the principal, jumped in, hoping to shift the focus. "You've made your point, Bonnie. We'll all try to use the proper procedure from now on. You can speak to Treasure about this situation privately. Let's move on."

If there was anything Bonnie hated, it was doing things privately. "I just feel that this is a teaching moment, Anita. And besides, I think we need to talk about the deeper issue here."

Knowing that a full report on the deeper issue would be given to the superintendent if Bonnie was thwarted, Anita yielded. "What deeper issue?"

"Well, the truth of the matter is," Bonnie paused dramatically, "I think Miss Blume is trying to buy the affections of her students."

The room began to squirm. Only Anita and Treasure seemed

paralyzed. From the back, the P.E. teacher drew her breath audibly. The librarian nudged his neighbor and began to whisper. Several teachers seemed to be examining their footwear closely. Treasure shot a glance over to the first grade group. Lucinda was nodding, clearly on board with Bonnie's train of thought. Kristen looked stung. She opened her mouth, then shut it, looking away from Treasure.

Bonnie continued, "And there was also the Pez incident with the Torres boy. We heard about that too." There was little that happened in the hive that escaped her notice.

"I'm trying to buy their love?" asked Treasure numbly, trying to grasp the concept. "With Sneetch shirts and Pez dispensers?"

"Well, maybe not intentionally," Bonnie flounced.

Treasure fought the urge to blurt. Because of her gift, she drew more than her fair share of insults and accusations. She developed a method for dealing with them. *I am a duck's back*, she mentally intoned. *These words roll off me like water.* But somehow the mantra didn't help this time. The sting clung to her, digging in with vicious spurs. She felt raw. How dare this woman question her intentions? To Treasure, intentions were sacred. She had learned long ago that she couldn't control outcomes. Outcomes often went awry. But she could control her own intentions. And in this case, her only intention was to help her students, sparing them feelings of embarrassment or exclusion.

In the silence, the accusation hovered over the teacher's lounge like an unpleasant gas. Bonnie sensed she was close to bringing Treasure down.

"After all," Bonnie went on, "it's clear you have to do something, since you don't seem to have the knack for making people like you."

Mentally, Treasure had been midway down the duck's back. But this statement shattered her mental duck completely. She began to spew words. "Just because you've never had an altruistic thought in your life, just because you never put yourself in those kids' place, just because everything for you is apparently perfectly typed and neatly filed . . ." Treasure gradually became aware that she was blurting and getting off topic as she did so (what did Bonnie's infuriating filing system have to do with this?). She must end the sentence, and soon, "You, um, can't imagine that someone else can. Have an altruistic thought, that is. That someone else might not be motivated by what other people think of them."

Bonnie inspected her nails. "I was only telling the truth. I pride myself on being truthful," she said. She didn't add that she counted it as her personal mission to weed the crop of first-year teachers, and Treasure was dandelion #1.

"Social Darwinist. You are the poster child for Social Darwinism!" Treasure shouted, pointing her own finger this time.

"I do not believe we descended from apes!" said Bonnie, now affronted.

Oddly, a strange thought flitted into Treasure's head. She wished Bonnie's name didn't start with B. It was a fine letter, one she'd always been fond of, especially since it was the first letter of her own last name. But now its association with Bonnie sullied it.

The thought gave her time to rebuild her mental duck. She was ready to respond more reasonably, when another teacher stood up. Treasure recognized her as one of the fourth-grade teachers, Dawn Robbins. She was built like a linebacker with no visible neck. Her honey-colored hair was done up in curls the size and shape of soda cans.

She put a hand on her hip and said, "Oh, Bonnie, back off. What you say isn't truth. It's your own opinion. And we are not required to listen to you tout it as truth."

An unpleasant shade of red began to creep up Bonnie's neck toward her face. She narrowed her eye and opened her mouth to speak, but Dawn cut her off.

"Anyone with half an eye can see that Treasure is doing good things for those kids. I have the Torres boy's sister in my class, and if Treasure can make any headway with that family, then I say she must be a miracle worker, with or without Pez and Sneetch shirts. As for buying their affections, then I'm guilty as well, since I just had a popcorn party last week in my class. It's not like we have any budget for supplements. We all dip in our own pockets. Maybe you'd know that if you were a teacher rather than a secretary."

Bonnie sucked her breath in through her teeth. Everyone on the faculty knew she held a never-used degree in elementary education.

Dawn didn't give Bonnie time to fire off another shot. Instead, she turned to Treasure, who was flabbergasted that someone would stand up for her. She'd never even talked to Dawn before, except to get the door for her when she was moving poster boards in one day.

"And, Treasure, really, I don't know why you threw Darwin in there.

You'll only mystify her." She looked back at Bonnie.

Bonnie glared at her, her attack foiled. How dare she throw her failed teaching career up in her face? "Well, you've made your allegiance clear, Dawn," she said.

"Yes, I suppose I have," said Dawn, plopping down in her seat.

Anita quickly stood and took control. "Thank you, Dawn, Treasure, and Bonnie, for bringing up these important details. Bonnie, please make a note." Her eyes flicked over to Treasure. "We have some resources. Let's see if we can carve out a little bit of money in the budget for a teacher's discretionary fund."

Bonnie nodded, but her pen remained in her hair.

"Since the bell will ring in two minutes, and the children are arriving, we will conclude this meeting and table the rest of the agenda."

As the meeting broke up and the teachers moved out, swinging in a wide arc to avoid her, Treasure found herself unable to move. Her moist palms left wet handprints on her denim skirt. She knew she needed to find Dawn and thank her, but she was certain it would come out a garbled mess. She caught sight of Dawn's broad shoulders as she weaved her way toward the door.

"You didn't need to," Treasure blurted.

Dawn halted and turned back. "Yes. I did. But I didn't do it for you. I did it for me. She's bullied this school from behind that desk for years." Dawn walked over and sat next to Treasure. "When she attacked you for all the good you've been doing, I couldn't sit there anymore."

Treasure looked toward the window. "But still, I don't want you to get into trouble because of me."

Dawn patted her arm. "Well, I didn't plan to battle with her today, but I knew it was coming. We've known each other for years, since college in fact. Don't fret about it." She hesitated, then continued. "I know that the other teachers haven't made life easy on you, and I should have made more of an effort at the start. But I've watched you and watched what you do. You remind me of how I was at the beginning. I know what you're doing for those kids. And that's what counts."

Treasure felt baffled again. She hadn't had an inkling that anyone was aware of her efforts. The thought warmed her like sun. She smiled. But the memory of Bonnie's words threatened to shut out all sunlight like Levolor blinds.

"I don't know why I let it upset me," said Treasure. "I usually handle that kind of stuff a lot better."

"No one handles attacks well."

"Well," said Treasure, "I've had a lot of practice."

"And you'll get more, before this is through. Bonnie is a devil," said Dawn, rising to her feet. "She may be worse, since she's better organized. Just watch your back. I'll be watching too." She left the room, limping slightly on her left leg as the bell rang.

· · · · · · · · · · · · · · · · · · · ·

Dennis Cameron turned his cell phone back on as soon as he left the building where his afternoon accounting class was held. The professor, a Pakistani woman who spoke more rapidly than a fry cook, despised cell phones. She had threatened to automatically fail the fool who answered a cell phone in her class. So far it was the only thing Dennis was sure that he understood. He tried not to resent the fact that he had taken out a student loan for this.

He jogged toward his van as he pushed buttons. It was about an hour before he had to pick up Micaela. He hated to be out of her reach. Every time he went to class, he felt like he was an astronaut rounding the dark side of the moon. What if she had an emergency? What if his mom did? And if he was honest with himself, he felt guilty for taking the class at all. It absorbed time and focus, both of which he could have spent with Micaela and his mother. He shook off the dark feelings and gave himself a mental pep talk. *I'm doing this for Micaela—so that we can have a better life.* He let these two statements play through his head, like a reader board at a bank, while he fiddled with his phone. There were two new messages. He opened his van door and sat down as he listened.

"Mr. Cameron, this is Bonnie B. Baumgartner calling. Micaela has had an accident and needs a fresh pair of pants. Please come to the front office as soon as you receive this message."

Dennis groaned and hit his head against the steering wheel, causing the horn to honk. The honk seemed to spur him into action. He started the van, stuck it in gear, and roared out onto the street. It had happened. His biggest fear. Micaela needed him and he wasn't there. Now his mental reader board read: *You're such an idiot. You're such an idiot.*

Of course, this would happen on the one day that he had an afternoon class. Of course it would happen when he was gone, and Micaela was at the mercy of Bonnie. Dennis had always tried to avoid her. He doubted she'd be kind and sympathetic toward Micaela. Once, he'd entered the office for her signature on something and had gone to wipe a dead bug off her usually meticulous desk. "Don't," she'd said. "It's an example. It's there so any other bug who tries it will know not to mess with me." Well, Dennis knew enough not to mess with her. But Micaela might not. He hit the button on his phone and listened to the next message, accelerating through a stop sign as he did so.

"Dennis, it's Sheila. I just got a call from that school about Micaela. It woke me up. You know I work nights. I told them I couldn't help them. I don't have anything of Micaela's anyway. If she peed her pants, it serves her right to have to sit in them. Don't let them call me again."

Dennis winced. His heart shriveled at the metallic sound of her voice. How could he have ever fallen for her? He guessed that if Sparkle Plenty ever had a wardrobe malfunction, the person who suggested that "it served her right" would have been stabbed with a stiletto heel. He stepped down harder on the gas pedal, checking his mirrors as he changed lanes.

How fast could he get there? Fifteen minutes? Maybe ten? How long ago did Bonnie leave the first message? He fumbled with the phone in his hand as he checked. Forty-five minutes ago. Not good. Forty-five minutes worth of Micaela sitting outside the office, on the stiff bench while Bonnie sat at the computer playing solitaire. Forty-five minutes worth of kids circling Micaela laughing and pointing at her wet pants. Micaela crumpling. Micaela sobbing. Micaela destroyed.

He had to get there. Now. He gunned the car through another intersection as the light changed from yellow to red. *Faster, faster, faster,* he thought, wedging his van into a space between a sports car and a Buick. If only he had his old Camaro. He sold it when Micaela was born. The van was safer and more practical, in case he ever got any catering gigs. Unfortunately, it was bred for comfort, not speed.

He heard the sound of the siren first, since he had stopped looking in the rearview mirror. He was no longer interested in anything behind him. When he did look back, he deluded himself into thinking that the officer just wanted him to get out of the way so that he could pursue someone else. He slid over to the right hand lane. The police cruiser pulled in right behind him. He slowed down and pulled onto the shoulder, the red and blue lights pulsing into his brain.

The rotund officer got out of his car and moseyed over to the van's driver side window. Dennis unrolled it and shoved his license and registration at him. The officer didn't make a move to take the documents.

"Do you know why I pulled you over?"

Dennis thought for a minute. This was not a question he wanted to get wrong. What offense should he pick? He had committed a veritable smorgasbord of traffic violations. He opted for honesty.

"That depends. How long have you been following me?"

The portly policeman was not amused. He took the documents from Dennis's outstretched hand. Before he replied, Dennis plunged ahead. "I know I was speeding, and that I ran that last light. But it's an emergency!"

The word *emergency* snapped the officer up straight. "What is it?"

Dennis swallowed hard. "It's my daughter. There's been an accident."

"Is she injured? I can call for lights and sirens," said the officer, hurriedly getting out his CB.

Dennis felt stupid. "Uhm, no. Not that type of emergency. She wet her pants at school."

The officer took off his shades and looked at the ground. For a minute, Dennis feared he might draw his gun and arrest him for lying. When he looked back up, he could see the officer was laughing and snorting. Now Dennis was not amused. Every second he watched this guy's beer belly jiggle was another second that Micaela was wet, ashamed, and uncomfortable. The cop paused to wipe tears away from his cheeks.

"Son, in my job, when someone says emergency, I think of someone smeared across a highway, not a little bodily fluid. I'll be back in a minute." He sauntered back to his car, shaking his head.

Ten minutes of torture later, he returned and handed Dennis a ticket for two moving violations. "You'll see I only wrote you up for two of the three violations I saw you commit, due to your, ah, extenuating circumstances," he said, his smile puckering. Dennis refused to look at his fat fleshy face, instead staring straight ahead. The officer sobered and put on his Safety Officer routine, "You need to take more care, son. Don't let your daughter's accident make you have an accident," he said, walking away from the car.

Dennis bristled at the guy calling him "son." *He's probably the same age as I am, the self-righteous pig*, he thought. *How can you be that fat and still be on the force?* He smiled as he pictured McGruff the Crime Dog taking a bite out of the officer's meaty thighs.

When he finally parked and sprinted into the front office, there was no Micaela. *They could have at least pulled her out of class*, he thought.

"Where is she?" he asked Bonnie. She reminded him of a gargoyle with teased violet hair.

She looked at him blankly. "Who?" she asked.

Dennis counted to ten before he answered. "I got a phone call about Micaela needing a spare change of clothes."

"Oh," the gargoyle said dismissively. "We tried to call your wife, but she sounded incoherent. Micaela was sobbing here on the bench when we talked to your wife. She made a wet spot. I had to clean it up with disinfectant wipes. I always keep them on hand to keep my desk free of germs from little noses and hands."

The way she said it made Dennis realize that she must see these children in those terms: not individuals, not people, but random body parts with germ-spreading potential.

"Where is Micaela now?" he asked through gritted teeth.

"Well," said Bonnie, "when it was clear that no one was going to come, I sent her back to class. After today, I bet she won't wet her pants again at school. You know, I always think a little taste of humility makes them try harder."

Dennis wanted to rip the glasses off her nose and make her eat them. He thanked the secretary. It would not be good to go off on her; she held way too much power. He speedwalked out to the classroom, intending to march right in. But when he thought about it, he realized that would only make things worse for Micaela. So instead, he looked through the rectangular window in the door.

Micaela was sitting in her desk, head bent over her work, so he couldn't see her pants. At least she wasn't bawling. Class was almost over. He stood watching while the teacher moved from desk to desk and then moved back to the head of the classroom, then dismissed them. Micaela was the last to get up and walk out.

He caught her at the door and held her. "Are you okay, baby? I'm so sorry I wasn't there when they called me."

"It's okay, Daddy. Do you want to see my bean sprout? We are going to grow lima beans in class. Miss Treasure says they aren't so good to eat, but they are fun to grow. I get to take the bean home with me and record what it does, and then we are going to plant them together when they sprout." Micaela got over things quickly. It was one of her gifts. Unfortunately, Dennis didn't have the same gift.

As he peered back through the window, he saw the smooth and dry rear end of Treasure Blume as she bent down to pick up scattered books in the book nook. The sight filled him not only with the dislike he had felt for her from the start, but also all the rage that he felt from the self-righteous piggy policeman, the gargoyle secretary, and his selfish ex-wife. The rage welled inside, a subterranean zit about to pop. Without even looking at Micaela's pants, he said, "Wait right here. Don't move." Then he walked in the classroom.

Treasure heard the door open. She expected it to be a student who had missed the bus. She expected to meet someone whose head reached to her waist, and she leaned down as she turned. She found herself looking into the belt buckle of Dennis, the lunch lady. She quickly straightened and smiled up at him. She liked what she knew about him, both from Micaela and from her own experience. From her own experience, she knew that he worked in the cafeteria to be close to Micaela and that he took extra care serving the food. From Micaela, she knew that he pretended to be a mad dog when he brushed his teeth. She knew that he reshingled the roof on his mother's house by himself. She knew that he planned a mermaid birthday party for Micaela, inviting all of her friends and creating a cake that looked like a mermaid. She was totally unprepared for the look in his eyes.

After all, she thought, she'd handled the crisis today well. She noticed Micaela's pants as the kids trooped back in from recess, and she pulled her aside then, asking her aide, Mrs. Gutierrez, to start the class without her. They were reading *The Spiderwick Chronicles* aloud. She'd talked to Micaela, who tearfully acknowledged the problem. Treasure had wiped her tears and assured her that no other kids had noticed yet. "That's right," Micaela had said, snuffling into her sleeve, " 'cuz I kept my back to the wall, until I had to turn the corner to come in here. That's why I was at the back of the line."

"I know," said Treasure. "You're never at the back of the line, so I thought something must be wrong. We'll get this taken care of."

School policy dictated that parents must be notified in a bathroom emergency. Bonnie had drilled it into her head, and after this morning, Treasure didn't want to be accused of violating policy again. She didn't like surrendering Micaela to Bonnie, but she comforted herself in knowing that her dad was probably around. She left Micaela and went back to class, but something nagged her that it wasn't right.

After fifteen minutes, when the groups started to work on their readers' theater, she made up her mind that she would duck out again. But when she peeked out, she saw Micaela coming toward the classroom, still crying, still wet.

"What happened?" she asked. She stepped out onto the ramp outside the classroom and shut the door.

"They . . . they said that they can't get a hold of my dad, and my mom wouldn't help me. . . so they sent me back here . . ." Micaela sobbed.

Treasure was still mad that her classroom was the farthest from the bathrooms. No other first-grade class was as far away. Of course the veteran teachers got close classrooms. Oh, that slick Bonnie. Momentarily, Treasure wished she had giant feet so she could stomp her like grapes.

"Stay right here," she said, hugging Micaela. She went back in the classroom. Mrs. Guitierrez gave her a funny look. She mouthed, "Keep going, I'm not here." She snuck to the closet and got out a bag filled with brand new pants (six different colors in three different sizes for both boys and girls) and Dora and Lightning McQueen underwear. She blessed her mother's admonition to be prepared. She slipped back out and into the hall.

In the hall, Micaela was delighted with the selection. She settled on a pair of panties with Dora as a princess and a pair of blue stretchy pants with butterflies. Miss Treasure also gave her a Ziploc bag to put the stinky clothes in. As they walked to the restroom, Treasure told her about a time when she was at school and wet her pants. Her mom couldn't be reached either, because she was on a field trip with her own class. She'd solved the problem by deliberately sitting in a mud puddle, so she could disguise the stain. "Did it help?" asked Micaela.

"Well, at least they made fun of me for sitting in a puddle rather than wetting my pants," concluded Treasure.

Micaela pondered the practicality of her teacher's solution. "But we hardly ever have puddles here," she said, sighing.

She went into the bathroom to change while Miss Treasure stood guard. When she came back, she handed the Ziploc to Miss Treasure who (as agreed) stuck it in her non-descript bag. Together they went back to class. Miss Treasure put the bag in the closet and started math time. She hadn't even had time to think about the episode until right now, with Micaela's dad staring her down.

"Mr. Cameron, I'm so sorry about the situation with Micaela today. I guess we couldn't get a hold of you . . ." Treasure started to say, intending to explain that she had handled the situation and that he didn't need to worry. But she didn't get that far before Dennis jumped in. It bugged him that she called him Mr. Cameron instead of Dennis, like he was an old man with a walker.

"Well, it's not like you tried very hard, from what I hear," said Dennis with heat. "Did you even try to find me? Or did you just hand her off to the office? Bonnie says she was sobbing, and for Bonnie to notice, it had to be bad."

Treasure glanced out the glass rectangle in the door. Micaela was absorbed in her lima bean observations, sitting on the concrete sidewalk. "Of course I took her to the office, Mr. Cameron. That's school policy."

"I don't give a flip about policy. I care about my daughter, and obviously, you don't."

So that's the way it's going to be, is it? thought Treasure. It wasn't an unfamiliar scenario. People often accused her of their own inadequacies. Projection. Her father had taught her the term.

"She trusted you, and you betrayed her . . ." Dennis said.

At this point, Treasure went icy. Accused of betrayal and buying the children's affections in the same day? She wasn't going to apologize for doing her job. And frankly, she was not in need of another verbal beating right now. "I'm sure I don't know what you're talking about. I do care about your daughter, and I didn't betray her, but obviously, you feel that you did," Treasure said.

"How I feel is none of your business," said Dennis. He felt his ears turning red. *Most likely, they'll explode off my head*, he thought.

Reacting to his obvious anger, Treasure began to blurt. "And obviously, based on your response time, you must not have thought it was much of an emergency at all."

Dennis was too mad to speak. He sputtered, trying to begin several sentences, unable to get them out. "Don't tell me to . . . You have no right . . . Of course I . . ."

Luckily, it gave Treasure time to imagine her mental duck. She drew a deep breath and started to speak in a low tone. "We took care of the problem. You'd know that if you had taken the time to talk to Micaela before you barged in here. Did you even speak to her?"

Treasure looked at him, waiting for him to spit out the venom that was clearly pooling in his throat. She wasn't angry anymore. Instead she was a little bit sad. She'd liked this man. She always chose his line for lunch, eager to see how he arranged the food on her tray. Based on his plating alone, he was more suited to Kitchen Stadium than the lunchroom.

With a nearly convulsive effort, Dennis swallowed and closed his eyes. He raised his hands and drew them through his surprisingly thick hair. Treasure had never seen it outside of a hair net before. It was nice: reddish brown and shaggy, a bit like the ears on an Irish setter. Then he looked up at her: "I want you to know that I blame you for this."

Not the first time I've heard that, thought Treasure, but instead she drew herself up and mustered all the dignity she could. "For what, Mr. Cameron? For the small capacity of children's bladders?"

"Yes," said Dennis, "and for poisoning her against lima beans. If she won't eat them, I'm holding you accountable." And with that, he slapped the top of a desk and left the room.

.... 7

The Circus Plan

TREASURE DIDN'T HAVE TIME TO WORRY ABOUT HER BIG BLOWOUT with Micaela's dad. With Grammy in her apartment, she frequently didn't have time to put on deodorant or shower. Grammy's wanderlust kept Treasure on constant alert. When Treasure arrived home, after that horrific day of school, Grammy wasn't there at all. Treasure counted to three before she began to panic. She stepped out of her front door, calling "Here, Grammy Grammy," much the same way she called for Howls when he went missing. In fact, Howls gave her the first clue that Grammy had gone AWOL. He was sprawled across Grammy's bed.

"Land, girl. Did you think I'd gone to the Yukon? I bet they could hear you out on the tundra," said Grammy, stepping out of Mr. Fong's apartment next door.

"Grammy!" said Treasure, hurling herself into her arms.

"Don't squeeze so tight. I haven't been on that Sally Field's Boniva for long. I doubt my bones can take it."

"You have to promise not to do that ever again, Grams."

"I'll die if I have to stay in there with that scraggly old cat all the time. I'm not a hamster. You can't lock me up in a cage. Besides, Mr. Fong is right neighborly. I think he's the perfect kind of man. He just nods at everything I say and keeps his yap shut. I have to say, I find that very attractive."

Treasure gave up. Poor Mr. Fong. She looked at Grammy sternly. "Oh, now what would Varden Moyle say about that?"

"That old coot got me in a heap of trouble with his ways. Mr. Fong's my favorite now."

Mr. Fong himself came to the door, nodding and smiling. He reached out and patted Grammy's arm. Then he reached over and patted Treasure's. It was his way of saying that they should stop fighting.

"Thank you for your hospitality, Mr. Fong. Grandma just said how much she enjoyed your company."

Mr. Fong could read lips, if Treasure went slow. He bowed slightly to show that he understood. He reached over and kissed Grammy's hand. It was his way of saying she was welcome in his home. Then he shut the door, waving good-bye.

Treasure and Grammy headed back in. At the sight of Grammy (who hissed at him), Howls streaked into the bathroom for another round of lurk and scurry with his new roommate.

Grammy plopped down on the couch. "Honestly, girl, why didn't you just text me?"

Treasure looked up at the ceiling. "You text?"

· · · · · · · · · · · · · · · · · · · ·

Every day since then had been just as jam-packed. For starters, Grammy still had Stepper practice on Tuesdays, Thursdays, and Saturdays in St. George. She insisted that she could drive it alone in Mullet. But Treasure didn't trust Mullet. For one thing, he sucked gas like a Winnebago. For another, he was only occasionally reliable. For an entire week, he only ran in reverse. It didn't phase Grammy though. She just bought herself some goggles and started driving backwards with her head out the window. Luckily, Treasure caught her before the cops did. She hid the goggles, but the image of Grammy backing down the Virgin River Gorge was enough to keep Treasure toting her Grammy over the roads three times a week.

And somehow, inadvertently, she'd managed to resume most of her Stepper gopher duties, like getting water for the girls, cueing music, and rubbing Bengay into cramped muscles. Randy averaged attendance at about one in every four practices, and he never provided Ben-gay service. Therefore, Ruby took him to task and demoted him in front of the entire company: twenty-five ladies all clucking and nodding their heads in agreement.

"You just don't seem to have the drive or the passion for the Steppers that your sister has," said Ruby. Randy had to agree. He didn't mention that unlike Treasure, he actually had a social life outside the geriatric set. That would only hurt Treasure, not Ruby. Publicly he took his demotion gracefully and vowed to assist the reinstated Head Gopher when his schedule allowed.

Ruby's tsking of Randy caught Treasure by surprise. She wasn't trying to roost him out. She just saw needs and filled them, like when Velva Lee's leg warmer fell off in the middle of "Pretty Young Thing" (it was part of their salute to Michael Jackson). Treasure just knew that if she didn't get that leg warmer off the floor, someone was going to slip on it during the samba rolls in the next section. And technically, she didn't have to learn the new routine (the Steppers added a new one every four months or so, just to keep it fresh). But what else was she going to do for three hours while Grammy practiced? She couldn't help it. She heard the music, and she just started moving. Ruby always complimented her on how quickly she picked up the dances. And Treasure was flattered, until she remembered that she was surrounded by women in various stages of dementia. Several couldn't remember the names of their first husbands.

And so, whereas Randy would disappear down the hall, or plug in his laptop and turn his back on the Steppers, Treasure danced, critiqued, caught leg warmers, and loved every minute of it.

"He was never really a part of us the way that you were, honey," said Ruby one night after practice. "And I cannot get over the change in Tabiona. She seems positively sane! She was within inches of getting kicked out. You know, all that crazy business with LuNae. But this is just the best solution for all of us!" Treasure nodded and did not mention that she had purchased this best solution at a high price: her time, just when it seemed she needed it most.

At school, they were ending the first term, and Treasure was working on several big projects with the kids. Parent-teacher conferences were looming, and Treasure had been warned by Dawn Robbins (who still had her back and sat by her at every faculty meeting) that they had never been successful.

"The parents that you most need to talk to never show up. Expect it to be a big waste of your time. I've about given up on it," said Dawn, shifting in her seat at the end of another Bonnie B. Baumgartner faculty production.

"So the traditional style just isn't working. Can we do something else instead?

"I don't know. Got any good solutions?"

Treasure just shook her head.

"Well, think on it some," said Dawn. "Maybe we can team up on this one."

At 2:00 a.m. after driving back from St. George, Treasure had it. The next morning, she ran to Dawn's class, just past the lunchroom, as soon as she got to work.

"What do you think about doing a circus?" she blurted to Dawn's back. Dawn's front was in the closet, getting out supplies for the fraction demonstration. She set down her graham crackers, started up her classroom computer, and googled "elephant rentals."

Treasure started to laugh.

Dawn scrolled down the page. "Who knew how easy it would be to rent an elephant?"

"This is Vegas, baby," said Treasure.

"The rumor alone should make Bonnie's hives flair up. So I'm willing. What do we need?"

"Well, I see it as a classroom production. We can make masks and easy costumes and cast the kids in all the roles."

"Like a lion tamer? And a trapeze artist? And a guy getting shot out of a cannon?" said Dawn thoughtfully. "I've got a couple of kids I'd volunteer for that."

Treasure turned serious. "What do you think? Will your fourth graders go for it? Especially if they're working with first graders?"

"Oh, they'll get into it. The question is, if we can get it past the powers that *be*," said Dawn, with a heavy emphasis on the last word.

"Not educational enough, huh?"

"For starters, it sounds fun. Bonnie hates fun." Dawn cocked her head. "But I think we can get Anita's support if we spin it the right way."

"So what's the right way?"

"We'll bill it as a mentorship opportunity for my kids and a hands-on learning situation for yours. "

Treasure nodded. "Plus we plug the creative, artistic, and physical education aspects of the project. I think we can make it work within our curricula."

"Oh yeah. And the science!" Dawn was a science junkie. "I'm excited just thinking about how I can use the trapeze act for a physics demonstration on force. Trust me, we can educationalize the heck out of this circus."

"And it doesn't have to be long," added Treasure. "We just do this short presentation, and then boom, all the kids and their parents are already there anyway, so we can still meet with them."

"What if we do it like a three ring circus, with something going on all the time? Then we can meet with parents as they come? We'll have to alternate duties a bit. I'll have my class do a ring, then yours, so one of us is free to talk with parents. What do you think?"

Treasure high-fived her. "Let's pitch our tent!"

After a conversation with an amused Anita, the circus (sans elephant) was a go. She was as ready as Dawn to try a creative approach to parent-teacher conferences.

Treasure was also working with the kids to create a portfolio to show their parents their progress in each major field. Most of it featured things they had already done in the class, like their finger painting projects, handwriting assessments, math worksheets, and scorecards from *Pass the Pigs,* a math game that taught addition using two miniature plastic pigs instead of dice. Treasure was delighted to discover how quick Liwayway was with numbers. She won the game and was crowned Super Mathlete. She shied away from the attention but accepted the prize of her own set of tiny porkers, along with the cheers of her class. In that moment, Liwayway was absolutely present with them, holding her pigs aloft, and dancing out of Octavio's reach. It was the most engaged she had been the entire year.

But Treasure also wanted to add something special to the portfolio, something to showcase their creative writing abilities. As a first-grade teacher, she dedicated a lot of her time to making sure each child could read and write at grade level. And so she started the Young Authors' workshop, in which each student would write and illustrate his or her own book, then Treasure would laminate the covers and bind them. She would also video each child reading his or her book aloud and burn it onto a DVD for the parents to take home.

"What are we supposed to write about?" asked Sharonda when Treasure explained the project to them.

"Well, anything you want," said Treasure. "But I hope you will write about your life. I want to make sure that you are in your own story."

"Does that mean we can make stuff up?" asked Spencer.

"Well, since it's your story, I won't be able to tell if you made stuff up. You're the author. You get to decide," Treasure told him.

"What if I write about how I can fly?" asked Spencer, testing her.

"Then I'll believe it," Treasure answered solemnly.

"Or that I have radioactive head lice and I'm using them to suck out people's brains so that I can take over the school?"

"Oh, I definitely believe that," said Treasure as the rest of the class grossed out.

The students loved the creative power of the project. It soon became their favorite part of the day, with story time in the book nook running a close second. Whenever the class would get too loud, Treasure would look at the clock and keep track of every minute wasted. She wouldn't say anything, except, "That's thirty seconds." The kids knew that anytime they messed around was shaved off from their young author time. Sharonda glared at the noisy kids until they shut their mouths. It did not do to get on Sharonda's bad side.

Micaela was particularly focused during this time. She didn't look up or talk to her neighbors. But it didn't seem like she was talking to anybody anymore. During recess, she would race to the swings alone and swing as high, hard, and fast as she could. The other kids would nag and beg her to take turns. But it was like she couldn't hear them. The only thing that made her come alive was books. She had devoured everything on Treasure's book spinners and asked for more. Treasure bought new books just for her and borrowed what she could from the library and the other teachers (those that were willing, like Kristen and Dawn). When she'd plucked up her courage to ask the General, she received a thirty-minute lecture about the dangers of taking new readers beyond grade level before they were mature enough. "They just burn out on the tough stuff!" the General chided her. Treasure listened, nodded, and wished she hadn't asked. Micaela's problem wasn't that she wasn't mature enough. It might just be that she was too mature. Treasure was worried. Her little shoulders sagged as she took off her backpack in the mornings. And now she had resigned her post as line leader for the week with little or no explanation.

Treasure hadn't gotten a chance to read Micaela's story. She'd read everyone else's. There were stories about lost teeth, about going to Disneyland, and becoming veterinarians. Even Eduardo showed Treasure his story. His story was about how he didn't cry when he got his tattoo and how he wanted to drive a Monster Truck. And while it disturbed Treasure, it was the least hostile project he'd created so far. But Micaela was secretive about her story. She refused to turn it in and kept it in her desk so that she could keep working on it whenever she finished her work early.

Finally, the projects were finished, and one by one, the students got to read their masterpieces in front of the class with Treasure filming.

Micaela climbed up the tall stool, her straight brown hair caught up in a fishtail braid, and began her story: "This is a story about a very sad dad," she said, holding her first page open. The illustration featured a man with red brown hair and a tall chef's hat holding a whisk. The man was frowning. She turned the page, "The sad dad wasn't always sad. He used to sing silly songs like 'I'm Being Swallowed by a Boa Constrictor.'" The words were accompanied by a picture of the man in the chef's hat holding a little girl's hand. Music notes came out from their mouths in big bubbles. A great big snake curled around their legs. The students giggled.

"But now the dad just moped. Why was he so sad?" Micaela turned the page. "Was it because his pants were too tight? Was it because the dogs like to fight?" The words were accompanied by a picture of a long, low orange dog snarling at a black scribble with beady eyes.

She turned another page. "I don't know why, because he wouldn't say. Instead he cooked. He cooked meatballs, and he cooked rice, and he cooked gnocchi." The accompanying page had plates filled with steaming piles of food. Treasure was amazed that she had spelled gnocchi correctly.

"But no one wanted to eat his food. The sad dad had a mommy who was sick. She couldn't eat all the food." This page showed a woman in a bed surrounded by more piles of food.

"And the little girl couldn't eat all the food either. What she wanted was for her dad to stop cooking and sing more silly songs. But he just kept cooking. The End."

Micaela slipped off the stool, went back to her desk, and put her head down. The class clapped. Treasure lowered the camera. The bell rang for recess, and the kids ran outside. Micaela didn't move. Treasure knelt beside her and put her hand on Micaela's back. She didn't say anything. Micaela started to cry. She unfolded herself from her desk and fell into Treasure's arms. As she held the sobbing little girl, Treasure thought about going to get Micaela's dad from the lunchroom, but she felt unsure. In the first place, it wasn't like they were even on speaking terms. But Treasure knew how much Dennis loved his daughter. He would want to be there right now. Still, though, he might just get angry about the story. He might be too close to help Micaela.

Treasure decided to ask. "Would you like me to get your daddy? I'm sure I could find him."

Micaela shook her head and wiped her nose on Treasure's sleeve. "No. I don't think he knows that I know he's sad. I think he thinks it's a secret, and I don't want him to know that I know his secret."

Treasure stroked her hair. "Micaela, I know your dad doesn't want you to be sad, even if he is."

Micaela got a fierce look in her eyes. She sat up and moved away from Treasure's reach. "He told me that Grandma is sick and she's not getting better. But while he said it, he was making a ragout. I hate ragout. All he cares about is food."

"That's not true. Maybe food is the only way he knows to make people feel better."

"But Grandma can't even eat. She gets sick when she eats. And I hate Fishstick. He fights with Puff, and he barks at me and nips my heels and tries to herd me like a sheep."

Wisely, Treasure decided not to ask about Fishstick. "Maybe that's why he is so sad."

"Because he can't herd me?"

"No, your dad. Because he can't do anything to help your grandma. Even the best that he can do doesn't help." Treasure thought for minute. "Maybe we can't help your grandma, but we can help your dad. What makes your dad happiest?"

"Besides food?" Micaela thought for minute. "Rain clouds."

"Rain clouds make me happy too, but I don't think we can make him a rain cloud. What else?"

"Kicking Fishstick?" she asked slyly, "but he doesn't really do it. He just threatens to, when Fishstick herds me." Micaela tapped her chin with her finger. Her forehead wrinkled in frustration. Finally, she gave up. "I don't know. I don't know if he knows how to be happy. He's happy when people eat his food."

"Well, maybe that's something we can work with," said Treasure. She hadn't been to the lunchroom for a while. Lately she'd been racing back to her apartment to check on Grammy. She thought back over the last couple of weeks. She hadn't heard any stories about weird food. And that was weird in itself.

She gave Micaela a hug. "Let's you and me think up a plan. You think about it tonight, and I'll think about it too, and tomorrow, we'll talk, okay?"

Micaela rubbed her eyes, nodded, and calmed down. She believed her teacher could fix anything. Her teacher was not so sure. The bell rang, signaling the end of recess. The kids trooped back in, and Treasure clapped her hands together: "Okay friends, let's gather for reading time!"

· · · · · · · · · · · · · · · · · · · ·

Unbeknownst to Treasure, Dennis was worried about Micaela too. But he had no idea that his little girl was worried about him. He thought that she wasn't getting enough iron in her diet. He didn't let himself delve deeper into what else might be wrong with her because if he did, he would have to delve deeper into what was wrong with him. And he didn't have time for that. He was cooking, yes. But he was doing so much more.

Three weeks ago last Monday, Dennis had gotten Micaela up, made breakfast for her, braided her hair, and taken her to school, just like every morning. But unlike every morning, as soon as the classroom door shut behind Micaela, he ran to his van, shucked his cafeteria gear in the back, and drove back to pick up his mom for an appointment with her oncologist. As they sat in the frigid room across from the cherry veneer desk, the doctor told them that the cancer was not responding. And so they had a decision to make. The doctor outlined their options. Either she could undergo more aggressive chemo, or she could stop treatment altogether in order to improve her quality of life. In either scenario, the doctor had used the word terminal. Dennis was caught at the doctor's first sentence: *The cancer is not responding.* As if they had invited the disease to a party and it hadn't returned the RSVP. It made Dennis want to shake the doctor.

"Just say what you mean," he'd say. Frankly, an organism was eating his mother from the inside out. She was being digested.

His mother pressed the heels of her hands into her eyes. She didn't say anything. It was Dennis who choked out, "How long?"

"With treatment, it's hard to know. Maybe five years. Maybe five months. Maybe five days, because of the risks. Without treatment, it would be more like five months."

Dennis had nodded and wheeled his mother out of the office and got her loaded into his van. The first things she said was, "You can't tell Micaela." Dennis didn't know what to say, but he nodded. His mom closed her eyes and settled her head back into the headrest. Dennis reached over and aimed the air vents at her. He couldn't remember a time when he hadn't taken care of his mom. His dad had walked out on them years ago. Dennis was used to being the strong man. But he didn't know if he could play the role anymore. "What do you want to do, Mom?" he asked.

"For tonight, I just want to go home, pat my dog, and see my granddaughter."

"Are you hungry, Mom? Is there anything I could get you that would taste good to you?" Dennis felt helpless.

Her smile was so thin it reminded him of prosciutto. "No, let's just go home."

From then on, he took her to every appointment. He was there on the next visit, when his mom opted to try the more aggressive treatment. Because he didn't have any extra time between the cafeteria and Micaela, he dropped his stats class. Driving away from the campus for the last time, he didn't feel any regret. He'd repay the loan somehow. He was just mad at the class for stealing him away from his mom and his daughter and giving him nothing in return. But that was his last thought about it.

Even inside the aftermath, Dennis still hadn't forgotten his lunch-room ambitions. His mom couldn't eat anymore. But the kids at school still could. He was haunted by the anonymous lunchroom donor and the idea that lunch might be the only meal some students would eat that day. The ideas buzzed like a low frequency radio station through his head. His talent with food could be his gift to these kids. He wanted to expose them to a higher level of cuisine. But it still wasn't working. The week after Thelma's warning hadn't gone any better than the week before it.

Thursday's gazpacho had been a bloody disaster. The lunchroom looked like the set from a WWII battle movie. And so, Thelma had decreed: no more high-class garbage. Dennis had agreed with her. What he was doing wasn't working for him or for the students.

But he didn't give up. Instead, he went back to basics. What was throwing him off, he decided, was making the food in huge quantities with lower quality ingredients. So he returned to his own kitchen to practice and regroup. He started testing recipes. What would happen if you quadrupled the recipe for salmon croquettes? Did the quality suffer? How about beef ragout? Could you make it in fifty-gallon batches? What was the cost per batch? He became Dr. Frankenstein, trying to infuse new life into old concoctions, obsessed with his work.

Food began piling up in every corner of their little kitchen. Every cupboard was a food stash. Luckily, Fishstick and Puff were devoted taste testers. If they wouldn't eat it, then he knew he had to trash the batch. If they sniffed it, walked away, and then returned to it, he would let them eat it. If they fought and snarled over it, he made Micaela try it. If Micaela liked it, he would load it up and deliver it to the local soup kitchen, and then he would make it again and again, to see if he could duplicate his results.

But Micaela soon grew tired of the game and refused to eat everything he shoved at her. He needed fresh blood. He tried hanging around the soup kitchen, listening stealthily for hints or clues about his food. But what he found was that the patrons were a close-mouthed crew. Finally, the program's administrator told him to quit harassing the homeless. If he kept bothering them, he would not be allowed to donate any more food. Dennis meekly apologized. He still brought food, but he needed feedback.

That's when he sought out Norman, the chubby fourth-grader who helped him discover the secret account. Norman had lost ten pounds, and his mom had agreed to let him off the lettuce and watermelon diet. But his gratitude for Dennis's help in his time of need had bonded them together. He was willing to eat anything for Dennis and give him an honest opinion. Dennis believed Norman had a future as a food critic. He had a great palate. He raved about the ravioli but told Dennis that the lettuce wraps would wilt before lunch time. He had suggested a dash of lemon to keep them fresh, and, he noted, the citrus taste added brightness and contrast to the richness of the pork. Dennis nodded and listened. He plotted the results as carefully as Darwin charted variations in species.

Soon he was living in his kitchen. He had only vague memories of what the other rooms in the house looked like. He saw them only as he passed through them, hunting for Micaela, or checking on his mother. His mother could see her son's OCD behavior, but she was too weak to stop it. The kindest thing she could say was "Smell's good!" It was the only comment that drew a smile from him. He abandoned his bedroom in favor of a cot in the pantry. That way, he didn't lose time. He'd set a pot of water on to boil while he brushed his teeth. If he got up early, he could get a couple of practice rounds in on his linguine before he had to get Micaela up and dressed. At school as he served Thelma's deep-fat-fried fare, his mind mulled the possibilities of sushi. Could he find unfishy-tasting fish that would tempt the kids? He'd have to consult with Norman.

· · · · · · · · · · · · · · · · · · ·

On the drive that night to St. George, Treasure put Micaela and Dennis at the back of her mind. She knew that it was one of the best ways to problem solve. She had great faith in this method. The ideas would fester and mutate into a higher life form, if she let them, just like three-week-old leftovers in her fridge.

But even if she'd wanted to, she couldn't concentrate on anything from school. Frankly, Grammy would not shut up during the drive. She warmed up by reading billboards (Hot Slots in Jackpot! Live Your Dreams in Mesquite!) and then moved on to the scenery. No one had ever seen so much in so little.

"You know, Treasure, these low mountains remind me of old men's ground down teeth. Don't they you?"

"I couldn't say," said Treasure. "I'm not as familiar with old men's teeth as you are," she teased, and then looked out her window. "I think the mountains look more like upturned faces. See, that peak there? It's a lumpy nose pointed toward the sky, and just above, see the stony eye sockets?"

Grammy nodded. "I see it. You've got good eyes, girl." She paused, still looking out the window. "I'm willing to share my desert with you."

The fact that her grandma regarded this stretch of country along

I-15 as her own personal wilderness made Treasure laugh. Only Grammy would claim to own the desert. But just the same, she felt honored that Grammy would share her kingdom with her. It was probably the closest thing she'd ever get to an inheritance.

Grammy turned toward her. "People think this place is barren, ugly, and empty, like a sea of land. But there are things here to surprise you, hidden deep inside, like the turquoise mines and the river gorge and the tiny orange geraniums."

Treasure reached over and squeezed Grammy's hand, "I love it when the geraniums bloom."

Grammy moved her sunglasses to the top of her head. "The dumb tourists are so busy rushing into every stupid casino that they never see the geraniums or the Joshua trees."

"Joshua trees always remind me of you."

"Now why would you say a thing like that?" asked Grammy, halfway offended.

Treasure told the truth. "Because they're prickly and prehistoric."

Grammy snorted, and her face relaxed. "They're also protected. By law. If you want to build a house on land that has a Joshua on it, you have to build the house around the tree. Remember that."

"I will, Grammy. I will." Treasure rolled her window down and let her hand surf the wind.

· ·

After practice, the outside world intruded on Treasure's mind and Grammy's kingdom. It was too dark for billboards and too dark for the landscape to push away their thoughts. The drives back to Vegas always deflated Treasure. Grammy was hammered from practice. In one month, the Steppers would perform during the halftime show at UNLV's homecoming football game in Sam Boyd Stadium. This invitation was a big deal, and Ruby had amped up the routine accordingly. They were country dancing to "She's a Pistol-Packing Mama" complete with silver toy six-shooters in white leather holsters. Randy, now the props manager, was in charge of ensuring that each pistol blew smoke at the appropriate moment. Grammy had a solo in the middle that featured her high kicks and ended in her doing the splits. But Ruby had decided that Grammy's would not be the only solo. Birdie Thompson would be doing her aerial cartwheel. Grammy half expected that. And after all, Birdie's moves had merit. But tonight when Ruby announced a third solo, Grammy nearly bolted from her seat. Only Treasure's steady hands on her shoulders kept her from completely spurting up out of her chair. LuNae would do the two-step with a plant in the audience. And the plant was Varden Moyle.

To the Steppers' credit, no one said a word. From across the room, LuNae smirked at Grammy, confident as Confucius. Grammy bared her teeth and growled like an animal. Treasure didn't say anything, but she didn't take her hands off Grammy's shoulders. Honestly, what was Ruby thinking? After all the commotion that got Grammy kicked out of the retirement village? Treasure tried to read it as anything but a direct insult to Grammy, but it felt like a ploy to get Tabiona Blume off the Steppers. She wasn't sure she wanted to know everything that was behind this move. How would she possibly keep Grammy from killing them? Luckily, Varden didn't show up, so she didn't have to see him, but the mere notion of him was enough to make Grammy sweat like a fancy cheese during the routine. She gnashed her teeth as she danced, but she made it through the entire practice and swept out the door without saying a word to LuNae.

Treasure was proud of Grammy's restraint. To be sure, she kept close to Grammy all night. In her mind's eye, she could easily see Grammy sneaking up on LuNae right before her solo and smothering her with her cowboy hat. But remarkably, Grammy didn't even make a move that direction. *Although she might just be biding her time.* Treasure would have to check Grammy's pistols before the performance, just to make sure that she didn't sneak a real piece into her holster. She didn't put it past Grammy to pack heat.

These thoughts ran through Treasure's mind as she navigated through the deep twists of the Virgin River Gorge. Grammy slumped in the seat beside her, as lost in her thoughts as Treasure. She muttered to herself. Treasure couldn't hear exactly what she said, but she did pick up the words "backstabbing old coot" and "spotlight-stealing hussy." Treasure knew Grammy wouldn't quit chewing on this of her own accord. She needed to get Gram's mind off Varden and the Steppers. She changed the subject.

"Grammy, I've been meaning to ask you, would you help me with something?"

Grammy looked at her, trying to focus her eyes. "What?" she asked. Anger made her less lucid.

"I need some help at school. Remember I told you about the circus we're doing for parent teacher conferences? Well, I need someone to work with our tight rope girls and the acrobats. All I can think for them to do is to walk on a line on the ground, and that's not very exciting. I know that you, with your performance expertise, can jazz it up. Would you consider choreographing a routine for them?"

Grammy sat back, perplexed. "Me? You know I don't choreograph. Ruby does that."

"But, Grammy, you've been doing this long enough, and dancing is in your bones. You can do it!"

Grammy reflected. "You were just going to have them walk on a line on the ground? That's for drunks."

Treasure nodded. "I know, but I've been so busy. I've still got costumes to make."

"You're making costumes?"

"Yes. Masks and clown pants for sure. We're trying to do most of it during art."

"Tightrope walkers don't wear masks. What were you going to do for them?"

Treasure checked her blind spot and pulled into the other lane to pass a semi. "I just don't know, Grammy. To tell you the truth, I'm a little overwhelmed. I've got the circus going on, the Young Authors' project, and my first parent-teacher conferences coming up. I feel stretched."

"Land, girl, you don't have to do everything yourself, do you? I'm happy to pitch in. I can help you with costumes. You know I have lots of old costumes from the Steppers we could use. And I'm a crack seamstress. I can bang out the costumes and help the tightrope girls."

Treasure looked at Grammy with relief. "You'd do that?"

"Of course I would. Why'd you wait to ask me? You're not in this alone, girl. I'd love to help out."

"It would mean coming to school every other day this week. The conferences are in three weeks."

"Okay, that's a start," Grammy said. She peered at Treasure's hands on the steering wheel. "You've been biting your nails again. What else is worrying you in that school?"

Treasure smiled. When she focused, Grammy picked up on things that no one else would, not even Randy or Roxy or her mother. She told Grammy about Micaela's story and their conversation. She even told her about the verbal beating she received from Micaela's dad and about how it had saddened her because she respected him. "Micaela's just wilting, right in front of my eyes," she said. "And she's counting on me to do something to help her dad. But I don't know what I can do or how I can help. He hates me. You should have seen the look in his eyes when he cussed me out over Micaela's wet pants."

Grammy furrowed her eyebrows. "What does that have to do with anything? Lots of people hate you. Hate shouldn't stop you from helping. You know better than that. That's using your gift poorly."

"I know, I know. Don't hate the haters," said Treasure, pondering Grammy's words. Sooner or later, it always went back to her gift. But Grammy was right. Why should she let this man's dislike paralyze her? Just because he didn't like her didn't mean he didn't need her. And Micaela definitely needed her. What if she let the General's dislike of her scare her off from the Sneetch party? That would have been a huge loss to her students. Treasure's mind wandered back over the events of the Sneetch party, particularly the moment when they were awarded the best costumes. Even Bonnie's nastiness could not tarnish the glow around that day.

Grammy spoke up. "That's right. It seems to me that this Micaela girl has already given you the answer. The dad needs people to eat his food. You just need to make it happen"

Treasure was still in Seuss land. Her mind had grasped a glimmer of an idea. It was slim, but it might work. "I think I can make it happen," she said aloud. She thought through the ramifications. She'd need Micaela's help, along with the cooperation of Thelma, the head lunch lady. Quickly she outlined the idea to Grammy, who clapped her hands together in approval. "That's the ticket, girl. I knew you'd come up with something!"

· · · · · · · · · · · · · · · · · · · ·

The next day at school, Treasure pulled Micaela aside and told her about her idea, and what she'd need to do to help. "You'll have to keep it a secret. You can't let your dad know what's going on. Do you think you can get your dad to make this?"

Micaela nodded confidently. "I can get Daddy to do anything. And I'll make sure it tastes good too."

"All right. You let me know when he's ready, okay?'

Micaela nodded again and scampered back to her seat. Treasure checked the clock. It was almost time, and she needed to prepare the students for what was about to happen. She returned to the head of the class and signaled to the kids that they needed to listen. "Okay, friends. Today we're going to work on our circus project. And to help us, I've brought in a very special lady. She'll be joining us in just a few minutes."

Right on cue, Treasure heard the roar of Mullet's engine as Grammy pulled into the parking lot. Treasure wished Grammy had not been quite so punctual. "This lady is my grandma. Her name is Tabiona Blume. And she'll be working with the tightrope walkers and the acrobats. She is a dancer."

Right then, the door opened and in walked Grammy Blume in all her glory. She wore a red sequined jumpsuit with yellow flames stitched into the bell bottoms. All the kids were dazzled by her brightness. Treasure shouldn't have been surprised. It was classic Grammy to make an entrance.

"I'm not just any dancer," Grammy picked up, just where Treasure let off. "I am the star of Ruby's Red Hot Chili Steppers!" And with that, she put down her bag and dropped into the splits. The kids didn't know how to react. Treasure put her hands together and began to clap. The rest of the class joined in.

Grammy clambered up off the floor. "Now, can any of you do what I just did?" No hands went up.

"That's fine. Now how many of you want to do what I just did?" Six or seven hands shot up. Several of the boys, including Eduardo, were shaking their heads emphatically.

Treasure decided to jump in. "As I said, Grammy is going to work with the tightrope walkers and the acrobats in the front of the classroom. I'm going to work with the lions and lion tamers by the book nook, and Mrs. Gutierrez will be working with the rest of you making masks."

Octavio raised his hand. "So if we aren't tightrope walkers, we won't work with her?" He indicated Grammy with a nod of his head.

"Don't you worry. I promise I'll work with all of you. I'm going to help with costumes too!" said Grammy .

Treasure couldn't tell if Octavio was excited or terrified by the prospect. She wondered if she could persuade Grammy to tone it down a notch. "Okay," she said. "Let's move to our stations."

The students scrambled out of their desks. Micaela was the first tightrope walker to reach Grammy. She reached out and touched a sequin on Grammy's bell-bottom. "Your costume is pretty," she said shyly.

"You think so?" Grammy asked. "Well, bless your heart, you've got taste. Now, what's your name?"

Treasure could see Micaela's smile from across the room. And she never left Grammy's side. Grammy looked up at Treasure and winked. She had a new disciple.

· · · · · · · · · · · · · · · · · · · ·

Dennis texted Norman as soon as he had the batch ready. *Eggplnt Parm rdy aftr school.* He didn't expect Norman to text him back. He thought he'd just show up like he usually did. But his phone started buzzing on the kitchen counter right before he was ready to open the oven. *Hmwrk. Talk ltr.* Dennis was disappointed but didn't dwell on it. He had other fish to fry. He wanted to try a halibut and calamari recipe that he found online in an English pub chat room.

He set the parm down and tried to regroup. For tonight, he'd have to find another tester. He looked at Fishstick and Puff, snoozing by the sliding glass door, and decided they would be useless. Puff didn't recognize eggplant as food. And even though Fishstick ate like a garbage disposal, his long, low-slung Corgi body posed a problem. If he gained any more weight, his belly would bottom out on the steps to the patio.

He checked his watch; it was time to pick up Micaela. The food would have to wait, even though he feared the eggplant would be rubbery, left to its own devices.

When he pulled up to the school, he couldn't see her at first. She was lying on the ground with her leg tucked behind her like Gumby. Dennis was sure she'd been wounded. He parked and bounded out of the car. "Micaela, baby, are you hurt?"

Micaela sat up and looked at him seriously. "I'm not hurt. I'm stretching. Grammy Blume says this is the best way to stretch your legs for the splits."

Dennis reached out his hand to pull her up. "Grammy Who says what? And since when was doing the splits part of first grade?"

Micaela grabbed his hand. "It's for our circus, Daddy. And Grammy Blume is Miss Treasure's grandma. She's a real live dancer! She had on glittery pants! And she's going to teach me how to be an acrobat, and a tight-rope walker, and a ballerina, and a tap dancer. And she's teaching me how to do the splits. Every true dancer, Grammy Blume says, works on her flexibility."

Dennis was amused by her enthusiasm but flustered by this new figure in his daughter's life. At home, he was still struggling to cope with the fact that every sentence out of Micaela's mouth started with "Well, Miss Treasure says . . ." Even though he realized what a jerk he'd been about the wet pants incident, he still winced when he thought about her. She just made him feel uncomfortable. And now she'd roped in her loony grandma to teach the kids? He wondered if the other parents knew. Didn't the school do background checks on these people? And of course she had to be a dancer. She couldn't just help with art. No, it had to be dancing, with its skimpy costumes and vulgar movements and brainlessness: everything he associated with his ex-wife. He wanted so much more for his daughter than that. But he couldn't deny the light in Micaela's face. It was the first time she'd been excited for days. As he drove and she chattered on about dancing and the circus and Grammy Blume, Dennis felt his anger abate. He'd forego the explosion for right now.

Micaela picked up the scent of the parmigiana when she opened the door. "Eggplant or chicken?" she asked, as she set her backpack down on the table.

"Eggplant," he answered. "And it's baked, not fried, so I think I could make it in the lunchroom. Would you try it for me?" He was prepared to beg and be turned down. But Micaela sat down on a stool and grabbed a fork. "I like chicken better." Dennis took that as a yes. He cut a piece and put it on a plate for her. She motioned for him to cut it in half. Dennis took the plate back, halfed it, and returned it to her. She took a bite and chewed.

"Well?" asked Dennis.

"It's a little soggy," she said, taking another bite.

"Dang it!" he cursed, slapping down his hot pads. "I really thought I had it this time. I knew I should have drained it longer!"

"Daddy, it's still good."

Dennis looked her squarely in the eye. "Would your friends eat it?"

"If they had to."

"That's not the answer I'm looking for."

"Next time, use chicken." Micaela swiveled back and forth in the stool as Dennis stared into the depths of his casserole dish. "Daddy, do you remember when you made me green eggs and ham? You read me the story, and I was sad that I'd never had it, and so you made it for me?"

Dennis barely heard Micaela. "I've got to figure out how to save it," he muttered. For a moment, he felt like an ER doctor observing a quickly fading patient on the table. Maybe he should call for a crash cart.

"Daddy!" yelled Micaela. "Daddy! Do you remember *Green Eggs and Ham*?" She yelled loud enough that both dogs started barking.

Dennis stopped doctoring the parm. He turned around to face Micaela. "Oh yeah. That turned out pretty good. We made spinach omelettes, with basil and garlic. And then we did a pesto sauce on the prosciutto."

"And it was good!" said Micaela. "Why don't you make that for school lunch? I bet the kids would eat it."

Dennis thought. "It's not a lunch-type food."

"But lots of times, we have breakfast for dinner. Why can't you make breakfast for lunch?"

Dennis considered. It might work. "And you really think the kids would eat it?" he asked.

Micaela nodded vigorously.

Dennis packed up the parmigiana. "But they won't eat this, will they?"

Micaela didn't want to, but she shook her head.

"Okay," said Dennis, shrugging. "Let's drop this off at the food bank and then swing by the market for ingredients."

8

Operation Green Eggs and Ham

A WEEK BEFORE THE CIRCUS, DAWN AND TREASURE SAT IN DAWN'S classroom after school, going over final details. Treasure was marveling at Dawn's ingenuity in creating a papier-mâché cannon large enough to fit one of her students. It also had compartments for dry ice and other chemical reactions.

"It would have been easier if Norman hadn't volunteered to be the guy shot out of a cannon. He's a husky kid. But I didn't have the heart to tell him no."

Treasure nodded. "I'm just so excited to see it work. Does he really shoot out?"

Dawn shook her head. "Not really. We just count on the dry ice and sparklers to distract everyone, and then he kind of lumbers out."

Treasure tapped her chin with one finger. "Could you fit someone else in there to push him out?

"I thought of that. But I'm worried that whoever was behind Norman would suffocate. I don't think any air could get past him"

"Maybe a spring?"

Dawn opened her mouth, but before she could answer, the classroom door was thrust open, and in swept Bonnie the Queen Bee followed by a lanky teenage girl.

"What is this I am hearing about the two of you creating some sort of unapproved circus at parent-teacher conferences?" asked Bonnie, clipboard in hand. The teenage girl never looked up. She had ear buds in and was scrolling through songs on her iPod.

Dawn stood up. "Nice to see you, too, Bonnie," she said pleasantly. "And it isn't unauthorized. We kept Anita in the loop on all our plans."

Bonnie was clearly enraged. For Dawn to imply there was a loop that she was out of infuriated her. "Even if the activity has been okayed, your collaboration has not. The only kind of collaboration that has been approved is grade-level cooperation. Fourth-graders and first-graders may not fraternize."

Treasure thought of Eduardo and his sister. "What if they're related?"

Dawn calmly replied. "Well then, I'm sure Bonnie would expect them to maintain the fraternization rules at home."

Bonnie ignored Dawn and turned the full force of her wrath on Treasure. "You're mocking me now. I see that. But you won't be. You won't be for long."

She turned to the lanky girl and snapped her fingers in front of her face to get her attention. "Aussie, we're going. Now." Bonnie stomped out, no doubt expecting the girl to follow. But she didn't. The girl pushed a swath of hair out of her face and looked out at Dawn and Treasure. Both of her eyebrows were pierced.

Dawn smiled at her. "Good to see you, Aussie. How's school going?" Aussie didn't answer. Instead she took in Treasure, from her sensible square-toed pilgrim shoes all the way up to her yellow angora cardigan embroidered with kittens. "Nice sweater. I ate a cat once in Vietnam," she said.

Treasure didn't have time to respond before they heard Bonnie barking from the hall. "Aussie, where are you? I've got reports to file and calls to make." Aussie's posture shifted. Her shoulder hunched again, and she scowled at them before skulking out of the room.

Treasure found that she had inadvertently been holding her breath. "Who was that girl? She has enough hostility to power an entire city grid."

Dawn shook her head. "That's Bonnie's daughter, Aussie. She used to be the cutest little girl. She'd always come by my classroom after school when her mom was working late and color pictures or play with play-dough. But I hear she's gotten in with a bad crowd. I think she got kicked out of her last school. Bonnie keeps a tight leash on her now."

Treasure shivered. She would not want to be on Bonnie's leash. "No wonder she looks like she's choking." She paused. "Maybe we shouldn't have antagonized her, Dawn. It really isn't the point. I don't want her to stop the circus."

"All she can do is huff and puff. She can't stop it without Anita's support. And remember, Anita approved this. We went through proper channels. It's not our fault if Anita didn't tell her. "

"I don't want a war. Especially with what we've got going on in the lunchroom tomorrow. I'm a teacher, not a fighter." Treasure crossed the room and looked down the hall.

"What's the worst she can do?" asked Dawn.

"Are you kidding?' asked Treasure. She was assailed with images of Bonnie shouting "Off with their heads," while a white rabbit scampered down a hole and giant playing cards, with teachers' faces, scrambled to escape her.

Dawn shrugged. "I'm not going to worry about it. How's your grandma doing with the acrobats and tightrope walkers?"

Treasure smiled. "She's been dancing and sewing like a woman possessed. It's good though. Then at least Mr. Fong gets some free time. She won't show me the full routine yet, but she's been working on it in her room at night. I keep fielding calls from the downstairs neighbors. Apparently some of the cottage cheese on their ceiling comes down when Grammy thumps around. In fact, I better get back to her. She's working with the kids right now."

Dawn waved good-bye, and Treasure started down the hall. Instead of going straight out to her classroom, she swung by the cafeteria. Thelma, the head lunch lady, was still working on the computer in front of the serving lines.

Treasure stuck her head in the door. "Thelma, are we a go for tomorrow?"

Thelma didn't look up from the screen but gave her a thumbs-up.

"Thank you so much. I really appreciate your help on this . . ." Treasure began.

Thelma cut her off. "No need. I should be thanking you. That account . . ."

Treasure put a finger over her lips, shushing Thelma, who had a voice that could easily be heard in the parking lot. "Doesn't exist," finished Treasure in a whisper.

Thelma nodded curtly and went back to her computer. Treasure hurried down the hall, looking side to side to make sure that no one had overheard them.

If Bonnie ever figured out there was a secret lunch account that could be traced back to Treasure, the consequences would not be good, for her or the kids. Thelma had figured it out by tracing routing numbers back to her account. Instead of confronting her about it, she'd just sent her an email thanking her and detailing the ways the account had helped particular children. At that point, there was no use denying it. Treasure responded, and they'd struck up a virtual friendship. Treasure felt a kinship with this woman, who was just as misunderstood as she was.

After listening to Micaela's Young Authors' project, Treasure had contacted Thelma. Thelma tutted over it and then filled Treasure in on the backstory on Micaela's dad. Treasure marveled at his previous successes and was sure that she'd watched a profile about him on E! a couple of years ago. It also explained a lot about his angst. Treasure was committed to easing that angst, if she could, for Micaela's sake. She ran her plan (Operation Green Eggs and Ham) by Thelma, who supported it enthusiastically, and together they worked out the details. All in all, they'd probably only spoken five words to each other via email. And that suited Treasure fine.

When she opened the door to her classroom, Grammy was straightening chairs. "Where are all the kids?" Treasure asked.

"I let them go early. I taught them a couple of visualization techniques and gave them copies of the music. They're supposed to work on the routines mentally tonight."

Visualization was one of Grammy's favorite exercises. "So how is it going?" asked Treasure.

Grammy clasped her hands like a little girl. "I am so excited by this! I've got them doing moves the Steppers could only dream of. They are so flexible, with their young little bones. That bossy one, what's her name?"

"Sharonda?" Treasure guessed.

"Yes. Sharonda. She's double-jointed, I swear. I had her doing backbends on day one. And that shy little Asian girl?"

"That's Liwayway," Treasure said.

"She's fearless. She just flips and flies! I swear she doesn't have any vertebrae! She must be descended from jellyfish. And that little Micaela, she's so dedicated. It takes her a little longer to catch on, but she practices and practices until she has it. She's only about five inches from the ground on the Chinese straddles. And she just loves it. That one has a dancer's heart."

Treasure's eyebrows raised. Liwayway fearless? She certainly had never seen that side of her. And her comments about Micaela—having a dancer's heart—was high praise indeed, from Grammy.

Grammy continued. "She's so cute, I'd just take her home in my pocket if I could."

"I don't think her dad would go for that," said Treasure.

Grammy leaned over and touched her toes a couple of times, stretching her back muscles. "Nonsense. She needs me." Grammy straightened up and grabbed her towel from the top of Treasure's desk. She patted down her armpits. "Have you got everything set up for the lunchroom shindig tomorrow?"

Treasure nodded. "I just talked with Thelma."

"I wish I could be there, but I promised Vard I'd drive up early to practice tomorrow and help him two-step."

Treasure's heartbeat accelerated. "You're doing what?"

"Two-stepping with Varden."

"It sounds to me more like you're two-timing with Varden. Do Mr. Fong and LuNae know about this?"

"Fongie is an easy-going guy. He keeps a lid on his steam. We're more like good buddies."

"And LuNae?"

Grammy took off her sweatband and fluffed her hair. "And LuNae can just kiss my grits."

Treasure looked at her reproachfully. "You know this will have repercussions. What are you thinking? And really, what is Varden thinking?"

"He's thinking he can't two-step without some practice, and LuNae has been too busy since she started selling Avon again."

"How did you even get in contact with him? Isn't there some kind of a restraining order?"

Grammy looked peeved. "Land, girl, we've got to find you a man! Maybe then you'd leave mine alone." She stood tall and mustered all the dignity she could. "There isn't a restraining order, if you'll recall, because he didn't file one. And FYI, he called me up, all worried about the big number and coming to Vegas. Sin City makes him nervous. He asked me to practice, and I said I'd help him out."

"You're playing with fire, Grams."

"Nonsense. I'm playing with ashes. Old coots don't have enough heat to roast marshmallows."

"Are you trying to kill me, Grammy? I'm going to have to lay down the law." Treasure slammed her hands down on her desk. "No heat. No fire. No way, Grams. You are not going alone to dance with Varden Moyle. "

Grammy pursed her lips, narrowed her eyes, and put her hands on her hips. Treasure did the same, without breaking Grammy's gaze. She knew if she flinched, she would lose. The standoff lasted two minutes and thirty-nine seconds, by Treasure's count.

Grammy backed down first. "Fine."

Treasure blinked and dropped the pose. "Fine?"

Grammy nodded. "Of course, fine. Do you think I'd go against you after all you've done for me, girl?"

"Actually yes, I do," blurted Treasure.

Grammy grinned at her. "Well, you're right. But I know where credit is due. And I also know that you keep me from drifting off into lunacy. I trust you, girl."

"That's a relief."

"So I'll just wait until you can go with me. I'll call Vard tonight and push back our private practice until Saturday."

Treasure slapped her hand against her forehead. It was no use.

Grammy picked up her purse and jingled her keys. "Wanna race me home?" she asked.

· · · · · · · · · · · · · · · · · · · ·

Dennis Cameron arrived for work the next day, hardly even aware of his desire for a lunchroom triumph. He hadn't slept much, on account of his mother. She was in enough pain that she needed to be on constant medication. But lately she had been refusing to take it.

"It makes me sleep, and I don't want to sleep my time away," she said, clutching Dennis's arm.

"But your body needs rest, Mom," he said.

She relaxed her hold on him and starting picking at the yarn on top of the coverlet. "Don't make me take it, Dennis," she begged, not making eye contact. "If it gets bad enough, I'll take it."

"Promise?" he'd asked.

She nodded. "Besides, I'll have plenty of time to sleep when I'm dead," she said, trying to laugh. The joke dumped both of their fears onto the bed beside them. Dennis tried to fight the hollowness by wrapping his arms around his fading mother. It helped some.

So now, when she slept, she made a low moaning sound that set the dogs howling. Fishstick would sing high, and Puff (who had a surprisingly deep voice for a Pomeranian) would sing low. The effect was harmonious but not conducive to sleep. Dennis had threatened the dogs to no avail. The only thing that stopped the mournful doggy lament was food. So instead of cooking for people, he had stayed up most of the night cooking for the dogs. This time he wasn't trying to create any culinary masterpieces. He was just trying to buy sleep time for Micaela. The time she spent working on her routine for the circus wore her out. She fell asleep at dinner. But she was so happy. She had started to sing and skip again. Dennis couldn't deny the joy present in his daughter's face. He even let her stay late to extra practices. Actually, the extra practices were a godsend lately. He'd been able to take his mom to her appointments and not worry about rushing across town to pick up Micaela right at 3:00.

The lunchroom was still dark when he came in, which was odd. Usually three or four ladies would be there, cleaning up after breakfast and getting started on lunch. He flipped on the lights and looked around. There was no sign of Thelma, and he couldn't see any boxes of heat-and-eat meat products defrosting. He supposed he should be worried, but instead, he found it oddly comforting to be there alone. He ran his hand across the smooth silver bars under the serving line, where the kids slid their trays. There was something beautiful about the way the overhead lights reflected off the clean sneeze guard. If he was a writer, he'd consider writing a haiku about it. Something like:

Fluorescent lights bounce
Reflect through glass on sneeze guard.
Rainbows in lunchroom.

The last line wasn't quite right. Still pondering the poem, he approached the computer in the center. Someone had stuck a yellow sticky note to the screen. He picked it up and read it.

> *Dennis,*
> *I'm running late. Our supplier didn't come last night, and I'm hunting him down. Can you handle the lunch rush? Now might be a good time to try out one of your new recipes. I hear you make a mean green eggs and ham. Check the fridge for ingredients. I'll be in before 10.*
> *Thelma.*

Dennis ran his hand through his hair. He wasn't sure he was ready for this. Count on Thelma to toss him into the thick of lunch without any warning. Well, he'd just have to cope. Her suggestion wasn't half bad. Hadn't Micaela asked about that same recipe just a few days ago? And it wouldn't take long to prepare. He could throw it together pretty quickly, if he had the right ingredients. He jogged back toward the kitchen, pulled out his keys, and opened the lock on the silver Frigidaire. Inside, he found stacks of egg cartons and a couple of packages of high quality prosciutto, wafer sliced, along with all the ingredients to make his pesto sauce. The thought flickered through his mind that this was a little too convenient. He was being set up. But he didn't care. The sight of all those beautiful ingredients moved him. There were sweet button mushrooms, along with shiny emerald bell peppers, fresh from the farmers market. His eyes watered, and he wiped them on the back of his sleeve. He opened a box and picked up one of the packages of meat. He cradled it like a baby. Just then, the bell rang. It made him jump, causing him to toss his prosciutto in the air. He dove like an outfielder to catch it before it hit the ground. "Yes!" he yelled as he felt the ham connect with the palm of his hand. He stood up, holding it aloft in his hand, showing off his catch. The catch gave him confidence. He could almost hear the roar of the crowd and the sportscaster's commentary: "Surely we are witnessing one of the greatest comebacks in culinary history! With this catch, Cameron has catapulted back to the top of his game. Look out, lunchroom!"

Just then he became aware of footsteps behind him. He turned around and saw the dumbfounded faces of the other lunch ladies.

"Well, don't just stand there," Dennis said. "Lunch is less than four hours away. I need you to dice. And you," he said, pointing to one of the dour-faced women, "I need you to go get Norman out of Mrs. Robbins's fourth-grade class." And with that, Dennis Cameron took command of his kitchen. He put on his hair net and started cooking.

· · · · · · · · · · · · · · · · · · · ·

Throughout the morning, Treasure kept close watch on the clock. Micaela would have too, if she'd been able to tell time. As it was, she raised her hand every fifteen minutes to ask what time it was. Treasure decided to channel her anxiety into a learning opportunity. She grabbed her set of laminated clock faces from the closet and taught a lesson on telling time. As the students moved the big hands and small hands, Treasure tried to lower her pulse. She didn't know why she was nervous. After all, she wasn't cooking anything. It was just lunch. But somehow it meant more to her than that. She really wanted Dennis to succeed. After talking to Thelma about him, she found herself thinking about his situation all the time. What he'd done in raising his daughter alone, taking care of his mother, and sacrificing his career had transformed her opinion of him. He wasn't just the angry parent who yelled at her after Micaela's accident. He was someone who cared more about other people than he cared about himself. And the fact that no one besides herself and Thelma knew about it even deepened the significance of his acts.

Treasure knew what it felt like to get kicked for trying to do good. It was a major theme of her entire life. She also knew how good it felt to get a win. And so she was ready to start something in order to give him that win, something that was sure to rub Bonnie the wrong way. Treasure didn't want to rub Bonnie at all. It was just that preserving the peace for Bonnie's sake was not her highest priority. She would deal with the fallout, if and when it came.

At 10:45, she collected the clocks and gathered her friends around her on the floor. "We're going to have story time," she said, sitting down Indian style.

"That's not right!" said Kysa. "We never have story time before lunch."

Treasure smiled at her. "We are today, for a very special reason. Micaela, will you bring me the book?"

Micaela sprinted over to the spinners and took down *Green Eggs and Ham*. Treasure cracked the cover and began to read. The kids perked up as they recognized it.

"Hey," shouted Spencer. "We've read this before! You read it to us during Dr. Seuss days." Treasure nodded but didn't stop reading. Micaela began to read along with her. "I could not, would not on a boat! I would not, could not with a goat! I do not like green eggs and ham. I do not like them, Sam I am!"

At first, the kids looked at Micaela like she was loony. But by the end of the book, every student, including Liwayway and Eduardo, were reading in unison along with her, getting louder as they turned the last page.

Treasure waited for the class to settle back down after the ending crescendo. When they all stopped, she asked them a question. "Why didn't the narrator want to eat green eggs and ham?" The question seemed to stump them.

Preston looked confused. "It doesn't say."

Treasure answered patiently. "I know it doesn't say. But why do you think he wouldn't want to try it?" She turned the question out to the whole class. "Are there times when you don't want to try something new?"

The kids nodded.

"How come?"

Octavio waved his arm. "'Cuz it might be gross."

Spencer nodded. "And it looks funny."

Rosita jumped in, "And someone might make fun of you."

Treasure agreed. "Yes, but what does Sam's friend discover when he tries it?"

Micaela raised her hand. "He finds out that he likes it!"

"That's right," said Treasure, putting down the book. "And he never would have known that if he hadn't tried. And so now, friends, I'm going to ask you to try something different. In just a moment, we are going to the lunchroom, and we get to be the very first class to eat. And guess what we get to eat? Green eggs and ham! Are you brave enough to try it?" The class erupted in clapping, squealing, and a few retching sounds.

Some of the kids squirmed. "I don't like my food to touch!" shouted Preston. Micaela put her head down, too scared to see her friends' reactions, but Treasure stood firm. "I am asking you to be brave. Trying new things is good! Even if it looks different. I expect you guys to set the example. I want you to imagine that you are soldiers when we march into the lunchroom. Brave soldiers. In fact, I even have a marching song for you."

She picked up her portable CD player, popped in her *Seussical* CD, and played the "Green Eggs and Ham" song. "We're going to change the words a little though." Treasure started to march in place. Micaela grabbed Rosy and Sharonda by their hands and led them to the front of the room and put them into rows. The three little girls started to march as Treasure sang, "Yes, I like Green Eggs and Ham. Yes, I like them Sam-I-Am. I would eat them on a boat. And I would eat them with a goat." Micaela started to sing with Treasure, and then Rosy and Sharonda picked it up. The other kids scrambled to join the ranks. "We're going to sing this all the way through the school and down into the lunchroom. Are you ready?"

"We won't get in trouble for being loud?" asked Octavio.

"Nope. You won't. I might, but you won't. Let's roll, kids." Treasure picked up the CD player and marched out the door and down the steps. She paused at the doors to the main building. The song faltered as the kids piled up behind her like cars at rush hour.

"Go past me!" said Treasure, holding the doors open. "Go toward Mrs. Robbins's room. We are going to pick up her class. Micaela, you lead out!"

Micaela stuck her chin out and started goose-stepping. The rest of the class followed. Treasure brought up the rear. Their song, a little softer since they came into the hallway, picked up momentum as they filed past the lunchroom doors. Treasure glanced through the small rectangular window and saw Thelma's face pushed up against the glass, her hand shading her eyes. Treasure gave her a salute as they passed, which Thelma solemnly returned.

As they rounded the corner to Dawn's classroom, Treasure sprinted ahead. Dawn was waiting at the door, with her students in rows. She high-fived Treasure. "We heard you singing all the way from the lunchroom!"

"Have you heard anything else? Besides our singing?" asked Treasure, more breathless and sweaty than she wanted to be. She fully expected Bonnie to show up with a cease and desist order.

"Nothing from Bonnie, but we have heard from Mr. Cameron, indirectly. He asked for Norman's help first thing this morning. Norman snuck back a few minutes ago and reported that all systems are a go."

Treasure exhaled loudly. "Well, that's a relief."

When she'd accidentally blurted out her plan to Dawn, she didn't anticipate such an enthusiastic response. After all, they were right in the middle of a circus. But Dawn definitely wanted to help out, mainly because of the change she could see in Norman, a kid with low self-esteem and a twisted home life. The other students ridiculed him. No one ever wanted to sit by him, and he lagged behind the rest of the class in nearly every subject. Dawn had just about given up. But then for the past couple of weeks, he was a brand new Norman. His hand was the first one in the air on the fractions unit, a unit that had the A+ kids struggling. But Norman never answered wrong. "Norman, what's gotten into you? How do you know all this?" Dawn asked him one day. He grinned at her and put his hands behind his head. "Cooking!" he said. "I've been quadrupling and octupling batches with Mr. Cameron from the lunchroom. And Mr. Cameron says I'm good at it. He says I could be a judge on *Iron Chef*! I could get paid to eat!" Those positive words alone won Dawn over.

Dawn's class fell in behind Treasure's, and the song gained strength as they filed out into the main hall. Treasure checked her watch: It was 11:58. The first lunch bell should ring in two minutes. Treasure signaled Dawn to quiet the classes as they crept passed the classrooms that didn't go to lunch until 12:30. As they turned into the first-grade hall, the lunch bell rang right over their heads. Treasure put her fingers in her ears. When it stopped, she raised her hands over her head. "Okay, friends, let it rip!" she said, and the song burst forth again, twice as strong as before. Earlier in the week, Treasure had emailed the other first-grade teachers (who also had the early lunch schedule) and invited them to participate. Kristen was the only one who had responded. Treasure spotted the General standing by her door. She frowned at Micaela as she led the parade by. "Let's have a little more respect for others' learning!" she said sharply. Treasure wondered what she was talking about, since the lunch bell had already rung, and Lucinda's students were lined up by the door, peeking out into the hall. Even though Treasure paused, Micaela didn't falter. She kept marching, sticking her tongue out at the teacher as she passed. Lucinda slammed her door closed. Treasure sprinted to the front and put her arm around Micaela. Somehow she knew this would get back to Bonnie.

They kept marching. Kristen's class was poised and ready by the door when the parade approached, her students sporting their hats and bow ties from *Cat in the Hat*. Kristen waved at Treasure as they approached. "We'll follow you!" she called as Treasure and Micaela marched past.

As they approached the lunchroom doors for the second time, Treasure squeezed Micaela's hand. "Are you ready to lead them in?" Micaela squared her shoulders. "Yes, ma'am, Miss Treasure," she answered smartly. She pivoted like a drum major and pushed open the cafeteria doors.

· ·

Dennis had been too involved in his preparations to know what was going on. The first strains of the song had been drowned out by the whistle and whine of his steamers and the sharp sound of ham crisping. The other lunch ladies kept sneaking over to the door, looking out to see what was going on. Norman was running back and forth like a happy golden retriever. Dennis could practically see his tail wag. Even Thelma seemed to be hanging around the dining room, keeping out of all the preparations. Something was up. But Dennis didn't mind. He was focused on his task, and he thrived on the responsibility. This was his menu, and he was going to do it his way. He looked up and down the two serving lines for final inspection.

"Remember, food is edible art," he said to the staff. "Appeal to the eye, as well as the palette. These are our patrons, and we will treat them like they are dining in a four-star restaurant." The ladies in the line sneaked sideways looks over to Thelma. Thelma nodded her head in agreement with Dennis.

"Are we ready?" he asked. The workers mumbled responses. Dennis shook his head. "That won't do. I asked, are you ready?"

Norman had a spatula stuffed through his belt like a sword. He drew his spatula and raised it over his head. "Yes!" he shouted.

"Good man, Norman," said Dennis approvingly. "How about the rest of you?"

The ladies still looked askance at Thelma. She pointed at Dennis. They looked back at him "Yes!" they replied, still bewildered by this strange new ritual. It was only lunch, after all.

"Well, it's a start," said Dennis, rubbing his hands together. "Thelma, you may open the doors."

As Thelma walked toward the doors, the first strains of the marching song reached Dennis's ears. At first he couldn't catch the words. Then he turned around to see his own Micaela marching at the head of a Green Eggs and Ham Brigade. The column snaked behind her, out through the doors and into the hall. The high ceiling amplified the song, lifting it up into the rafters. Dennis was dumbfounded. He couldn't move. He just stood there, at the point where the serving lines split, bug-eyed. Micaela marched right passed him and grabbed her own utensils. Dennis still couldn't move. The lines swung out around him. The normal clatter of students gathering trays and silverware was swallowed by their unified song. It was the second time that day that his eyes watered—and not because of onions. He put a hand over his face, overcome. When he removed his hand, he paused on the face of Micaela's teacher, that crazy Blume woman. She was tucking a strand of strawberry hair behind her ear, bending over to pick up a tray, when she noticed Dennis's gaze. She winked at him. That wink made him laugh. She looked joyful and guilty at the same time. She obviously had something to do with this. "You?" he asked. She shrugged and pointed over at Micaela, who was eating at the nearest table.

"Micaela, what do you think?" he shouted at her through cupped hands.

She swallowed and shot her dad a thumbs-up.

Dennis shook his head. There was no way Micaela pulled this off, all on her own. He looked back at Treasure Blume and bowed to her like she was his sensei. Then he ran back into the kitchen to join the serving line. One of the lunch ladies fell back, offering him her spot. He jumped in and started plating the spinach omelettes, the spinach chopped so fine that it gave the omelettes a soft green tint. He added swirls of pesto sauce. Beside him stood Norman, who placed his basket-shaped, prosciutto-stuffed bell peppers at a 45-degree angle from the omelet. Dennis was proud of each tray they created.

The song continued to ring through the lunchroom, even though the original singers were seated and eating. Every successive class that came to lunch picked it up. It was a full twenty-five minutes before the song dwindled completely. And even weeks afterward, Dennis could still hear it in his head, and it made him smile.

9

Under the Big Top

TREASURE AND GRAMMY BLUME STARTED WORKING ON THE FINAL costumes for the circus right after dinner. Earlier, they'd hit the thrift stores for raw materials. Grammy was a great believer in thrift store scavenging, especially in Vegas. Once, Grammy found an entire white Elvis costume, complete with thousands of rhinestones, for only $19.95. It just took some digging and a creative eye. Grammy had assured her that with a little sewing, she could turn orange disco pants into manes for the lions with minimal effort. Treasure had agreed and started stitching. With parent-teacher conferences coming in two days, they didn't have a minute to lose. While they worked, Treasure filled Grammy in on the lunchroom events from the day before.

As she listened, Grammy stopped sewing. She pressed both hands over her heart. "The whole lunchroom kept singing, even after your class left? Why, that story just warms my cockles, girl. I am so proud of you."

Treasure stopped. "Your whats?"

"My cockles. The cockles of my heart."

Grammy's cockles had been stone cold for at least fifteen years, by Treasure's recollection. She rarely felt sentimental. "Are you going soft on me, Grams?" she asked in a skeptical tone.

Grammy's response was to flex her bicep. "Soft? Look at this? Do you see any old lady sag here?" She jiggled her arm back and forth.

Treasure wisely said nothing. She returned to the original subject. "And the food, Grams. It was fabulous. Everybody liked it, even the picky kids. The omelettes were fresh and bright, with just a bit of creeping

125

heat in the sauce. You know how I don't like mushrooms because they turn into sponges? Dennis maintained their texture. I can see how this guy used to be a big deal in the food world."

Grammy bit a thread with her teeth. "It sounds like it went real well."

Treasure picked up her scissors. "But the best part was the look on his face when Micaela marched into that room. He just looked love at her. You know what I mean?"

Grammy stopped sewing. "No, I don't. How do you look love at people? That seems like a dumb-fool thing to say."

Treasure stood by her statement. "Yes, you do. It's not a dumb-fool thing to say. You know what it looks like when someone gives you the love eyes."

"Oh. Like the way that scraggly cat looks at you when you open a can of tuna? Well, then say what you mean, girl."

Treasure sat back in her chair. "It was more than that. It made me want to cry and jump and shout and run away all at the same time. I still get shivers when I think about it."

Grammy glanced over at her granddaughter. Obviously this wasn't all about Micaela. "Sounds like you've had quite a change of heart."

Treasure straightened her posture and stabbed her needle through some of the loose sequins. "There's just more to him than I thought. And he loves his daughter, enough to sacrifice his career for her. It's something I can appreciate, that's all."

Grammy didn't turn. She hunched over the sewing machine, threading a bobbin. "Whatever you say."

They were ripping seams on one of Grammy's old costumes when the phone started to ring. They heard two verses of "When the Saints Go Marching In" before Treasure found the handset deep in the bowels of her couch. She fished it out. It was probably her parents, or Randy, or Roxy. There was an outside chance it was Patience, who was supposed to be flying into Vegas soon. She looked at the display screen. The number was completely unfamiliar. She thought about letting it go to voice mail but decided to answer in case it was Dawn.

"Hello?" she answered.

An unfamiliar and brusque male voice responded to her query. "Yes. I am looking for Miss Treasure Blume, first-grade teacher at Elbert Edwards Elementary. Is this the party to whom I am speaking?"

Treasure was flustered. Who could this be? "Yes?" she responded.

"This is Dr. Robert D. Baumgartner, superintendent of schools for Clark County."

Treasure's knees buckled. She felt behind her for the couch and perched on the edge. She took a deep breath. "Yes, Dr. Baumgartner. What can I do for you?"

"I understand that your parent-teacher conferences are coming up on Friday. Is that correct?"

Treasure nodded and then remembered that he couldn't see her. "Yes, that's correct," she squeaked. Howls jumped up beside her and curled his head into her hand. She patted his head and waited for a response, loose fur sticking to her sweaty palms.

She heard the muffled sound of papers being shuffled on the other end. "I've received a report about you utilizing some rather unorthodox teaching methods. I understand that for parent-teacher conferences, you've organized some sort of performance art, or something of that nature."

"A circus," Treasure squeaked. "We're doing a circus."

"Yes, that's what I've heard," said the voice in the same tone as the Terminix man would say, "Yes, you've got an infestation."

Treasure began to panic and blurt simultaneously. "Is there something wrong? Are you going to tell me that I can't do that? Are you going to cancel it? We've worked so hard!"

The pause that followed was not reassuring. "That's fallacious thinking, Miss Blume," said the deep voice. "Just because someone works hard on something does not mean it's worthwhile, educationally speaking. That's not the kind of thinking that I like to see in my teachers. It disgruntles me."

"I don't want you to be disgruntled. I want you to be fully gruntled!" Treasure wailed. She clapped a hand over mouth. She desperately wanted it to stop spewing stupidity. She could only pray that her brain would transmit the message to her mouth before it was her turn to talk again.

"Ah, yes. Well, my motive in calling you was to determine the educational value of this, uh, endeavor. You are, of course, familiar with this county's foundational document outlining the aims of elementary education?"

"Of course," bluffed Treasure, hoping he didn't quiz her down.

"I'd simply like a report, ten to twelve pages, outlining the way that your activity follows and exemplifies those aims. I need it on my desk by noon tomorrow, so that I can have time to go over your input before I make a decision on your activity."

Treasure bowed her head. How in the world was she going to do that? It was Wednesday night and she was knee deep in clown pants. She looked in the kitchen where Grammy was still seated at the table, humming "Green Eggs and Ham" as she ran the fabric through the machine. She squared her shoulders. "I can do that, Dr. Baumgartner. May I have your email address so that I can send the document to you directly?" She got the rest of the information and hung up. She felt ten years older than the Treasure who answered the phone ten minutes before. She stumbled into the kitchen, while a worried Howls twined between her ankles.

"What was that all about?" asked Grammy. "Was it that chef in lunch lady clothing, calling to say thank you?"

Treasure shook her head. She still felt shocked. "It was the superintendent," she whispered.

"The superintendent!" said Grammy with a start. "That nasty secretary's brother? I didn't know he was real! I thought he was just a myth, like narwhals."

"Narwhals are real," said Treasure tiredly.

Grammy decided not to argue about the obvious fictional nature of a horned fish. She probably thought unicorns were real too. But it was obvious that the poor girl was distraught. She looked like she might break apart into tiny motes of dust if someone blew on her. "What did he want?" she asked in a more gentle tone.

Treasure melted into the chair beside her grammy and spilled out the whole tale. "Bonnie warned me that I'd be sorry, that she'd make me sorry, but I didn't listen. I should have listened," she finished, snuffling into her sleeve.

Grammy slapped Treasure on the knee. "Now you're talking nonsense. You did good things! You know you did. Just because you don't get good results, that doesn't mean you shouldn't have done them."

Treasure smiled wanly. "No good deed goes unpunished?"

"Something like that. You know that your Green Eggs and Ham thing was a success right? Now does it matter what this secretary says?"

"I just thought she'd confront me directly, like she did last time. Instead she called in the big gun."

"Snakes seldom make the same move twice. And the worst snakes are those who strike from the side. Besides, you know better. You don't give up on good things just because you run into some opposition."

Treasure knew her grammy was right, but she felt too defeated to speak.

"What were you saying about the change in Micaela since the circus started? And the other kids? Weren't they getting excited about learning?"

Treasure nodded her head.

Grammy continued, "Now, from what I can see, this guy didn't shut you down, which is what this old biddie wants, right?"

Treasure looked up, confused. "What's a biddie?"

"It's a chicken. And calling her brother in to keep tabs on you, that's a cowardly, chickeny move to make. Now don't sidetrack me, girl. Did he shut you down?"

Treasure wrinkled her forehead. "I'm confused. First you called Bonnie a snake, and now she's a chicken? Pick a species and stick with it."

Grammy just looked at her. "Don't sidetrack me, girl. Did he shut you down?"

Treasure shook her head, trying to clear it. Images of both reptiles and poultry with Bonnie's face cluttered her brain. She refocused on her grammy. "No. He wants me to document how this circus provides for the educational aims."

"Well, it looks to me like you've got a shot, if you do it right. He's obviously talked to Anita and found out that you had her support. That's probably why you've even got this option at all. I say, buckle down and get it done."

"But there's so much else I have to do! We've got costumes, and practices, not to mention that I need to teach other subjects tomorrow."

"Don't get whiny. You know I hate whiny. I'll do my part, and some of yours. After all, you've got all night."

Treasure snorted. "Who needs sleep?"

"That's right," said Grammy, patting her hand. "Besides, you can sleep when you're dead."

· · · · · · · · · · · · · · · · · · · ·

Right after her conversation with Grammy, Treasure called Anita and confirmed what Grammy had guessed. The superintendent wanted to call off the whole circus completely, but Anita had urged him to talk to Treasure and investigate how closely this activity aligned with the curriculum and his own aims.

"I'll email you the aims right now," said Anita sympathetically. "That's about all I can do."

"That helps a lot," Treasure assured her. "And I'm sorry about the Green Eggs and Ham thing, if that disrupted anyone's learning."

Anita laughed. "I thought it was great! In fact, I think we should do it every year."

"But I'm sure it upset Bonnie."

"Bonnie was looking to be upset. She gets some kind of thrill out of it."

"Well, I didn't mean to antagonize her."

"Look, Bonnie's been looking for a way to thwart you on this circus since she found out about it. The *Green Eggs and Ham* thing just spurred her into action. But the superintendent is a reasonable guy. If you can give him good specific details, he'll back off. He isn't that much like his sister."

Unable to restrain herself, Treasure blurted out a question she had always wondered about. "Why do you keep Bonnie on?"

Anita took it in stride. "Why don't I fire her? Well, she's a really good secretary. You'd be amazed at how many details she keeps track of, and how many things she takes care of on her own. Of course, I have to put up with some of her power plays, but I know who really runs the school. Her obsession with minutiae frees me up to deal with the important stuff. This school really couldn't run without her."

Treasure felt humbled. She thought Anita was just cowed by Bonnie. It never occurred to her that Bonnie might be good at her job. She had always just thought of Bonnie as a demon. "Thanks for your support, Anita. I'll meet his deadline, or die trying."

"You won't die. Good luck, and I'll see you tomorrow."

· · · · · · · · · · · · · · · · · · · ·

It was about 4:00 a.m. when Treasure got her second wind. Grammy was stretched out on the couch with Howls curled around her head like a turban, the two of them snoring together in a pile of circus garb. Treasure removed Howls, woke up Grammy, and walked her to her bed. Then she came back to the glow of her laptop, cracked her knuckles, and returned to her task.

At 7:30, she finally attached the document and hit send. She felt good about what she'd created. Luckily she had recorded some of the practices, so she attached a few video clips to demonstrate the students' learning: Octavio subtracting as he juggled, Liwayway showing the other girls the steps to the tinikling, a traditional Filipino folkdance, and Eduardo the lion tamer talking to the camera about the social structure of prides.

She jumped in the shower, washed, toweled, dried, and then jumped in her car, her hair wadded into a damp bun. She would not give Bonnie the satisfaction of seeing her roll into school late.

That morning at school was a blur. She taught like she was on automatic pilot. The numbness protected her. It made it so she could fight back the nausea every time her students mentioned how excited they were for the circus tomorrow, which happened about fifteen times an hour. Treasure was so numb that she failed to notice that no one from the office came to give her a list of announcements. She also didn't notice that a load of construction paper and scissors that they were using for invitations hadn't arrived either. She finally noticed that no one had come to pick up her class roll (which she usually put outside the door of her classroom) when she stepped on it as she led her class to lunch. Treasure walked to the lunchroom in a trance. She left the kids at the lunchroom door, then turned and walked in the other direction.

From the serving line, Dennis saw her and felt a twinge of disappointment. He wanted to thank her and to have her try his new seafood mac and cheese. Bolstered by the success of the previous day, he and Norman had come up with a new menu plan: new twists on the classic kid favorites. It was so simple. Dennis didn't know why he didn't think about it before. Why not make what was familiar to the kids, but just make it better? He'd contacted one of his old buddies in the food supply world, who was willing to donate some of his leftover food. Today he had shrimp and Gruyère cheese.

"It's a tax write-off, right?" his buddy said. "Plus some idiot double ordered the shrimp today anyway, and it won't last."

Dennis blessed the idiot in his head as he scooped up a serving, bubbling, steaming, and cheesy, and poured it back into the pan. He didn't even really want to talk to her. What would he say? He was just disappointed that he wouldn't get to see the look on her face as she ate. He pulled on his plastic gloves. *Why should I care what her face looks like when she eats?* he thought. Frankly, she was a sloppy eater. He had noticed that yesterday. She chomped, slurped, and only occasionally chewed with her mouth closed. He was positive she had gotten pesto sauce on her shirt. Why did he want to see her eat this? He didn't have any more time to ponder before the first tray slid before him and the lunch rush began.

Zombie teacher Treasure wandered up to the office with her attendance roll in her hand. She wasn't even aware enough to avoid Bonnie, who was sitting at her desk, sipping a cup of noodles from the microwave. Treasure slipped the roll on the corner of Bonnie's desk without saying anything. She didn't want to talk. She didn't want to fight. She turned to walk out toward the parking lot. Maybe she'd drive home to see Grammy and pat Howls. Before she could get out the door, she heard Bonnie's voice.

"Is there something I can help you with, Miss Blume?" Bonnie asked sweetly.

Treasure shook her head and started to pull the door open.

"Because if there is, I'd be happy to hear it," said Bonnie, settling back into her chair.

Treasure paused, her hand on the door. "Someone forgot . . ."

"To deliver your construction paper and scissors?" Bonnie finished.

Treasure let the door close and walked back toward Bonnie. "I was going to say that someone forgot to pick up my roll and deliver announcements, but now that you mention it, I didn't get that order yet."

Bonnie flicked a piece of lint off the lapel of her cement-colored suit. "I just didn't think you'd need that order, since the circus isn't happening anymore."

Treasure was so tired and numb she could hardly muster an answer. "So it's over. You've heard from the superintendent."

Bonnie smirked. "Oh, this is rich. I get to be the one to tell you. I thought he was going to call you last night, but letting me do it is so much better."

"He did call me last night, but not to cancel. He requested a report on how the circus aligned with his educational aims."

"Did he?" asked Bonnie, in a tone so acid that Treasure feared it might curdle the Styrofoam cup she was holding.

Treasure refocused. There was a little hint of doubt buried in Bonnie's eyes. Of course, it was hard to tell Bonnie's expressions, since her eyebrows were drawn on with a pencil. Treasure straightened up. "Yes, he did. And I delivered the report to him this morning. So if you haven't heard from him since then, then I'd guess that my information is more current than yours."

Bonnie dropped her cup, spilling noodle juice all over her spotless desktop. As the citrine-yellow lake spread, Bonnie tried to dam the flood with a stack of manila folders. She grabbed her disinfectant wipes, but they failed to absorb any liquid. Treasure walked over to the restroom and came back with a pile of paper towels. "Here, use these," she said, holding them out. Bonnie snatched them from her outstretched hand and swabbed her computer keyboard. "This will probably melt my hard drive," muttered Bonnie.

"No, it won't," said Treasure. "Your hard drive is right here, under your desk. It might short out some of your keys, but I think you got it in time."

"Well, that's a relief," said Bonnie. She turned to Treasure. "Well, now, I guess it's my turn to ask. Do you know if he's read the report?"

Treasure shook her head. "No. I'm on hold until he lets me know if we can proceed or not."

Bonnie wadded the paper towels into a ball. She caught Treasure's eye as she aimed at the garbage can. The wad flew like a perfect half-court shot. "I wouldn't count on proceeding if I were you," she said, settling back into her desk and picking up the phone as it began to ring.

Treasure didn't reply. She just turned around, retraced her steps to the door, and walked out. She stood in the blazing heat, blinking. Before she could get to her car, or even make her feet move, she heard the unmistakable roar of Mullet. She watched bewildered as Grammy turned into the school lot and parked in a drop-off-only zone. Grammy barely cut the engine before she barreled out of the car and into Treasure's personal space. She was waving a piece of notebook paper in her hands like a flag.

"That superintendent called on the home line!" she said. "I told him that you were at school, of course. Where did he think you'd be? So he said he'd call the school instead, and I said there was no way he was getting off the phone without telling me what his decision was."

"And?" Treasure asked, still afraid of the answer.

Grammy threw her bony arms around her granddaughter. "And it's a go! He thought your report was thorough and demonstrated the aims admirably. That's what he said! Admirably!"

Treasure felt overwhelmed. She sat down on the curb. Grammy plopped down beside her. "And I just couldn't wait for you to find out. I just had to come tell you. Besides, we've got our dress rehearsal to do now!" She hopped up, with the vim and verve of a woman half her age, and held out her hand to her sleep-deprived and zoned-out grand-daughter. Treasure leaned on her Grammy as they walked back into the school.

As they walked passed Bonnie, Grammy yelled excitedly, "Have you heard? We're going to have a circus here tomorrow!"

Bonnie didn't look up. "That's what I heard as well," she said with a sniff, deeply involved in a blank yellow legal pad.

Treasure perked up. That must have been the phone call that Bonnie received right when she walked outside. "Then can I get that order of construction paper and scissors right now? I want to get the invitations made before the end of school today."

Bonnie heaved a sigh, as if Treasure's request was a heavier burden than a wheelbarrow full of rocks. She pushed herself back from her desk and rolled her chair over to an adjacent table that had the package on it. She picked it up and handed it to Treasure.

Grammy crowed like a rooster. "I'm so proud of my girl I could spit!" she said.

"Yes, she has that effect on people," replied Bonnie, manufacturing an artificial smile. "I hope it goes well," she said in a tone that very much implied that she did not.

Grammy got it. She drew herself up (and Treasure along with her) and stuck her nose in the air. "I'm sure you do," she said in a tone that implied that she felt that Bonnie B. Baumgartner, Queen Bee of the ele-mentary school, was a bug that should be swatted as soon as possible. And with that, Treasure and Grammy Blume swept past her.

"Old biddie!" Grammy muttered under her breath.

· ·

Micaela knelt next to the bed so her grandma could put her hair into a bun. As her grandma slid bobby pins into her hair, Micaela chattered on about the circus.

"Grandma, I wish you could come. I've got to be there on time to get into my costume. Miss Treasure said 6:15. Is it 6:15 yet? That's when the big hand is on the three and the little hand is on the six. The clock kind of looks sad like that. My costume is so beautiful. It has swirls of pink sequins. Swirls! And Grammy Blume is going to help me with my makeup. It must be tasteful, she says. She doesn't approve of painting babies, she says. I'm not a baby, but anyway, she says I have to remember to look up and stand tall. I'm supposed to imagine that there is an invisible cord that connects my chin to the ceiling. I wish you could come too," she said, finally turning around and looking at her grandma who coughed into her hand before she replied.

"I do too, sweetheart. But your daddy will be there. Now, come give me a hug. It's almost time."

Micaela sprang up from her bedside, hugged her grandma, and ran smack into her dad's legs as he walked down the hall. They collided with an oof that turned into a hug.

"Daddy, did you know it's time to go? I can't be late. I'll be out in the car waiting for you."

Dennis patted her head. "You look like a princess with a crown. I'm just going to make sure Grandma is okay, and then I'll be out."

Micaela shook a finger at him. "You have two minutes. I'm counting." She started toward the garage door yelling, "One Mississippi, two Mississippi . . ."

Dennis shook his head and looked in on his mom. "I don't think I can take much more of her enthusiasm, can you?"

His mom smiled at him. "I'm so happy to see it. She talked to me when I was doing her hair, just like she used to. She was Mile-a-Minute Micaela again. "

Dennis chuckled at the nickname. He'd given it to her when she was two, and only knew about ten words. She'd string those ten words into garbled frantic sentences that only he could decipher. But she wasn't a baby anymore. She was so grown up it killed him. He sat down beside his mother on the bed. She was rubbing her arms.

"Doing her hair made you arms sore? You should have gotten me," he said.

"I wanted to do this for her. And I miss having hair," said his mom, slumping back against the pillows. "She's so excited. Every other word out of her mouth was about Miss Treasure and Grammy Blume."

"Yeah, I've noticed that too. I hope it doesn't bother you for her to call someone else Grammy."

His mom got a drink of water from the bottle on the nightstand, downing some pills. "Not at all. I love to have other people love my granddaughter. She needs all the love she can get. And I can tell, just by talking to her, that these two ladies love her."

Dennis thought about Treasure Blume's face, lit up from the lunchroom lights, her freckles all speckly as she winked at him. It made him chuckle. "Yeah, it's funny. I really didn't like her teacher to start with, and now . . ." He couldn't finish the sentence, because he didn't know how he felt about this woman. He felt squirmy just thinking about it.

His mother waited before prompting him, "And now what?" she said.

"Now, I have to go," he said, tucking the covers around his mother and turning on the oscillating fans. "I put the dogs in the backyard. We'll be back as soon as we can," he said, turning off the light in the room. Just then the front door banged open, and he heard Micaela's voice from the steps below. "Time was up twenty-five Mississippis ago!" she shouted.

· · · · · · · · · · · · · · · · · · · ·

The invitation that Micaela had brought home from school indicated that the circus/conference would be in the lunchroom. Dennis felt a little territorial. It was strange to walk in there without anyone expecting him to prepare food. But as soon as he looked up, he got off his possessive trip. The lunchroom was unrecognizable. A giant red and white striped canopy stretched across the ceiling, with balloons tied to every corner. Behind the center ring, a red curtain was hung. A few of Dawn Robbins's fourth-graders were already juggling. Dawn, with a big curly black mustache, was obviously the ringmaster. Beside her stood Treasure, dressed in yellow and green striped clown pants, with a red rubber nose, enormous shoes, and a rainbow-colored wig. As Dawn welcomed the crowd and introduced the next act, Treasure slapped her way toward them. He'd seen ducks waddle more gracefully than she did. She stretched her hand out to Micaela, who grabbed it with both her own and began swinging her arms.

"Micaela, your hair looks so pretty! Did your daddy or your grandma do it?"

Micaela beamed from the compliment. "My grandma did it. Daddy can only make buns out of dough." That made both Dennis and Treasure laugh.

"It's true," said Dennis with a shrug.

Treasure squatted down to Micaela's level. "Grammy's behind the red curtain getting the rest of the acrobats and tightrope walkers ready. We just finished the costumes. Can you head back there?" Micaela nodded and took off without a backward glance at either of them.

Slowly, Treasure straightened up and looked at Dennis. This was the first time the two of them had been face-to-face since the wet pants incident. She supposed that she should start conferencing with him about Micaela, just as she had done with other parents as they arrived. But for some reason, she had a hard time concentrating. Her heart had decided to flutter. *Don't be stupid*, she told herself.

Luckily Dennis didn't notice her fidgeting. He'd caught sight of Norman, decked out in a lime-green leotard and cape ensemble. He had a scuba mask over his eyes and gel in his hair. He was posing superman style against an enormous papier-mâché cannon while his anorexic mother took photos of him. He noticed Dennis from across the room and waved. Dennis nodded at him. "Come meet my mom," Norman called. Dennis started to move before he remembered that Treasure still stood beside him. "Did you want to say something?" he asked. Treasure balanced on the balls of her feet. She shook her head. "I just wanted to talk to you about Micaela's progress, but I can do that later. Enjoy the circus, and make sure you pick up her portfolio. They're by the door." And with that, Treasure turned away and walked behind the tent where Grammy and the acrobats were about to go on. "Chicken, Chicken, Chicken," her giant shoes squawked at her with each step. She should have just talked to him. He was right there in front of her.

Grammy was applying a tiny bit of blush to Sharonda's cheeks as Treasure approached. "Suck in those cheeks like this, girl," said Grammy, demonstrating a fish face. "That's it." She looked up as Treasure came over beside her. "How's the turnout?" she asked. Grammy herself was wearing one of her more understated costumes: a basic black leotard with a few fuchsia sequins scattered across the top and a ballroom length bubble gum pink satin skirt with dyed chicken feathers sewn into the hem.

"It's pretty good. I've gotten to talk to almost six families so far and more are trickling in. How about your crew? Are they ready to go?"

The little girls were solemnly stretching on the floor. They each wore stretchy black yoga pants and shiny polyester tops with sequins in different bright colors: Sharonda was green, Rosy was blue, and, of course, Micaela was pink. Looking at the costumes now, Treasure had to hand it to Grammy. She doubted that anyone would guess that they were pieced together from throwaway materials. She scanned the girls backstage, counting heads.

"We're missing Liwayway," she said.

Grammy nodded. "I know. Do you think she'll come?"

"If she doesn't, what are you going to do? Isn't she lead on the dance?"

"Yes, but I can improvise if I have to."

Treasure cocked an ear. Dawn was announcing the trapeze act. It was right before the tightrope and acrobat act. "I think you're going to have to, Grams."

Grammy reached down and fluffed her feathers. "That's why I came prepared, for such an occasion as this. Girls! Gather!" she said, clapping her hands. The little girls sprang from their stretches and circled about her. Grammy knelt down and gazed at each girl at eye level. Except for her blue bouffant hair, she could have been one of them. "We are about to perform. I will take Liwayway's position, and I will carry out the lengths of bamboo as planned. I would like you all to fold your arms and link pinkies with the girl next to you as we pray for guidance and vision during our performance."

As Grammy prayed and the girls swayed with tightly closed eyes, Treasure offered up a prayer herself. At the amen, they heard Dawn's voice announcing their act. Grammy rose and turned to the girls. "It's showtime! Now remember: dignity and energy, that's what I want from you." She turned to Treasure. "Do I have lipstick on my teeth?" she asked. Treasure shook her head. "Well then, let's get on with the show!" The girls scampered out in front, and Grammy, carting several lengths of bamboo, pulled up the rear. For a moment, Treasure thought she might just stay backstage. Then it wouldn't be as visible as she cringed. It wasn't that she didn't trust Grammy. It was just that this wasn't Grammy's show. And applause was Grammy's favorite fix. She just hoped Grammy could resist enough to let the girls shine. She stood still for a minute before walking back out to watch. She decided she'd better be within glaring distance to make Grammy behave.

· · · · · · · · · · · · · · · · · · ·

Dennis had found a seat two rows from the front about five minutes after meeting Norman's mother. She had bleached hair and the kind of ropy hard arms that marked her as a fitness junkie. She wore a sports bra and running pants. Who comes to parent-teacher conferences dressed like that?

"Well, you're the man that Norman's been spending all his time with?" she cooed at him as he approached. "Not that I blame him," she said, as she sized up Dennis's pec muscles beneath his shirt. "Do you work out?" she asked.

"Not intentionally," said Dennis, feeling naked before her. And the conversation went downhill from there. As soon as she started talking about health supplements from South American tree bark, he knew he had to escape. He made a remark about needing to talk to his daughter's teacher as he scanned the crowd for Treasure. He couldn't see her giant suspenders or striped pants anywhere. Why did people think clowns were scary? Women like Norman's mom were scary. Clowns were positively soothing. He'd have paid money to see a clown right now. It took five minutes for him to disentangle himself, and when he finally sat down, he was shaking. Not even for Norman would he go down that road again. He had to close his eyes and breathe deeply before the panic went away.

He was just starting to calm down when Micaela's act was announced. She and two other little girls held hands as they walked into the center ring. Behind them marched an elderly lady in a feathery pink skirt. Her thick blue hair swept back from her ears like wings. Dennis blinked. It was like Willy Wonka's fairy godmother had just been dropped into the lunchroom. He could only assume that he was staring at Grammy Blume. He pried his eyes off her and focused on Micaela. He couldn't see her face because her chin was pointed at the ceiling, but her outfit was cute. It did have swirls of sequins, but Dennis was relieved to see that it wasn't too tight or too revealing. Part of his disgust with dancing was that it made little girls look like showgirls. These costumes didn't do that. Score one point for the Fairy Granny.

The girls stopped and faced the audience. Grammy nodded and some eerie New Wave music began playing. All three little girls dropped into backbends. Grammy slid three bamboo poles into position behind them. In unison, each girl went from a backbend to an unassisted handstand. Dennis had no idea that Micaela could even do that. The little black girl on the end drew her legs up tall and straight and then suddenly mule-kicked onto her feet and onto the bamboo. Dennis could only assume she must have prehensile toes. Then Micaela and the other girl followed suit. The audience erupted in spontaneous applause, with Dennis cheering the loudest of all. The three little girls acknowledged their audience with an incline of their heads. Grammy handed each girl a concealed prop, and then poised herself on the frontmost bamboo pole. At a wave of her hand, they walked the bamboo as if it were a tightrope, with sharply pointed toes. At the end of the pole, at exactly the same moment, each girl (and Grammy) opened an umbrella, which they had held concealed in their right hands. Still in unison, they tossed their umbrellas in the air and caught them as they came down. Then they dropped down into the splits. The audience gasped. Honestly, Dennis was more pleased with Micaela's umbrella catch. She'd always had terrible hand-to-eye coordination.

After the applause, the girls and Grammy rose to their feet and bowed. Then two of the girls sat down Indian-style inside two of the bamboo sticks. Grammy and Micaela stood off to each side as the girls picked up the ends of each stick. In unison, they thumped the sticks against the ground twice and then hit the sticks together. The sound cracked across the lunchroom. The girls continued thumping the sticks: *pound pound thwack, pound pound thwack*. Then Grammy and Micaela started to dance in between the bamboo poles, going faster than doubledutch jump-ropers. Micaela was quick and nimble, as if she were dancing on water. But Grammy was no slouch. She danced as smoothly as a spider. Even as the beat got faster, she kept her feet clear of the trap. The audience started to pick up the beat, clapping along with the dancers, as the dance accelerated. At the end, the sound was deafening, and it was hard to pick out the hollow thwack of the bamboo poles under the sound of people cheering, stomping, and clapping. At the climax, Grammy and Micaela turned around and do-si-doed without missing a beat. The two other little girls stood, bringing the bamboo poles with them to shoulder height, before dropping them to the ground with a heavy thud. Then all four dancers bowed.

The audience cheered, and Dennis wolf-whistled. He was so proud of Micaela. She had never missed a step. How had she managed to do all that without him even knowing? He watched as Grammy gathered the other three girls into a fierce hug before waving to the audience and picking up her bamboo poles. Dennis pitied the next act. He hoped it wasn't Norman.

And it wasn't. A Little Tikes Cozy Coupe was rocketing up the center aisle. When he saw it, Dennis felt nostalgic; he'd bought one for Micaela when she was two. Then he started to get worried. This sucker was flying. Usually these little plastic cars didn't go very fast because they were foot-powered, a la Fred Flinstone. But it was obvious that foot power had nothing to do with this ride. Because stuck out through what would have been a windshield in a normal car were Treasure Blume's giant red floppy clown feet. Treasure herself was scrunched into a ball, apparently bracing for impact. She rolled to center stage, nearly knocking over the mic stand, and dizzily got out of the car, giving herself a good shake as she unfolded. Dawn Robbins hung onto the mic stand, laughing. "Trust Miss Treasure Blume to make an entrance!" she said. "Is there something you want to say?" she asked Treasure.

Treasure bobbed her head up and down. "The dance that you just saw was the tinikling, a traditional folk dance from the Philippines. It was taught to us by Liwayway, one of our students who couldn't be with us tonight. But I just wanted to be sure and mention her." The audience clapped politely. "Who was the old lady?" someone shouted from the back.

Treasure answered. "That was my grandmother, Tabiona Blume, who volunteered to help with choreography. We'd like to thank her for her help with costumes as well."

Dawn took the microphone from Treasure. "You might recognize Mrs. Blume from her performances with Ruby's Red Hot Chili Steppers. Would you like us to bring Grammy back out?"

The audience hooted and clapped. Treasure shot Dawn a warning look. "What are you doing?" she hissed.

Dawn whispered in her ear. "Don't worry so much."

"Easy for you to say. You don't know what Grammy is like with an open mic! There's no telling what might come out of her mouth . . ." whispered Treasure back.

Grammy had started moving back to the center stage when she heard her name. She curtsied to the audience as if she were standing before royalty. She held up her hands to quiet the crowd before she began to speak. "Thank you for your support tonight. You truly have remarkable children. I hope you can see all the work that these two teachers have put into this event, and the work they've put into your children's learning. I am honored to have been part of this night," she said bowing again and then leaving the stage.

Treasure drew a deep breath and folded herself back into her tiny car. Grammy's lucidity seemed to be holding.

"How about another hand for Tabiona Blume!" said Dawn. "She will be appearing with her dance troupe during halftime at UNLV's home game next Saturday!"

Treasure cringed. That kind of plug would bring Grammy back out on stage for sure. And Treasure wanted the focus on the kids. She had to shut Dawn up. She climbed back into her tiny car and rammed it into Dawn's legs.

"On with the show!" said Treasure, as the audience laughed.

Dawn rubbed her shin, then spun Treasure around, aimed her car back down the aisle, and gave it a shove. "Please remember to speak to your child's teacher before leaving and pick up their portfolios. We will be conducting conferences until 8:30 p.m.," said Dawn, as her fourth-graders rolled out the huge papier-mâché cannon. Treasure tooted the horn as she sped back down the aisle.

Dennis hadn't been planning on sticking around for the whole show, but he was glad he did. While the cannon itself was amazing, Norman's part was a little anti-climactic. They lit the cannon, and suddenly the dry ice started smoking and a large boom echoed through the room. Dennis wondered how they could have gotten that cannon to make that sound. Then the nose of the cannon pointed down, and out rolled Norman, doing somersaults across the floor. At the end, he jumped to his feet and struck a superman pose. It was cute, but not as strong as Micaela's dancing. She was the star, as far as Dennis was concerned.

After the circus ended, Micaela scampered back to him and jumped into his arms. "Was I good, Daddy?"

"You were terrific!" he said, hugging her.

She disentangled herself and tugged on his hand. "Come on. I want you to meet Grammy Blume."

Dennis felt a little like he was being dragged to meet the Wizard of Oz. Tabiona, the great and powerful, was intimidating to him, and not just because of her wacky appearance. Suddenly he was standing before her.

"You must be Micaela's father, the lunch lady," said Grammy, looking him over from every angle. "And you're the one who's all soured on dance."

Dennis winced. There would be no "Hi, how are you?" with this woman. He started to try and explain, but it sounded so stupid coming out of his mouth.

"I get it. You've got issues with your ex. But this isn't about your issues. It's about your daughter and her talent. She needs some formal training. She has heart."

Dennis shook his head. "We just can't afford it right now, and I don't know anyone I trust enough to teach her." Micaela looked down at the floor.

"Well, you know me now," said Grammy. "And who said anything about money? I'd like to teach some private lessons. And of course it would be free. What do you say?" Grammy fixed her sharp golden-green eyes on him, reminding him of a raptor. And he felt like the prey. He shifted his feet and looked down at Micaela. She hugged his arm with her whole body and looked up at him like a puppy. "PLEASE?" she begged.

Since Dennis was solely responsible for the care and upkeep of two leftover dogs, the puppy eyes didn't budge him. In fact, the look annoyed him. He hated being put on the spot like this. "We'll see," he answered.

Micaela started to cry. "That means you'll take forever to decide!" she wailed.

Grammy turned her sharp eyes on Micaela. "I can't abide whining, Miss Micaela," said Grammy, as if she was talking to a new army recruit. "Dancers need emotional strength. I want to see you turn off the faucet and suck up that sad face. That's not the way you speak to your father."

Micaela sniffed and bowed her head. "Sorry, Daddy," she said.

"That's better," said Grammy. She refocused on Dennis. "Now, you can take your time. Just remember that I'm old. I could keel over at any minute. I'll tell you what. Why don't you come see the halftime performance next week at Sam Boyd Stadium? Then you can see my team in action and decide if it's what's best for Micaela or not. What do you say?"

Dennis was still mystified by this woman's ability to stop Micaela's outburst. Was she secretly a kid whisperer as well as a dancer? He smiled at Micaela, then at Grammy. "I think that's a great idea."

Grammy nodded. "Good. Then it's settled. I have some complimentary tickets that I'll get to you. We'll see you next Saturday. Keep that chin up, girl, and keep practicing." And with that, Grammy waved goodbye and walked back stage.

Dennis checked his watch. It was almost 8:30 and he still hadn't talked to Treasure. "Let's go get my portfolio, Daddy," said Micaela, tugging on his arm again.

"Micaela, quit pulling on my arms," said Dennis. "You're going to make my right arm longer than my left." He followed her to the table and picked up the folder. "Tell me what all these things are," he said.

Micaela started digging. "That's my math sheet. It tells you how fast I am on all the timed tests. I'm not the fastest in the class, but I'm pretty fast. . ." She explained each sheet except for something laminated tucked in the back. "That's pretty much everything," she said, snapping the folder shut.

"What about that last thing in there?" Dennis asked. "That thing with purple covers?"

"That's just my story from the Young Authors' project," said Micaela.

"You wrote a story? I want to read it."

"No, Daddy, it's . . . it's not very good. I don't want you to see it." She tried to grab it out of his hands. Luckily, since she was only as tall as his waist, he could easily hold it above her head.

Micaela jumped and made another grab when Miss Treasure walked up behind her and placed her hands on Micaela's shoulders. "Let him read it, Micaela. It's okay."

Micaela stopped fighting. Dennis pulled out *The Sad Dad* and began to read. Micaela drooped against Miss Treasure's legs. Treasure held her straight. She watched Dennis's face as he read. His bright blue eyes started to cloud. By the end, he looked like a wounded animal.

"Are you mad at me, Daddy?" Micaela asked, hardly daring to look up.

Those words snapped Dennis out of his funk. His eyes looked glassy but calm when he looked at Micaela. "No, baby. I'm mad at me." Then he managed half a smile. "I thought you did a great job on that story. I especially like how you drew the gnocchi, and your picture of Fishstick and Puff. Puff looked tough!"

Micaela smiled back and straightened up. Treasure was glad. She didn't know how much longer she could have held up Micaela's weight. Her legs felt shaky from being crammed into her tiny car.

The awkward moment stretched until Treasure decided to break it. "Micaela, did you remember to pick up your other clothes back stage? I don't want you to forget them."

Micaela snapped her fingers. "I forgot," she said. She turned to run backstage. "I'll be back in a minute, Daddy," she said.

Dennis was thumbing through the story again and shaking his head. "How could I have been so dumb?" he asked. "Boy, she sees right through everything, doesn't she?"

"She's a perceptive little girl," said Treasure gently.

"I had no idea that she had absorbed so much of what was going on around her," Dennis muttered, finally placing the story back in the folder. "Are all kids like that?"

Treasure considered. "Kids are aware of a lot more than their parents think they are. I bet most parents would be mortified if they knew every-thing that their kids told their teachers." She meant her last statement to soften his embarrassment, but somehow it seemed to heighten it.

"So at least I'm in company with other bad parents," he said, looking across the room to where Dawn Robbins was handing balloons to the remaining kids. Micaela was pointing at a yellow balloon in the center, and Dawn was struggling to untangle it.

"You aren't a bad parent," said Treasure. "Believe me, I can see the difference. You are a good parent. You love her and care about her, and you're there for her. And Micaela is special. She's gifted. She's easily the best reader in the class. And she wouldn't be, without your help."

Dennis smiled. "We did spend a lot of time reading books when she was little. She loved pop-up books. There was one with a pink cover and farm animals. You know how some kids have a blankie or a stuffed animal that they haul around? She had that book. We hauled it every-where. She named it Sophie."

Treasure liked seeing his face like this, when his worry lines softened. "Don't worry about your daughter. I've seen a big change in her in the last little while. She isn't the same girl that wrote that story."

"Why didn't you tell me about it?" All his anger was gone, and he just looked lost.

"Maybe I should have," Treasure conceded. "But Micaela begged me not to . . ."

"And that's when you hatched the *Green Eggs and Ham* plot with Thelma. I knew you had more to do with it than you let on."

Treasure blushed and rocked on the balls of her feet. She hastily looked under the table for something. "I've got something for you." She held out a copy of *Pride and Prejudice* that she had dug out from her bag.

"Um, thanks?" said Dennis, making it into a question. "But I'm not really a classic-reading-tea-and-crumpets-sort of guy."

Treasure giggled. "I bet you could make a mean crumpet. But anyway, it's for your mother. Micaela said how much your mom liked the BBC miniseries, and she was so excited when she found out that it was based on this book. I think that she and your mom could read it together."

Dennis took it skeptically. "Isn't this a little advanced for her?"

"Well, maybe a little," said Treasure. "But not much. Micaela has read everything I could get my hands on for her. She likes a challenge. She's so hungry."

Dennis shook his head. He looked deflated. "Hungry, huh? I don't think I've ever been accused of that before."

"That's not what I meant," exclaimed Treasure, putting a hand on his arm. Why did she use that word? "There's more to hunger than food. She's hungry for words, Mr. Cameron. Sometimes it's like there aren't enough words in the world for your word-starved little girl."

Dennis relaxed and exhaled. He could see the truth in what Treasure was saying. "Words. Right. Sorry about that. And please call me Dennis. I'm sort of touchy about hunger. I've just been so worried about the kids at school here. A while ago, Thelma told me that lunch might be the only meal that some of these kids eat. So that's why I want to make lunch something special for them."

Treasure nodded sympathetically, then realized her hand was still on his arm. She snatched it back. "I know. I worry about that too." More than he knew. She changed the subject. "So as you can see, Micaela is doing well in every subject. She's a model student. I just want to challenge her a little more, so I'm finding her more books. From testing, we can see that she's actually reading at a fifth-grade level. And I know I could take her higher if her comprehension caught up. That's why I thought Jane Austen might be good for her. It will test her comprehension. Just make sure when you and your family read together that you ask her questions about her reading."

Dennis watched her. It was very disconcerting to have a circus clown talk to him about his daughter's academic progress. For a minute, he wanted to reach up and honk her nose. He pushed the random thought aside. "By the way, I really enjoyed your circus. And I loved seeing the tinikling. I haven't seen it for years"

Treasure's face brightened. "You know it?"

"Yeah. I spent about three years in the Philippines."

"Doing what?" Treasure asked.

Dennis laughed. "Well, some kids run away to join the circus. I ran away to learn how to cook Spanish-Asian fusion dishes at a four-star resort."

"That's incredible!" said Treasure. "One of my students, the one who was supposed to dance with Micaela's group, is a refugee from there. She's one that I'm most worried about. The culture shock is a lot to deal with, let alone the language barrier. Do you speak the language?"

"Some. I'm pretty rusty, though. I don't have much of a chance to work on my Tagalog skills."

Treasure seized on his answer. "Would you be willing to try?"

Dennis hesitated. He didn't know what he was getting himself into. "For what?" he asked.

"It's just that I want to visit each of the children that didn't make it to the conference tonight, just to talk with their parents. And so someone who could speak Tagalog would be a real help to me."

Dennis raised his eyebrows. "You want to make a house call to every kid who didn't show up tonight? Do teachers make house calls?"

"This one does," said Treasure, lifting her chin. "And it's only three kids. And they're the ones who need help the most."

Dennis admired her dedication. He caved. "Okay, I can come with you for this one little girl. But can it wait? I'm swamped this week. I'm working on an upscale beans and wienies dish," he confided. "And now

I've got to make time to come see your grandma perform in the halftime show on Saturday."

"Why?" blurted Treasure.

Dennis sighed. "Because she asked me to, and because she wants to teach Micaela private dance lessons."

Treasure raised her hand to her forehead.

"I take it this is the first you've heard of this?" Dennis asked.

Treasure let her hand slid off her face. "Yes, it is. But I think she'd do a great job. She's spoken very highly of Micaela's talent and abilities. I just wasn't aware that she had decided to start her own studio."

Dennis shrugged. "Micaela's been bugging me about dance lessons ever since she was three. And she loves your grandma. It might be a good fit for her."

"Why haven't you let her dance before?" asked Treasure curiously. Micaela had never said why he felt so strongly about it.

Dennis cleared his throat. "My ex-wife was, well is, a dancer on the strip. I didn't like the lifestyle, or the people, or even the costumes for that matter. The whole scene seems so hollow. It's all condensed selfishness, flash, and sleaze. I guess I just didn't want Micaela involved in that world."

Treasure fought the urge to hug him. "Well, I can reassure you. Not all dance is like that. Grammy's team, the Red Hot Chili Steppers, is made up of ladies over sixty. Their idea of nightlife is hitting the early bird specials at the buffets. And the costumes are glitzy but they're designed to cover as much skin as possible."

"How do you know so much about it?" asked Dennis.

"I'm, uh, kind of a volunteer manager for them."

"So you'll be there?" asked Dennis eagerly.

Treasure was taken aback. Could this be the same guy who vowed he'd blame her forever if his daughter didn't eat lima beans? "Um, yes. I'm in charge of water bottles and Bengay distribution."

Dennis laughed. "Then we'll see you there. Your grandma said something about complimentary tickets."

"Oh yes," said Treasure. "We got quite a few for this performance. I'll make sure that you get some. I'll send them home with Micaela. Just so you know, the Steppers' fans usually sit together. It's kind of a rowdy bunch."

"It's fine. I'm sure Micaela won't let me forget," he said, looking around for his daughter as he spoke. He found her sitting at the refreshment table, cramming her face with brownies with her yellow balloon tied to her wrist. He cupped his hands and yelled at her, "No more junk food!"

Micaela turned and opened her mouth, showing him the train wreck inside. He started to walk toward her, then turned back to Treasure. He shook her hand, placing his other hand behind hers, creating a hand sandwich. "It was really nice to talk with you, Miss Blume. Thank you for all you've done for Micaela."

Treasure felt as limp as overcooked pasta. She watched as he walked away and then called weakly, "You can call me Treasure!"

Dennis turned and flashed her a smile to show that he heard her.

10

Halftime

WHEN TREASURE GOT UP ON SATURDAY MORNING BEFORE THE STEP-pers' homecoming performance, she could barely move. She felt old enough to be Grammy's grammy. She needed some Tylenol and a walker. She hobbled into the kitchen, accidentally stepping on Howls's tail. Howls squalled, more offended than actually hurt. He hid under the table and reached out a claw to scratch Treasure's ankles as she walked over to the fridge to get milk for her cereal. She heard the toilet flush and the shower turn on in the bathroom. Grammy was awake and belting out Broadway hits. Treasure could hear "I like to be in A-mer-i-ca. Okay by me in A-mer-i-ca" from *West Side Story* coming through the wall. How could she be so perky? The week following the circus hadn't been any less hectic than the week preceding it. The Steppers had been holding practices almost every night, plus Grammy and Treasure had been two-stepping with Varden Moyle on the side. In fact, that's where they'd been last night. It had taken them a lot of hours, but he was fully prepared for his part now. LuNae, it seemed, was far more interested in showing off Varden than in spending time with him.

The first time they'd driven out to his ranch, he said he was just tick-led to see them. Treasure, who was always apprehensive about meeting new people, hung back. But Vard wouldn't let her. "This must be your beautiful girl," he'd said to Grammy, taking Treasure's hand in his and kissing it with the courtesy of a knight. His wide smile stretched out all his wrinkles so that Treasure could see his eyes. They were the color of faded denim—worn, comfortable, and real. Right there, she'd been able to let go of all her baggage about him, her concerns about his effect on her grammy's lucidity, her worries about the LuNae vs. Grammy battle, and her fears that both she and Grammy were being disloyal to Mr. Fong. As far as she could judge, Mr. Moyle's intentions were honorable.

· · · · · · · · · · · · · · · · · · · ·

It wasn't until last night when they were practicing at his ranch that the subject of LuNae had even been broached. Vard seemed genuinely surprised that he was a node in the hottest geriatric love triangle in Steppers' history. It all came out when Grammy lost her patience with his mistakes and started yelling at him.

"You're a disgrace to the name of cowboys everywhere! Honestly, Vard, how did you get yourself roped into this?" screeched Grammy, hand on her hips, after Varden had accidentally tromped her toe with his Tony Lamas.

Vard had hung his head for a minute, then shrugged his shoulders. "It beats me. I wasn't asked. I was told. LuNae called me up and told me that I'd been selected. It was the first time I'd heard from her since that date when you nearly broke my nose."

Grammy's arms dropped to her side. "You haven't been seeing her?"

"Nope. I've been out here on my lonesome for months. I don't know how my name got tossed into this."

"Then what is LuNae up to?" asked Treasure from the side where she'd been watching.

The old man took off his hat, revealing a horse-shoe shaped bald spot on top. Neither Grammy nor Treasure had ever seen him without his Stetson on. It was like seeing him in his underwear. "I don't know," he finally mumbled.

"But you were willing to do it anyway?" Grammy asked, still perplexed. "Why?"

"Well, because it meant that I'd get a chance to see you. I hadn't seen you since you whisked your way down to Sin City. And so I plucked up my courage and called your son. He gave me the number so that I could call you. I knew you wouldn't leave me high and dry, like old LuNae."

Grammy embraced him and held him fiercely. "You old fool. You didn't have to agree to dance with my nemesis at a halftime show to get my attention."

Vard grinned wide, showing a gold molar. "I wish I'd a known that before today. Looks like we're stuck with it now."

Grammy pulled back and patted his cheek. "Don't count us out yet. Treasure and I'll get you two-stepping in jig time. And I'll know that when you're dancing with that bony old crone, you'll be thinking of me."

Vard leaned down and started to pucker up, intending to plant a big one on Grammy. But Grammy would have none of it. She shoved him away. "Not now, you crazy coot! My granddaughter's watching, and we've got dancing to do."

Grammy stiffened up into her teacher posture and beckoned Treasure over. "I want you to dance with Treasure. She's lighter on her feet and better at partner dancing than I am. Remember, you've got to lead her."

Vard ran his hand over his head then put his hat back on. "This whole thing would have gone a whole lot smoother if you'd have let me lead in the first place."

Grammy nodded. "I know. It takes a strong woman to let a man lead her. I've never been good at that. My girl is stronger than me."

Treasure just gaped at her grandma. Stronger than her? How could that be true? She could think of WWE wrestlers who wouldn't dare take on her Grammy. "I don't know about that, Grammy," said Treasure.

"Well, I do, so just shut your yap," said Grammy. "Now get into position."

Treasure obliged. Varden put his hand on her waist. Behind him, Grammy poked him between the shoulders. "Frame, Vard, Frame. I want to see you use those core muscles that you built up steer wrestling. Hold that frame and look into Treasure's eyes. Ready?" Grammy stepped back and Vard began to dance. Treasure followed and tried to encourage him with her eyes. His first steps were tentative and awkward, but by the end, he gained confidence. He dipped Treasure, and then sprang up like a teenager. "I did the whole thing! And I didn't step on your toes once, did I, honey?"

Treasure high-fived him. "Not one misstep. You did great!"

Grammy whistled through her teeth at them. "Now that was a show-stopper! Let's do it again. The beginning was still a little rough. I want the whole performance to be smooth as spam. Ready? And one, two, three . . ." Grammy clapped the rhythm, and Treasure twirled through the dance, responding to Vard's every step. By the time they left last night, it was a quarter to midnight, but he'd done the whole routine perfectly five times.

But today, Treasure was paying for every dip, shimmy, and kick. How on earth could she be so sore? She finished her cereal and rinsed the bowl in the sink.

Grammy walked in with her hair up in a towel. "Good morning, sunshine!" she said, stretching her arms over her head. "I feel like a spring chicken, just hatched! This is going to be a good performance, I know it!"

Treasure watched her grammy grudgingly as she started humming more *West Side Story*. "I feel more like unshine than sunshine," she said, sinking back into a kitchen chair.

"Well, Unshine, you better kick it into gear," Grammy said, as she ticked through their agenda on one hand. "First, we've got to get over to the stadium ASAP for that run-through at 8:30. Then you've got to swing out to the airport, right? Isn't Patience flying in today?"

Treasure groaned. She didn't know if she had what it took to deal with Patience today, on top of everything else, and she'd pushed her sister's layover out of her mind. She let her head smack against the table, forehead against Formica.

Grammy pursed her lips. "I sense some distress from you about this. You've known about this for weeks. What's the matter now?"

Treasure kept her forehead against the table. "Besides Patience's penchant for ulterior motives? I don't know. It's just that this time, Dennis will be there with Micaela, and I don't know if I'm prepared for him to meet Patience. Once people, especially men, meet Patience, it's like there isn't anybody else in the room."

Grammy plopped into a plastic chair beside Treasure and started massaging her neck. "What've you got to worry about? You're just as pretty as your sister. In fact, you look just like her."

Treasure snorted. "On what planet? Patience is a knockout, and you know it."

Grammy made a face. "Patience's polish is about an inch thick. Strip away her highlighted hair, spray tan, and fake nails, and what have you got left? You."

Treasure sat up. "But men want veneer. And I should know. My lack of veneer has held me back since puberty."

Grammy shook her head. "I don't think that's the case with your lunch lady. I get the feeling he's more into substance than style."

"He's not my lunch lady," said Treasure, massaging her sore forehead. "He's just my friend."

Grammy knew she better tread softly here. "Have you talked to him much since the circus?"

Treasure shrugged. "Not much. I see him at lunch, but he's so busy, all I can say is 'Hi' or 'I just loved the kielbasa in the beans and wienies.' He usually gives me extra breadsticks, though. And when I gave him the tickets, he said he was looking forward to it."

Grammy stopped rubbing. "Extra breadsticks, huh?"

Treasure shook Grammy's hands off her. "You're reading too much into this, Grams."

"You don't need to get touchy about it. He's your friend, then, and that's good. And he'll stay your friend, even after he meets your sister. I can just about guarantee that."

"That doesn't sound ironclad."

"Well, when you're dealing with men, you always have to build in a stupidity factor."

"Grammy! That's mean. What about Varden?"

Grammy snorted. "If he didn't have a stupidity factor, he wouldn't be dancing with LuNae today at halftime."

Treasure stood up, creaking as she did so. "I still wonder what she's up to."

Grammy rose too. "So do I. And I intend to find out about it before today is through." She looked at the Kit-Cat clock on the wall. The eyes and tail flicked back and forth. It was almost 7:45. "Get a move on, girl. We've got to hustle."

. . . .

As Dennis drove to Sam Boyd Stadium that afternoon with Micaela, he wished he had come up with an excuse not to attend. Not that Micaela would let him. She had marked Grammy Blume's performance on every calendar in the house with pink highlighter. But there had to have been some sort of excuse that Micaela would have accepted. His mother was as adamant as Micaela was that he attend, so she was no help. She'd even scheduled a nurse to come and stay with her while they were gone. Maybe if one of the dogs had to go to the vet? He should have scheduled a flea-dip. That might have worked. He snuck a peek back at his daughter through the rearview mirror. He could only see her eyes. From her nose down, she was covered by a giant poster that rested against the toes of her sketchers. She'd worked on it all last night, using all her favorite stickers and her red glitter glue. It said, "Grammy Blume is our favorite Stepper Star!" There had been a panic-filled moment when Micaela had misspelled "favorite" on the poster. But Dennis dried her tears and managed to turn a *u* into an *o* with minimal mess. There was no way Micaela would have let him out of this.

He didn't know why he felt nervous about it. Well, that was a bit of a lie. It would be a huge crowd, and he always got afraid that he'd lose Micaela. She could slip through people's legs like an eel. After three stranger-danger lectures, he'd given her strict warnings that if she let go of his hand, she would not get to have dance lessons with Grammy Blume or anyone else. But it wasn't just that, and he knew it. It was one thing to see Treasure at school. But this felt weird. He would be completely out of his element, hanging around with the Steppers' groupies and Treasure's family. And frankly, he doubted the sanity of both sets of people. Treasure's family couldn't be normal. The law of apples and family trees told him that. He was just starting to admit to himself that he liked her. He wasn't ready for grilling yet.

"Get a grip!" he muttered to himself. He was treating this like way too big a deal. Why couldn't he just take it at face value? He was going to watch his daughter's potential dance teacher perform. That was it. And then maybe after, they'd swing by the organic produce warehouse that he liked so much. They had the best broccoli he'd ever seen. He could make that broccoli, Portobello, and cheese soup that his mom liked. The idea perked him up. As he pulled the van into a parking space, he felt himself relax a little. He'd just keep the image of the broccoli in front of him, and then he could cope.

Micaela unbuckled her seat belt and jumped out of the van before he could even turn off the car. "We're here!" she squealed, clasping her sign to her body. "Let's go, let's go, let's go! I want to see Miss Treasure and Grammy Blume!"

Dennis turned off the car and jumped out himself too quickly to mull over anymore ramifications. "Micaela! What is the rule?" he asked as he bounded over to the pavement to where she stood.

She rolled her eyes at him. "Stay with Daddy."

"That's right. And you just broke that rule. You can't go jumping out of the van in a parking lot. You could be run over. You're only three feet high! Drivers can't even see you."

"Daddy, I was just getting out of the car. I'm still in your parking space." She indicated the yellow line two inches to her right.

Dennis didn't want to hear it. "What's the rule?"

"Stay with Daddy."

"That's right. In fact, let's amend that rule. The new rule is: never leave Daddy."

"What if I have to go to the bathroom?"

"You'll go in the men's room."

"NO, I WON'T!" Micaela shrieked.

"Fine," said Dennis, taking her hand. "I'll just go in the ladies." It was going to be a long day.

. . . .

At the very same minute, Treasure Blume was thinking the very same thing. She and the Steppers were buried deep within the warren of tunnels under the stadium, awaiting their call time. The Steppers were restless, penned in their dressing room like wild ponies. As the ladies stretched and primped, Treasure hoped that everything would go as smoothly as the morning run-through, even though Varden Moyle hadn't shown up.

"Are you sure this man is coming?" Ruby had asked LuNae when Treasure and Grammy arrived at the stadium. "Because if he's a no-show, he could ruin the show, you know?"

LuNae looked unconcerned. "I spoke with him last night, and he assured me that he'd be here. I believe he had some prior commitments this morning," she said, patting her elaborately curled hair.

Grammy looked tempted to jump into the discussion. She had been right by Varden's side, listening in, when he fielded the call from LuNae. Varden had a true emergency. He had to rush over to his son's ostrich farm. (Dale had been attacked by one of the big birds. And that started a fight between father and son. Varden himself didn't like the "big chickens," but Dale swore they were the meat of the future.) But LuNae didn't deign to tell the Steppers the truth. And it made Vard look flaky, when really, she was the flake. Grammy visibly bristled. The nerve of that woman! She hadn't listened to him at all. She'd just run through the dance number over the phone, giving him cryptic instructions: "Right after Birdie finishes her aerial, step out onto the floor. Just turn to the left on the second downbeat, and then we'll do the pretzel." Grammy was disgusted by her sloppiness. How could anyone learn to dance over the phone?

Treasure sidled up behind Grammy and laid a calming arm around her shoulder. Grammy quit seething and clamped her mouth shut. It would do no good to call LuNae out now.

"Well, that really handicaps our practice for today. We can't even go through that section without Varden," said Ruby, starting to sweat. She had never gone into performance day without having every move carefully planned and charted. To head into a performance this huge with practically no practice on a solo made her head swim. Treasure left Grammy's side and fetched Ruby a water bottle. She stood by Ruby as she drank. "Thank you, Treasure," said Ruby, patting her arm.

Treasure cleared her throat. "I can step in and do Varden's part for the practice, if you need me to. I know his part."

Grammy glanced over at LuNae to watch her reaction. If LuNae was surprised, she didn't show it. Ruby seized on Treasure's words. "You do? Well, bless your heart, honey. That would be a real help today. Aren't you a wonder?" Ruby clapped her hands to get all the Steppers' attention. "We're going to go through the whole number, and I want you to do it full out. Don't just mark it. Treasure will step in for Mr. Moyle."

LuNae frowned a little. "How did you happen to learn the steps, Treasure?" she asked.

Treasure smiled at her. "Just by watching you run through it at practice. You made it look like so much fun that I thought I would try it. "

LuNae looked flattered. "Well, it is a lot of fun. And I know I make everything look easy. That's the mark of a great teacher. "

Treasure looked past her to Grammy, praying Grammy would not comment on LuNae's easiness or teaching methods.

Grammy put a hand to her mouth and mimed locking it with a key. Treasure focused back on LuNae. "Now where is Mr. Moyle's seat?"

· · · · · · · · · · · · · · · · · ·

By the time that Dennis and Micaela climbed up to their seats, the first quarter of the game was ending. Dennis didn't need to count stairs to find the Steppers' section. Three entire rows wore scarlet and gold T-shirts that said "Steppers Support Squad" emblazoned across the front. On the back, each shirt screamed slogans like "My Granny is hotter than your Granny," "Who Says Sixty isn't Sexy?" or "My Sweetie Sweats with Steppers." Dennis was amazed by the sheer variety of people in the section. He'd expected the Steppers' husbands to be there, of course, but he hadn't anticipated all the babies (in tiny Stepper onesies that said "Future Stepper in Sixty Years") or kids Micaela's age. And he could see at least five couples in their early thirties, sporting Stepper shirts and holding hands.

Micaela scampered up the steps and then ran back down to her dad, no doubt mindful of the injunction to keep hold of his hand. "Daddy, I want a shirt like that," she said, tugging on his arm again.

"Micaela, you sound like Veruca Salt," said Dennis, continuing to climb the stairs. "Are you going to ask for an Oompa Loompa next?"

"Nope. Just dance lessons," said Micaela with glee. She handed her dad the sign and started climbing over people's knees to get to their seats, which were smack dab in the middle. Dennis, still boggled by all the scarlet, followed, apologizing as he went.

"Sorry," he muttered, climbing over an older man with a sparse comb-over, before he finally sank into the seat beside him.

"No need," said the man, standing up and stretching out his hand. "I'm Gary. My wife is Ruby." He looked at Dennis expectedly. Dennis drew a blank. "Oh. That's nice," he stammered. Gary looked a little hurt. He twisted his shoulders so that Dennis could read the back of his shirt, which said "Ruby Rocks my World!"

"You know, Ruby . . ." He looked at Dennis incredulously, as if he couldn't believe he had to explain to anyone who Ruby was.

Finally it dawned on Dennis, "As in Ruby's Red Hot Chili Steppers,"

"That's my baby!" said Gary, settling back into his chair. "I'm kind of the unofficial chairman of their fan club. And I drive their bus."

"High honors," said Dennis, because some sort of reply seemed to be expected.

"That's right. Those ladies couldn't get along without me. Now, who are you? And why aren't you wearing the colors?"

Dennis looked down at his light blue polo shirt. "I, uh, I'm a friend, I guess, of Treasure Blume. She's my daughter's first grade teacher. And

Grammy . . . I mean, Tabiona Blume asked us to come and watch today."
His face felt as bright as Gary's T-shirt.

Gary perked up. "Oh! So you're Treasure's friend? Well, you should
know how highly we all think of her. She's just an angel with those ladies.
Without her (and me and Ruby, of course), there might not be any Steppers at all. She does so much. Puts all her vim and verve into the job. I'll
tell you, when she moved down here, Ruby worried for days. We found
a replacement, of course, but it just wasn't the same. Have you met her
family? Her parents couldn't come today, but her brother and sister are
here." He cupped his hands and shouted down in front of him, "Hey,
Randy, come up here for a minute."

Three rows down, a guy with a backwards baseball cap turned around
and waved. He climbed out over everyone in his row with an easy gait,
not even upsetting a scarlet infant car seat perched beside him. He jogged
up the stairs and over to an empty seat right in front of Dennis. He knelt
backward in the chair and stuck out his hand. "Hey, I'm Randy Blume,"
he said. Dennis examined his face for traces of Tabiona and Treasure.
The similarity was there, in the nose and shape of the eyes. He had sandy
blond hair and the kind of skin that looked like it had been sunburned
too many times.

Dennis quit examining him and stuck out his own hand. "I'm Dennis
Cameron, and this is my daughter, Micaela," he said, shifting in his chair
to indicate Micaela, only to discover her chair was empty, except for the
huge sign slanting toward the ceiling. The panic must have been evident
on his face, because Randy pointed over at the stairs where Micaela was
dancing with three other little girls.

"I'm Treasure's brother," said Randy. "And Grammy Blume's grand-
son. I've heard all about Micaela. Thanks for coming." He leaned in
closer to Dennis. Gary, meanwhile, had become engrossed in the game.
"Treasure tasked me with helping you to feel welcome. I know the Steppers' section can be a little intense." Dennis noticed that unlike all the
other fans, Randy's red shirt didn't sport any slogans. Before he could
ask, they were interrupted.

"I was wondering where you had gotten off to," said a glittering
blonde, who had magically appeared beside Randy with two large drinks
in her hand. Like Dennis, she didn't wear Stepper scarlet. Instead she
had on a trim blue boat-neck top with a sheer silk scarf wrapped around

her neck. She handed a drink to Randy, keeping her eyes on Dennis as she did so. "I'm Patience. I'm Treasure's sister." Dennis could see the resemblance. Patience looked a lot like Treasure, just with different coloring and more upgrades: perfectly manicured nails, perfectly tanned skin, and a perfectly proportioned figure. Dennis doubted that any of these features were natural.

"You must be Dennis. She told us you were going to be here. She just talks and talks about you."

Dennis started to feel sweat bead on his forehead. She was talking about him to her sister? It was worse than he thought. "I don't know her that well," he said, dazzled by Patience, who smiled at him with a toothy grin. *That's a lot of teeth*, thought Dennis. He wondered if they grew in rows, like shark teeth.

Randy rolled his eyes. "Shove over, Patience. You're blocking Gary's view."

With a graceful step, Patience stepped over the row of seat backs and slid into Micaela's seat. "Is that better?" she asked Randy. Randy didn't say anything. "So have you seen Treasure yet?" Patience asked, sipping on her straw. Dennis had a hard time focusing. For one thing, now Patience blocked his view of Micaela. "You'd think she'd at least come up to see you, after she invited you here." Dennis peered around Patience's silky hair. He could still see Micaela out of the corner of his eye, if he craned. She was on the steps, chanting, dancing, and dodging people who were climbing up to their own seats clasping hot dogs and pretzels.

"Is that your little girl?" asked Patience without bothering to look behind her.

"Yeah," said Dennis. "I wish she'd come back over and sit down. I can just see her tripping and rolling all the way down to the field."

"She's fine," said Patience, eyes still on Dennis. "Randy can go over and make sure she's okay. Right, Randy?"

Randy rose up slowly. "I can do that." He had his cell phone out and was texting furiously.

"She didn't invite me," Dennis offered, remembering Patience's last question. "Your Grandma did."

Patience arched one perfectly groomed brow. "You must have made quite an impression on Grammy. We're not that close," she said, leaning in to whisper in Dennis's ear. "To tell you the truth, I think she should be in a home, but I might as well be talking to myself. After all, my sister can barely have a life since she's become Grammy's guardian. Not that she had one before. I can't count how many times I told her to get a life. Treasure just doesn't have much vision. Myself, I'm not into the past much. I'm more proactive. For me, it's all about the future," stated Patience, leaning on the arm of her chair.

If she gets any closer, she'll be sitting in my lap, thought Dennis. The thought didn't please him.

He straightened up. "Well, they seem like a good team to me."

"Who?" asked Patience.

"Your Grandma and Treasure."

"Oh," said Patience, looking at her manicure. "Of course. They've always been tight. But there's so much more to life than hanging out with children and old people. In my life, for instance, I travel. I'm a flight attendant."

Dennis didn't quite know how to handle the abrupt shift in subject. He craned his neck again to see Micaela. "Up until a couple of years ago, I would have agreed with you. But travel's kind of taken a backseat to my priorities these days."

"Well, timing is everything. You've just got to think outside the box. It's easy to cram your life full of minor priorities," noted Patience dismissively.

As Dennis worked at not boiling over to this clueless woman lecturing him about priorities, he looked down. It was at that moment that Treasure Blume appeared below him at the portal, red cheeked from the effort of running all the way from the tunnels. She climbed the stairs and started down their row. "Randy texted me that you were here!" she said, tripping over Gary and co. Gary finally gave up and moved to a different seat. "Sorry, Gary," Treasure called to his retreating back. She slipped into his chair so she wouldn't block anyone's view of the game.

Treasure's hair was pulled up into a wispy ponytail that swung as she walked. Flyaway strands waved gently around her face. "Here," she said dumping a Steppers' T-shirt into his lap. "There's one for Micaela too. I wanted to get this to you before the game, but I just couldn't get back up here." Her face fell when she looked past him to see her sister perched on the seat beside him with her legs crossed seductively.

"I was wondering when you'd show up," said Patience. "What kind of manners do you have to invite someone here to a performance and then not even come up? I've had to keep poor Dennis entertained the whole time. That's downright inconsiderate. You know, she was late picking me up at the airport today," she said to Dennis as if Treasure weren't standing in front of them.

Treasure fought the urge to blurt out a statement regarding Patience's penchant for being inconsiderate. "I came as soon as I could, both times," she said. Then she began to pan the crowd for Micaela.

Dennis recognized the look. "She's on the stairs," he said.

Treasure sat back. "Well, I hope you enjoy the show. I'll try to come up and talk with you afterward. It's a little bit hectic right now."

"I can imagine," said Dennis, overwhelmed himself by the sea of red faces and Treasure's gleaming older sister. She was beautiful, like an Italian race car: trim and chrome, built for two. And Dennis could appreciate that beauty. But it made him nervous. And after talking to her for five minutes, he was sure he didn't want to drive her. He knew the cost of maintenance and upkeep too well. He really just wanted her to move so he could see his daughter better.

He expected Treasure to rush off as quickly as she had rushed in. But despite her declaration, she stayed put beside him. She closed her eyes and leaned back into the chair, resting her head against the back. Her face relaxed, and she drew a deep breath, letting it out slowly. Dennis found himself breathing along with her. His sweat glands calmed down. He closed his eyes too and just kept breathing. The whole stadium disappeared: the yells of irate fans screaming at the referees, the odor of thousands of bodies baking in the glaring sun, even the feeling on the back of his thighs of his skin sticking to the plastic seat.

"Did you ever notice how many colors you can see when your eyelids are closed?" asked Treasure.

Dennis hadn't considered. Wasn't dark just dark? He tilted his face more toward the sun. "Oranges and reds. Horizontal stripes," he said.

"You must be facing the sun. Turn away, toward your left," Treasure advised. "Now look."

"Browns and tans," he said.

"Still stripes?"

"Yep."

"You must not be looking at the same place that I am. I can see spots, in all these metallic tones: bronze and rust and platinum. I don't want to move."

Dennis cracked an eyelid and looked at Treasure. The sun washed across her face, turning her downcast eyelashes golden. Her face shimmered with constellations of freckles, some light, some dark. No wonder she saw spots.

"When I was a little girl, we went camping in Yellowstone. And one day we were swimming in the Firehole River. At dusk, all these bright, metallic dragonflies came out and skated on the river. They hardly looked real, like they'd been spray-painted. That's the only place I've ever seen colors like this before."

And as she spoke, Dennis started to see the dragonflies, vivid and dazzling, skimming the surface of the water, swirling back up to a sunset sky. From beneath his eyelids, it was like he was there, beside Treasure in her memory.

He started to say something (he didn't know what) when they heard an announcement blare over the loud speaker. "Miss Treasure Blume, please report to room 16B. Miss Treasure Blume, report immediately to room 16B."

Treasure sighed and sat up. "That was the closest thing I've had to a nap in weeks." She swiveled in her chair, stretching her back.

Dennis sat up too. "Hey, when did Patience leave?"

Treasure opened her eyes. They wouldn't refocus. Now all she could see were black splotches. "Did she go?" she murmured, standing up and shielding her eyes with her hand.

"I guess she isn't into eyelid gazing," joked Dennis.

"I guess not," replied Treasure, still looking. "But I better go before they page me again."

As Treasure stumbled back down the steps, Dennis felt someone punch him in the shoulder.

"Daddy!" shouted Micaela, who had just snuck up beside him. "You let that fake lady who was sitting in my chair crush my sign!"

. . . .

Treasure could hear loud voices, cackling and screaming, before she even opened the door to the Steppers' room. If the audio clues left her guessing, the visual didn't give her any more info. In her first glimpse, all she could see was a cluster of Steppers circled around something or some-one. The Steppers were already in uniform: red satin cowboy shirts with white piping and fringe, with gun belts slung low across their hips. The costumes were the reason Treasure couldn't see what was in the middle. The silver sequined cowboy hats blocked her view. She waded into the knot of women without thinking. "What is going on?" she demanded, throwing an elbow into someone's side. "Let me through. If someone is hurt, I can help." The Steppers panicked, their voices getting shriller as they crushed against each other tighter, pushing Treasure back.

Treasure got mad. "Ladies!" she hollered. "Shut up and step back. We have a show to do." The Steppers on the outer perimeter looked ashamed and scrambled back. Each band of ladies shifted outward until Treasure could reach the innermost ring. At the center knelt Ruby with both hands poised protectively over her hair like a helmet. On the floor lay LuNae, one hand over her eye, twisting and writhing in pain. Sitting beside them Indian-style, with a hand on both, was Grammy Blume.

Treasure shook her head. "Grammy, what are you doing in the middle of this?"

"Me?" asked Grammy. "I am just an innocent bystander."

Both LuNae and Ruby harrumphed at the statement.

Grammy glared at them both. "Fine. I am the long arm of the law, here to ensure that each sister gets her due."

Treasure felt doomed. It was always a bad sign when Grammy decided to dish out vigilante justice. She never should have left her, even for fif-teen minutes. "Clear out, ladies. There's nothing to see here. I'll handle this. Start stretching. We're on in ten minutes." At Treasure's announce-ment, Ruby let out a wail and the Steppers scattered.

Treasure squatted beside the three figures. "Now, Ruby, why don't you tell me what this is about."

"Why don't you start with me?" asked LuNae, hand still over her eye. "I'm the one who's been maimed."

Treasure turned toward her. "Okay, LuNae. Tell me what happened."

LuNae drew a shuddering breath. "Well, I was just going to put on my false eyelashes, and someone knocked me over. You know how sticky that glue is. The lash landed on my cornea, and I think it's stuck."

Treasure fished her cell phone out of her pocket. "Did anyone think to call a doctor about this?" she said, jabbing numbers.

LuNae nodded. "Yes. You know my youngest girl married an optometrist. He's on his way here, but he lives in Mesquite. He'll be here as fast as he can. In the meantime, he told me to hold this compress over my eye."

Treasure noticed a washcloth clenched in LuNae's fist. "Okay. So do you need any other medical attention?"

LuNae shook her head, then winced.

"Okay," said Treasure, taking a deep breath. "I guess the next thing to sort out is who bumped LuNae." She was afraid to ask. Her gaze settled on her grandmother.

"Don't look at me," said Grammy. "I didn't do it."

Treasure glanced over at Ruby, whose cheeks burned as bright as her name. "Ruby?" asked Treasure in disbelief.

"Yes, it was me," said Ruby, hands still poised over her hair. "I didn't mean to hurt her. It was an accident."

"That's a lie!" screeched LuNae.

Treasure looked at Grammy. Grammy pursed her lips. "I hate to rule in LuNae's favor, but I saw it for my own eyes. LuNae is right. That wasn't an accidental bump. Ruby came out of nowhere and just plowed into her."

"She blindsided me," whimpered LuNae.

Treasure turned back toward Ruby, mystified. "Why?'

Ruby rocked back and forth on her knees. "I don't know. I swear I didn't plan on doing it. I was just so worried about this performance, and because of LuNae, we haven't ever done the full routine, with her two-step with Mr. Moyle. So I looked at her, and I got so angry, I just ran her down."

Grammy nodded, confirming Ruby's recital of the event.

"But," said Treasure slowly, trying to figure this all out. "You gave LuNae that solo to begin with. If you didn't want her to do it, why'd you give her the part?"

Ruby started to cry again and tried to slide away.

Grammy kept a firm grip on her ankle. "That's what I was trying to figure out," she said. "I came over when Ruby leaned over LuNae, and LuNae reached out and grabbed a hunk of her hair. That's when the other girls started to crowd around us. And it didn't help that Ruby was screaming like she'd been scalped."

Treasure thought back briefly to the five minutes that she had sat beside Dennis. Those five minutes of peace up there had cost at least forty minutes of cacophony and craziness down here. She prayed she could get this sorted out, especially since the Steppers were expected on the field at any moment. "Okay, let's just talk this through . . ." she started to say. But she couldn't finish her sentence before Ruby broke down.

"It's no use. I've ruined everything. Now we won't get to perform, and it's all my fault!" she continued to sob.

"Shut your mouth," hissed LuNae.

"No, LuNae. I'm tired of this game. I'm spilling it all."

"No!" LuNae yelled. She reached out to grab Ruby's arm, but her depth perception was off, and she grabbed air instead. Grammy took advantage of the situation and put LuNae in a head lock.

"I'll kill you!" LuNae said.

"I'll haunt you," said Grammy, unperturbed. "Now Ruby, you go ahead."

Ruby drew a breath and began to talk. "You're right, Treasure. I was the one who gave LuNae that solo. She'd been nagging me about one for weeks. Every time I came in to get my hair done, she asked about it. But I kept saying that unless she could do some sort of special trick, she couldn't have one. And that's when she said that if she wasn't special enough on her own, she'd do a partner dance. I told her we don't do partner dances, but she said that's why it would be so special. I still didn't want to, and that's when she threatened me. She said she'd tell everyone my secret."

Treasure and Grammy exchanged mystified glances.

Gingerly, Ruby let her hands drift to her side. She bowed the top of her head. Treasure and Grammy raised up and peered. "What are we supposed to be seeing?" asked Grammy.

Ruby reached up and carefully lifted off a section of bright red curls, revealing shiny white skin beneath. "I wear a wiglette," she whispered.

Grammy released LuNae. "It looks like a Commanche tried to snatch you bald!" she exclaimed.

Ruby shook her head. "I lost a section of my hair as a teenager in a motorboating accident. I took a blade to the head, and it severed my follicles. That section of hair never grew back. And I dye the rest of it."

Grammy and Treasure sank back down. LuNae glared at them with her one good eye.

"Lots of people dye their hair," said Treasure, slipping an arm around Ruby. Ruby dug out a Kleenex from her pocket and blew her nose.

"That's right. Almost everybody here, in fact," said Grammy. "And a couple of the other girls wear wigs. You know that."

"Well, maybe. But I'm different. I'm Ruby. And my hair is the reason for our colors. That's why we're red hot. And wouldn't everybody snicker if they knew about my wiglette?"

"That's not true," said Treasure. "You are Ruby, with or without your hair. It's your talent that makes you our leader. No one can choreograph like you."

At that, LuNae let out a snort.

"That's enough out of you," said Grammy, raising herself up. "I think that it serves you right, blackmailing and scheming. That's not appropriate Stepper behavior and you know it. Threatening to reveal Ruby's hair secrets, well that's low. Isn't there some sort of a hairdresser's code that says that whatever people say in your chair is confidential? Privileged information?"

Treasure cocked her head to one side. "You're thinking of lawyers, Grammy, and doctors."

"Well, there should be a law of confidentiality for hairdressers as well. I'd strip your scissors myself, if I could. Not to mention," Grammy said, rising to her full height, "that this was a lowdown dirty trick to pull on Varden as well. Why did you rope him into this?"

LuNae turned away from them. "Of course you wouldn't under-stand. You're always in the spotlight. Front and center, that's where you always dance. You don't know what it's like to be shoved in the back row."

Grammy brushed her comment aside. "Okay, but why involve Vard? You didn't even practice with him. Did you want to make him look like a fool?"

LuNae turned back around. "He certainly made me look like a fool at the dance. I just thought I'd return the favor. And after what happened on our first date, I mostly wanted to show you up."

"I suspected that it was more about me than about him. Look, LuNae, I am truly sorry for wading into your date. I never should have. And I have no excuse, except that my reason escaped me." Grammy glanced sideways at Treasure. "But I can see more clearly now. I just wish you hadn't involved poor Vard. You've treated him shabbily, and that's a fact. But for my part, I am sorry."

LuNae glared out of her good eye. "Your words can't make it better, Tabiona. I'm done dealing with you." She looked over at Ruby, who was wiping the mascara off from under her eyes. "Ruby, I'm sorry, but as of this minute, I'm resigning from the Steppers."

Ruby looked panicky. "But we've got to go on in ten minutes. What do you expect us to do?"

"Well, I refuse to dance beside this showboating hermit anymore! It's either her or me," LuNae said, her voice rising higher.

Ruby looked helplessly back and forth between the two women. Then she straightened her spine and made a decision. "LuNae, I've had it with your ultimatums. Strip out of your uniform, and hand it over."

"Fine!" shouted LuNae, popping the pearl buttons and shimming out of the pants. She threw her gun belt at Ruby's feet. "Good luck going on without me," she said, one hand still clutching her wounded eye. She stalked out of the room as spitefully as she could in her underwear.

Treasure let out a whoosh of air. "That wasn't pretty," she said. "And now we have two minutes before we've got to be on the grass."

Ruby picked up LuNae's guns. "I guess I'll go tell them that we won't be going on."

"Wait a minute," said Grammy, grabbing Ruby's arm. "Treasure can go on in LuNae's place. She knows the whole section with Varden."

"Me?" said Treasure. "Why not you, Grammy?"

"If I take over LuNae's spot, my spot will be empty. Besides, I already have a solo. And I'm not good at partner dancing." Grammy picked up LuNae's uniform and held it out to Treasure.

"Yes, it's the only way," said Ruby.

LuNae was at least two sizes smaller than Treasure. "Just suck in your breath," said Grammy, as Treasure tried to tug the zipper up on the pants.

"This can't be happening," said Treasure. "I don't meet the age requirement."

Grammy laughed as she jammed the cowboy hat on Treasure's head. "You may not be old, honey. But you're old at heart. Now get that shirt on. We've got to get out on the field."

· · · · · · · · · · · · · · · · · ·

After Treasure left, Dennis felt like he could almost enjoy the game. He checked on Micaela, who was still playing on the steps. It turned out that her two new friends were twins, and their mother was sitting right next to them. She assured Dennis that she was watching all three. Micaela begged to be able to sit with her friends, and he had agreed. Then he made a quick call home to check on his mom and finally settled back to watch the game. He hadn't been able to watch a game since he moved in with his mother and yielded the remote control to her.

Randy, who had disappeared earlier, came back over and sat down beside him. "So, you're the guy with all the gourmet grub," he said, handing Dennis a hot dog from the concession stand. "I hope this dog doesn't offend you."

Dennis opened the wrapper. "Mustard and onions? I'm touched. How did you know?"

Randy shrugged. "You seemed like a mustard man to me. It's Dijon, by the way."

Dennis bit into the dog, smearing mustard over his chin. "That's good," he said through a mouthful.

"All beef. Costco's finest. We supply the stadium. I asked the guy who runs the concession stand to get one that hadn't been on the rotator for hours," said Randy, biting into his own dog. They chewed together in companionable silence.

"So where'd your sister go?" asked Dennis, swallowing.

"Treasure or Patience?"

"Patience. Treasure's with the Steppers, I assume."

"Patience ran into an old friend, and she's sitting with him."

"I didn't even know Treasure had a sister. Does she usually come to the shows?"

"Nah. She's just here on a layover. Usually she wouldn't bother making contact with us, but I think she wanted to hit Grammy up for some money."

Dennis started choking on his dog. "She shakes down Grammy?" He couldn't imagine someone having the nerve to do that.

"Yeah. Patience pretty much sees her family as a resource to be strip-mined. She only surfaces when she needs something. We haven't heard from her for months."

"What does she want money for?" Dennis asked curiously. "She certainly looks like she's well taken care of."

Randy laughed. "Oh, she is. That's why she doesn't have any money of her own. She spends it all on herself. You could see her latest invest-ment, right?" said Randy, looking down at his own chest and then back up at Dennis.

Understanding flooded Dennis's mind, and he felt his cheeks go pink. "Ohhh. So that's why she's more, uh, proportional than Treasure."

"Yep," said Randy. "By the way, if you're ever asked by either one of them, this conversation never happened."

"Got it," said Dennis.

Randy looked relieved. He resumed their earlier topic of conversa-tion. "So now Patience wants money to go on a cruise around the world."

"Isn't she a stewardess?"

"Yes, but she insists that she needs to experience the world from a new vantage point, leaving footprints on the waves or something like that."

"But will Grammy go for it?" Dennis asked.

"What do you think?" Randy replied. "My guess is that my parents turned her down and so she thought she'd try Grammy. She must be desperate."

No wonder she looked like a shark. The thought of Patience bleeding Treasure's family dry turned his stomach. He reached in his pocket for a Zantac.

"She's nothing like Treasure, is she?" Dennis asked, popping the antacid.

"Glad you can see it," said Randy. "I'm a little worried. The Steppers should be on the field by now. I ran down there for a second to double-check their pistols, and Treasure didn't even see me. One of the ladies had a hand over her eye, and Treasure and Grammy were trying to help her."

"I hope she's okay," said Dennis, wiping at a mustard stain on his shirt.

"If she wasn't, Treasure would have called the paramedics." Randy finished his last bite of dog and crumpled up the wrapper. The clock showed two minutes until the end of the half. The UNLV crowd was going wild because of an interception.

"Do you want to get closer to the field, so we can see better?" he asked.

"Can we do that?" asked Dennis.

"Sure, we always get closer to the field for halftime. Let's grab Micaela, and then we'll head on down."

Dennis beckoned to Micaela, who left her friends and dutifully ran toward her dad. "We're going down closer to the field to see the performance, okay?"

"Yes!" said Micaela. "I want to see Miss Treasure too. I didn't get to talk to her before."

Randy squatted down to her level. "She wants to see you, too. I know she was excited that you came. You probably won't get to see her during the show. But I'm sure she'll come up before the end of the game. Are you ready?"

They started down the steps and the buzzer sounded. They soon found themselves fighting the tide of people who were headed for the concession stand. "Stay right behind me," Dennis said to Micaela, using his shoulders to muscle through the crowd.

"I'm staying with you, Daddy," said Micaela, hooking her fingers into his belt loops. Randy led them to some empty seats about three rows from the field where Gary and other Stepper supporters had already set up camp. Gary was setting up a tripod for his camcorder. "I want to get the zoom angles just right," he said to Randy.

Randy shook his head. "Don't zoom. Ruby wants wide shots, remember?"

Gary looked injured. "Do you think I'm a rookie at this? I'm only going to zoom on the solos." He turned his attention back to his camera.

The football fans continued to the concessions in a mass exodus as the Stepper fans descended to the front rows. Dennis watched the rivers of people and leaned down to Micaela. "Just don't say you need to go to the bathroom right now."

"I'll hold it," said Micaela, looking determined.

The Stepper fans began to chant and clap. "S-T-E-P-P-E-R! Ruby's Red Hot Steppers are superstars!" They heard static rumble over the PA system.

"Look, there they are," said Randy, pointing to the concrete walkway that led to the field. The Steppers, with Ruby at the head, were lined up five abreast, in shimmering satin and fringe. The cowboy hats made it hard to see their faces.

"I can't see!" said Micaela, jumping up and down. Dennis reached over and put her on his shoulders.

The announcer cleared his throat. "Fresh from their performances at the Jon Huntsman Senior Games, please welcome the pride of St. George, Utah: Ruby's Red Hot Chili Steppers!" The Stepper fans went wild while the rest of the stadium (those still in their seats) sent up a half-hearted clap. Ruby raised her arm over her head and blew a whistle. The Steppers began to march out onto the field in precise rows. When they were in an exact square, five by five, Ruby's arm went up again, and the Steppers stopped. In one fluid motion, they dropped their heads and crossed their legs, cocking one cowboy boot toe down, while their right hands went to the brim of their hats, and their left hands hovered over their pistols. "Good unison," remarked Randy.

The Steppers stood poised. On Dennis's shoulders, Micaela began to twitch. "When's the music going to start?" she asked Randy.

Randy put a hand to his ear. "Just listen," he said. The first notes blared over the system at too high a level, creating a painful screech. The crowd put their fingers to their ears, mimicking the unison of the Steppers themselves.

But the Steppers didn't flinch. On the first blaring note, they started to dance. They each kicked a leg high in the air and shot their pistols. Clouds of smoke raised above them, as they continued to move. The ladies started a clogging sequence. Dennis was astounded. The music was fast, but the Steppers kept stepping. In some parts, they weren't just in time with the music, they were double-timing their moves. If he hadn't known that these ladies were over sixty, he never would have guessed.

The Steppers moved into a pinwheel formation. The ladies on the ends had to move three times as fast as the ladies on the inside, and yet the lines stayed as straight as if they'd been drawn with a ruler. They intertwined arms and started doing a kick-line that ended with each lady putting her leg up on the waist of the lady next to her. Then the innermost ladies started to bow. The move rippled through the lines at exactly the same time. The entire crowd clapped. Then the ladies on the inner part of the pinwheel swung out from the center to form a giant U-shape. The ladies threw their hats across the U in the air, and shouted, "Yee-haw!" The hats flashed silver in the sunlight before each Stepper on the opposite side pirouetted and caught them. As they put the hats back on, one Stepper stepped to the center of the U. "Look!" said Micaela, pointing. "It's Grammy Blume!"

Randy looked up at the sky. "I don't want to look. I get so nervous when she dances."

"It's okay. Daddy got nervous when I played soccer," said Micaela, patting Dennis's head.

Grammy stood in the center of the field, looking like Annie Oakley in the Great Old Wild West shows. She twirled her guns once, twice, three times, and then sent them flying. She caught them, turned, and with great flare, she lifted her pistols high in the air and dropped down into the splits, shooting her guns as she slid. The audience got on their feet as Grammy climbed to hers. She waved to the crowd, then spotted Micaela, to whom she blew a kiss. She hightailed it back to her place as the next solo Stepper pranced onto center field.

"She did great," said Randy, with evident relief. "Now I can relax. This is Birdie's solo," he said. "It's even better than Grammy's, but don't tell her I said so." They watched as Birdie threw her hat behind her into the air. She looked determinedly at the field and started her tumbling path. She did three cartwheels before ending in the aerial. She landed with perfect precision. Dennis doubted that an Olympic gymnast could have done any better. Micaela was clapping along to the music, and Dennis found himself moving to the rhythm too.

Randy leaned over. "Now this is the new part that I haven't seen yet. It's with Grammy's friend Varden Moyle and her arch nemesis, LuNae. I know Grammy and Treasure have been working with him. See, he's sitting over there." Dennis looked over to see an older gentleman in a gray Stetson. He looked as nervous as Dennis had felt sitting next to Patience. He missed the next dancer stepping out because he was concentrating on the old man. He heard Randy say, "What the?" and then Micaela shrieked. "That's Miss Treasure! Look Daddy!" She grabbed his ears and turned his head. Dennis looked at the dancer standing in the center.

"It can't be," said Randy. Just then the dancer turned around. The silhouette from behind left no doubt. It was Treasure Blume in a painted-on Stepper costume. She lifted her head to the nosebleed section and tossed her hat in the air. Her hair fanned around her face as she twirled and drew her pistols. She took huge skipping steps toward the audience, pistols held high. She shot once and then twirled them into her holsters, stopping just short of Mr. Moyle. She inclined her head and held out her arms. Mr. Moyle shakily stepped forward. He clasped her waist in his hands and started two-stepping. Treasure followed him, smiling toward the sky. When they reached the center, Mr. Moyle jerked Treasure toward him. Dennis thought for a minute that she might fall, but she slid under his arm in a complicated twirl and came out on the other side. They did the move again, faster and faster as the music crescendoed. They were a blur of flying fringe. Treasure's hair looked like a low-lying strawberry cloud. The Steppers in the background were moving forward in an arrow formation. They fanned out behind the dancers and started twirling too. Finally, on the last note, Mr. Moyle dipped Treasure backward to the turf. The rest of the Steppers dropped to one knee. They grabbed their guns and shot again, just as Treasure sprang up into Mr. Moyle's arms.

The entire audience stood up and cheered. They were on their feet. Dennis whistled until his mouth went dry. Micaela clapped both hands on her dad's head. Randy pumped his fist in the air and yelled, "Way to go, Steppers!"

The PA announcer said, "Let's hear it for Ruby's Red Hot Chili Steppers, with special guest Varden Moyle." Mr. Moyle waved both hands at the crowd. He planted a kiss on Treasure's cheek and jogged back to his seat. Treasure stood in front of the crowd and closed her eyes. She took two deep breaths and smiled. Birdie and Grammy came forward and grabbed her hands. Together they bowed.

When they came back up, Dennis found himself yelling her name. "Let's hear it for Treasure Blume!" Treasure's eyes searched the crowd until she found Dennis. She grinned at him, her scarlet lipstick smeared. He looked back at her, and this time, he winked.

After the Steppers left the field, Dennis found himself rooted to the ground. He finally lifted Micaela off his shoulders after she knocked on his forehead like a door. "Earth to Daddy!" she yelled. "Let me down. I'm going to see Miss Treasure and Grammy Blume."

Randy stood beside him, still shocked. "I guess LuNae was too hurt to perform. I can't believe they let Treasure go on."

"Did you know she could dance like that?" asked Dennis, visions of Treasure twisting and twirling like a flame still playing through his mind.

Randy shook his head. "She can dance, I've always known that. But I didn't know she could dance like that." They stood shoulder to shoulder looking out across the empty field. Football fans were starting to filter back to their seats.

"She's . . ." started Dennis, struggling to define exactly what he wanted to say about Treasure.

"What?" asked Randy, defensively.

"Talented."

"Oh. Yeah. She is that," said Randy, relaxing his posture a little.

"And it was something more. There was just such joy in her. It was like she was really alive, you know?"

"Yep. I saw it," said Randy. He looked like he was going to burst if he didn't say something more. "I also saw how my little sister can fill out a pair of wranglers." He shook himself, trying to pry the image out of his head.

Dennis had noticed too, but he wasn't going to say anything about it to her brother.

Randy looked over at Dennis. "Dude, I'm sorry. Please, don't say anything about it. It's weird to say my sister looked hot dancing with a bunch of grandmas."

"But she did," said Dennis appreciatively. He still felt dazzled. Who knew she had that figure? He'd only ever seen her in lumpy sweater sets with pleated skirts and once, a clown suit. He knew she had a kind heart, but really, he never suspected that there was a hottie buried underneath all that polyester. For all Sheila's trashy glitz and exposed skin, she had nothing on Treasure today.

Randy suddenly pointed. "I see Treasure walking Micaela over here. They're on their way back toward our seats."

Dennis unrooted. "Let's go meet them."

They met about halfway up. Micaela was wearing Treasure's cowboy hat pulled down well over her eyes. Treasure held Micaela's hand, steering her around obstacles. She still wore the Steppers' uniform, sweat rings staining the satin under her arms. One of the bright pearl buttons had popped open at her neck. Randy rushed over and hugged his sister, lifting her off the ground.

"Miss Treasure took me to the bathroom," said Micaela, pushing her hat back so she could see.

"I'm so glad," said Dennis, looking into Treasure's eyes, half a smile on his lips.

The four of them stood there, oblivious to the yells of the football fans around them. UNLV had just scored a touchdown.

11

All Hoincked Up

TREASURE, YOU DORK, HE JUST ASKED YOU OUT," WHISPERED RANDY, as they watched Dennis and Micaela make their way down the stairs.

"No, he didn't," said Treasure, turning to face her brother. The game was over, and people were beginning to filter out of the stadium.

"Yes, he did."

"No, he didn't. He just asked me if I liked to eat Asian food," said Treasure, setting her silver sequined cowboy hat back on her head.

Randy grabbed her arm. "Yes. With him. He asked if you'd like to eat Asian food *with him.* "

"No," said Treasure, shaking out of his grip.

"For real, Treas. You drowned out his question with your enthusiastic response about New Fongs, and then Micaela started pulling on him.

Treasure stopped and looked her brother in the eye. "You can't be serious. Quit making fun of me this way. It's not funny."

Randy looked back at her, exasperated. "I'm a guy. I know what I'm talking about. He was definitely asking you out."

Treasure turned away and began to pick up all the trash around them.

Randy ran a hand through his hair and then turned around himself. He looked at the lady sitting behind them in the stadium seating. She wore a UNLV visor and a sweatshirt that said, "Put on your big girl panties and deal with it!" He appealed to her. "Excuse me, ma'am? You just saw the whole conversation between my sister and the man with the little girl, right?"

The woman took a sip of her Big Gulp and nodded.

176

"Did that man ask my sister out?"

The woman sipped and nodded again.

"Thank you!" said Randy.

Treasure's eyes bugged. The woman's straw struck air.

Treasure was sure she was going to hyperventilate, like when she had gone snorkeling with Roxy in Hawaii. She had breathed in through her nose and wound up with a lung full of seawater. She'd started to panic, then Roxy made her stand up. The water was only up to her waist.

"Oh," she said, the realization hitting her. Then she started to panic. "Randy? What do I do?" She directed the question both at her brother and at the big panties woman behind them.

"Call him?" Randy offered.

"Leave him alone?" panties lady suggested.

"Call him," Randy said firmly.

Panties lady shrugged.

"Do you know his number?" Randy asked.

Yes. Yes she did. She sang the phone number song out loud. "But I can't call him."

"I'll do it for you," said Randy.

"Have my big brother call? That's too lame for words."

"I'll do it if you don't," Randy threatened, his fingers poised over the keys in his cell phone. "You already sang the song."

Treasure wavered as Randy pushed the first number. "Fine," she said, snatching his phone. She should just be grateful that Grammy was downstairs with the rest of the Steppers.

"Hi, is this Micaela's dad?" she said.

Randy slapped his hand to his forehead. *Stupid, stupid, stupid,* Treasure thought. *You don't refer to a guy who just asked you out as anybody's dad.*

Then she heard Dennis answer. She could hear Micaela in the background. "Daddy, I can see my friends up there by the fountain. I want a drink."

"Can you hold on a second?" Dennis asked. She heard him talk to Micaela. "We're going home. No friends, no drinks, no potty. NOW. I'm on the phone. Quit yanking me!" The background noise surged.

The pause was just long enough for Treasure to feel stupid. That's how the prospect of romance affected her. What would she say when he shifted his attention back to his phone? She felt a blush crawl up her face and was devoutly glad he couldn't see her.

"Uhm, yeah. Sorry about that. Who is this?" He hadn't been able to check the caller ID.

"This is Treasure . . . Blume" Well, duh. In case he would confuse her with any other Treasures he knew.

Silence from Dennis. She could hear Micaela saying, "Daddy, come on!"

What was he thinking? She must not let him think. If he thought, he might regret. She plowed ahead, hoping to disrupt his thought chain. She looked at Randy. He had both thumbs up, for encouragement. She squeezed her eyes shut and prayed for her blurting powers to kick in. "Uhm, I guess I didn't hear you before, when we were talking, but my brother tells me that you asked me out."

"No, don't mention me!" Randy mouthed, dropping his thumbs,

"I mean I just wanted you to know I like Chinese food," she stammered.

Dennis started to laugh. "Yeah. I got that you liked Chinese food. (Stop it now Micaela, or you'll be grounded from dancing.) I'm glad your brother was listening. I wondered if you wanted to go out, like maybe next Saturday. I'd love to try New Fongs with you. I hear it's got fabulous egg rolls."

I must remain calm. Must act casual. Must act like I get asked out every-day. Must swallow. Must not let eyes bug out of head. Must answer! I must answer. Oh no. Treasure couldn't talk. This was bad.

Micaela continued to riot. "Okay, you are officially grounded," Dennis growled. Micaela started to bawl. "Look, Treasure, I've got to get Miss Cranky Pants home. I'll pick you up on Saturday, around seven. Okay?"

She opened her mouth. Nothing came out. Nothing.

He tried again. "Okay?"

"Kay," she croaked.

"Right," he said, and the line went silent.

Treasure stood rooted to the cement floor while people elbowed their way past Randy and her to get to the end of their row. She didn't even hear the panties lady snort and heave herself to her feet. Randy grabbed Treasure in a triumphant hug and spun her around, banging her ankles against the yellow hard back of the seats in front of her.

It was only then that she remembered to shut the phone.

. . . .

Back in the dressing room, Grammy Blume was peering into the mirror with the other Steppers, wiping lipstick off her teeth and teasing her hair. She'd already shimmied out of her costume and back into her street clothes when Randy came running through the door, yelling and fist-pumping the air.

"Randy! What are you thinking? You can't just barge in here. We might not all be decent!"

Randy laughed. "Sorry, Grams, but I really don't care! Treasure has big news."

"Ah-ha! I bet this was just a ploy to catch us in our birthday suits," said Ruby from across the room.

Randy shuddered. He shook the wrinkly image out of his head and turned a cartwheel instead.

"Heavens, boy!" said Grammy. "I always knew you were ADHD even though your mom was afeared of putting you on medication. What's this news about Treasure?"

Treasure had not even entered the door yet. Randy craned his head around. "She was right behind me. Where could she be?" Randy rushed back out of the room and found Treasure leaning against a wall, staring at the door with the expression of a coma patient. "What are you doing out here?"

"Randy, I can't go through that door."

"Sure you can. Grammy told me I'm not supposed to, and Ruby accused me of being a pervert, but they're all waiting for you."

"That's not what I mean," said Treasure, sliding down the wall. "I mean the door of hope. Because you'll tell Grammy, and she'll announce it to all the Steppers, and you'll call Mom and Dad, and then everyone will get their hopes up and think that this date will lead somewhere, and it won't."

"Why can't it lead somewhere?"

"It just won't. It never has. It never does. It just hurts. I can't walk through that door." Treasure melted into a puddle.

Randy assumed a sergeant pose and began to bark orders at her. "Treasure Rhonda Blume! Did this man kick you in the head?"

"No."

"Did he abuse you and call you names?"

"No."

"Did he, in fact, express interest in you?"

"I guess so."

"Answer yes or no."

"Okay, yes."

"Did he in fact ask you out on a date, a feat which has rarely happened in the history of Treasure Blume?"

"Yes."

Randy dropped the threatening pose. He sat next to his sister and put his arm around her. "Well, then. That is hope. You don't have to be afraid. You are justified in feeling some hope. I know I feel it. I just spent the whole game with him, and he likes you. He really does."

Treasure quoted, "Hope is that thing with feathers."

Randy hugged her. "Whatever that means. I swear, Treasure, you deal better with mistreatment and nastiness than you do with kindness and hope."

Treasure blinked. "Well, I have more experience with them."

Randy stood up and held out his hands. "Enjoy this moment. Feel the hope. No matter what happens next. We can't control what happens next, but we can celebrate what we feel right now."

Treasure took his hands and pulled herself up. "Celebrate. That's what we'll do."

"That's right, and you can't celebrate without the Steppers." Randy put his hand on the doorknob, and turned.

"Even if I give them heart failure?"

Randy cocked his head to the side. "Now that Lorna has a pacemaker, I think you're safe."

Treasure shook her hair out, nodded at Randy, and walked through the door. "Grammy, you'll never believe what just happened to me!" she sang.

Randy let the door close behind her. He stood in the hall while she had her moment with the Steppers. When he heard hooting and whistling, he came back in.

"My girl, you've got a date? A bona-fide hot date? With the lunch lady?" asked Grammy with both hands pressed over her heart.

"Your cockles warm again?" asked Treasure.

Grammy nodded mutely.

Treasure was about to speak again when she was enveloped by a nest of Steppers, all aiming to hug her. "It's what we've been praying for!" Alice Allen said. The rest of the Steppers were high-fiving.

Grammy stopped clutching her heart and got down to business. "Well, now we've got to plan. We're going to get you all hoincked up!"

Treasure feared for herself, and not just because she couldn't breathe. She didn't know what hoincking was, but it sounded frightening on Grammy's lips.

"What does hoincked mean?" she asked as Alice released her.

"It's a cross between hoisted and plucked."

Treasure's fears increased. She saw herself dressed as a rotisserie chicken, answering the doorbell for her date.

"I'll do your tanning and waxing!" cried out Beverly, who ran Beverly's Bake Your Bod. "And I'll do your nails too."

But Grammy would hear none of this. "I'm supervising this. We'll hire professionals for that stuff. But I'm taking her shopping! And none of you girls are horning in!" Grammy glared at Beverly and then cast her eye upon all her teammates.

Treasure looked in horror at Randy. "Help me!" she pleaded.

Randy sprang into action. "Well, I'm not a girl. Can't I horn in on the hoincking?"

Treasure looked at him gratefully.

Grammy narrowed her eyes. "Why would you want to come?"

"I can offer a fresh perspective. After all, I am a man, and I do go on dates."

Grammy looked at Treasure. "What do you think, girl?"

Treasure drew a deep breath, "I say, let's get hoincked."

· · · · · · · · · · · · · · · · · · ·

The hoincking began the following week, three days before the date. In order to sidestep the Steppers' connections, Randy called an old girlfriend, a former Junior Miss Clark County, and asked for a salon recommendation and appointment. The girl assured Randy that the stylist would a) be nice to Treasure, b) make her look cute, and

c) ignore all of Grammy's suggestions. This treatment would come at a rather high price (namely restarting a high-maintenance relationship), but Randy was willing, even eager to do it, for the sake of his sister.

The hair appointment went well. Randy lined up Varden Moyle to spend the afternoon with Grammy. Junior Miss Clark County made an appearance and gushed as she introduced Treasure. Treasure knew enough to keep quiet, and the artist, Mr. Philip, was intrigued by the unique color and texture of her hair. He deemed it a challenge worthy of his expertise. Randy stayed by her and handled the small talk. In the end, Treasure did not (as she had so many times before with LuNae as the stylist) wind up with poodle curls and a perm scald. After the cut and dry, Mr. Philip began to brandish both the curling and straightening irons that he wore slung around his waist in twin holsters.

"I should change my name to Rumpelstiltskin!" he exclaimed as he tore the cape off Treasure's neck and swiveled her chair to face the mirror. "Because I have spun straw into gold!"

Treasure hardly recognized herself in the mirror. She actually had a hairstyle. Soft layers fell across her forehead, framing her face and accentuating her eyes. It was still Treasure, but better, sharper, more focused, and positively modern. Randy grinned at her. "Look, Treasure, now everyone will know you're an angel. You've got the halo to prove it."

Treasure snorted. "Yep. Angel to cats, kids, and codgers. That's me."

The hair turned out so well that, after a quick make-up lesson by Junior Miss Clark County, Randy had high hopes for the shopping day. He'd asked for the name of some of the stores that she shopped at. She made him a list with her new number emblazoned across the top, and "Call me!" written in suggestive letters. But it was not to be. Randy contracted strep throat and had to let Treasure and Grammy shop unchaperoned. From his sickbed, he armed Treasure with the shopping list and a list of Ten Commandments:

- You may not purchase a sweater set or any other old lady gear.
- You may not shop in any store that you and Grammy usually frequent. In fact, if Grammy likes it, you should seriously doubt purchasing it.
- You may not buy anything with embroidered animals on it. ("What about seasonal embroidery?" Treasure asked, "like

fall leaves, or rcindcer?" Randy's answer was as unyielding as the Almighty. Treasure chalked it up to his high fever).

- All fabrics must be natural fibers. ("But polyester doesn't wrinkle," Treasure pleaded to no avail.)
- You may not purchase anything that is loose and baggy.
- You may not purchase anything that is tight and bunchy.
- Do not purchase shirts with horizontal stripes and do not purchase pants with vertical stripes.
- You must purchase one bling item to draw attention to your face (but Randy pointed out that Treasure should not ever say the word *bling* aloud, because if someone heard her, they'd probably beat her up for trying to act street. "I am street," said Treasure, posing. "Yeah, Sesame Street," said Randy).
- You should find something in a pink tone, since pink is a power color for women ("Really?" Treasure asked. "But it will clash with my hair." But Randy shook his head, wise as Yoda. "Find one that does not. Trust me," he said).

He also had photos clipped from magazines of outfits he thought would be flattering on her. "Try on a skirt, especially an A-line. That should balance you out a bit. You have a great figure, sis."

"Whatever," said Treasure. She felt uncomfortable in this conversation but also impressed. Who knew Randy had such expertise?

"You do! As long as you don't drown it in polyester. Don't be afraid to show your curves. They are an asset. Definitely an asset."

Treasure hugged him. "I never knew you were such an expert in women's fashions."

Randy looked amused. "After all the hours I spend folding capri pants at Costco, I was bound to learn something."

"You don't get all that from folding pants."

"I watch *What Not to Wear*."

"Just accept the fact that you have a gift."

"Right. And so do you."

"I'll trade you straight across!" she teased, squeezing Randy's hand and finding it clammy. "Is there anything I can get for you? You really are sick. I shouldn't go. I should stay here and help you. I don't need new clothes for this. I'll just dig out something from my closet."

"NO!" Randy shouted, nearly tumbling out of his bed. "You need this. Really you do. I want this guy to see you, to really see you. I've worked too hard to have this fall apart. Please go."

"Really?"

"Yes. Go. But take Grammy's opinions with a grain of salt. Remember, this is the woman who once wore an African mumu to Dad's college graduation. In fact, take pictures with your phone and send them to me. That's my tenth commandment. I want veto power."

"Complete veto power." Treasure raised her hand. "Jeez, Randy, don't worry so much. We'll be fine."

· · · · · · · · · · · · · · · · · · ·

"You sure you want to go to these stores, girl? These ditzy salesgirls wouldn't know quality if it slapped them upside the head," said Grammy as Treasure pulled into a parking space outside the outdoor mall.

"Grams, I let you have your way at the underwear store."

"Foundational garments are an essential part of hoincking. It's scaffolding, see. And don't deny that you were mightily impressed by the 'This-End-Up' panty slimmer we found."

"I admit, Grams, it's a marvel. That's why I bought seven pairs."

Grammy waxed philosophical. "Good underwear, it's like fine architecture. Now some undies are just cheap and sleazy, like the hotels down on the strip: all façade and no support. But these: solid and elegant and firm, like gothic arches. This underwear will bear you up on the toughest of days."

Treasure was oddly comforted by the thought of being buoyed up by her underwear. She released her seat belt. "Gothic arches, huh. Should I insert the flying buttress joke here?"

"Mind your manners, girl. I'm just trying to help you out."

"You are, Grammy, you are. You've been my only underwear consultant since puberty."

"And don't you forget it." Grams settled her sunglasses on top of her head and surveyed the stores. "So Randy thinks this is the place for hip and swanky. Well, let's get to it." She shut the car door and made for the store entrance.

Grammy's resolve gave Treasure little time to be intimidated by the photos of shirtless male models looming overhead as she walked into the darkness of the store. The music boomed and lights pulsated. A spurt from a fog machine made Treasure instinctively search her purse for her inhaler.

Grammy had found a pile of shirts next to a thumping speaker. "See what I mean?" she hollered. "No quality. Why I can see right through this top!"

Treasure yelled into Grammy's ear. "I think that's kind of the point, Grams!"

"Well, what do you think?" Grams asked, tossing the shirt to her. Treasure examined it. Grammy was right. The fabric was thin and cheap, but the shirt was not.

"Structure!" bellowed Grammy. "Loosy goosy just won't do!"

Treasure agreed. This place just wasn't right. Even Randy would have been able to see that. "We can stay and look, if you want," said Grammy through gritted teeth. They had yet to see a sales clerk at all. Treasure felt sure that if they stayed, she would wind up with a headache and an asthma attack. *Sorry, Randy*, she thought, *we did our best. Now it's time for store number two.*

As they went to leave, Treasure bumped into someone with her shoulder. "I'm sorry," said Treasure. The girl turned around and flipped her limp dishwater hair behind her ear. She scanned Treasure and sprinted toward the door, hostility rolling off her like waves.

Treasure shrugged and walked toward Grammy, who had gotten sidetracked at the accessory spinner. "Are these the type of blings that Randy told us to find?" she asked, holding up a shark's tooth necklace. Treasure didn't answer. There was something about the girl that nagged her. She knew that girl. She did. But from where? The girl was almost to the door, her dark lanky shape silhouetted against the brightness of the desert sun outside. Treasure snapped her fingers. "It's Aussie."

"The necklace?" asked Grammy.

"No, the girl," said Treasure.

Then the alarm sounded, and out of the recesses of the back room, two salesclerks swarmed the front door. Treasure held her hands over her ears. Grammy fumbled to turn off her hearing aid. The sound went off as the lights came up.

"Thank heavens," said Grammy. "I was beginning to think this was a store for bats." The other shoppers, nearly invisible until now, squinted against the light, like underground cave dwellers.

"Now, who's this girl, girl?" asked Grammy, but Treasure was already approaching Aussie from the side, where she was held firmly by the pimply salesclerk. It was clear he wasn't listening to her. *He must be talking to the manager on his headset*, thought Treasure. She watched him nod and frown as he clutched Aussie's arm. The other salesclerk, with broad shoulders and a ponytail, stood impassively in front of the door.

"Right, yeah. I see. So I'll need to take a look in your bag, miss."

Aussie glared. "I don't have to show you anything."

The second clerk moved forward.

Treasure stepped up. "This is just a misunderstanding. This girl is my niece. She was bringing an item to show me, and she thought that I was at the front of the store. She didn't mean to trigger the alarm."

The pimply clerk looked at Treasure suspiciously, "Your niece. Right. Look, lady, are you even sure you're in the right place?"

"I am now," answered Treasure.

Aussie glared at her and wrenched her arm away from the clerk. "That's right. I just wanted to show this to my aunt." She opened her bag and fished out one of the skimpy shirts that Grammy had critiqued. The clerk went to take the shirt, but Aussie didn't let go. He tugged harder, and then they all heard a ripping sound.

Grammy had made it to Treasure's side. "What are you doing?" she muttered to Treasure.

Treasure leaned over and whispered in her ear. "Don't hate the hater, remember?"

Pimply asked Ponytail, "Are you buying this?" He refocused on Aussie. "Because I'm not. What are you, like fourteen? I think I better talk to your *mother*."

Aussie winced at the word.

Treasure took the shirt from clerk's hand and smoothed it out. "I see what you mean, but I don't know if your mom will like it. What do you think, Aussie?"

Aussie just rolled her eyes, bored of the game already.

"Look, I don't know what the three of you are trying to pull," said the clerk. "But I can have the cops here in five minutes. You've damaged the merchandise. You can pay for the shirt and walk away, or you can wait for the cops in the storage room." The ponytail clerk started to pull Aussie back deeper into the store.

Treasure smiled at the clerk. "We'll take the shirt, and then we'll go."

"I don't want it anymore," said Aussie.

"Well, you're getting it now," said Treasure, taking out her purse.

Outside the store, Treasure introduced Aussie to Grammy Blume.

"Grammy, this is Bonnie B. Baumgartner's daughter, Aussie."

"Bonnie B. Whosewhatsits?" asked Grams.

"Bonnie. The secretary?" Treasure waited for recognition to dawn on Grammy's face.

Grammy's mouth formed an O. "Well, I'd think you'd want to thank Treasure for getting you out of that mess back there."

"Whatever," said Aussie, pulling her cell phone out of her bag and beginning to text. She turned to stalk off, but Grammy put an arm around her and then snagged her phone. Treasure would never have dared touch her. That kind of anger was bound to burn skin on contact. But this was no sweet grandmotherly hug. It was the Grammy equivalent of a headlock, the same type she'd used on LuNae.

"Now listen here, you little bit of trouble, my granddaughter just pulled your tootsies out of the fire, even though your mother has done nothing but make her life miserable. Why do you think she'd do that?"

"She's pathetic?"

Grammy put the phone on the ground, managing to make every move look menacing. "Try again."

"I don't know, and I don't care."

"Strike two," said Grammy, poising her strappy cork wedge over the phone. "Strike three and the phone gets it."

"Hey! You can't break my phone!"

"Oh, yes I can. What are you going to do? Tell your mother?"

Aussie's eyes widened, and she shook her head.

"Because then you'd have to tell your mom this whole escapade. And that's what my granddaughter was trying to avoid in the first place, I think. So let's just start over, and this time, play nice." Grammy cautiously let her out of the headlock.

"Fine," Aussie said. Her shoulders slumped, and her tough girl routine dissipated like the canned fog in the Vegas heat.

Grammy picked the phone up. "Treasure's a good person. And she took a risk for you. That demands a little respect. And a little gratitude."

"Fine. Thank you. Can I go now?"

Grammy considered. "No, you may not."

"What? You can't hold me here against my will."

Grammy slipped the phone down the front of her blouse. "I'll just keep this here for safe keeping."

Both Treasure and Aussie shuddered. "Now I'll have to boil it before I can ever use it again," lamented Aussie.

Treasure didn't disagree. "There's still the matter of the shirt."

"I didn't even want the shirt."

"Then why were you trying to steal it?"

"To see if I could."

"What would your mom think?"

Real fear entered Aussie's eyes. She scratched at her elbow. "You won't tell her? Will you?"

"I don't want to. I don't think that would help you. And that's really what I want to do."

"Why do you care?"

Treasure shrugged. "Maybe just because I know something about being mad at the world. Maybe just because I know your mother. Maybe just because I wish sometimes that someone would give me a break." Treasure held up the shirt. "So here it is. Your break. What are you going to do with it?"

Aussie took the shirt.

"That's what I like to see," said Grammy, grinning. "Now, we need your help. You see, my granddaughter has a hot date, and we need to pick her out an outfit. And we think you'd be the perfect person to give us a fresh perspective. Our fresh perspective has strep throat. What do you say?"

"Do I have another option?"

"Prison or telling your mother," said Grammy, patting the front of her shirt.

Aussie drew a deep breath. "Fine. Let's shop."

The next store was at least more brightly lit. The polished concrete floor and industrial lighting reminded Treasure of Costco. But that was where all comparisons ended. The cubic furniture was glossy white and all the elongated fixtures, included the clothing racks and hangers, were polished silverwave shapes. None of the mannequins had heads. Aussie kept her hand over her face to avoid being recognized by anyone she knew. Grammy and Treasure separated and started to slide hangers, with Grammy keeping a hand across her cellular hostage.

"Skimpy, skimpy, skimpy," Grammy exclaimed. "I don't see how you can find anything in this place!" she shouted across the store to Treasure. One clerk, a size twelve in a size six outfit, shot Grammy a "what planet are you from?" look as she walked back with an armful of rejects from the dressing rooms. But she didn't offer to help, which relieved Treasure. The clerk shook her head at Grams.

"I'm sure there are lots of things here that might work," Treasure said, holding up a V-neck fishnet tunic.

Aussie shuddered.

"Well, what would you pick?" Treasure asked her.

Aussie shrugged, then picked up a neon green faux crocodile belt.

"I meant for me."

"So did I," said Aussie, snickering.

"Okay," said Treasure, pursing her lips. "I really do need your help. This isn't a joke to me. But if you're going to make fun of me and dress me like a bigger freak than usual, then you can go. I'll dive down Grammy's blouse myself to get your phone. Really. I don't need anyone else here who is going to make this harder than it already is. I am terrified. If you haven't experienced that feeling yet, let me help you. Have you ever tried to look really good for a special occasion and just ended up looking stupid?"

Aussie didn't respond.

"Well, I have. In middle school, I wore parachute pants on a ski trip. People drew cartoons of me for months. I don't want a repeat of that." Treasure moved toward the clearance racks in the back, leaving Aussie bewildered in the middle of the store. For a minute she looked like a lost kid. Treasure half expected to hear an announcement: "Shoppers, we have a little lost girl in our store . . ." Then the moment passed, and Aussie was back to being the hostile awkward teenager. She skimmed through clothes, making the hangers squeal, until she wound up a rack away from Treasure.

"Parachute pants, huh?' she said, without making eye contact. "That's pretty bad. One time, my mom dressed me up in lederhosen so that I could showcase our German heritage. That was a dark day."

Treasure laughed but didn't look up.

"So it's a first date with a guy you like."

"It's a guy I really want to like, but I'm afraid."

Aussie nodded, eyes on the clothes. "Maybe something like this?" she said, pulling out a short-sleeved silk top in a rich eggplant.

"Silk? What if I sweat through it?"

"You'd layer something underneath it. See, it's a little sheer, so it can breathe, but a little bit of sheer is good, on a date with a guy that you really want to like."

"Really?"

"Trust me."

"Okay, what do I put with it?

"Skinny jeans and boots?"

Treasure cocked her head. "I'm not that cool."

"Granted," said Aussie, getting into it. "Scratch the skinny jeans."

"My brother suggested an A-line skirt."

Aussie considered. "Maybe. A skirt. That's got possibilities. Of course, I hate skirts. But for you . . . But something with a little more kick than an A-line. Hang on." She ran to the front of the store and grabbed a matte black skirt with a trumpet flair.

"Really?" asked Treasure.

"Try it on," said Aussie.

Grammy approached, clutching a dozen hangers adorned with loathsome selections. She reached out a hand toward the skirt. "Kind of boring, I think. No sequins, rickrack, or even fringe to make it sing. I like my special occasion wear to be special."

Treasure took it as a positive sign that Aussie didn't even roll her eyes. And with that, they headed into the dressing room.

After six different train wrecks, including a gangsta rap inspired ensemble and a plaid jumpsuit, Treasure tried on Aussie's selection and faced the mirror ready to cringe. But when she looked, she liked it. The color didn't clash with her hair, and the seaming under the bust emphasized her waist. And with her new shaper (Grammy had run out to the car to get it for her), the skirt looked stinking fabulous. At least that's what Aussie said, when she walked out to show them.

Grammy clasped her heart: "My girl! I'm getting palpitations!"

Treasure laughed. "If that's an effect of this outfit, then I'll take it!"

Aussie, after her initial declaration, jumped up and ran out. She came back in with three different necklaces. "I was thinking this longer one, with the three strands."

Treasure slipped the necklace over her head. The polished jet beads looked so sleek and civilized. Could she really pull it off?

Grammy was getting misty. "And there's the bling. It's something, girl. Not what I would have picked in a million years, but it's right. I know it is." And with that, she grabbed Aussie into a hug. Aussie didn't fight back or even try to retrieve her phone.

"It's not pink, but Randy will have to get over that." She had Grams snap a picture and send it to Randy. His answer: "Pink Shminck! Buy the whole thing!"

Aussie grinned. "I told you to trust me."

"I do now," said Treasure. Grammy nodded, fished out the cell phone, and handed it back to Aussie. Aussie seized it and began to text. Grammy looked over at Treasure, who shrugged. Aussie looked up. "I was just answering my mom's eighty-five texts asking when I'd be back. You can check if you want." She held the phone out to Grammy.

"We believe you," said Treasure. "Now I owe you. Can we drop you off at your house?"

Aussie's eyes got huge.

"Or a couple of blocks away from your house?" said Treasure.

Aussie nodded.

In the car, no one spoke. Outside the mall, back in the world, the dynamics were different again. Grammy tried to fill the space. "Now, how ever did you get a name like Aussie?"

Aussie looked out the window. "It's geographical. Australia. It's where my dad is from."

Treasure and Grammy exchanged glances. Treasure had never heard Bonnie ever mention her ex-husband.

"Well now, that's interesting," said Grammy. "My name's geographical too. Tabiona's where I was born."

"Never heard of it."

"Well, you probably wouldn't. It's in Utah. My momma wanted to name me Utahna, for the state, but Daddy won. And I'm sure glad he did. Can you imagine being saddled with a handle like that?"

No one answered.

"Of course, I've known of worse names. Just be glad your dad wasn't from Bulgaria or Svalbard."

"Svalbard?" Treasure mouthed, catching Aussie's eye in the rearview mirror. Aussie swallowed a giggle.

"I once knew twins who were called Whim and Dim," Grammy mused. "The one just did whatever he wanted, spur of the moment-like, and the other one followed him. 'Course, Whim and Dim weren't their given names, but the effect was just the same."

Treasure tried to change the timbre of the conversation. "I'm sure you heard all sorts of interesting names when you were in Vietnam, Aussie. I'd love to hear about your experience there."

Aussie traced patterns on the window. "I've never been to Vietnam. I've never been anywhere," she said.

Treasure looked at her again in the rearview mirror. "Oh," she said. "But I thought you said . . ."

Aussie shifted in her seat. "Well, you thought wrong."

Treasure turned the corner and pulled over. "Is this where you said you'd like us to drop you off?" she asked Aussie, who nodded, opened the door, and climbed out. She started to walk away without a word, arms crossed and fists clenched.

"Hey," Treasure yelled. "Don't forget your shirt," she said, holding out the bag.

"Thanks," Aussie said, grabbing it. She started to walk away again. Then she paused and turned back. "Good luck on your date."

"Thanks," said Treasure, "for everything."

Aussie cocked her head to the side. "What do you think my mom would say about what you did for me today?"

Treasure laughed. "Oh, probably that I was trying to buy your love."

Aussie gave her a puzzled look and then started walking home, swinging her bag as she walked.

12

First Date

AT T-MINUS TWO DAYS UNTIL HER DATE WITH DENNIS, TREASURE began to feel the nausea creep into her stomach, the same feeling she had when she waited in line for the teacups ride at Disneyland. *Why am I putting myself through this?* she wondered. The whole date would probably be a lot like her Disneyland experience—a very short thrill proceeded and followed by long bouts of heavy sweating and nausea. In order to avoid vomiting, she forced her mind away from any moony, lovey-dovey Dennis-related thoughts, edging all perimeters with barbed wire and imaginary rottweilers.

Instead, she focused on her students. As soon as the Steppers stopped sucking up all her spare time, Treasure started to seek out the families of the students who hadn't attended the circus. The first of these visits took place around 3:00 a.m. at Denney's on Thursday night. Treasure had talked with Kysa's dad as he washed dishes. On the phone, he seemed baffled and annoyed that Treasure wanted to meet with him at all. But Treasure's persistence eventually won out. He finally agreed to let her come during the slowest part of his shift, and his mood perked up considerably when Treasure started to rinse.

Cleaning soothed Treasure's nerves and her propensity to blurt out. Somehow it was so much easier to talk about Kysa's progress side by side rather than face-to-face. Treasure could talk to a sink full of suds much easier than a human being.

For Kysa's father's part, he couldn't hear most of Treasure's words. They were drowned out by the sound of the sprayer. But the crazy teacher lady rinsed and dried quickly, freeing him up for a quick smoke out by the dumpster. He hoped that he could ditch the teacher on his way out, but she barreled through the "Employee Only" doors, waving a folder full of Kysa's work in his face, until he finally took it and looked through the contents. Treasure could see his chest swell when he saw Kysa's blue ribbon for best bean sprout. He fingered the ribbon, running the smoothness against his calloused palm. It was only then that he looked up at Treasure and smiled.

· · · · · · · · · · · · · · · · · · · ·

Across town, Dennis Cameron was up too. Earlier that afternoon, his mother had finished her last round of chemotherapy and insisted that she was hungry again. She'd asked for baked ziti, but Dennis fixed her a banana and mango smoothie instead, hoping that she'd be able to keep it down. No such luck. He heard his mother heaving and retching in her bed. She hadn't had the strength to make it to the bathroom. Dennis carried her into the bathroom and started stripping the soiled sheets. His mother stumbled out of the bathroom and leaned on the doorframe until Dennis carried her to the rocker by her bed. He ran into the kitchen to grab his OxiClean, a sponge, and a bucket. When he returned, he could see that his mother was still shaking. He grabbed the afghan from the footstool and wrapped it around her.

"I'm sorry," she whispered.

"No, Mom. Don't apologize. I'm just glad I heard you."

His mother grimaced. "Well, I'm not."

Dennis rolled his eyes. "Enough, Mom. No more martyr routine. I get to help you. Don't apologize anymore."

She shrugged. "It's just I know you've got so much else to handle. You have work in just a few hours, and Micaela to take care of. And I want you to have a life too."

Dennis snorted as he scrubbed. "Me, a life? Do you think I can just buy one on eBay?"

"Well, I know you have a date this Saturday. That's a start."

"At this point, I think I better cancel," said Dennis, squirting Oxi-Clean onto the bed.

"Why?"

Dennis threw his sponge and ran his hands through his hair. "This,

Mom. This disease that is eating you alive. I can't go out on a date if I'm worried about you. What would have happened if I hadn't been here? What if it had been just you and Micaela? I can't go."

He retrieved his sponge and started scrubbing again. His mother was silent. She started to rock. Dennis liked the combined rhythm of the rocker and the scrubbing. It erased all thought from his head.

Then his mother broke the rhythm. "Dennis, I am your mother. I don't play that card much, but I'm playing it now. You are going on that date."

Dennis looked up. "Why? It doesn't matter."

"It does matter," said his mother. "It matters because I'm not going to be here very long. We both know that. And I want a good woman in your life. I want a good woman in Micaela's life. And this Treasure Blume is a good woman."

Dennis fought down the panic. It sounded like his mom wanted him married off before she croaked. He did not want to hear this. He covered his ears with his hands. "Jeez, Mom. It's a date, not a lifetime commitment."

"But you care about her. I can tell. There's something there, isn't there?"

Dennis thought about Treasure. In his mind he could see her leading the first graders into the lunchroom, singing. He could see her dancing at halftime in the arms of the geezer cowboy. He knew she was good, but he wondered if his mother would think that if she actually met her.

Dennis dipped his sponge in the bucket of warm water. "You don't even know her."

"I know her through her actions," said his mother. "And I know her through the light she brings to Micaela's face . . . and to yours when you talk about her."

Dennis left his sponge and knelt beside his mother's chair. "But she's different in person. I don't know if I can handle having you meet her. It's like . . . It's like that time that I made shrimp and spinach cream cheese puffs, remember? And Micaela whined and yelled and told everyone how much she hated spinach, but then after I got her to take a bite, she loved it and ate it all?"

"Yes," said his mother, propping her face up with her arm.

"Treasure's like that."

"She's like a finicky little girl?"

"No, Mom. She's like spinach. It's like everyone hates her at first, even the idea of her. I did too. But once you try her—well, you realize how flavorful and versatile and good for you spinach is. And you're glad that everyone else doesn't like spinach, because then it would be sold out." Dennis picked at the carpet, embarrassed by his passionate diatribe on the virtues of the green and leafy.

"So you're dating a vegetable," said his mom in an amused tone. He looked up. She was smiling deeply enough that Dennis could see the dimple in her cheek.

Dennis cocked his head to the side. "In a way, yes."

Their eyes met, and they both started to chuckle.

"That's good. You love vegetables. You were the only little boy on our block who loved to eat his veggies."

"I know," he said.

"But you don't want me to meet her."

"Not yet."

His mother eased herself forward on her chair and patted her son's cheek. "You worry too much. I'll love her."

"No, Mom. Really. You won't."

"But see, I'm a step ahead of you. I already love her. And the rest, I'll learn to love."

"What about leaving you and Micaela alone?" Dennis fretted, arms around his knees.

His mom leaned over the arm of the chair and moved a strand of hair out of his eyes. "You leave that to Micaela and me. We'll work it out." And in that one minute he believed her. She was his mom again. The one who could make things work out. The one who made all his friends stop teasing him when they caught him wearing an apron.

"Okay," he said, picking himself off the floor. "You can meet her later. I promise. Just two conditions."

His mother nodded.

"One, you do not mention marriage, lifetime commitments, or me needing a good woman in my life."

His mom nodded again. "And two?"

"You never tell her that I compared her to spinach."

When Dennis showed up at Treasure's apartment on Saturday night, he thought he had the wrong address. After all, her complex backed up against a trailer park and an auto salvage yard. But then he saw the cardboard cutouts of chubby vampires on her door, the same ones that she had up in her classroom. And when he spied a *Sassy Senior's Weekly* magazine in the mailbox, he knew he had the right place. He hesitated only for a minute, sniffing his palms. He wished again that he had worn Ziplocs over his hands before he chopped onions for the lasagna his mother mysteriously requested. He knocked against the widow's peak of the fat vampire and waited.

Almost instantly, he heard caterwauling seeping through the door. It sounded like someone was shoving a cat through a meat grinder. He put his fingers discreetly to his ears. The door cracked, and Grammy Blume's fierce eyeball peaked out at him.

"Get back, you mangy animal!" Grammy yelled.

Dennis stepped back.

"Not you, Mr. Lunch Lady," she said, acknowledging him. "I'm wrestling with Treasure's blasted feline."

Dennis looked down to see the source of the sound—a baleful, sparsely-furred black and white tomcat wedging his face out the cracked door. His eyes protruded like a pug dog. Dennis was briefly reminded of Puff, who also enjoyed accosting visitors.

Grammy gave the cat a shove with her foot. He hissed at Grams and streaked back into the apartment. Grammy Blume held up a hand. "Wait right here," she said, chasing the cat.

When she reappeared at the door, she looked more relaxed. "Come on in, Mr. Lunch Lady. Treasure's just finishing hoincking."

Before Dennis could even wonder what hoincking was, he knew he needed to sort out the name issue. "Dennis," he said. "Call me Dennis."

Grammy Blume shook her head. "No. I just can't seem to remember that. Pick something else."

Dennis was at a loss. "I promise that's my name. It's on my driver's license and everything."

Grammy gave him a look. "You're about as smart as creamed corn. I know that's your name. I can't get a handle on it. That's why I call you Lunch Lady. That I can remember."

Dennis pondered. "Uhm. Okay. But since I'm not a lady, it doesn't work for me. My daughter calls me lunch daddy. How about that?"

"That'll do," said Grammy. "Take a seat, Mr. Lunch Lady."

"Lunch daddy," Dennis corrected. "What would you think if I called you dancer man?"

"That you were going blind," said Grammy with a grin as she grabbed her purse. "All right, Mr. Lunch Daddy, I've got to scoot. Just sit down right here and Treasure'll be out in a minute. Don't worry about the cat. I've got him locked up."

"Where are you going?" asked Dennis politely.

"Over to your place," said Grammy, digging her keys out of her fuchsia handbag. "Micaela said you were fussing about leaving your mother. So I'm headed over to stay with them while you two go out."

Dennis scrambled in his head for something he could say to prevent this from happening. This was not his idea of a solution to the problem. But what could he do? He'd been outmaneuvered from both ends. If his mother couldn't meet Treasure herself, she'd get the next best thing. He hadn't forbade her from meeting Grammy Blume. His shoulders slumped in defeat. "You know how to get there?" he asked.

Grammy nodded. "Micaela googled it for me," she said, unfolding a map from her purse. "Don't look so worried. We'll be fine. You two just have a great time," she said, patting his cheek on her way out the door.

Dennis wondered briefly what it was about his cheeks that compelled women to pat them. The door closed behind Grammy Blume, and he sank down on the disco-gold couch. He leaned back and shut his eyes. Then he heard shotgun blasts echo from the parking lot. He sprang up and collided with Treasure, who had just walked in.

"We should probably get going," he said, gripping Treasure's shoulders.

"What for?" said Treasure, rocking back on her heels to keep her balance.

"I knew this was a bad neighborhood," said Dennis, crossing over to the windows and drawing the blinds.

Revelation spread across Treasure's face. "Oh. That wasn't a gunshot; that was Grammy starting her car." She stepped over to the window and put the blinds back up. She turned to him and smiled. "See, look out here."

Dennis peered out the window. A faded putty-brown El Camino with orange racing stripes sputtered onto the street.

Treasure followed his glance. "That's Mullet, Grammy's car."

Dennis snorted. "Of course. She can remember Mullet, but she can't remember Dennis?"

"What?" asked Treasure as they watched Grammy screech to a stop at a red light. Dennis explained to Treasure his previous conversation with Grammy. Treasure shook her head. "I'm so sorry, Dennis. But you know, I think lunch daddy has more sizzle."

"You do, huh?" said Dennis, looking Treasure over for the first time. She'd done something different to her hair, so it framed her face and didn't straggle down her back. Makeup played up her eyes and toned down her freckles. She had on cute, well-fitting modern clothes that emphasized her best features. Dennis hadn't thought she could look any better than she did in her Steppers' uniform, but he was glad to be wrong.

Treasure noticed his glance and twirled for him. "Do I pass?" she asked. Dennis couldn't even answer. It was surreal to watch her try to flirt. Instead he cleared his throat. "Wow. You're the one that has the sizzle."

Treasure looked at him shyly. "Do you know that's the first compliment I've ever received from a boy?"

"Well, I'm glad to be that boy. I'm sure it won't be your last," said Dennis, holding out his arm. "Are you ready to go?"

Treasure took his arm and tried not to think too much about Gene Kelly. The only thing better would be if he burst out into song. But she knew Dennis. Song wasn't his style. He was more likely to burst out into salami. "Yes, I'm ready for anything," she said as they walked out the door.

· · · · · · · · · · · · · · · · · ·

When they got into his van, Treasure pointed the air conditioning vents at her armpits and willed herself not to sweat. Dennis checked his rearview mirror and paused. "So I guess we start with the parent-teacher conference part of our date, right?"

Treasure looked relieved. "I was really hoping you'd say that. I didn't know when I'd get another opportunity. I finally tracked down the place where the family is, and Liwayway's mother is home tonight. It won't take long, I promise. "

"Just give me directions," said Dennis, straightening the wheel and pulling out onto the street.

Ten minutes later they were sitting outside a half-finished house, just bare studs jutting into the sky. It was surrounded by ten more houses just as abandoned. "This can't be right," said Treasure, wrinkling her forehead. Dennis didn't speak. He got out of the car and began to prowl around the house. "Come here," he called softly. Treasure unbuckled her seat belt and joined him. At the bottom of a small hill, in a corner of the lot, they could see a makeshift village. It made Treasure's neighborhood look like Bel Air. Wordlessly, they stared. It was like entering a third world country. Dilapidated camp trailers and automobiles teetered on cinder blocks. A few plywood and tin huts leaned up against them. Half-naked children scampered through gravel, broken glass, and weeds as mothers stood in a clump, babies balanced on their hips, picking through something in a plastic Walmart bag. Skinny dogs lay panting in the shade, watching out of the corners of their eyes for the chance to dart through an unguarded doorway.

"Do you want to go through with this?" asked Dennis gently.

Treasure blinked. "Yes," she said. "Although my perspective just shifted. I'm not so concerned about the days she missed. I'm just impressed with how frequently she's come."

Dennis nodded. "Jeez, and I thought I was going through a rough patch. I didn't know places like these existed here," he said soberly.

Treasure took a deep breath and squinted. "It's the one with the pink flamingo stuck through the roof. You ready?"

Dennis nodded again and held his hand out to her. "Let's do this."

At the shanty door, which was a plywood plank tied on with orange string, they paused again. It was a strange moment. For an instant, Dennis felt like he and Treasure were missionaries, preaching the gospel of education in a faraway land.

Treasure was rooting through her purse. "I wish I'd thought to bring them something. I was just so distracted, thinking all about myself and how my hair looked and stupid, stuff like that, that I didn't plan very well."

Dennis looked at her fondly. "Don't worry about that. Just smile and follow my lead."

"I found a bag of Skittles," said Treasure, triumphantly holding up the shiny red package.

"Put your Skittles back in your purse," muttered Dennis through his teeth as someone on the inside shoved the door aside.

Treasure stowed away her Skittles, and Dennis smiled. They found themselves face-to-face with a tiny balding grandmother without any teeth. She started talking to Dennis in a fluttery melodic language that reminded Treasure of birds. From the look on Dennis's face, she could tell it wasn't Tagalog.

Dennis stammered something back. The old lady waved her hand at him, chasing his words off as if they were flies. Dennis persisted. He cleared his throat and started using his hands to talk. Treasure couldn't do anything but look at the old woman and smile. The woman looked at Treasure and shrieked. She tugged the door shut, leaving a flummoxed Treasure and Dennis in her wake.

"That went well," said Dennis, leaning his arm against the doorframe.

"What happened?" asked Treasure. "She wasn't speaking Tagalog, was she?"

"No," said Dennis, straightening back up. "I think it was Illongo. It's a language spoken in the southern part of the Philippines. I spent all my time in the North, near Boracay."

"So you don't have any idea what she said," asked Treasure.

"Not so much," said Dennis, watching a dog approach him from the side. "What do we do now?" he asked.

Treasure put her hand out to the dog.

Dennis moved to stop her. "Don't go touching strange dogs! You don't know where it's been. Even if it's only been here, that's bad enough!"

Treasure giggled as the dog nosed her hand. Since she had no food, it merely sniffed, then went back to lie down.

"You're such a dad," said Treasure, turning to face the door again. "So now we try something else." She knocked again. A few seconds later, the door was shoved aside again, and the same little lady stared at them. Looking at Treasure, she shrieked again and grabbed her heart. Treasure started to speak in bad Spanish. "*Soy la maestra de Liwayway. Conoces Liwayway?*"

The little lady stopped clutching her heart. "Liwayway?" she asked.

"Sí," said Treasure. "Yes," said Dennis as the two of them nodded emphatically.

The lady backed away from the door, but she didn't tug it back into place. In two seconds, she returned with Liwayway by the hand. Liway-way looked at them with big eyes. Treasure opened her arms and stepped forward. Liwayway hesitantly stepped into her embrace.

"You came," she said.

"I told you I would," said Treasure, stepping inside.

Standing inside, the shanty looked larger than it had from the out-side. Her eyes adjusted to the dimness, and she could make out sleeping bags and two or three children asleep on top of them. In the corner stood a shiny karaoke machine.

Liwayway stepped back from Treasure and looked up at Dennis. "Who's that?' she asked.

Treasure followed her glance. "That's Micaela's dad. He's my friend, and he used to live in the Philippines. He came here to help me talk to your mother." Treasure motioned Dennis forward. Dennis squatted down to Liwayway's level and started to speak in Tagalog. The little girl's eyes lit up, and she responded rapidly. Treasure could tell Dennis was thinking hard to retrieve all the right words from his memory banks. But it was clear he understood her.

He nodded and turned back to Treasure. "That was her grand-mother. Grandmother was raised in Cotabota, so she speaks Illongo, not Tagalog. But Liwayway assures me that her mother speaks both. She says she's over at the cooking place, but that she will be back as soon as she can. Liwayway and her grandma are tending the babies. Liwayway says for us to wait here while she runs to get her mother."

Treasure's eyes started to tear up. It was so good to hear Liwayway speak so much, and for someone to understand her. Liwayway scampered away as Treasure reached out and squeezed Dennis's hand.

"Thank you so much," she said.

"I didn't do anything," said Dennis, surprised.

"You understood her. I haven't been able to do that all year."

Dennis returned the squeeze and stood holding Treasure's hand as the tiny grandmother shooed flies away from the pile of sleeping, sweat-ing babies.

In about five minutes, Liwayway returned with her mother. She held a tarnished silver pot clasped between two mismatched hot pads. Like Liwayway, she was short and slight, with bright eyes and thick dark hair. She set down the pot and bowed before her guests. Dennis stepped forward, speaking a steady stream. He shook her hand and then indicated Treasure, who stepped forward and offered her hand. Liwayway's mother took it, still talking to Dennis.

Dennis nodded and started to translate. "She welcomes us to this place, which is only a temporary home, until she can find another. She is grateful to meet you."

Treasure smiled, hoping that her sincerity would overpower the potency of her gift. "Ask her why Grandma freaked out when she met us," she said. Dennis nodded and began to speak. Liwayway's mother shrugged and turned. It was clear she was more comfortable speaking with Dennis than looking at Treasure. She started speaking the melodic tones of the bird language to the grandmother, who responded with musical sounds and wild gestures. Liwayway's mother started to laugh, and so did Liwayway. When Liwayway's mother explained it to Dennis, he started to laugh too.

Dennis wiped his eyes. "She thought you were a ghost. Wait. That's not quite it."

He asked Liwayway's mom a word. The woman nodded in the affirmative.

"Angel," said Dennis. "That's it. You are so white that she didn't think you could be human. She thought you were the angel of death coming to take her away. She's been having chest pains. But then, when you talked to her in Spanish, she knew that you must be from this world."

Treasure laughed too. "I don't mind being mistaken for an angel."

Liwayway's mother continued to speak, and Dennis translated, "Maria has invited us to dinner. She has cooked a feast for us and begs us to join her. What do you think?"

Treasure looked, back at Dennis. "I don't know. What do you think?"

Dennis whispered in her ear. "It would be very bad manners not to eat with them. I think she's spent all day in preparation for this."

Treasure nodded and Dennis turned and bowed to their host. Liwayway flew to the other side of the room and rummaged in a cardboard box. She brought paper plates and cups and plastic silverware. Carefully, she set the table, which was a large scrubbed NO LEFT TURN sign propped up by bricks.

Treasure came over to help her. She held up one of the cups. "This is my favorite design, Liwayway. I love sunflowers."

Liwayway beamed at her. "Flowers for you, teacher," she said. It was easily the longest sentence she had ever heard Liwayway speak in English.

Dennis continued laughing and talking with Liwayway's mother while Treasure and the Grandma woke the babies and got them ready for dinner.

"Hey, Dennis," Treasure said, cuddling a sleepy toddler, "ask if these are all Liwayway's little brothers and sisters." Dennis translated. Liwayway's mother shook her head. She kept talking as she began to dish up helpings of the meal onto the paper plates.

Dennis came beside Treasure. "No, only one of them. The little boy with a thumb in his mouth is her brother. The mother says that she also has an older son, about nineteen, who works as a dishwasher in a casino on the strip. That's how they make money. She says that the grandmother runs a day care for all the shantytown families with little ones while the parents go out to find work. She also says that Liwayway's father is still somewhere in Mindanao. There was a militant religious group bent on killing unbelievers. And Liwayway's family were part of the religious minority. They got separated, and they haven't heard from him. She just feels lucky to have gotten out alive."

Treasure rocked the sleepy toddler, afraid to ask any more questions. Dennis kept talking with the mother as she dished the food. Treasure looked at the profile of Dennis's face and felt grateful to have him by her side on this adventure. Somehow, with him there, her gift didn't feel like the giant obstacle that it usually did.

Together the family came to the table and sat on newspapers Liwayway had carefully spread on the dirt floor. Treasure had to hike her skirt up a bit as she and the grandma busily cut the food into bites for the hungry children. If she had known this was what she would be doing on her date, she wouldn't have worried so much about her outfit.

"Dennis, what are we about to eat?" she asked as she sat down. "Anything I'll need a tetanus shot for?"

"No," said Dennis, easing his long legs beside her under the table. "It's chicken adobong. At least I think it's chicken. I'll ask." As Dennis asked, the grandmother served up sticky rice from another pot.

"Chicken," said Dennis, rubbing his hands together. "It looks authentic, though. Smell those spices." Dennis took a bite and chewed. He gave a big thumbs-up to the chef, who inclined her head.

"Good?" said Liwayway's mom in English.

"Excellent!" said Dennis, taking another bite. Treasure took a bite too and felt the spices invade her mouth and take her taste buds captive. Was she really in the same world that she had been this morning?

"What do you think?" Dennis asked. "I was planning on taking you to New Fongs for dinner,"

"Mmm . . ." mooed Treasure. "Who needs Fongs after this?" She kept eating steadily until she cleaned her plate. The grandmother looked at her approvingly. She leaned over and served Treasure more chicken. Then she twittered something in the singsong language that made Liwayway's mother laugh. Finally the comment trickled through the language barrier to Treasure.

"She's never seen an angel eat so much," said Dennis.

Treasure tried to scrunch her shoulders down smaller. "I'm sorry."

"Don't apologize," said Dennis. "Enjoying their food is probably the biggest compliment you can give them."

Treasure smiled and took another bite. She chewed once, hard, and then held her hand over her mouth. "Dennis," she whispered in his ear. "Dennis, do they use all the parts of the chicken?"

Dennis finished chewing and swallowed. "Traditionally, yes," he said.

"Would they use the head?" asked Treasure.

Dennis nodded. "It's a possibility. Why do you ask?"

"Because I'm fairly sure that I have the beak in my mouth right now," said Treasure, trying to stay calm.

"Well, whatever you do, don't spit it out," said Dennis.

Treasure's eyes went big. "What am I supposed to do with it?" she hissed.

"Swallow it," said Dennis.

"I can't swallow it!" said Treasure.

"Yes, you can," he said, taking her hand away from her mouth. "Just focus on me and swallow." Treasure fastened her eyes on Dennis and took a giant gulp.

"Good girl," said Dennis, still holding onto her hand. "I knew you could do it."

Treasure smiled wanly. "Okay, but I don't think I can eat anymore," she said, pushing around the last sliver of chicken on her plate.

"Don't eat it all," warned Dennis, "or they'll think that you're still hungry."

After dinner, Treasure and Liwayway showed her mother her portfolio. She had Dennis tell her about how Liwayway taught the girls the Tinikling and about the circus. The mother explained that they had missed the circus because they didn't have a way to get to the school. And, said the mother as she smoothed Liwayway's hair, everyone worked at night, so Liwayway was needed to watch the little ones.

Treasure nodded, subdued by the thought that at six, Liwayway was no longer one of the little ones herself.

The mother got off the floor and clapped her hands. She pointed to the shiny karaoke machine in the corner and began speaking.

"Oh boy," said Dennis. "She says tonight we must have music. And you and I are the first ones invited to sing."

"How do they have power?" asked Treasure.

Dennis pointed to a long orange extension cord. "She told me that she hooks it up to a friend's generator. Do we really have to do this?" he asked Treasure. "Can't we just mutter our polite excuses and go now?"

"If I had to eat a beak, you definitely have to sing," said Treasure.

"One song," said Dennis.

Treasure sorted through their selections. "Eighties rock. Air Supply must be big in the Philippines."

Dennis looked over her shoulder. "How about that?" he asked.

"Okay," said Treasure. They stood together in the corner, gripping the tiny microphone while the children circled around them, waiting for the music.

The opening chords sounded, and Treasure jumped into the music with the self-assurance of an American Idol reject. "I can't fight this feeling anymore. And yet I'm still afraid to let it flow . . ."

Two little kids started to cry. Treasure apologized and tried to turn down her volume.

Dennis shook his head. Too bad she didn't sing as well as she danced. He jumped in on the third line. "What started out as friendship has grown stronger. I only wish I had the strength to let it show."

Treasure gazed at him gratefully and joined in on the chorus. " 'Cuz I can't fight this feeling anymore!" Together they kept singing, Treasure trying desperately not to show on her face how much she liked Dennis.

"I've forgotten what I started fighting for," sang Dennis. He had a great voice. It was deeper than Gene Kelly's, but she could easily imagine

Dennis singing in the rain, and it almost made her swoon. Her near swoon triggered her mental rottweilers, who started to bark at her for triggering the lovey-dovey alarm. She stopped swooning and looked away from Dennis for the rest of the song.

At the end, all the little kids clapped. Dennis went forward to shake Liwayway's mother's hand. "Thank you for opening your home to us," said Dennis in Tagalog. Treasure hugged each baby, then Liwayway, then the grandma, before hurrying over to Dennis's side.

"Thank you so much," she said. The mother bowed and began to speak. Dennis smiled and said something Treasure couldn't follow. Liwayway ran over and hugged Treasure's knees. Dennis bowed and ushered Treasure out the door. They left as the sound of eighties rock blared from the hut again as the tiny grandma took over on lead vocals. Outside Dennis was relieved to find his van still there—tires, CD player, and all. He opened Treasure's door, then got in himself. When the clock flashed 9:30, he couldn't believe it. "I guess we kind of lost track of time in there."

"I guess so," said Treasure. "I lost track of place too." And Dennis knew what she meant.

"It's not what I planned," said Dennis, as he merged onto I-15 toward downtown, "but I'm really glad that I got to be part of that."

A silence filled the space between them.

After a couple of minutes, Dennis cleared his throat. "I have a place that I'm really excited to take you."

Treasure perked up. "Yeah?"

"I know you're going to love it," said Dennis, changing lanes so he could exit.

"Where?" asked Treasure eagerly.

Dennis grinned at her. "Munchkins."

"Munchkins?" asked Treasure. "Like from the *Wizard of Oz*?"

"Well, kind of. It's a dance club. But they only play show tunes."

"Are you serious?" screeched Treasure, as she grabbed his arm.

Dennis inadvertently swerved. "Wow, I knew you liked show tunes, but I had no idea you liked them that much."

Treasure bounced in her seat, unable to keep herself still at the mere prospect. "And you're going to dance with me?"

"Well, I'm no Varden Moyle," said Dennis, "but I'll try."

After they parked, Treasure skipped to the door, dragging Dennis behind her. Once they were inside, Treasure couldn't look around fast enough. Lots of people were dressed up in costumes from the musicals. She could see the entire Von Trapp family at the bar. The walls were lined with old movie posters from *The Sound of Music, Carousel, Thoroughly Modern Millie,* and *West Side Story,* as well as *Wicked* and *Mama Mia.*

"Oh, I love this song!" said Treasure, as "You're the One that I Want" from *Grease* blared through the enormous speakers. She tugged Dennis out onto the floor, where he tried desperately to keep up with her hand jive.

"Why didn't you tell me? I could have dressed up!" said Treasure, as they walked off the floor toward a table.

"That's exactly why I didn't tell you. I knew you'd make me dress up too."

"Oh, but you'd be so cute! And Grammy would have sewed us costumes."

Dennis shivered at the thought of being spotted by his friends in a musical-inspired Grammy creation. He shook it off, unaware that Treasure was mentally dressing him up as a sailor, a la Gene Kelly in *On the Town.* He was about to suggest that he go get them a couple of water bottles from the bar when Treasure squealed again.

"Oh, we have to dance to this one!" she said. "It's 'Dancing through Life' from *Wicked.*" She grabbed his hand and whisked him out onto the dance floor. Dennis was sure he had never danced this much in his life. He tried desperately not to look awkward as he twirled Treasure around.

Privately, Treasure thought it was a shame that he didn't dance as well as he sang, but she could work with him on the dancing. Toward the end, he started to relax and have fun, without thinking too much about where his feet where.

"Now I have to have a break," said Treasure after Dennis dipped her to the floor with his best Varden Moyle impression.

"Okay, if you can't keep up," wheezed Dennis.

"You've got me," said Treasure, who was barely winded. Stepper routines lasted for seven to ten minutes, and Ruby was always trying to stretch their stamina.

"I'll be back," she mouthed, grabbing her purse from the table.

Dennis sat down and watched her walk away, enjoying the view. He ran his hands through his hair. Who could have predicted this night?

Certainly not him. He couldn't even predict Treasure. Was she the same woman he had fought with about Micaela's accident? He could hardly recognize her, stripped of her sweater sets. And she was tough. She swallowed a beak. The thought made him laugh. It just felt right to be with Treasure. He didn't want to analyze it. Tonight, he just wanted to enjoy it.

Dennis checked his cell phone. No new messages. No texts. Grammy Blume and the gang must be doing okay. He wondered what Fishstick and Puff thought of Grammy. He figured they were probably hiding under the bed. He made his way over to the bar to get a couple of water bottles, when he spotted her, dressed in a black leather jacket with spandex pants and silver heels, a la Sandy in the finale of *Grease*.

For a minute, Dennis thought it might not be her. But then she turned, and her thick glossy ponytail fanned out behind her. There was only one ponytail like that in the world. Okay, maybe two. But one was on Micaela's head. And this one belonged to Sheila, his ex-wife. She dangled a silver-haired man on her wrist like jewelry. The man wore dark glasses and had a cell phone to his ear. It was then that she caught his eye and lifted her glass to him. If only he had been invisible. He stood paralyzed as she started to walk toward him, dragging the man with her. At the same moment, he could see Treasure walking toward him too. He felt trapped. Both women would converge on him at the same moment. There was nothing he could do. He would have to introduce them. He stood as stoic as a marine in the face of an oncoming storm.

"Sheila, what are you doing here? I thought you said this place was out," said Dennis. In his head, he could hear her saying it just that way: "Oh, Munchkins is so out." It was one of the reasons that he dared bring Treasure here. Because he'd been certain Sheila wouldn't be.

Sheila raked her eyes over Treasure, who had just come to Dennis's side. She smirked at Dennis and then turned to her date, who was currently talking on his cell phone. "Out is the new in. That's what Rodizio says," she said, squeezing his arm. Rodizio put one finger in his ear and turned his back on the three of them.

"Rodizio is a producer. We're here scouting locations for my new music video," said Sheila.

"But you don't sing," said Dennis skeptically.

"You don't need talent to sing. Rodizio says all we need is really good sound equipment. And branding. Rodizio is all about branding," Sheila purred.

Dennis pictured Rodizio in his dark leather coat, with a phone to his ear, on horseback, dragging Sheila to a fire, iron in hand.

"Besides," Sheila said, "we won't release here. Rodizio is all about the Asian market. We're shooting for Taiwan. He says I'll be huge there."

"Apparently Taiwan is the new Japan," said Treasure, venturing into the conversation.

Sheila looked back at Treasure. "Who are you?" she said, acknowledging Treasure's existence for the first (and last) time.

Dennis refocused his eyes. He'd been lost in his own personal nightmare. But that was no excuse for not being polite. "Oh, I'm sorry. Sheila, this is Treasure Blume. Treasure, this is Sheila." He might as well introduce them before he ran screaming out the door.

"Great stage name," said Sheila.

"No, it's my real name. I don't do anything on a stage," said Treasure, who apparently hadn't gotten the memo about the awkwardness. She held out her hand. "It's nice to meet you. I have your daughter in my first grade class." She hiccupped. Apparently dancing after eating a beak gave her hiccups.

Sheila shot a glance at Rodizio, who was just snapping his phone closed when Treasure stuck her hand out. She disregarded the hand and glared at Dennis. "Oh, you must be mistaken," she said, still looking at Dennis. "I don't have a daughter." Rodizio's phone rang.

"Dennis, could I speak with you privately?" asked Sheila, taking his arm and steering him toward the tables at the side. She flashed a simper at Rodizio and mouthed "I'll be back in five" at him. He gave no indication that he heard her. It was impossible to tell what his reaction was beneath his dark glasses. He never stopped talking on the phone.

Dennis looked at Treasure as Sheila dragged him away. She shrugged at him and turned back toward the music, swaying her hips in rhythm to the beat.

Sheila dug her nails into his arms. "How nice that you're making friends. Really is that all you can dig up on your own?" she said, indicating Treasure with a tilt of her head.

Dennis ignored the remark. "What do you want, Sheila?"

Sheila turned back at him. "I don't know if you're aware, but your little dish almost ruined my life."

"Really? You seem to be able to do that on your own," he said, folding his arms across his chest.

"Rodizio doesn't know I have a kid, and he can't, because he already said that would ruin my chances with the pre-teen demographic."

"Treasure didn't know, so don't blame her. Excuse her for thinking that just because you gave birth to Micaela, you were her mother."

Sheila shot a glance over to Rodizio.

"Bet he doesn't know how old you are either," Dennis mused. "Should I tell him that? Let's see, you were twenty-five when I met you, and you were twenty-five when you had Micaela six years ago, and you were twenty-five when we broke up . . . so that must make you . . ."

Sheila cut him off. "Don't threaten me, Dennis."

"Don't threaten *me*, Sheila."

"Look, I'm not going to make you wear your little girlfriend's mistake, Dennis, but don't mess this up for me."

Dennis shook his head, still baffled by his worlds colliding. "Look, Sheila, I'm on a date here. And I know it's in my best interest for you to be huge in Taiwan. Treasure didn't know, so don't blame this on her."

"Fine," Sheila spat at him. She hoisted a happy façade over the top of her anger and turned toward Rodizio, who had wandered toward them, phone clenched between his shoulder and his head, two drinks in hand. "You're so thoughtful, Daddy," she beamed.

Dennis peered over her head, looking for Treasure. She was still swaying to the music on the edge of the dance floor. She looked back at him, with a quizzical expression on her face.

"Come here," he mouthed. Treasure came just as Rodizio's pants began to ring. Since he was already on one phone, he used his other hand to methodically pat down his pants.

"Hold on," he said, shoving his drink at Treasure, slopping some over the side as he did so. She grabbed for the stem but missed, spilling it all over the floor and Sheila. Rodizio didn't notice. He found his other phone and now had one to each ear. Sheila spun on her silver wedge, spat a curse word at Treasure, and shot one murderous glance at Dennis. She grabbed Rodizio by the arm and steered him out of the club.

Once they were out of sight, Dennis wanted to slump on the floor. The conversation had drained him. He covered his eyes with his hands, blocking the pulsating light, and tried to soak in the restful darkness.

When he opened his eyes again, Treasure was on her hands and knees. Armed with paper towels from the restroom, she was mopping up the puddle on the floor. He sank to his knees and covered her hands with his own.

"Don't," he said. "It's not your job."

Treasure sat back on her haunches, obviously angry. "No," she said. "Cleaning up her messes has always been your job, hasn't it?" Her sincerity threw him off. He couldn't say anything.

She kept scrubbing, harder and harder, until the paper towel bunched and tore. She went to stand up, to get another, but Dennis stopped her. He hugged her until he felt the anger melt away from her frame. Then he looked into her eyes. They surprised him. Up close, they were beautiful. Early on, Dennis had dismissed them as muddy hazel. But they weren't. At least not today. Today they were green with a ring of gold around the iris. Actually, they looked a lot like her grandmother's. But where her grandmother's eyes looked fierce and metallic, Treasure's were soft and luminous. The gold ring in Tabiona's eyes reminded him of a bird of prey, but the gold in Treasure's eyes was soft, like feathers, maybe. He looked closer. Not feathers, petals. A burst of petals. "Sunflowers," he murmured. The gold around Treasure's iris looked like the petals on a sunflower. It was a little like looking into a meadow—a field of deep green, with the iris as the heart of the sunflower. He took a step back. He had never looked that closely into someone's eyes. It was like falling out of a picture, he'd been so deeply engrossed. He wasn't in his own personal nightmare anymore. He wasn't even on the floor of an out disco-tech with throbbing music, pulsating lights, and a spilled drink soaking through the knees of his pants. He felt something unfamiliar. Something on the floor? No. Something inside him. Peace. That's what it was. He felt at peace and safe. He reached out and drew the sunflowers toward him. The rest of Treasure's face came too. He tilted her face with his hands and kissed her lightly on the lips.

· · · · · · · · · · · · · · · · · ·

Treasure didn't entirely know how it happened. One minute she was scrubbing the floor, ruining her new 1940s-inspired suede pumps.

And then Dennis was kissing her. Not exactly how she pictured her first kiss, but hey, she'd take it. She'd take the look on Dennis's face when he looked into her eyes too.

13

Squash

AFTER THE FIRST DATE AND FIRST KISS, TREASURE'S MENTAL ROTTWEI-lers went soft. They abandoned the barren and lonely perimeter of Treasure's rational mind for the lush green meadows of her daydreams, where they frolicked in fountains, chewed on bones, and panted in the shade of trees, tongues lolling. And whenever Dennis showed up there, they wagged their tails and ran to him, eager for pats and ear scratches. Treasure gave up. She couldn't help it. She trusted him as much as the mental dogs did. And she couldn't evict Dennis from her thoughts, just like she couldn't evict him from her life.

He'd kissed her again at the door that night, not even jumping away when they heard the roar of Mullet in the parking lot below. After he left, Treasure felt dizzy, like she'd spent too much time looking in fun-house mirrors. She collapsed onto the couch, dazed.

When Grammy came in, she waved a hand in front of Treasure's face to get her attention. Treasure didn't respond. Grammy shook her shoulders. Treasure was only dimly aware.

"Girl! Are you in there? Or am I going to have to get Fongie in here to give you mouth-to-mouth?"

The mention of Mr. Fong and mouth-to-mouth snapped Treasure back into her rational mind. Grammy might do it. She re-collected herself. "Jeez, Grammy, I can still breathe. Leave Mr. Fong alone."

Grammy made an O with her lips. "Oh. I see. You've already had some mouth-to-mouth tonight."

"Grams!" said Treasure. "Where did you get that idea?"

"Well, there is nothing else in the world that will addle your brains quite like a good kiss. And you look plenty addlepated," said Grammy, setting down her purse on the couch. "I was afraid that your lunch lady wouldn't have enough moxie to lay one on you."

Treasure giggled, thinking about Dennis planting one on her on the floor of the club in a puddle. "Oh, he's got moxie. He's got moxie coming out of his ears."

"Well, he better watch his moxie. A little bit goes a long way," said Grams, reaching a hand out to Treasure to pull her off the couch. "Now you go to bed. We'll talk more about this tomorrow, girl."

Treasure took her hand and stood up. "Grams," she said, "I like him." It was the first time she'd admitted it out loud to anyone, even herself.

Grammy gave her a hug. "Well, thank heavens for that. If you didn't and you'd smooched him, I would have had to disown you. Who wants a shameless hussy as a granddaughter?"

"I didn't think that a kiss or two was hussy-making material," commented Treasure, bending over to pick up her shoes.

"Well," said Grammy, "it depends on the kiss. And if you ask me, your lunch lady seemed as addlepated as you when he left. He got in the wrong van and tried to drive it home. Didn't you hear the car alarm?"

Treasure cocked her head to one side. "That wasn't in my head? I thought my mental dogs just shorted out the system. "

Grammy shook her head. Now the girl wasn't making any sense at all. "That wasn't just a car alarm. That was a love alarm."

Treasure smiled and turned a pirouette. "Now I know why Eliza Doolittle could have danced all night."

"Well, we need to dance all day tomorrow. So you better sleep tonight. We've got Stepper practice in the morning." And with that, Grammy shoved Treasure into her room.

· · · · · · · · · · · · · · · · · · ·

Dennis himself couldn't wipe the stupid grin off his face. He wore it in the house to check on his mom, who said that everything had gone very well with Tabiona. "She's a colorful piece of work," his mom reported. "She ate three big platefuls of your lasagna. But she also danced with Micaela, cleaned the oven, gave her a bath, and put her to bed. Micaela loves her, even if Puff doesn't. He didn't quit barking until we locked him up."

"Well," said Dennis, "I've never thought much of Puff's taste in women, anyway." He absently kissed his mom on the cheek and went in to check on Micaela. Dennis's mother was mystified. She had been fully expecting him to grill her regarding Tabiona. The fact that he didn't spoke volumes.

Dennis tucked the covers around Micaela, who didn't wake up when he came in. She was twisted around sideways, with her feet against the wall. He tugged her dead weight back into normal position. She had red smooch marks on her forehead, the same color of lipstick that Grammy Blume wore. Normally, he would have washed it off, but tonight it just made him smile. He patted Puff's head and tripped on Fishstick, who was stretched out on the floor.

· · · · · · · · · · · · · · · · · · · ·

He was still wearing the grin when he went to work on Monday. He tried to push it down, but it kept creeping back up on him, at the silliest times, like when he was supposed to be gutting squashes for his butternut boats for lunch. Objectively, he knew he was looking at a squash, but in his head, all he could see was Treasure—maybe because they were the same shape.

"Hey Dennis, are you going to marry that squash or hack it up? We need to get those innards stewing," called Thelma from across the kitchen.

Dennis picked up a squash and kissed it. "I might. Don't we make a cute couple?"

Thelma's expression didn't change. "Fine with me. I don't judge. Just come over here and add the spices to this batch. I'm not some fancy shmancy chef."

Dennis abandoned his squash and went to Thelma's side. He started to pick up bottles, sprinkling and dashing the contents into the first stewed squash pot. "Here, taste," he said, holding the spoon up under Thelma's faint mustache.

Thelma had not been hand-fed by a man ever in her fifty plus years. It struck her as a strangely intimate thing to do. She looked around to make sure that all the other ladies were occupied before tasting a bit on the end. She looked at Dennis solemnly as she rolled the squash over her tongue.

"Tasty," she said.

"Tasty?" said Dennis. "That's all you can come up with?" He took a bite himself off the same spoon. "The cinnamon is home and holidays and warmth, and the chili powder is heat and passion and adventure. I've given you a love sonnet in a pot and all you can come up with is tasty?" He brandished the spoon at her accusingly.

"Really tasty?" she said.

Dennis put his spoon down and walked away. "I give up on you."

"Fine," said Thelma to his retreating back, relieved to have him out of her personal space. "Just don't give up on lunch."

"Did you say that I shouldn't give up on lunch? Or that I shouldn't give up on love?" Dennis asked, returning to his station and picking up his favorite knife.

Thelma shrugged. "Take your pick."

· · · · · · · · · · · · · · · · · · · ·

While Dennis couldn't wait to see Treasure, Treasure quaked at the thought of seeing Dennis. While he had spent his morning composing rhapsodies in squash, she taught spelling and went over worse case scenarios. What if he ignored her? Or regretted everything? What if when he saw her again, he was utterly repulsed and ashamed? What if she was trapped in some Shakespearean comedy in which Grams paid Dennis to take out Treasure, when he was really interested in Patience?

Maybe if she just taught through lunch, the kids wouldn't notice. She finished spelling time and started ramming subtraction down their throats. The kids were not amused. Not one of them got their math books out. Spencer started to point at the clock. She knew she shouldn't have taught them to tell time. She hemmed and hawed until they were five minutes late. Finally, Sharonda put her hand in the air but didn't wait for Treasure to call on her.

"Miss Treasure, what is wrong with you?" she asked. "Don't you know it's lunch time?" Finally Treasure acquiesced and led the students to the cafeteria. She paused at the door, causing Octavio to bump into her, starting a chain reaction through the entire line.

"Aren't you going in, Miss Treasure?" asked Octavio.

Treasure panicked. "You guys go ahead. I've got something to take care of at the office," she lied, pushing Octavio through the door. She hurriedly turned and walked out, not even daring to look toward the serving line. She hustled toward the office. A nice, brisk lap around the school. That was what she needed. Then she could face Dennis.

As she rounded the corner to the office, she paused. She had been so concerned about avoiding Dennis that she hadn't even worried about avoiding Bonnie. She peeked around the corner. She could make out a black clad figure near Bonnie's desk. But since her other option was going back toward the lunchroom, she decided to move forward. She took a deep breath and started walking. *If I look like I have a purpose, then she won't stop me*, Treasure thought. She was halfway past the office when she dared look back. Aussie was sitting Indian-style on top of her mom's desk, ear buds in, her hair hanging over her face. Bonnie was nowhere in sight. Treasure let her breath out audibly and walked over to the desk, happy to find a distraction. She tapped on Aussie's shoulder. "Aussie! It's so nice to see you. What are you doing here?"

Aussie shook her hair back and took out one bud. She glared at Treasure without a glimmer of recognition. "Do you need something? 'Cuz my mom is at the library."

So that's how it's going to be, is it? thought Treasure. She stepped back. "No, I just . . . wanted to say hi."

Aussie gave her the "yeah, whatever," teenager look. "Hi," she said, sticking her buds back in.

"Yeah. So now we've said hi, and so now I guess I'll go," said Treasure, backing away.

Aussie started scrolling down her playlist.

Treasure resumed her lap. She just didn't get it. Teenagers baffled her. She could have sworn that she and Aussie were friends after the shopping trip. Treasure shrugged. She decided to duck into the bathroom. She could stall in a stall. She picked one, closed the door, and sat down. She could stay here until the bell rang. That wouldn't be weird, right? She spent a few quiet minutes until she heard the door open.

"Treasure Blume, are you in here?" called a voice.

Treasure didn't answer.

"I know it's you. I can see your dorky pilgrim shoes," the voice resumed. "I just wanted to find out about your date."

Treasure stood up and opened the stall door. "Aussie?" she asked as she crept out.

Aussie was perched on the counter top, her iPod out of sight. When Treasure came out, Aussie flashed her a smile.

"I am totally confused," said Treasure.

"I couldn't take that chance of my mom coming back and finding us talking. If she finds out we're friends, we'll both get it," said Aussie. "So I followed you here."

Treasure had a hard time shifting gears. "For somebody who claims to be my friend, you sure do a good impression of someone who hates me."

Aussie inclined her head. "Thank you. I try. Now tell me about your date. Did he like the outfit?" Treasure chuckled. "Yeah. The outfit scored me some points. He made me twirl around in it."

Aussie looked skeptical. "He made you twirl?"

"All right, I twirled voluntarily, but he appreciated it. He said I sizzled."

"Sizzling is good," said Aussie, rubbing her hands together. "So the whole date . . . was it good?"

"Really, really good," said Treasure, frowning at herself in the mirror.

"If it was so good, then why are you making a stink face?" asked Aussie.

Treasure didn't want to get into it. "What are you doing here right now?" she asked.

"Oh, it's sort of like an internship, a take-your-daughter-to-work thing, only I get credits for helping Mom on Mondays. It's her latest form of torture for me and my uncle's last-ditch effort to make sure I graduate from high school. Why are you changing the subject?" said Aussie, flicking her hair back over her shoulder.

Treasure gazed at her levelly. "Do you really want to know?"

Aussie considered. "It's better than stapling packets with my mother."

"Okay," said Treasure, squeezing her eyes closed and beginning to blurt. "The date wasn't just good—it was really, really good. And he kissed me twice, and I liked it both times, and when we went to Liwayway's house, it felt like we were a couple, and we just worked together really well, and I kept wanting to touch him and hold his hand. Then I ate a beak for him, and he took me to a dance club that only plays show tunes, because he found out that I like musicals, and no one has ever cared enough to find out what I like, and he did and we danced, and I wanted to dress him up like Gene Kelly, but then his ex-wife showed up and was nasty to him, and I wanted to kick her in the shins, and that's when he kissed me. And now I don't know what to do, because I'm afraid if I see him again, that he'll regret everything or that he'll say, 'I was just kidding,' or something like that. And I don't know if I can take that because I really, really like him. I just might love him. My mental guard dogs already love him. I don't know. But I don't want to see him, but I don't think I can avoid him, since he's in the lunchroom." She ran out of breath, and the flow of her words subsided.

Aussie leaned back, as if she'd been standing too close to an explosion. "Wow. You just vomited words at me. That's intense."

Treasure clapped her hand over her mouth. "Sorry. I have a tendency to blurt."

"It's all right," said Aussie. "It's just a lot to process. Now what did you say about him being in the cafeteria?"

"He's one of the lunch ladies," said Treasure.

Aussie's eyes widened. "Shut up."

Treasure drew herself up. "You don't have to be snotty about it. I know it's not a glamorous job, but it's one of my favorite things about him."

Aussie shook her head. "No, I'm not trying to be snotty. It's just, well, my mom has big issues with workplace romances. Last year she spotted the gym teacher and one of the part-time teacher aides at an IHOP. The aide was fired, and the gym teacher was suspended. Trust me, you've got to keep this quiet. If my mom found out about you two, you'd both get canned. You're already her number one target. The only thing worse would be if he was a parent."

Now it was Treasure's turn for eye-widening. "He's a parent too. His daughter is in my class," she squealed.

"Shut up," said Aussie in a deadpan voice.

Treasure put her hands over her mouth. "I am shutting up. But what am I supposed to do?"

Aussie shrugged her shoulders in a helpless gesture as Treasure turned away from her and began to mutter under her breath. "What was I thinking? Why did I even entertain this idea? Of course I'm not meant for love and happiness. I am meant for cats and kids and old people. Love is too complicated. This is all too complicated. I don't like complication. I like a good musical and Chinese take-out."

Aussie jumped off the counter and put her hands on Treasure's shoulders. "Get a grip. Just because my mom is bent on the destruction of your happiness doesn't mean you should buy into it. She's bent on my unhappiness too, but do I do what she says? Of course not. And you can't either. You're just going to have to be careful, that's all. You can get around her."

Treasure stopped muttering. "You think?" she asked Aussie.

"Absolutely. And I'll help you. Hiding things from my mother is my special talent. It's the only thing I know how to do really well." The idea of helping Treasure defy her mother perked up Aussie. She looked gleeful at the prospect.

"I don't know, Aussie. I'm not so much a sneaking-around sort of gal. I'm more of a clear transparent wear-whatever-I'm-feeling person."

"Think Lady Gaga," said Aussie wisely.

"How is wearing a dress made of meat going to solve this?" asked Treasure.

"Poker face. That's what you need. Put on your poker face," said Aussie, looking in the mirror. "Watch me." Aussie donned the glimmerless resentful expression that she had been wearing the first time Treasure met her.

Treasure blanched. "I can't do it. Whatever I'm feeling just spurts right up on my face."

"Yes, you can. And you've got to, if you want this thing with this guy to work out. Now practice."

Treasure and Aussie spent fifteen minutes practicing Treasure's poker face in the mirror. She could maintain it easily when Aussie said nasty things to her, but it would shatter like glass whenever Aussie alluded to her date or mentioned Dennis's name.

"It's your eyes," Aussie finally said. "Too much light in them. When I say his name, they get all hopeful and excited and scared. You've got to control that."

"Right," said Treasure, focusing.

Treasure tried until Aussie finally gave up. "Well, just look at your shoes, then, if someone mentions him to you directly. I've got to get back to the office. Mom's going to freak."

Treasure looked at her watch and started to panic. "Lunch is nearly over. What do I do?"

Aussie started to open the bathroom door. "Go teach your class?" she said, looking at Treasure like she was an idiot.

"Right," said Treasure, fighting off the feeling of disappointment that welled up from her stomach. Now that she'd successfully stalled, she felt empty. She wouldn't get to see Dennis at all. She didn't know if she could muster the proper enthusiasm to teach the color wheel to the kids. She started to walk slowly back to her classroom, but each step tugged her backwards, like she had a rubber band wrapped around her ankles. She turned mid-stride and started marching determinedly toward the lunchroom.

· · · · · · · · · · · · · · · · · · · ·

Throughout the entire lunch hour, Dennis kept one eye on the door as he served. He saw Treasure's class come in without her and tried to stay calm. She probably had an errand to run. She would be here. She would. He didn't lose hope until five minutes before the bell, when all the children had come, eaten, and left the lunchroom. He dropped his lonely vigil and went to help Thelma clean up. On the way back, he scooped up his last, lonely, butternut boat and cradled it in his hands. He started to walk back toward the dishwasher, when he heard the unmistakable slap of her shoes against the linoleum. Dressed in an embroidered orange cardigan that clashed badly with her hair, she hustled toward him like a mall-walker. She stalked over to the trays and grabbed one, slapping a napkin and silverware into their proper slot. She had an uncomfortable look on her face. Dennis wondered if she had an upset stomach.

"Are you still serving?" she asked, plopping her tray down on the metal bars.

Dennis felt his goofy smile spread across his face. "Sure. And I saved the best for the last." He placed the squash boat on her tray.

Treasure looked down at the little boat, the top flecked with nutmeg and chili powder. It was as beautiful as art. The boat told her that he didn't regret anything. She didn't trust herself to look at him. "Thank you," she said to her shoes.

Dennis couldn't help himself. He reached over and lifted her chin up. "I'm up here," he said, cupping her face in his hand.

At first, Dennis could see the welcome response in Treasure's eyes. The golden ring around the iris expanded and softened. It was his favorite look, the look that made him want to kiss her. He leaned in a tiny little bit, and Treasure jumped back. She lost her balance and fell on her rear end. When she stood up, her face wore its uncomfortable expression, and her voice was all business.

"I didn't mean to be so clumsy," said Treasure, dusting herself off. "Well, it was nice to see you. I better eat my food. We're covering the color wheel today," she said brightly as she picked up her tray and rushed off before Dennis could say anything else.

He left the serving line and went to the alcove by the silverware stand. He stood brooding and watching as she ate. She never looked up. She took three bites of squash, then swished a swallow of milk around her mouth before dumping her tray in the trash and hurrying back to her classroom.

Dennis stood rooted to the floor. He couldn't have felt worse if he'd had food poisoning. He jogged over to the trash and retrieved his forlorn little squash boat from the trash. He could see how her fork marks only skimmed the very top of the surface. He examined it closely, until Thelma yelled at him to come and man the sprayer nozzle.

· ·

Treasure managed to find some enthusiasm for creating color wheels with the students. She knew it came from the knowledge that Dennis seemed pleased to see her. She didn't let herself dwell on what had happened at lunch. When she saw him in a Bonnie-free zone, she'd be able to reciprocate those feelings. She'd call him as soon as she got off school grounds.

The thought of talking to him made her imaginary rottweilers start wagging their tails as soon as the last bell rang. After the kids left, she scurried up and down the aisles, bending over to pick up all the tiny snips of paper. She heard the door open and turned around, only to see Dennis standing in the doorway.

"This feels like déjà vu," Treasure said. "The last time you came in and found me bent over picking things off the floor, you cussed me out. Where's Micaela?"

Dennis didn't smile. "I told her to wait for me by the front desk."

Treasure put her handful of scraps in the wastepaper basket. She checked the window. Bonnie hardly ever came out to the trailers, but it wouldn't hurt to make sure. She walked over to Dennis and put her arms around him.

Dennis shrugged off her embrace.

Treasure stepped back, confused. "Dennis, what's wrong?"

Dennis took the little squash boat out of his pocket.

Treasure looked at him quizzically. "Is that my lunch?" she asked.

Dennis nodded. "I'm not going to lie. It hurt."

"What?" asked Treasure.

"When you didn't eat this. I was so excited to see you, and you were just cold."

Treasure put her hands on her hips, exasperated. "Should I have just wrapped myself around you there in the lunch line?"

Dennis shifted back and forth on his feet, looking at his boat. "It would have been nice."

Treasure just looked at him. "Really? Because I just found out that if Bonnie knew that you and I were dating, she'd get us fired. I thought I would try to maintain some decorum and save our jobs."

"You call falling on your behind maintaining decorum?" asked Dennis.

"You call trying to kiss me in the lunch line decorum?"

"I wasn't going to kiss you," said Dennis.

"Yes, you were," said Treasure, mad. "I can recognize that look on your face."

"Well, don't worry, because you won't see that look again," said Dennis, shoving his boat back into his pocket.

Treasure rubbed her hands over her eyes. "Okay. Let's start over. If I acted cold, I'm sorry. I was really happy to see you. I just wanted both of us to keep our jobs, and I was talking to Bonnie's daughter Aussie in the bathroom, and she warned me against going public."

Dennis traced a circle on the floor with the toe of his shoes. "Okay, I get that. But what about the food? You only took three bites."

"You watched?" asked Treasure.

Dennis nodded.

"Dennis, it was good, really. It's just that I wasn't hungry because of how nervous I was about seeing you, and then the conversation with Aussie really keyed me up, and I just couldn't eat."

Dennis took out the boat again. "This boat is my heart, and you squashed it."

Treasure cocked her head to one side. "So you're saying I squashed your squash."

"Exactly," said Dennis.

"And it was your heart," said Treasure, putting her hand on his chest.

"Yep," said Dennis, pulling her closer. He didn't seem dedicated to maintaining his anger anymore. "Let's go back to the part where you said you were nervous to see me. Why?"

Treasure's heart started to beat faster, just from his proximity. "I thought you'd regret our date."

Dennis picked her hand up off his chest and moved it to his mouth. He opened the palm and kissed it. It tasted like paste.

"No."

Treasure's eyes were already closed, so she didn't get a chance to recognize the look on his face before he kissed her.

When they broke apart, Treasure nestled her head into his shoulder. "I'm sorry I squashed your heart."

Dennis laughed. "It's okay. It's pretty squashed from riding around in my pocket anyway. Besides, you can have a chance to make it up to me, tonight at dinner."

Before Treasure could answer, the door to her class room banged open again. "I knew it!" said Aussie triumphantly. "Did you even hear what I said in the bathroom? At all? What if I'd been my mother?"

"Aussie, meet Dennis. Dennis, this is Aussie," said Treasure, stepping back from Dennis.

"Yeah, whatever. Just don't do this kind of stuff here. I can't protect you if you're stupid."

"So you're going to protect us?" asked Dennis, smiling at Aussie.

Aussie blinked, clearly dazzled by Dennis's ocean-colored eyes. "Um, yeah. I guess so." She looked over to Treasure. "So does this mean you two are together?"

Dennis slipped his arm around Treasure's shoulder. "Oh yeah. I'm in too deep to back out now," he said.

Treasure beamed at him. Aussie glared at her. "Seriously, your poker face sucks. Both of you. And you," she said, pointing to Dennis. "Don't you have a daughter to take care of? She's hanging out in the office irritating my mother. She's dumped out all her paper clips to make a necklace. You're lucky I talked her into letting me come out to find you."

Dennis checked his watch. "It's only been ten minutes," he said.

"My mother has a low tolerance for children," said Aussie.

"Right," said Dennis, snapping back into parent mode. "I'm on my way." He pulled his squash boat out of his pocket and handed it to Treasure. "Tonight, at seven?" he asked.

Treasure gripped the boat and nodded.

Aussie held the door open and waited until Dennis walked out. "He's kinda cute," she said to Treasure. "But old."

14

Spurts and Spats

THEIR SECOND DATE WAS FOLLOWED BY A THIRD (DINNER AT FONGS), A fourth (country line dancing, with Grammy and Varden), and a fifth (an international folk dance festival). Both Grammy Blume and Dennis's mother knew what was going on, but all parties involved thought it was best to keep Micaela (and everyone else at school besides Aussie) in the dark about their new relationship. Micaela had been told that Miss Treasure and her father were just good friends, and Grammy helped out by teaching Micaela dance lessons during dates, so Micaela was too excited to wonder where her daddy was going.

For their sixth date, Dennis surprised Treasure when Grammy was over dancing with Micaela. He showed up at her door with mahi-mahi and his rice cooker. "Let me make dinner for you. Then we can just hang out and watch a movie and eat, and maybe . . ." Dennis moved in to kiss her. Treasure held up her hand in front of her like a stop sign.

"What's wrong?" asked Dennis as Howls twined around his ankles. They had negotiated a treaty: Howls would accept Dennis if Howls could shine his ankles, and Dennis would try his best to ignore it.

"All this kissing has got to stop. It scatters my brains like birdseed. And I need my brains," Treasure said, holding her pose as firmly as a crossing guard.

Dennis took a step back. Maybe he was moving too fast. Although it felt slow to him—glacially slow. He peered into her eyes. "Haven't you ever been in a serious relationship before, Treasure?"

Treasure pushed away thoughts of Howls (three years and counting!)

and answered him honestly. "I've never been in a relationship before, period. My only experience has been from reading books. Lots of books."

Dennis chuckled. "As long as you don't expect me to be Mr. Darcy, I think we're good."

Treasure clapped her hands together. "You've been reading with your mom and Micaela! Oh, what does she think?"

Dennis shrugged. "Well, we all like Elizabeth. Her sassiness reminds us of you. But Darcy—jeez, what a loser." He disentangled Howls with his foot and moved past Treasure into her tiny kitchen.

Treasure came over and helped him unpack his supplies. "I know girls are supposed to identify with Elizabeth, but I always sympathized with Darcy."

"Even in the beginning?" asked Dennis, wrinkling his nose as he sniffed the fish.

Treasure smiled. "Especially in the beginning."

Dennis snorted as he tied his apron on. "Really? When he insults Elizabeth and refuses to dance with her?"

Treasure nodded as she searched to find Dennis a cutting board. "I bet he didn't intend to come off that way. I bet he had great intentions, but maybe he just blurted that out without thinking."

Dennis looked sideways at Treasure. She had two Hello Kitty barrettes holding her bangs out of her eyes, and she wore a teal argyle sweater over her ratty Hawaiian print housedress. But Dennis knew what was buried beneath all that frump. "You look adorable, by the way."

Treasure looked down at herself and yelped. She had been fully hoincked on every date she'd gone on with Dennis. And here she was, sans scaffolding, sans makeup, and sans big, sexy hair. She looked down at her dress. It had chocolate handprints around the pockets. Randy had been threatening for years to burn it. She wished he'd followed through. Treasure bolted to her bedroom and slammed the door, frightening Howls, who began to yowl.

Dennis gathered up Howls in one hand and put him out onto the patio. "Don't change now. Besides, I've seen how well you clean up. Just come out here and be comfortable."

Treasure reemerged in the same outfit. "Maybe it'll help you keep your lips on your own face."

Dennis shook his head. "You really are a grandma trapped in a hottie's body. Your morals come straight out of 1945. I've never seen anyone so prickly about a few measly kisses." He looked at her ensemble critically. "But you're right. The outfit does help. Someone should market it as boyfriend repellent."

Treasure couldn't help it. She flew across the room and wrapped her arms around him. "So you're my boyfriend now?" she asked, rolling the word in her mouth to taste how it felt. She hadn't used it since her preteen episode with Petie Peterson.

Dennis picked her up off the ground. "Well, I think so. I'd be happy to prove it to you with a little smooch, but I understand that we are in a strict smooch-free zone."

"That's right," said Treasure, struggling to put her feet back on the ground. "But it isn't a food-free zone. Let's cook," she said, rolling up the sleeves on her hideous sweater.

"Argyle never looked so good." Dennis sighed, then shook himself and focused on his fish. "Okay, can you dice celery without cutting your finger off?"

· · · · · · · · · · · · · · · · · · · ·

After dinner, Treasure insisted on cleaning up the dishes while Dennis lounged in the living room. He was supposed to be sorting through her DVDs to find a movie, but he had yet to discover anything filmed in this century. Did she have anything that wasn't a musical? He finally settled on *Arsenic and Old Lace* with Cary Grant. He tapped the case against the heel of his hand as he looked around the room. He'd never really looked at it closely before. The far wall was painted a cheerful yellow with black and white family pictures in matte black frames. Behind the gold couch, an enormous old brown, orange, and yellow quilt dominated the wall. Dennis looked closer. Four squares had elaborate patterns stitched on them. He took a step back, trying to make sense of the piece as a whole. While the four squares were meticulously detailed, the rest of the quilt defied organization. It looked like it had been designed by sleep-deprived truck drivers.

He touched the scratchy fabric and drew his hand back quickly. No wonder they put it on a wall. It couldn't hurt anyone there. He stood there examining it, until he started to feel uncomfortable. It was like the quilt was inspecting him, some disapproving old aunty who measured him and found him wanting. Dennis shivered and turned his attention to a high white shelf that ran the length of the wall above the window. On the top of the shelf, hundreds of different colors of glass bottles stood, some short and squat, some elegant and long. Some had patterns engraved along the sides. He pulled a chair over and climbed up so he could see better. He picked up a bright blue bottle and examined it. The bottle had dirt embedded into the deep grooves that ran around the sides. He held it up against the window. The light played through the glass, refracting it into rainbows. It reminded him a little of his sneeze guard experience in the lunchroom.

"Okay, now I can relax," said Treasure, coming into the room with a tray stacked with Pepperidge Farm mint milano cookies.

Dennis still stood on the chair, mesmerized by the colors that the light teased out of the tiny blue bottle. "Where did you find this?" he asked, hopping down from his chair, the bottle still in his hand.

"Oh," said Treasure, setting the tray down on the couch. "I found them on my grandparents' ranch when I was a little girl. Apparently, part of it was used as a dump in the thirties and forties. I gathered these bottles and washed them out. I just thought they were beautiful."

He held it up to the light again. He could see the intricate raised design etched around the edges. It was beautiful. "So these are antique, then?" he asked, handing the bottle to her.

"Well, I doubt they're worth anything, but yeah, you could say that," said Treasure, turning it over in her hands.

"Antique bottles, antique blankets, antique people. Is there anything old you don't like?"

Treasure shook her head, handing the bottle back to him. "I haven't found anything yet."

Dennis ran his thumb around the grooves. "What do you think it was used for?"

"Grammy thinks it was a laxative bottle," said Treasure, tucking her legs underneath her.

Dennis laughed. "Only you would rescue an old laxative bottle."

"But it's pretty, right? I think beauty is always worth rescuing," said Treasure.

Dennis came over and sat beside her on the couch. "So what's the story with this quilt? I don't think you can claim beauty as its most prominent feature."

Treasure got quiet. She looked at her hands. "It's beautiful to me, but I can see why you don't see it."

The mood in the room shifted. Dennis didn't say anything. He sensed that Treasure needed his silence right now. Slowly, he threaded his fingers through her fingers and held her hand.

She looked up, and he was surprised to see tears bright against her lashes. "I didn't mean anything by what I said," he said.

Treasure shook her head. "No, it's just . . . it's just . . . Well, I think there's something that I better tell you that has to do with the quilt. Since you're asking about it, now is just as good a time as any. You should know about this, now that you're, well, my *boyfriend*." She nearly choked on the last word.

Treasure took a deep breath and started to talk, lifting the curtain to expose her family's peculiar history. She told him about Experience Mankiller and the white-skinned shaman and his pronouncement of the gift. She recounted Grammy's reawakening after Treasure hit puberty. She even mentioned Petie Peterson. She pointed out the hundreds of stitches, tiny as grains of rice on Thankful's square. She couldn't quite look at him as she talked.

Dennis listened attentively, and his eyes never left her face. He wanted to say, "Come on, who believes in this stuff?" But something about her downcast eyes stilled all his questions. He could tell that Treasure believed it. And if he started to think through his own first impression of her, and even the conversation he'd had about her with his mother, it all jived with the wild story she was telling.

Treasure's words dribbled into quiet. She leaned back into the couch and looked up at the ceiling. He could see the tension in her neck.

Dennis let go of her hand and copied her posture. "So people hate you, huh?" he asked the ceiling tiles.

Treasure nodded. "With a hatred usually reserved for members of washed-up boy bands."

"With acronyms for names?" Dennis added.

"Exactly," said Treasure.

Dennis couldn't help it. He cracked up, his shoulders shaking with laughter. Treasure broke her staring contest with the ceiling and swatted him. "Hey, I'm bearing my soul to you," she said.

"I'm sorry," said Dennis, sitting back upright. "It's just kind of funny.

"Funny," said Treasure, perplexed. "How can you say that? I thought you'd be running for the hills when I told you about this."

"You thought I'd run?" asked Dennis. "Just from a little, tiny, teensy, weensy family curse?"

"Gift," Treasure corrected.

"Right," said Dennis. "Gift. Sorry. Now explain to me how this thing is a gift?"

"Well, it's all in how you look at it," said Treasure, settling back into the couch more comfortably. "See, I never have a problem with door-to-door salesmen trying to weasel their way into my house. They shut the door in their own faces, just to get away from me."

Dennis considered. "And it kept all sorts of slimy teenage boys at bay during your delicate, formative years, which I can appreciate," he said, sliding his arm around Treasure.

"That's right," said Treasure, nestling close against him. "And I've never once considered applying to be on *The Bachelor*. So it saved me from making a fool of myself in a hot tub on reality television. Not to mention how it's kept the paparazzi from stalking me."

"Well, that right there, that's priceless," said Dennis. "I can't leave my house without the paparazzi hounding me. So," he said, kissing the top of her head, "the way I see it, this is the best gift anyone could ever have. Much better than something useless like being good at football."

"Yes," said Treasure emphatically. "What good would it do me to be good at football?"

"Or X-ray vision, or reading people's minds, or flying."

"Flying is a lousy gift. Look at Patience."

"Exactly," said Dennis. "I agree. All in all, I think you're one of the most blessed creatures on the planet."

Treasure sat up and looked into his eyes. "I think that now too."

It was just too good. He couldn't pass it up. He had to kiss her. And this time, she wasn't going to stop him. He kissed her until she melted beside him like chocolate chips left in a hot car. *Arsenic and Old Lace* lay forgotten, kicked under the couch. They didn't even hear Grammy rattle her keys in the lock.

"Gracious, I am going to have to string up chicken wire to keep the two of you love birds respectable," said Grammy, hands on her hips as the two of them slid apart.

Treasure tried to pat back her flustered hair. "Hey, Grammy. How did Micaela's lesson go?" she asked.

"Oh, no you don't," said Grammy. "You aren't going to sidetrack me out of this. And you, Mr. Lunch Daddy, you have got to go. Folks are waiting at your house to read more of that swoony old book. I will escort you to the door."

Dennis stood up, then leaned down to peck Treasure's cheek. "I'll see you tomorrow at lunch," he said.

"None of that," scolded Grammy, hooking her thumb into one of Dennis's belt loops and towing him toward the door. "If this keeps up, I won't ever be able to leave you unchaperoned. And what will become of Varden and Fong, I ask you? Selfish, selfish man." She started to shut the door on his face.

Dennis tried to stick his foot in the door to buy him a little more time, but Grammy was having none of it. She stomped on his toes. Treasure could hear him yelp on the other side of the door.

"Grammy!" exclaimed Treasure standing up. "You hurt him." She rushed toward the door.

Grammy barred the way with her body. "A little pain will clear his head. I should do the same to you," she said, holding her heel over Treasure's bare feet. Treasure hopped up on the couch, as if she'd seen a mouse.

"On second thought, I think I'll go to my room," she said, jumping down and then squeezing past Grammy. Grammy started to pace the length of the apartment, stopping briefly at the window to watch Dennis climb into his van. She didn't cease her patrol until he pulled out onto the street.

"These shenanigans are going to make me old before my time," she said, shaking her head as she trotted off to the bathroom.

· · · · · · · · · · · · · · · · · · · ·

For their seventh date, Grammy refused to let them spend any time alone together in either apartment, so they were headed to the movies. As they waited for Dennis (who was going to pick them both up and then drop off Grammy at his house on the way), Grammy lectured Treasure. "I have my doubts about the two of you going somewhere alone together in that van."

Treasure rolled her eyes. Now she knew how Aussie felt having her mother bird-dog her every move. "Grammy, we are adults. Please give us a little credit."

"I'd tail you in Mullet if I didn't have a dance lesson to teach."

"There's no way you could be stealthy, Grams. Mullet roars like a cougar."

"Well, just the same, you remember yourself, girl. Imagine that I'm sitting there behind you, in that movie theater, along with his mother, holding Micaela on my lap."

Treasure could clearly picture it now. She had finally met his mother last week. She thought the interview had gone well. Dennis had explained Treasure's special gift to his mother so that she could be prepared. But when Treasure walked in, Dennis's mother declared that she must be immune. "That's weird," said Dennis. "Didn't you think she'd feel it?" he asked Treasure.

"Maybe it's because I've already heard so many positive things about you," his mother said, smiling encouragingly at Treasure.

Treasure shook her head. "Believe me, I usually erase any good word of mouth in the first five minutes. Ask my last blind date. Are you sure you're not just in denial?"

His mom shook her head. "Not at all. I'd tell you if I didn't like you."

Her statement convinced Dennis. "She really would tell you. What do you think?"

Treasure scrunched her forehead as she thought about it. "You're within the age limits," she said. "I just can't figure it out." Then she snapped her fingers. "I've got it! It must be because you're close to leaving this life! That's one of the stipulations," she said, pleased with herself for figuring out the mystery.

But Dennis didn't look pleased. It only took a few seconds for Treasure to realize that she'd just pronounced a death sentence on her boyfriend's mother in her hearing. Dennis didn't say anything. He balled up his fists and walked out of the room.

Treasure felt waves of horror wash over her. She began to sputter apologies. "I am so sorry, Dennis's mom . . ." she began. She clapped her hand over her mouth when she realized that she didn't even know her first name.

But it didn't seem to bother Dennis's mother. "I think you should call me Collete," she said laughing. She held out her hands to Treasure and motioned for her to come and sit beside her on the bed. "No, I'm glad you said it, Treasure," she reassured her. "It's the truth, and he needs to hear it."

Then Collete immediately violated both conditions that Dennis had forced her to agree to. She pressed her hand into Treasure's and told her how glad she was that Treasure was now a part of their lives.

"The only thing I can't quite figure out is why you're a cat person," she said, nudging Fishstick with her toe, from where he was passed out, belly up, on the end of the bed. Fishstick, unlike Puff, seemed unfazed by both Grammy and Treasure.

Treasure had laughed and tickled Fishstick's chin. "Well, I haven't been around dogs very much. And I haven't had much luck with people," she said.

Collette thought carefully about what she was going to say before answering. "You might be a people person. You just haven't been around the right people. Don't give up on that." She sat up a little straighter and looked Treasure squarely in the eye. "My son loves you," she said. "Oh, I'm sure he hasn't said it yet, but I want you to know that he does."

Treasure felt the air whoosh out of her lungs audibly. "How can you be so sure?" she croaked.

His mother patted her hand. "He compared you to spinach. And trust me, that's a good thing."

The spinach comparison amused Treasure. She embraced the frail little woman. "Now I know why my life has been so full of manure. Optimal spinach-growing conditions."

Treasure adored the memory of that moment. It was one of the only times in her life that someone didn't hate her after meeting her. And Collette thought he loved her! It was almost as good as hearing him say it himself. She wanted to stay in that golden moment, rather than listen to Grammy drumming dating rules into her head.

"And if he so much as tries to take your coat off during that movie, you just give him a hi-yah karate chop to the gut. Like so," said Grammy, demonstrating.

"Grammy, Dennis is an upstanding guy. You've got to loosen up on the reins. Do I ask if you and Varden are behaving yourselves? No. I trust you. I don't even worry when you go out on dates."

"That's just because he can't undo any buttons when his arthritis acts up."

"Grammy," pleaded Treasure. "You've got to back off, or you're going to scare Dennis off."

Grammy looked thoroughly shocked. "If he's scared by a loving and protective relative, I say good riddance."

"Not good riddance. I don't frighten Varden, do I? I don't grill Mr. Fong, do I?"

"Well, Fong and I are just friends. There's no reason to grill him. And if you're going to grill Varden, why don't you ask him why he won't pop the question and fork over my engagement ring. At this pace, we'll both be dead before he gets around to it."

Treasure brightened. "Grammy, are you serious? This is huge news. I didn't know you guys were considering marriage."

"Well, apparently, neither does Vard," Grammy grumbled.

"Is that why you've been so cranky these last few weeks, Grams? Have you been taking out your frustration about Vard on Dennis?" Treasure asked, putting her arm around her grandmother.

Grammy shook off Treasure's arm. "I don't know. But there's not much I can do. I just have to be patient. I'm a very patient woman."

"You're patient like a mental patient, Grammy," said Treasure as she heard Dennis's knock at the door.

Grammy looked waspish. She narrowed her eyes to make a smart remark when Dennis came through the door with a bouquet of flowers. "One for my girl," he said, handing roses to Grammy. "And one for Treasure," he said, whipping out sunflowers from behind his back.

Grammy sniffed the flowers as she accepted the bouquet. "It's good to see you've got some manners, boy."

Treasure looked rapturous. "Sunflowers! That's my favorite domesticated flower. How did you know?"

"I didn't," said Dennis. "They remind me of your eyes. What do you mean by domesticated?" he asked, scratching his head.

"This one's got a thing for weeds," said Grammy as she went into the kitchen to find vases. "She won't even let me spray dandelions."

"They're my very favorite," said Treasure, hugging Dennis and leading him to the couch. "We'll get these in water, then we'll be on our way."

Dennis shook his head. There was something about dandelions that nagged his memory. But he couldn't come up with it. He shrugged it off. "So you're saying I could have saved fifteen bucks and just weeded my yard?"

....

After they dropped Grammy off, Dennis and Treasure bought tickets for the show. The short, skinny man at the ticket counter obviously didn't like Treasure. He reminded Dennis of a flying monkey from *The Wizard of Oz*.

"Can I see some ID?" he asked Treasure condescendingly.

"What for?" asked Dennis. "We're watching *The Dark Knight Rises*. It's rated PG-13. Don't you think she looks older than 13?"

Treasure didn't say anything. She just handed over her license.

"I don't care to make any comments on her personal appearance," said the guy. "Although I doubt that you weigh what you have listed here," he said, smirking at her.

Dennis fought the urge to smack his smug monkey face. Treasure didn't respond. It was like she hadn't heard. She took the ticket and Dennis's arm and went into the theater.

....

After they found good aisle seats at the movie theater, Dennis simmered down and tried to forget the obnoxious ticket guy. It was obvious that Treasure wasn't thinking about him. He opened his messenger bag and motioned for Treasure to take a look at the contents.

"So you've got a purpose for carrying a purse. I thought you were doing it to prove how secure you were in your masculinity," said Treasure.

"It's a man bag, not a purse. And yes, I'm secure. Now look."

Treasure peered down. "You snuck food into the movie theater?" she asked. "But that isn't allowed."

"Well, if I didn't, we'd be stuck eating that nasty movie butter popcorn. Now this," he said, grabbing a bag of earthy brown popcorn with red spots, "is my Cayenne Cheyenne popcorn blend. You've got to try it."

Treasure did and immediately started choking. "Did you bring any water?" she gasped.

Dennis stopped whacking her back and dug through the bag. "Uhm, no. I guess I'll have to go the concession stand after all. I'll be right back."

Treasure nodded and continued to wheeze and gag as Dennis jogged up the aisle. Her eyes watered off all her carefully applied make-up. She managed to stop coughing just before she thought she was going to pass out.

She sat with her eyes closed, taking deep breaths when she heard Dennis's voice. He had returned, but he hadn't sat down or said anything to her. Instead he was chatting with a beefy Polynesian man in the aisle.

Dennis was saying, "Oh, no Micaela has done really well this year. Life without Sheila is just happier for all of us."

The guy nodded. "Well, that's good to hear. Napua and I have been worried about you. Since you left the restaurant, it's like you just fell off the planet. Where are you cooking now?"

Dennis glanced behind him at Treasure. "Oh, nowhere special. Just a place that lets me be close by Micaela. She's in the first grade now, you know. And she reads at a fifth-grade level. She's started reading Jane Austen."

Treasure expected Dennis to introduce her at this opportune moment, since she had lots to say about Micaela's reading level, if that was the chosen topic of conversation.

The guy obviously thought he might introduce her too at this point. His eyes had followed Dennis's glance toward her. Once his eyes met Treasure's, the jovial happy look on his face disappeared and was replaced by one of baffled annoyance. Obviously her gift was working on him. "That's great," he said. "So are you here with anyone tonight?"

Dennis moved so that he blocked Treasure completely. He made some sort of muffled sound that was impossible to understand. "How's Ricky?" he asked. "Does he still have that crazy hair that the ladies love?"

The guy refocused on Dennis. "You know it." The guy laughed. "How's your mom doing?"

Dennis's face clouded. "Not well. Cancer. The doctor told us . . ." Dennis continued in deep conversation with this guy, revealing all sorts of information that Treasure didn't know about. It was clear that this was no casual acquaintance.

The house lights dimmed and Treasure expected Dennis to introduce her then. He didn't. Instead he gave the guy a big back-thumping hug. The guy refocused on Treasure's face. He whispered loudly in Dennis's ear. "Look, do you want to come and sit up with us? I think there's an empty chair, and then you won't have to sit with . . ." He left the rest of his sentence unfinished but indicated Treasure with a lift of his eyebrows.

Dennis laughed him off. "No, I'm good here. But let me know if you need somebody to whip your kitchen into shape again," he said too loudly.

"Will do," said the guy, after shooting another annoyed look at Treasure. Treasure could tell that Dennis's friend thought she was rude for eavesdropping on their conversation. He waved to Dennis and walked down to the front of the theater.

Dennis sat back down by Treasure. "Here's your water," he said, without looking at her. "I hope this movie is good. I know it has lots of special effects."

Treasure could not muster up an answer. Would he have noticed if she had passed out as her lungs originally intended? She doubted it. She grabbed the water from him and chugged it, hoping it would dampen her anger. Dennis seemed unaware, absorbed in his gourmet popcorn, of which Treasure did not take another bite.

· · · · · · · · · · · · · · · · · · · ·

After the movie, Dennis noticed something was wrong. Treasure sat silent on the ride home, only answering questions in monosyllables. That wasn't like her. Dennis walked her to her door. He planned to spend some time alone with her and then go pick up Grammy and bring her back.

After Treasure slammed the door in his face, Dennis knew it couldn't be his imagination. She was ticked about something. He'd have to bite. He knocked on the door. "Treasure, what's wrong?"

Treasure wrenched the door open. "You make me wish I had claws," she spat out.

Dennis smiled. "Like Howls? Reow." He mimed spitting and growling.

"No, like a lobster," said Treasure, about an inch from his face. "I'd latch onto your nose and tear it off your face."

"But then I'd just boil you and eat your claws," said Dennis, catching her around the waist.

Treasure was grateful that she had attended Grammy's earlier karate-chop demonstration. She used the skill now, whacking Dennis right in the solar plexus.

He oofed with surprise and took a step back. "Oh. So you're mad."

"Just figure that out, Captain Oblivious?" Treasure said tartly, sounding just like Grammy Blume in a mood. She walked into her apartment and hung her keys and purse on the stand behind the door. Howls uncurled from his place on the couch. He arched his head against her skirt. Treasure didn't even move to pat him. Instead she clapped her hands and shooed him into her bedroom, slamming the door closed behind him.

Dennis had only seen Treasure like this twice before, once over Micaela's wet pants, and once mopping up Sheila's wet mess. Why was liquid always involved? "So tell me," said Dennis, stepping over the threshold, shutting the front door, and leaning against it.

"You didn't even introduce me to your friend. You just ignored me."

Dennis shrugged. "Who, Larry? I worked on the line with him at the last restaurant I was at." He considered for a minute. "He would have hated you anyway, right?"

"So what?" said Treasure, turning around to face him.

"Well, I just wanted to spare you that," said Dennis, folding his arms over his chest.

Treasure looked up at the ceiling tiles. They were so much more sensitive than her boyfriend right now. "So what are you going to do? Keep me in a cave? Build me a cabin on a high and lonely hill? Lock me in a tower that no one but you can ever enter?"

Dennis moved closer to her. He was positive she couldn't stay mad at him long. "Would that be so terrible? For it just to be me and you?"

"Then I'm your prisoner, not your girlfriend."

Dennis looked hurt. "That's not what I meant."

"Isn't it?" cried Treasure. "That's what my family wanted to do. Shield me and protect me from every life experience. That's how I've lived my life. And I don't want to do that anymore. I want to be on my own. That's what moving here was all about."

Dennis put his hands up, like a thief caught by police. "I don't like to see you hurt. That guy at the ticket counter was so nasty to you—I wanted to slug him. And I hated it when Sheila was so awful to you."

Treasure looked at him squarely. "I don't even listen to jerks like the movie counter guy anymore. I just let it roll off me. And Sheila—she just ignored me, which is exactly what you did tonight."

Dennis ran his hands through his hair, perplexed. "I just wanted to protect you."

Treasure wasn't buying it. Her voice got steadily louder as she walked into the kitchen. "No. You didn't. You were trying to protect yourself and your big fat stupid chef ego. You didn't want your buddy to meet me and say, 'Jeez, what's Dennis doing with her?' "

Dennis felt like he'd been slapped. That thought had flitted through his head (the memory of how Treasure bungled the introduction to his mother was still fresh), but he assured himself that it wasn't his primary motivation. Still, how could she be so stinking perceptive? He opened his mouth to talk, but no sound came out.

"Maybe this isn't going to work," said Treasure, her hands gripping the sides of the kitchen sink, her eyes fastened on the garbage disposal.

Dennis started to walk toward her. "The garbage disposal? I fixed that last week."

Treasure turned around to look at him. "This isn't a joke to me, Dennis. I can't live like this."

Dennis gave up trying. This conversation was absurd. He just spared her some pain, that's all. "But you can live with people treating you rudely, making fun of you, and tromping on you with big muddy boots."

Treasure lifted her chin. "Yes."

Dennis was at a loss. "But you just would have said something stupid."

Treasure couldn't say anything. She turned away from him again. His words hurt so much she couldn't take a deep breath. "What I say at first, it isn't who I am. You know that. But it is part of me. And you'll have to cope with it, if we're going to be together."

He didn't know what to say. "Well, I don't know if I can," he mumbled.

Treasure slumped against the sink. "Then this isn't going to work."

Dennis exploded. "So you're going to throw it all away because I didn't introduce you to a guy who would have hated you?" His voice was loud enough to rattle Treasure's bottles from the dump.

Treasure felt exasperated. "Well, if you remember, you didn't love me the first time you met me."

"So I'm a hypocrite," said Dennis, his ears heating with anger.

Treasure felt small, but she held her ground. "It's just that you can't be mad that everyone doesn't see me the way that you do now. You have to forgive them, and let it go. That's how I cope. I can't live my life hating everyone that hates me. It takes too much energy, and it's useless." She paused for a minute, looking at Dennis's sneakers. "And

I don't want to be with someone who is ashamed of me," she finally whispered.

Dennis ran his hands through his hair. "I wasn't ashamed of you. I wanted to protect you."

"You can't," said Treasure flatly. "You can't protect me or hide me away. You've got to deal with it the same way that I've learned to deal with it. Or else this won't work."

Dennis felt the muscles in his jaw twitch. She'd said that it wouldn't work three times. It sounded like she was already convinced. The words burned his ears, sending spirals of pain down through his entire body. He didn't need this. "Then I guess this is good-bye," he said. He turned and walked out the door.

· · · · · · · · · · · · · · · · · · · ·

When Grammy returned, she found Treasure curled in a ball on the floor, surrounded by the yellow petals from her sunflowers. In her hands, she clutched the bald stems. She turned her swollen eyes on her grandmother. Grammy knelt on the floor beside her, stroking her hair. "Oh my girl, I'm so sorry."

"You heard?" Treasure asked Grammy.

Grammy nodded and fingered the petals. "I guess this means he loves you not?" she asked. Treasure couldn't answer. All she could do was sob.

Cleaning Up

WHEN TREASURE WOKE UP THE NEXT MORNING, SHE HAD ONE BRIEF happy moment of ignorance before the events of the previous night came crashing down on her. She cracked her eyelids and willed her eyes to make sense of the shapes in the room. As her eyes began to focus, so did her mind. Each fragment of their disastrous date hit her like a frozen snowball to the head. Thwack: Dennis nearly let me choke to death. Thwack: Dennis wouldn't introduce me to his friend. Thwack: Dennis claimed he was protecting me, but it was really because he was embarrassed about me. Thwack: Dennis and I broke up.

The last hit was more than just a stinging little snowball. It felt like an avalanche, threatening to bury her. She felt the weight of it press down on her chest, pinning her against her mattress. She couldn't breathe and she couldn't move. Nothing she had known before compared to this pain. Not the rejection of a thousand bad dates. Not the snide remarks of previous crushes. Not even the humiliation of Petie Peterson's junior high crudeness.

In the next room, she heard Grammy wrench the blinds up. As much as Treasure loved her grandmother, she couldn't stand the thought of talking to her right now. She didn't want to listen to any nuggets of wisdom featuring farm animals.

Treasure mustered her strength and shoved the boulder of pain aside. She got out of bed and quickly dressed, hoping to escape before Grammy noticed that she was gone. She slipped out the front door before Grammy had even started singing. Standing outside on her own front doormat, Treasure felt lost. She had no idea where to go. She needed to think. That meant she needed to clean. She did some of her best thinking that way. She knocked on Mr. Fong's door.

Despite the fact that it was 7:30 on a Saturday morning, Mr. Fong seemed genuinely glad to see her. He gestured for her to come in, and waited patiently for her to explain what she was doing. Treasure tried to enunciate so Mr. Fong could read her lips, but every time she tried to get a word out, she produced a sob instead. She shook her head and tried again to speak. The sob turned into a wail. For a moment, Mr. Fong looked grateful he was deaf. He came over to Treasure and put his arm around her shoulder. Treasure lurched against the slender Asian man. She felt him sway and tried to pull herself together. She straightened up and put her hands over her face and focused on breathing. Mr. Fong trotted over to his living room table. He picked up a paper and pen and thrust it against Treasure's hands. Treasure took the pen and paper. Quickly, she scribbled a note. "Good Morning, Mr. Fong," it said. "May I scrub your toilet?"

If Fong was fazed, he didn't show it. He just led Treasure to his stash of cleaning supplies under the sink. Treasure selected Tidy Bowl, rubber gloves, and a bristly U-shaped brush, and followed Mr. Fong into the bathroom. He stayed with her until she seemed to be in control of her emotions. Then he went into his living room to begin his morning Tai-Chi routine.

Treasure squirted and scrubbed furiously. She felt like an avenging angel wielding a sword of doom, wiping out entire germ cities in a single swath. It felt soothing to channel her pain into something productive. She could think now. Perspective, that's what Roxy would tell her she needed. The thought of Roxy made Treasure homesick. She hadn't talked to Roxy in so long, not since her first date with Dennis. She pulled out her cell phone and dialed Roxy's number. She cradled the phone against her ear and continued scrubbing.

Roxy answered on the third ring. "Treasure!" she said. "I was just thinking about you. What do you think of calla lilies as the design motif on your wedding invitations?"

"What?" said Treasure, caught off guard.

"Oh, I've just been playing around with different designs for your wedding invitations. I really like the calla lilies, but—"

Treasure cut her off, unable to hear anymore. "Stop it, Roxy. We just broke up." She started to cry.

Roxy shifted mental gears quickly. "That idiot. What happened?"

Treasure stopped scrubbing and related a summary of last night's events. By the time she finished, she could feel Roxy's anger streaming through the phone lines. "I wish I was there. I'd take my weed killer and burn the words 'Dennis Cameron is a jerk' on his lawn."

The thought made Treasure giggle. "That's a beautiful thought, Rox, but I need some perspective. That's why I called you."

"Fine," said Roxy. "Although I'd like to waddle over to his house and give him an earful. But you want perspective, not justice. Okay. Well, you've been in pain before."

"Yeah, I practically own real estate there," said Treasure. She could seldom recall a day in which she didn't have cause to cringe.

"You have the skill set for dealing with pain," Roxy reminded her.

"I know, but it's not working. See, usually, the pain just stays in my head. But this time, it's like the pain is alive. It's seized control of my heart, my lungs, my spleen, even my gallbladder, and it's threatening to open up new chasms in my other organs. "

Roxy listened to Treasure's description before replying. "So the question is, why is this pain more debilitating that any other pain you've dealt with?"

"I don't know," said Treasure as she pulled her rubber gloves off. She stayed motionless and closed her eyes. "That's why I called you."

Roxy waited for Treasure's brain to come up with the obvious answer. Finally she couldn't wait any longer. "Love," she said. "It's because you love him. And you haven't been in love before."

Treasure opened her eyes and felt the jolt of truth hit her. She hadn't been in love before. That was why the pain hadn't just stopped at her head this time. But what could she do to stop the pain from drilling through her? Her vision blurred again, whether from her emotions or the toxic fumes of the cleaners, she didn't know.

"So you're up against a new kind of pain. What are you going to do? Lie there and let it consume you? Or are you going to fight it?" Roxy asked, refusing to let Treasure wallow.

Treasure wiped her eyes with a piece of toilet paper and put her gloves back on. Roxy made it sound so easy. "Fight it?" she asked in a whisper.

"Darn right," said Roxy. "So your heart has been destroyed. Big whoop. That happens to people every day."

"How do they function?" Treasure wondered.

"I guess you'll learn how," said Roxy.

"Maybe I'll just grow a new heart. Like a starfish's arm, or a lizard's tail," Treasure said, remembering Darth the salamander.

"That's right. If they can do it, you can too," said Roxy with characteristic enthusiasm.

Treasure cracked a smile. "You're right. I can do that. They're lower life forms, and I have all the benefits of evolutionary science on my side." The idea made Treasure laugh. And laughing felt so much better than crying. Her laugh infected Roxy, who started to laugh as well.

"Treasure, I've got to go, but you can do this. Have some faith in yourself."

Treasure said good-bye to Roxy, buoyed up by her positive energy. She put down her phone and flushed the toilet, sending blue bubbles swirling down in concentric circles. *Now that's what I call a clean toilet,* she thought, patting the porcelain bowl. She got off the floor, gathered her supplies, and searched out Mr. Fong.

"The toilet is clean now," she said to Mr. Fong, bowing. "Do you have anything else that requires scrubbing?" she asked.

Mr. Fong looked at her eager face and shrugged. Then he pointed at his kitchen floor.

· · · · · · · · · · · · · · · · · · · ·

It was not a typical Saturday morning at Micaela Cameron's house either. For one thing, the kitchen sat dark, empty, and odorless, nothing simmering on the stove top. For another, her daddy was still sacked out, face down on the couch wearing last night's clothes. He hadn't even changed into his jammies.

"Daddy," whispered Micaela into his ear. "It's morning time. You need to wake up."

Her daddy remained motionless.

"Come on, Daddy," said Micaela in a normal speaking voice. "We always cook together on Saturday morning. How come you're still sleeping?"

Nothing.

"Daddy!" Micaela finally yelled. "I want crepes today. Wake up and make crepes with me!" She stamped her foot.

Dennis didn't even turn over. "Get some cold cereal. I'm not cooking today," he mumbled into the couch cushions. Micaela didn't know what to make of this. Her father had never, ever, in all her six years, refused to make her food. She burst into tears, setting both dogs off, and ran into her grandmother's room. Dennis Cameron didn't even bother to move.

· ·

When Treasure re-entered her own apartment, she was ready to face Grammy. After all, Grammy cared about her. She had stood beside Treasure through hard times before. Tabiona Blume was a loyal friend and a fearsome enemy. For a moment, Treasure pitied Dennis Cameron for breaking her heart. He had guaranteed himself the full measure of Grammy's wrath.

Grammy was chopping up potatoes and whisking eggs in the Kitchen-Aid mixer that Dennis had bought for Treasure as a gift. She hummed, "Oh, What a Beautiful Morning" from *Oklahoma* as she cooked.

"I'm making omelettes, along with my famous cowboy biscuits and potatoes," Grammy announced as Treasure sat down at the table. "We have a lot to discuss, and we can't rehash without hash browns."

"Oh, Grams, I don't think I can give you the play-by-play from last night," said Treasure, putting her head down on the table.

Grammy held up a hand. "No need. Dennis told me when he drove me home."

Treasure lifted her head up. "What did he say?"

Grammy shrugged. "Well, first he quizzed me down about our family gift. Then he said something about you getting all feisty when he didn't introduce you to his friend."

"That lying sack of pirate," muttered Treasure. "It was about more than that, and he knows it."

"Of course he knows that. I knew it too," said Grammy. "So that's when I smacked him upside the head."

Treasure cracked up. "Did you really?"

"Yep," said Grammy, stirring green peppers into the omelet. "This is a family gift fight if I ever saw one. Your grandpa and I got in fights like that daily."

"That doesn't reassure me, Grams," said Treasure, examining the salt and pepper shakers.

Grammy flipped the omelet. "It's normal, that's all I'm saying. Besides, I think he'll come around."

Treasure shook her head slowly. "I don't think so."

"Well, judging by his response when I smacked him, I think there's hope."

"What did he do?"

Grammy slid the omelet onto a plate and put it in front of Treasure. "He said, 'Thank you. I deserved that.' "

"Huh," said Treasure, picking up a fork. "Maybe he isn't Captain Oblivious after all."

"Well, I still think it's going to take some time. It's one thing for him to know about this gift. But it's a whole other thing to live with it. He'll have to decide if that's something he can do."

Treasure nodded and swallowed, fighting to keep the bite of omelet down. Her empty stomach wanted to reject any form of comfort.

"Now," said Grammy. "I've got some bad news that I need to share with you."

Treasure put down her fork and clutched the edge of the table with her hands. What could be worse that what happened last night?

Grammy wiped her hands on her apron and sat down beside Treasure. "While you were out, I got a call from Ruby. Lorna Sims has tested positive for swine flu."

"Oh," said Treasure, recovering from the dread that flooded her system. It wasn't what she had expected. She heaved a sigh of relief, then immediately felt guilty for being relieved at Lorna's expense. "Is she going to be all right?" she asked.

Grammy nodded. "Well, if she didn't shovel food down her gullet, she'd be better. But it doesn't seem to be a very serious case."

Treasure wrinkled her forehead and strained to understand her grandmother's logic. "Grammy, are you implying that Lorna got swine flu because she eats like a pig?"

"If the snout fits," said Grammy, raising her fork to her mouth.

"That's impossible, Grams," said Treasure. "Swine flu is a virus."

"Well, just the same, I've never seen a woman hoover down bacon like Lorna. But here's the worst part: Ruby has suspended all Stepper activities until the beginning of the new year."

"Oh, Grammy," Treasure said, noting how her grandmother seemed to sag as she delivered this news. "I'm so sorry. I'll miss the Steppers too."

Grammy shook off Treasure's attempt to console her. Instead she hopped up and checked her biscuits browning in the oven. "Just right," she said, reaching in with an oven mitt. She set the pan on the counter. "Now don't you fret, girl, because I've already picked out something to occupy my time. At the last Stepper practice, Alice Allen was telling me about this." She took out a flyer from her pocket and handed it to Treasure along with a biscuit.

Treasure unfolded the flyer. "Competitive gift wrapping?" she asked Grammy. "I didn't know such a thing even existed."

"CGW is a nationwide sport," said Grammy, slightly injured by Treasure's incredulous tone. "And there's going to be a big meet right here in Vegas. I know I've got what it takes. I used to wrap all the Christmas presents for all you kids. Look here," she said, leaning over Treasure's shoulder. "It's got three different rounds: the speed round, the flair round, and oddly shaped parcels. I think I could be competitive in all three."

Treasure was amazed by her grandmother's determination. "You are something else, Grammy. If you want to get into this, more power to you."

"Thank you," said Grammy, slipping the paper back into her pocket. "You know, throwing yourself into something is the best way to beat heartbreak. The main reason I'm doing it is so I don't sit here and fret about Vard. You should try it too."

Treasure shook her head. "Gift wrap isn't my thing."

Grammy looked exasperated. "Well, then find something that is. Because if you don't, you'll turn into a goat."

Here it comes, thought Treasure, readying herself for a farm animal onslaught. "A goat?" she asked, afraid of the answer.

"Yes, a goat. Remember when I told you about the sheep and the goats? And how you had to use this gift to sort them?"

Treasure nodded.

"Well, one of the biggest dangers with this gift is turning into a goat yourself. See, sheep live together in herds and flocks. Goats live alone, stubbornly, and try to convince themselves that they like it. Remember, I used to be the poster child for goats. I don't want that to happen to you."

Treasure was touched by Grammy's concern. "I promise not to turn into a goat. I have my students, you and the family, even Aussie and Dawn. That should be enough to keep me from entering goathood."

Grammy exhaled loudly. "Well, I hope so. But just the same, you better be on your guard."

Treasure patted Grammy's hand. "I will be, Grams. Now, should we head on over to Costco to get you some practice wrap?"

· · · · · · · · · · · · · · · · · · · ·

During the next couple of weeks, Treasure took Grammy's advice to heart, or rather what was left of her heart. *Getting on with your life is as much fun as digging out an ingrown toenail,* Treasure decided. She poured herself into her work and cooperated with the other first-grade teachers (even the General) to construct a full-scale Thanksgiving feast, complete with brown paper bag pilgrim hats and feathered Indian headdresses. The fact that the event centered on food and Dennis wasn't involved pricked Treasure's internal organs afresh. But Treasure stitched up the bleeding parts as firmly as she could with big messy stitches and kept going. The stitches might not hold forever, but they were good enough for now.

She avoided Dennis by going home for lunch (when she didn't have playground duty). Grammy had a present for her to open every day. Granted, the gifts were usually just household items or her own things all wrapped up (socks, the can opener, a bag of cat food), but seeing them bedazzled made her appreciate them in a new way. Treasure had to admit that Grammy's new hobby was helping them both to heal. Grammy's relationship with Vard seemed stalled as well. Treasure hadn't seen him since before she and Dennis broke up. But the shine and shimmer of bright paper and curling ribbons excited them both. Grammy was focused on improving her flair. She would cut out different designs from the wrapping paper, mount them on a contrasting color, glue the whole shebang onto the wrapped gift, then outline the design with grosgrain ribbon. It created an effect as elegant as origami.

While Treasure could avoid Dennis, she couldn't avoid Micaela. And looking into Micaela's face threatened to rip out all the stitches in her heart. Micaela had sunk back into her former silent self, the way she had during the Young Authors' project. This time, Treasure couldn't reach out and solve it. She reminded herself that Micaela had a father, and that it was his place to step up and help her. But deep inside she knew that Micaela only floundered when Dennis did. That's when she asked Grammy to contact Dennis.

"Micaela needs those lessons with you more than ever," said Treasure as she timed Grammy one night for her speed round. "I don't know what's going on with Dennis, but it can't be good, judging by Micaela."

"Hush up. You're taking my mind off the game," grumbled Grammy, jabbing tape onto a box.

"Sorry," said Treasure. She waited until the buzzer on the microwave sounded and then began to count packages.

"How many?" asked Grams, biting her fingernails.

"Twenty-nine," said Treasure.

"That's three better than last time," said Grammy. "These pop-up tape dispensers you got me really helped." She started to gather up her supplies. "Now let me get this straight. You want me to call your ex-boyfriend and beg him to let me teach his daughter dance lessons, when I've only got less than a week to go before my first meet?"

"Pretty much."

"Well, I'll do it," said Grammy, stuffing tubes of wrapping paper into her blue canvas organizer and zipping the top. "Because I care about her. In fact, why didn't the two of you knotheads think of this sooner? Do you think the world revolves around your love life?"

Treasure got out her cell phone. "No, Grams, I do not think that." She punched in Dennis's number and handed the phone to Grammy. "Here. It's ringing."

· · · · · · · · · · · · · · · · · · · ·

Dennis muted *Dancing with the Stars* and answered the phone. He felt his stomach flip when he saw the incoming number flash on the screen. He tried to hide his disappointment when he discovered it was Grammy calling about resuming dance lessons with Micaela. He quickly agreed, hoping that the faster he talked, the more he would forestall Grammy's efforts to chat him up or ask him about his feelings. They decided on a time tomorrow, and then Grammy hung up. Dennis resumed his slack-jawed position. Since his breakup with Treasure, he'd bought himself a new flat screen. Who needed real friends anyway? His TV friends were witty, charming, and beautiful. Why had he neglected to spend time with them before? He found that he couldn't pry himself away from his programs to fix food for Micaela anymore. And his mom couldn't eat anyway. So why bother? If he paused live TV, he might miss something vital on the other channels. Typically he watched three or four shows at once. Right now he was flipping between *Dirtiest Jobs, Dancing with the Stars,* and *Iron Chef.*

Micaela walked into the room and stood in front of her father, hands on her hips. "You never let me watch that much TV, Daddy. You tell me that it turns my brains into goo."

"Can you please move? I can't see what Morimoto is doing."

"Daddy, I'm worried about your brains. And I'm hungry. Aren't you going to make dinner?"

Dennis sighed and paused the TV. He'd either have to miss the first ten minutes of Battle Crab, or the judge's comments about the cha-cha. With Herculean effort, he shifted his weight and snagged his wallet out of his back pocket. He fished out a credit card and handed it to Micaela. "Order a pizza," he said.

Micaela twisted the card, trying to snap it in half.

"Hey!" Dennis yelled. "Give it back. I'll order the pizza."

Micaela handed over the card. She didn't want to fight him anymore. She gathered Puff in her arms from where he was curled up next to her dad and started to walk down the hall.

"By the way, you have a dance lesson tomorrow night," Dennis called after her.

Micaela acted like she didn't hear. She locked herself in the bathroom.

Dennis unpaused his program and dialed the pizza place. He could watch while he was on hold.

· · · · · · · · · · · · · · · · · · · ·

Treasure forbade herself from moping the next night when Grammy headed over to Dennis's house to teach Micaela about grand jetés and chaîné turns. Instead she geared up to visit Eduardo and his mother. It was the only parent-teacher house call that she hadn't been able to complete.

"Are you sure you should be going down there alone?" Grammy asked, zipping up a jacket over her bright purple leotard.

"I'll only be there for fifteen minutes. I'll be fine," said Treasure, grabbing her own keys.

"Okay, but I'm calling you after the lesson. If you aren't back, I'm coming to look for you," said Grammy.

Treasure hugged her. "That's good incentive for me to be back. I don't want you roaming the mean streets of Vegas alone."

"Right back at you," said Grammy.

They walked out to the parking lot together and got in their respective cars. Grammy honked her horn when she turned left to go to Dennis's subdivision.

· · · · · · · · · · · · · · · · · · · ·

Dennis bolted as soon as Grammy showed up. He let her in, then mumbled something about errands. Judging by the state of the living room, Grammy figured it was the first time he'd left the couch for days.

Micaela confirmed Grammy's suspicion. "He only goes to work now, and comes right home and flips on the TV. He's ordering take-out and eating it in here. I've never been allowed to eat in here," Micaela said, picking up a Chinese takeout box (not from New Fongs, Grammy noticed) with her finger.

Grammy pursed her lips. "Well, let's clean it up. We can't dance ankle deep in dirty Styrofoam boxes." Together they worked, Micaela talking to Grammy as she followed her around with a garbage bag.

"And even at school, he doesn't make anything good for lunch anymore," Micaela said. "He just serves wiener tots and chicken nuggets—all those things he hated before."

Grammy patted Micaela's head. "Don't fret. Your dad will come out of this. How's your grandma?"

Micaela shook her head. "I don't know. Worse, I think. We got a nurse that comes and checks on her now, every day. Dad told me that I have to stay out of her room. That I could bring her germs. He's never said that to me before." She choked back a sob that turned into a hiccup.

"Well, this will never do," said Grammy Blume. She stalked down the hall and tapped on the door. "Colette, it's me. Tabiona Blume. Are you in there?" Grammy gently pushed the door aside. Dennis's mother was sleeping in her bed, curled in the fetal position. In the corner, a petite Asian lady sat reading *Ladies' Home Journal*. She put her fingers to her lips, motioning for Grammy to be quiet. Grammy didn't make any noise, but she did put her hand on Dennis's mother's hip. She felt like a pile of bones. Grammy stood for a moment, watching the rise and fall of the frail woman's breathing. The Asian lady motioned for Grammy to leave the room. "Hospice?" Grammy whispered. The nurse nodded and shooed her away. Grammy shut the door. She straightened up and walked down the hall to the little girl, who sat waiting in her pink tutu. She grabbed Micaela in her arms and gave her a fierce hug. "Now, let's dance," she said.

Micaela impressed Grammy by her progress. "You've been doing those strengthening exercises I taught you, haven't you, girl," said Grammy approvingly as Micaela demonstrated her high kicks.

Micaela nodded, happy to hear Grammy's praise. "I've been focusing on my flexibility too," she said. "Watch this!" She grabbed her heel and stretched it up to the ceiling.

"That's mighty impressive," said Grammy. "Now we need to work on your core muscles, and spotting.

"What's spotting?" asked Micaela.

"It's how dancers keep from throwing up when they're doing a big bunch of turns in a row. Here, watch this," said Grammy, demonstrating with chaîné turns.

Micaela clapped. They worked on spotting until they heard Dennis's car pull into the driveway. He came in the door loaded with boxes from Gordito's Taco Palace.

"Micaela, it's dinner time," he called, putting the food down on the table.

Grammy leaned over and whispered in Micaela's ear. "Can you go play in your room for a minute? I need to talk to your dad right now."

Micaela nodded gratefully. She skipped down the hall, happy to have an ally willing to take on her dad.

Dennis had his back to Grammy when she first came in. "Dennis," she said, "we've got to talk."

He turned around. "I thought you couldn't remember my name," he said, reaching in the pantry for hot sauce.

"I know your name, boy. I know you better than you think. And you need to listen to me. You've got to pull yourself out of this funk. You're ruining your little girl, turning her old with worry. If you go scooters, she'd have nothing to cling to anymore. And I looked in on your mother."

"The cancer is spreading to other organs. The doctors can't do any- more," stated Dennis in a matter-of-fact voice. He put a bottle of hot sauce on the table.

Grammy pursed her lips. "It looks like tough times are ahead for you."

"Tough times are here right now," said Dennis, grabbing a pile of napkins.

"That's a fact," acknowledged Grammy. "But you don't have to wallow in it. And you've been through tough times before. When your wife left. When your mom was first diagnosed. When you came to work at the school." Grammy ticked each episode off on her hand. "You need to think about someone other than yourself. Treasure is. She's out meeting with Eduardo's family tonight."

Dennis couldn't take in all the information Grammy had thrown at him. His ears snagged on what she'd said about Treasure. "Well, hurray for Treasure for moving on. I'm not like that. Besides, I have more than just a break up to deal with." He stopped for a minute and then ran his hands through his hair. "And why in heaven's name would you let her go visit Eduardo's family by herself? Don't you know what might happen to her in that neighborhood?"

Grammy looked at him stubbornly. "Treasure can take care of herself. That's kind of the point. Yes, she's hurting, more than you could ever know. But she's still going—which is what you need to do."

"Thanks for the advice," he said, slamming down a tray of tacos on the table. He really didn't want to talk with Tabiona anymore, but he couldn't stop himself from speaking. He slumped into a chair and looked at his hands. "I'm having a hard time without her. But with her doesn't work either. I don't think I can take the pain of watching her get kicked in the teeth daily. Not on top of the pain I'm already feeling. I don't want any more pain."

Grammy sat down at the table. "Of course you're afraid of pain. Everyone is. Men more than women. But that's not what Treasure brings to you, and you know it."

Dennis put the heels of his hand over his eyes. "You just don't get it. This relationship with her, it's just so complicated. Why does love have to hurt?" he asked.

"Folks have been asking that old question as long as they've been picking their noses. And I don't have an answer for you," said Grammy. "But I can tell you this. Beauty, love, and pain. They're all tied up together." She gazed out the kitchen window. "It isn't hard to find beauty in something beautiful. Anyone can find beauty in Hawaii, looking out over ocean sunsets and sandy beaches. But not everyone can find beauty here, in sagebrush and June grass and heat and desert."

Dennis had no idea what the old lady was talking about. He wished she would go away.

"But Treasure does," Grammy continued. "It's who she is. She finds beauty in everything—in balding cats, and throwaway children, and saggy old women in spandex."

Dennis caught on and smiled involuntarily. "In old laxative bottles and scratchy quilts?"

"Yes," said Grammy, nodding. "And in a well-plated school lunch too."

Dennis moved his hands and reached out to straighten the tray of tacos.

"Hidden beauty longs to be recognized and praised. And that's what Treasure does. It's why she's done so well with that class of hers. Why, I bet you money that if you take her anywhere in the world, she'd be able to find the beauty."

Dennis considered Grammy's words, toying with a taco as she spoke. Grammy was still looking out the window. He didn't say anything.

"That's her real gift. You just watch her and see what she brings back to life around her. She brought me back. I was an ornery old woman who had given up on life. Never left my recliner if I could help it. But she worked a resurrection on me. I wouldn't be here if it wasn't for Treasure Blume."

Dennis cleared his throat. "But that was you. You're family. I . . . I walked out on her. When she said it wouldn't work, I agreed with her. Then I left."

Grammy whipped her head around and met his gaze. "Sometimes, boy, I fear you are so dumb you might try to milk a duck. Try walking back in. She'll let you. She loves you—I know she does. She knew you weren't coping, just because of Micaela. That's why she asked me to call you and set up a dance lesson."

"She did this?" asked Dennis, cocking his head to the side.

Grammy nodded. "Her idea. She wouldn't want to see any of you hurting this way. Walk back in, and she'll help you find the beauty in where you are."

Dennis wiped his eyes. When did they start to water? He stood up from the table. He looked down on Grammy Blume. "Want to stay for dinner?" he asked.

Grammy picked up the taco that Dennis had been playing with and inspected it. "Will you throw out this junk and make something decent?"

Dennis threw back his head and laughed. It felt so good to laugh, to feel it deep in his belly. "Of course," he said.

"Then I'm game," said Grammy. "I'll go fetch Micaela."

16 ....

Gift Wrap

WHEN TREASURE AND RANDY WALKED INTO THE LAS VEGAS CON-
vention center for Grammy's first Competitive Gift Wrapping Rally,
they felt dwarfed by the cavernous space.

"She said this sport was big, but I didn't think it would be this big,"
said Treasure, looking up at the ceiling rafters. Randy focused his attention at eye level. "It looks like Christmas elves threw up all over this
place," he said, noting the colorful mishmash of paper, ribbons, and para-
phernalia surrounding each wrapper's station. The wrappers themselves
were garbed every bit as brightly as their tables. Most sported Santa hats
or elf ears, along with colorful holiday sweaters, even though it was a
steamy eighty degrees inside.

The sight of so many embellished sweaters brought out covetous
thoughts in Treasure's mind. After hearing about Treasure wearing her
ratty housedress during a date, Randy had staged an intervention. He
broke into her house, ran the dress through a paper shredder, and stole
her sweaters (anything embroidered with bells, pumpkins, bunnies,
shamrocks, leaves, ladybugs, teddy bears, or cats). He allowed her to keep
two, just for sentimental reasons. Then he took her shopping.

But Treasure still mourned. Sure, her new clothes fit and were more
attractive, but it just wasn't the same. Without Dennis, it didn't matter
how she looked.

"Missing your sweaters again?" asked Randy, nudging her with his
shoulder.

"The one with the Christmas tree would have been perfect for today.

When you press the star at the top, it plays 'O Tannenbaum.'" She sighed.

"Yes, but then you'd blend right into this mess," said Randy, dodging a squat man who carried two spools of curly red ribbon on his shoulders. He shuddered. "Let's go find Grammy," he said, grabbing Treasure's hand and leading her through the crowd.

Grammy's station sat square in the center of all the crazy. She was measuring paper with her yardstick, wearing her pop-up tape dispensers over her hands like brass knuckles. Beneath the jingling reindeer antlers poised on her head, she looked wired and wild-eyed. And no wonder. She had gotten up at 5:30 to practice.

"I've got to gear up for this," she told a sleepy-eyed Treasure that morning. "I know I've got it going on in the speed round, and my creative wrap can't be beat. But oddly shaped parcels, that's my waterloo. They could throw anything at me today, and I've got to be ready."

When Treasure got up two hours later, Grammy was gone, but she had wrapped all the furniture in the living room, including Treasure's lamps, recliner, coat rack, and coffee table. Treasure heard a meow coming from the kitchen. "Howls?" yelled Treasure, panicking. She followed his cries until she found him under the table, trying to free himself from the candystriped paper Grammy had enveloped him in. Luckily, she left his head sticking out, with a red bow on top. When Treasure finally freed him, he streaked away and hid under the toilet until Treasure lured him out with a can of tuna.

But clearly Grammy's early morning practice round had invigorated her. Now she was wrapping with full steam. "I thought you lazies were going to miss the whole show," said Grammy, slitting the paper with her razor scissors.

"We aren't that late, are we?" asked Randy, checking his watch.

Grammy raised her eyebrows. "Oh really? You already missed the novice speed round. In which I took second place," she said, drawing their attention to a silver ribbon pinned to the front of her booth.

Treasure clapped her hands. "Oh, Grammy! I'm so proud of you."

"Well, don't be," said Grammy, straightening her apron. "I didn't win, and I've still got two more rounds to go. Flair is next," she said, "and detail is key here."

"What's your concept?" asked Treasure, coming around to Grammy's side of the table.

"Currier and Ives. I'm doing a whole scene: one-horse open sleigh, a snow-covered cottage, and lamp posts, using four different types of paper."

"Can I help?" asked Treasure. She noticed Randy wandering off toward the concession stand.

Grammy nodded toward Randy. "Grab me a Coke. But no caffeine. I need steady hands for flair."

As they stood in line together, Randy started to bail. "Treasure, you know I want to be supportive, but I may go crazy if I have to stay here all day." He jumped to the side as a big lady dressed as Mrs. Claus brushed by him, dragging her wheeled gift wrapping caddy behind her.

Treasure laughed at him. "Go. I'll stay here with Grammy. Just check back in with us later, okay?"

"Thank you," said Randy with obvious relief. He ran off without buying anything. Treasure paid for the Coke and then headed back over to Grammy's station.

Grammy started stressing an hour before the oddly shaped parcel round. She flexed her fingers to keep them limber. Treasure had seen thoroughbreds more calm. "Grams, you've got to hold it together," she said. "This can't be any more stressful than a Steppers' performance."

"But with the Steppers, I'm out there with my team. Here, it all rides on me," Grammy said, rolling her wrists. "And you know this is my most difficult round."

"You'll be fine," Treasure reassured her. "You know you don't have to win, right?" she said, in her first-grade teacher voice.

Grammy snorted. "I don't have to breathe either."

"Just have fun, Grammy."

"Where's your lazy big brother?" Grammy suddenly asked.

"He'll be back before you go in the ring," said Treasure, massaging Grammy's neck.

Grammy shook her off. "Go check. I can't have you hovering over me like this, girl."

Treasure didn't take offense. She left Grammy and walked back toward the entrance, calling Randy on her cell. He answered after the first ring.

"Treasure, I'm in the parking lot. And you won't believe who I've got with me," he said.

"Mom and Dad?" Treasure guessed.

"No. This is way better. Here. I'll hand the phone over to him."

Treasure heard Randy's muffled voice as he passed the phone over to someone else. "Why Miss Blume, it's an honor to speak with you," said a gravelly gentleman's voice.

Treasure couldn't believe it. She nearly dropped her phone. "Varden Moyle?" she screeched.

"Yes, ma'am, in the flesh."

"What are you doing here?' she asked, hustling toward the door. She caught sight of Randy and Varden just outside the gate. Randy had the phone again. "We see you. Just let us get through and we'll talk in person," he said. Treasure snapped her phone shut and stood on tiptoes, waiting for the two of them to come through the gate.

When she met them, she couldn't help herself. She hugged Varden so hard she knocked his Stetson right off his head. "Well, missy, I doubt I deserve a greeting like that," he said. Randy picked up his hat and dusted it off before handing it over.

"Did you come to support Grammy?" Treasure asked. "Oh, that will make her so happy! Let's go tell her you're here," she said with the overeager enthusiasm of a golden retriever.

Varden held up both hands. "Just wait a minute."

"Treasure, you can't tell her that you know Varden is here," said Randy, grabbing Treasure's arm.

"Why not?" asked Treasure.

The two men exchanged a look. "Think we better tell her?" Randy asked Varden, who nodded. He reached inside his jacket pocket and fished out a tiny black velvet box.

"Is that what I think it is?" Treasure asked, clutching her heart.

"Crack it open and find out," Varden invited.

Treasure did. Inside was a tiny twinkling diamond, set in old-fashioned filigree scrollwork. "It was my mother's," he continued, his voice cracking a little. "My wife was buried in hers, so I thought this would do."

"It's beautiful," said Treasure, lifting it out of the box. "She'll love it," she said reverently. "But can I ask you a question? I haven't seen you for weeks. And now you're here with a diamond. What's going on?"

Varden resettled his hat on his head. "Well, you remember when you were teaching me to dance? And your grandma said that she had a hard time letting a man lead? Your grandma is opinionated. And I didn't want to be bullied into marriage. No sir. I had to do it my way."

"You wanted to lead," said Treasure, handing him back the ring box. "I can understand that."

"So can I," said Randy. "So what's your plan?"

Varden squinted his eyes. "She's going to be in the next round, right? I figured I'd slip this into the pile that she's wrapping. What do you think?"

Treasure thought for a second before answering. "I think it's a lovely idea. It's just, well, if it hurts her chances for winning . . ."

Varden nodded. "It might. But I'm hoping to tame her crazy competitive streak a bit."

"Good luck with that," Treasure blurted.

"Well, we've got to move," said Randy. "They just announced her round."

"Oh no," yelped Treasure. "Randy, go find Grammy and distract her. Varden and I need to talk to the judges and get this gift into her pile."

They split up, Randy jogging back to Grammy's station, Varden and Treasure hustling to the main ring.

When they finally got there, Treasure had no time for pleasantries. She spotted the head judge and rushed right up to him. "Are you the head judge for this round?" she asked, trying to be properly impressed by his authority.

The man pointed to the judge's pin nestled in his chest hair and clicked his heels together in assent.

Treasure bowed her head, trying to look meek. "We have a special request. This man," Treasure said, tapping Varden on the shoulder, "wants to propose to my grandmother here today. He would like to slip a wedding ring into her gift pile. Can you help us make that happen?"

The judge glanced at Varden's outstretched hand—clutching the velvet box—before speaking. "Absolutely not," he sniffed. "That parcel isn't oddly shaped at all."

Treasure grabbed the box and opened it. "What if we just submit the ring? It's rather unusual to wrap a ring without a box. And it's definitely unconventional."

The head judge hesitated before going over to his fellow judges to confer. When he shot a glance back at her, Treasure channeled back all the humility and admiration she could muster in a single look. Varden wasn't any help. He shoved his hands in his pockets and looked at the toes of his Tony Lamas.

Treasure watched for Grammy, nervously craning. She could feel giant sweat tacos blossoming under her arms. She cursed her silk shirt. Her sweaters never would have betrayed her this way.

Finally the judge returned. "Since this is merely the novice round, my fellow judges have agreed to humor your request. But know this. We will not be making a habit out of this," he said, one finger in the air, much like Bonnie B. Baumgartner.

"I'm only planning on proposing the one time," said Varden, bewildered by the man's serious expression.

The judge pointed toward the very end of the long table that had been set up for the round. "We will channel your grandmother into that station. If you would hand me the item in question, then I will take it back to our parcel master." He held out his hand.

"Wait," said Treasure, suddenly worried that Grammy would just wrap the ring without realizing that it was for her. "We need to add a tag." She walked over to the wrapping station, stole a cardboard cutout of a poinsettia, and handed it to Varden, along with a pen.

"You better write it down," she said.

Varden didn't seem to be in any hurry to take the items from Treasure. "I'm not a hand with writing words and such. Maybe we should just bag the whole idea."

The judge shifted his substantial weight from one foot to the other.

"No!" said Treasure. "It won't take much to make this happen. You can do this!" She looked at him in the same steady, encouraging way that she had when they two-stepped together at halftime.

Varden straightened up and took the pen and poinsettia. Quickly, he scrawled the note: "Tabiona Blume, marry me."

Treasure thought he was wise to command Grammy rather than ask her. She looked across the ring and saw Randy jumping up and down to get her attention. "She's just getting her number on," he mouthed.

Treasure nodded, and Varden handed the ring to the judge, who whisked it away. Varden looked shaky, as if his knees might buckle at any moment.

"Let's go find you a chair," said Treasure.

"I feel a bit dizzy," Varden acknowledged, glad to have Treasure steer him through the crowd.

"Maybe that's why men get down on one knee to propose," Treasure mused. "Because the thought of marriage makes them light-headed."

Varden couldn't answer. He sat down, his face a fishy pale. Treasure hoped he wouldn't throw up. She looked around but couldn't see a garbage can. She decided she'd snatch the hat off his head, if needed.

The microphone screeched, and Treasure saw Grammy give Randy a hug before entering the ring with the other novice gift wrappers. She stood tall and straight, as grimly determined as any warrior. Only the tinkling sound of the bells on her antlers marred the effect.

"Attention competitors. You will have ten minutes to wrap the gifts at your station. After ten minutes, you will walk away, while the judges deliberate. Each contestant will be evaluated on tape seams, complete coverage, and overall attractiveness," the judge announced.

Grammy bobbed her head to demonstrate her understanding. She crouched over her table.

"You may remove the blanket over the gifts when the buzzer sounds. Are you ready?"

The buzzer went off. Grammy tore the blanket off her pile and started sorting. She grabbed a BB gun first. She turned it up on its butt, and wrapped the paper around it, securing it with tape strips in long bold strokes. She finished it in less than one minute. Next she grabbed an upright mixer. She popped off the beaters and rolled them up in paper like a burrito, before moving on to the base. She had it wrapped in fifty seconds. Then she taped the beater burrito to the base package and moved it to the other side. She never looked up at the other wrappers.

Next she grabbed a pair of Mickey Mouse ears. She frowned at the hat as she folded the ears back and forth, trying to figure out a plan. She finally shrugged, and wrapped each ear individually before she attacked the crown.

Next she lugged a four-foot, fully assembled weather vane onto her wrapping space. The gigantic rooster at the top spun as Grammy evaluated. Treasure feared for her grandmother. How would she manage to make this look attractive? But Grammy didn't hesitate. Instead, she began wrapping paper over each individual arm of the weather vane and then over the rooster himself. Finally she wrapped the base. She used efficient folds to create tight, tiny corners. When she finished, Treasure thought the weather vane looked much more appealing. She would have mounted it on her barn fully wrapped.

Grammy grabbed the final large gift from her pile, a light-up globe, trailing an extension cord.

"Wouldn't most people just put it in a box before they wrapped it?" whispered Randy, who had snuck up behind Treasure.

Treasure shushed him before answering. "Yes, but I don't think CGW is grounded in practicality. This is art."

Randy decided not to argue. Practicality had never been Grammy Blume's strong suit either. "Well, she's certainly the fastest wrapper up there," he said. "That other lady is still struggling with her BB gun."

Treasure looked over at Grammy's nearest competitor, who was swinging her gun back and forth like an elephant's trunk, clearly perplexed. "I hope that thing isn't loaded," Treasure whispered back to Randy and Varden.

"Let's duck, just in case," said Randy, scrunching down in his chair.

"The safety's on," said Varden, still pale and pasty.

In the meantime, Grammy had devised a plan for her globe. She set it square in the middle of a sheet of paper, Antarctica side down. Starting first with four equidistant tape strips in Brazil, Indonesia, Africa, and the Pacific Ocean, she taped the edge of the paper to the equator. Then she began to pleat, in crisp, neat folds. Next she wound the cord around the equator. When she finished with that, she wrapped the top half the same way, matching the pleats exactly. She ran a ribbon around the seam at the equator, disguising the cord.

"Wow," Randy breathed. "I've got to say, that is artistic."

Grammy threw her hands in the air like a calf-roper at a rodeo. "Done!" she yelled.

The head judge shushed her. "Let's keep it quiet for the other competitors," he said severely.

"But she's not done," Treasure hissed at Randy. "Where's the ring?"

Randy half stood up, still covering his head in case any BB guns went off. "I can't see it," he said.

Treasure could not stand to let time tick away like this. She stood up.

"You're not done, Grammy. Look around your station. There should be one more very small item."

Grammy started to scour. "How can I find it if I don't know what I'm looking for?"

The other four competitors had paused in their wrapping. They each craned over at Grammy.

The judge glared at Grammy and Treasure. "Please do not disrupt the proceeding. Wrappers, you have two minutes until this round ends."

Grammy got down on all fours, examining under the table. "I found it," she yelled, trying to straighten up and bumping her antlers in the process.

She held the delicate ring in one hand as she reached toward her scissors and paper.

"Don't wrap it. Read it!" Treasure urged.

"Young lady, one more outburst from you, and you will be removed from the gallery!" the judge huffed.

Grammy stood up, then squinted at the poinsettia tag trailing from the ring. Her eyes widened and her lips mouthed the words. She looked up at the crowd, struck dumb.

At that point, Treasure and Randy unitedly hauled Varden to his feet, where he rocked back and forth, threatening to tumble over. Treasure and Randy each put an arm around him, supporting him from behind.

Grammy managed to find her tongue. "Do you mean it, Vard?" she asked.

Varden Moyle firmed up his stance and looked out at his lady. "Yes, m'dear. I certainly do. I want you to marry me, Tabiona Blume."

Grammy couldn't help herself. She rushed across the ring, kicked her away over the velvet rope, and threw herself into Varden Moyle's arms, scattering spectators as she went. The crowd and the other wrappers started to clap. "Is that a yes?" Varden asked.

Grammy couldn't even speak. Giant tears hovered on her lashes. She nodded her head, then looked Varden in the eye and kissed him fiercely.

The crowd looked askance at the geriatric smooch fest. Even Treasure had to turn her head.

The buzzer sounded, ending the spectacle and the round. Two other wrappers, besides Grammy, had finished. Another threw her scissors, obviously frustrated. One poor wrapper had been so immersed in the drama, she hadn't even started her globe.

The judge seethed at Grammy and Varden, then finally at Treasure. "We will now deliberate," he said. It was clear that he wished he had never let this little drama upstage his final judging round.

Grammy was too happy to glare back.

· · · · · · · · · · · · · · · · · · · ·

When Grammy left the convention center that evening, she had two ribbons pinned to her apron: a second place from the novice speed round and a first from the novice flair division. She would have had another, the judge had explained to the oddly shaped parcel crowd, but she had been disqualified for unsportsmanlike behavior. The crowd had booed at his pronouncement. For Grammy's part, she blew the judge a raspberry and flashed her diamond ring at him.

"I'm walking away with the grand prize," she said, holding Varden's hand.

Vard grinned at her. "I'm glad you feel that way. Treasure and I wondered how you'd react if I hurt your chances to win."

"Well," said Grammy, straightening her ribbons. "You're just lucky that I won a first place in flair."

17

Snow Day

Liwayway had missed two entire weeks of school. Treasure felt sick. After visiting Liwayway's family, she felt responsible. After school ended on Friday, she stress-cleaned her classroom but came up with no solutions. She finally left her trailer, determined to talk to Dawn and get her take on the situation. But when she stepped out of her classroom, it felt like she'd entered the arctic. The temperature had plummeted. She exhaled and saw her breath crystallize in front of her. Low dark clouds swirled away the sunlight, making it look much darker than 4:00 p.m. She held out her hand and felt the unmistakable brush of snowflakes against her skin. She looked skyward and watched the white plummet toward her. Sure, it was December. But this was Las Vegas. She looked down at the ground, where the snow had started to coat the dirt and gravel. It wasn't melting. Treasure didn't stop to think about the ramifications of a snowstorm in Vegas. Instead she drew her new suede jacket around her more tightly and sprinted toward the double doors to the school.

. . . .

Dennis Cameron was still at school too. He and Thelma were planning menus and going over the food orders. Thelma didn't change her expression when he told her that he was ready to start cooking again. She just pulled a pencil out of her hair, reached for her order forms and said, "So you're going to rejoin the living, huh? What did you have in mind?"

Dennis explained his concept for Israeli falafel on pita bread with chopped vegetables. "I'm not sure how the kids will respond to harissa, but I figure it's worth a shot," he said.

Thelma sighed. "Are we back to this again? Gourmet garbage that the kids hate? Don't you remember the beginning of the year? What about new takes on kid classics?"

"I'm going another direction," said Dennis stubbornly.

Thelma put her hands on her hips. "Yep. You'll be headed down to the unemployment line." She peered into his face, moving closer into his personal space. "What's with you? One day you're making squash love boats, then, all of a sudden, you're serving nuggets like a coma patient, and now you're trying to force feed African hot sauce to the kids. What's up with the mood swings?"

Dennis didn't want to respond. What could he say that wasn't tied up with his feelings for Treasure? After his conversation with Grammy, he had gone to bed determined to talk to Treasure the next day. But he just couldn't. He overheard a couple of the other first-grade teachers making fun of her as they went through the lunch line. Lucinda, the one Treasure called the General, was particularly catty, mimicking her bouncy walk and expressive hand gestures. For days afterward, Dennis fought the urge to spit in her food when he saw her coming down the line.

The anger steamed his resolve until it was as limp as overcooked asparagus spears. What would he say to Treasure? Nothing had changed. Yes, he thought he loved her, but he still didn't know how to deal with her peculiar gift without wanting to kick people. Introducing her to his friends would be agonizing. It would be a replay of the Larry situation every time. And as much as he didn't want to be selfish, it did bruise his ego. And that made him mad. He really wanted to take that snotty teacher by her ears and rub her sarcastic face in Treasure's goodness and kindness. "That's what a teacher is supposed to do," he'd yell, thrusting the General's face into Treasure's classroom. But he couldn't. He was sure Treasure would frown on that.

Thelma tapped him on the head with her pencil. "Your face looks like it's going to explode. Do you want to talk about this?"

Dennis looked down at the tile floor. "Have you ever been in love, Thelma?" he asked.

Thelma was taken back. Now it all made sense. She knew she'd been too familiar with him, letting him spoon-feed her that day. As much as she was flattered by the boy's attentions, she was old enough to be his mother. "I've been married for twenty-five years. And I've never entertained the notion of stepping out," she said, a warning implicit in her voice.

Dennis felt embarrassed. "No, Thelma. I'm not . . . I mean, I value your friendship, but I . . ." He cleared his throat. "I'm in love with someone, at least I think I am, and the relationship is just complicated. I don't know if I can do it."

"What's complicated? If you love her, and she loves you, then what's the fuss?" asked Thelma, deeply relieved (and a little disappointed) to find out she was not the object of his affection.

Dennis stood up. "What if you were with someone, Thelma, that no—one—else—liked?" He punctuated the last four words with giant pauses.

Thelma shrugged. "If I loved him, then it wouldn't matter what anyone else thought."

"Really?" said Dennis. "Even if every friend, every coworker, every waiter you ever introduced him to hated him? It still wouldn't matter?" He moved in closer, about two inches from her nose.

She could smell the onions on his breath. She dug in her pocket and handed him a mint. "Nope. Not to me. What somebody thinks of you, that's not who you are, right? Take me for example. Sometimes people think I'm pretty gruff. But I don't let that bother me. I know it's not who I am, so I let it go. I didn't become head lunch lady by listening to fools' opinions."

He popped in the tic tac and sat back down. "I know other people's opinions of her aren't true. That's what makes me mad. I just want to pound people and make them shut their mouths and open their eyes and see what a great person she is."

Thelma contemplated his words. "Not everybody wants or needs that kind of recognition. Take our anonymous lunch donor. She went to great lengths to make sure that no one knew who she was. It took me forever to ferret out that information."

Dennis sprang forward. "You know who the donor is? You've got to tell me."

"No, I do not," said Thelma testily. "Forget I said it. Besides, that's not what we were talking about. And how did I become your relationship counselor anyhow? That's not in my job description. Let's talk about menus."

"Oh no, you don't," said Dennis. "You can't tease me like that. If you didn't want to share that info, you wouldn't have mentioned it. Just tell me."

"You'd blab it all over, and she wouldn't like that," dismissed Thelma. "Now, I can authorize falafel if you drop the harissa," she said, starting to write on her order form.

Dennis leaned back. "I'm not a blabber."

Thelma ignored him and turned away. She wouldn't crack.

Dennis folded his hands behind his head and closed his eyes. He thought about the time that Treasure told him to look at the colors beneath his eyelids. It made him smile. Thelma and Grammy were right. So what if no one else liked Treasure? He loved her. It didn't matter that she didn't want everyone to know how great she was. The last thought stopped him cold. She didn't want recognition. Just like the secret lunch donor. He wanted it for her, but she didn't want it for herself. An image coalesced in front of his eyes. Dandelions—the icon for the secret account—Treasure's favorite undomesticated flower. How could he have missed it? Dennis snapped back up to an upright position as if he were preparing for landing.

"Thelma," he said in a low voice. "If I guess who the donor is, will you tell me if I'm right?"

"Dennis, I'm trying to figure out how many boxes of boneless skinless chicken breasts we'll need for the next month," said Thelma, leaning over her desk.

"It's Treasure Blume, isn't it?" he whispered.

Thelma swung around toward him, pencil still poised over her ordering sheets. "How did you figure that out?" she asked, mystified.

"Because she's the girl I'm in love with."

. . . .

Treasure found Dawn sitting at her desk grading papers. "Hey, Dawn, I had something that I wanted to talk with you about," she said, slipping into one of the child-size desks.

Dawn looked up, happy to see her. "Treasure! Just when I needed a break from these anyway." She set her stack of papers aside and brought out a bag of Holiday M&Ms from the top drawer of her desk.

"What's up?" she asked, pouring a handful into Treasure's hand.

Treasure funneled the candies from one hand to the other as she explained about Liwayway's absences and her living situation.

Dawn looked at her in amazement. "They invited you over? You actually went into their house?" she asked in disbelief.

"Well, it's not really a house."

Dawn stood up. "My guess is that they moved somewhere else. They may have thought that you would tell INS or something. You may have spooked away the whole community."

Treasure gaped at her. "I was trying to help."

Dawn plopped down beside her, exasperated. "We're all trying to help. But when the family is trying to fly under the radar, the fact that you took an interest in Liwayway at all probably frightened them. They don't like authority figures of any kind."

The enormity of Treasure's naiveté hit her. Her actions (even with her good intentions) could have negative repercussions for everyone involved. What could she say? What could she do? "I'm sorry. I feel like an idiot."

"You should," said Dawn bluntly.

Treasure couldn't look at Dawn. She picked up her M&M's and rolled them around in her sweaty palms. They left red and green smears. "How can they say that these don't melt in your hand? Look," she said, holding up her hands.

Dawn was not amused. She opened her mouth to say something when they heard the PA system rumble. Bonnie's voice echoed through the empty halls. "Attention all personnel: please come to the office as soon as possible. All personnel, no exceptions."

"What could that be?" said Dawn, rising to her feet.

"Well whatever it is, I doubt there are very many people still here. It's Friday night," said Treasure.

Together, she and Dawn hustled down the deserted halls until they came to the office. Treasure nearly bumped into Lucinda, who was coming from the other direction, looking at her watch. They found Bonnie standing on her desk with a bullhorn.

"Let's remain calm, people," she said, blasting the three of them out of their skins.

Aussie sat in her mother's chair, arms crossed, feet up. She had dyed her hair purple since Treasure last saw her. While Bonnie spoke, Aussie blew enormous bubbles with her bright pink gum.

"Jeez, Bonnie, it's just the five of us," said Dawn. "Do you think you could lose the megaphone?"

"We are in an emergency situation," said Bonnie through the bullhorn.

"Well, so am I," said Lucinda. "I have a Pilates class that I'm teaching at six." She had already changed into her spandex workout clothes.

This remark clearly infuriated Bonnie. "I have no patience for people who underreact," she said severely.

Treasure felt guilty for not panicking.

"What's the emergency?" asked Thelma, the head lunch lady, as she entered the office with Dennis Cameron by her side.

"What are you doing here?" blurted Treasure at Dennis. "Aren't you usually home by now?" Everyone turned and looked at her. She instantly regretted her outburst. They hadn't spoken since the night they broke up.

Behind her mother's back, Aussie drew her finger across her throat in a knifing motion.

Dennis remained silent. Thelma thought Treasure had directed the question at her. "We've been going over menus and food orders. We do this every other Friday," she said, defensive that anyone would question her right to be at the school any time she pleased.

Bonnie disliked the shift in focus. She raised her megaphone to her mouth and continued blasting them. "People, please. Allow me to explain the situation. The city of Las Vegas is experiencing the worst winter storm that the city has ever seen."

Treasure couldn't stop herself from commenting. "But I just came in from the trailers. The snow wasn't that deep."

"Meteorologists are expecting three to ten inches overnight on the strip, and several feet in the foothills," said Bonnie, with a challenge in her voice.

Dawn nudged Treasure. "It won't take much snow to shut this city down. I doubt we have any snowplows. So when you combine slick roads and people who don't know how to drive on ice, you get traffic snarls that last for hours."

Bonnie looked gratified by Dawn's explanation. "That's exactly what I've been trying to say," Bonnie huffed.

Everyone exchanged mystified glances. Bonnie had not mentioned anything about the impact of snow on surface streets.

Bonnie continued. "As I was saying, several roads have been closed due to hazardous conditions."

"We'll all be careful going home," said Dennis, reaching for his keys.

Bonnie finally put down the megaphone so that she could jab her finger at him. "You're not going anywhere. No one is," she said, with the peculiar glee of a prison warden. "The roads around the school are closed. And one of our buses, with twenty children aboard, slid off the road. They are stranded half a mile away, down by the dry cleaner."

Everyone gasped. Bonnie finally received the kind of response she had been looking for, except from one person.

The General inspected her fingernails. "Aren't we overreacting here, just a weensy bit? I'm sure it's just a fender bender or something like that. The bus driver will figure it out. It's his job. I have other priorities. I have Pilates students who need me to put their feet on the path to learning."

Dawn looked disgusted. "I'm impressed you can direct other people's feet," she said, "because you've just put your own in your mouth. We've got to take care of these kids."

Lucinda ignored Dawn and puffed up. "Bonnie, I have to go. That's why God invented four-wheel drive. I cannot stand here anymore. Excuse me for being the voice of reason," she said, turning on her heels and walking toward the door.

Bonnie watched in open-mouthed shock as her favorite ally abandoned her.

"If that's the voice of reason, I'm delighted to be counted among the crazy," Dawn muttered under her breath.

"I guess we've finally got her commitment level pegged down," said Treasure. They watched the General sprint out to her Ford truck, slam the door, and plow her way out of the parking lot.

"Where's Anita?" asked Thelma, after the din of the General's engine had subsided.

Bonnie was still trying to recover from Lucinda's desertion. "She's at that convention in Reno," she said, inflating her lungs and shifting her focus. "And that means that I am the senior ranking official here."

Dennis raised his hand. "I'll go get the kids and bring them back here," he said.

"So will I," said Treasure.

"And I will too," said Aussie, surprising everyone (especially her mother).

"No," said Dennis. "I can do this. You guys stay here."

"Oh, take off the cape, Dennis," said Thelma. "You can't haul all those kids back by yourself. The little ones will need to be carried. You're going to need help."

Dennis evaluated Treasure's sling-back flats and Aussie's platform flip-flops. "I doubt either of you could make it in those shoes," he said.

"Just hang on for a minute," said Dawn. She had her phone out and was texting with both thumbs, faster than Aussie. "My husband, Don, says he can get through on his four-wheeler. He'll load up blankets and sleds. He says he can get to the place where the bus is. Dennis, you go down to meet him. He'll haul the kids back up the hill."

"Your husband's name is Don?" Aussie said, snapping her gum. "That's weird."

Dawn glanced at Aussie's Barney-tinted hair. "Yep. The world is a weird place."

Bonnie sputtered objections at Dawn's solution. It rubbed her the wrong way that someone else had come up with it. "But the roads are closed. It's dangerous. How can he be so sure he can get through?"

Dawn heaved an exasperated sigh. "He's from Idaho. Snow doesn't scare him. Plus, he's used to driving eighteen-wheelers from Canada to LA. Trust me, if anyone can make it through, my man can."

"Well, when those kids come back, they'll be exhausted and hungry," said Thelma. "We don't have much food on hand. Our suppliers won't come until Monday. But we'll have to think of something," she said, looking at Dennis.

Dennis jumped up from where he had been slouching against the wall. "Can your man grab us some grub too?" he asked Dawn.

Dawn shrugged. "I'll ask him to bring whatever we have in our freezer."

"We'll make do," said Dennis. "I'm heading out. What's Don's ETA?"

"He figures he can do it in fifteen minutes," Dawn said.

Dennis looked over at Bonnie. She was still standing on top of her desk. "Bonnie, what have you heard from the bus driver?"

"The bus is stuck. No one is hurt, but all emergency responders are bogged down. They can't get there for hours. So far the driver is keeping the heat on and the kids inside."

"That's the best plan for now," said Dawn. "I doubt any of those kids have decent coats. Just tell him to sit tight until Dennis and Don get there. We'll call parents and let them know."

Bonnie nodded and went over to the CB. They listened while she relayed the message. Then they started to move.

Treasure followed Dennis to the lunchroom where he left his coat. "I'm going with you."

Dennis turned around. "Please don't. Just let me and Don handle this."

"Why, because I'll just be in the way?"

Dennis zipped up his jacket. He pulled his phone out of his pocket. "Look, will you call Micaela? She's home alone with my mom. And I know you need to call Grammy Blume too. Will you handle this for me?"

Treasure relented. "Keep your phone. I'll call on mine," she said, reaching in her pocket for her own phone. She fiddled with it in her hands. "Is it because you don't want to be around me?" she asked. "Because I promise I won't make it awkward," she said awkwardly. "At least I'll try."

Dennis stifled a laugh and waited until he was sure she wouldn't verbally erupt again. "No," he said. "It's because I don't want you to slip and fall. Knowing you, you'd probably crack your tailbone."

"Since when did you care about my tailbone?" asked Treasure.

"I care more than you know," said Dennis, kissing her gently on the forehead and then heading out into the storm.

Treasure Blume felt the moist spot on her forehead with her hand, completely flummoxed. She felt as mystified by his conduct as a penguin in Tahiti. She let her hands thump back against her side and walked back to the office, which Bonnie had temporarily re-titled "Operation Headquarters."

When she walked back in, Dawn, Aussie, and Bonnie each held a cell phone pressed to their ears, engaged in various stages of conversations with parents.

"Here's your list," mouthed Bonnie to her. "We're a man down since Thelma went back to the kitchen."

Treasure began to quake inside. Had Thelma witnessed her forehead kiss with Dennis? And what did that one little action mean? She wasn't sure. She just really hoped she wouldn't have to explain it. She started calling. Somehow reassuring and soothing parents worked to soothe and calm her too.

After the fourth phone call, Treasure dialed Grammy's cell and started pacing. Grammy answered after two rings. "Ho ho ho!" she caroled as a greeting.

Relief seized Treasure when she heard her grandmother's voice. "Grammy, how are you? Don't try to go anywhere. The city's a mess. I need you to stay put."

"Well, that's my plan. I just got here. Isn't this weather beautiful? When that storm hit, everybody on the road started driving like old ladies, which is a good thing, if you ask me. Except for some hot shot in a Mustang. He tried to zip out around me, but I just swung Mullet out in front of him and slowed him down. And we all just kept going sure and safe."

Treasure was grateful the Mustang driver didn't rear-end Mullet and send Grammy spinning. "Where are you?" she asked.

"Well, it's the funniest thing. I was just stitching on that old quilt. I decided it was high time to embroider my square, what with all the blessings I've received lately,"

Treasure interrupted. "You're restitching your square? Like you told me that you would? Oh, Grammy." Her own heart cockles started to warm as she thought of Grammy running new bright thread through the old holes in her square.

"Well, you know, with Vard proposing, and winning first place in flair, and living with you. And none of it would have happened except for our family gift. That's what drew you and me together. So anyway, I was stitching and counting blessings, and I got to thinking about little Micaela dancing, and then the strangest feeling came over me."

"What?" asked Treasure, realizing that Grammy still hadn't told her where she was.

"It was like I heard a voice and it told me to get over to Micaela's house right then for a dance lesson."

"Is it like the last time you heard voices, Grammy? Because that's when Dad put you on that medication."

"I didn't say I heard an actual voice. I just felt it. And I just knew I needed to get over here. So I bit off my thread and hopped in Mullet."

Treasure found that she had been inadvertently holding her breath during Grammy's story. She let it out with relief. "So you're with Micaela and Collete. Are they okay?"

"Happy as lambs. We've got the nurse here too. We're listening to some Lionel Ritchie, and I'm whipping up a beef stew. Collete looks like a person again. She's rallied. Last time I was here, I thought we better start casket shopping. But she's managed to cheat death. She told me to tell you that she's borrowed one of your mangy cat's lives. So we'll need to tell Howls he's down to eight. She's here in the front room watching us dance. Did you know that Fishstick, that long little dog of hers, can stand on its stubby hind legs and turn in a circle? I want to figure out a way to get him on stage with the Steppers. We could call it Corgi-ography!"

Treasure was so wrapped up in Grammy's world, she almost forgot why she called. "Grammy, I'm still at the school. Dennis is too. We're here with Dawn, Thelma, Bonnie, and Aussie. The roads are closed, and we've got twenty kids coming here to spend the night. We can't get home."

"I knew there was a purpose for me coming here today. I'm just glad I heeded the call," Grammy said. "Now you've got power, right? And heat?" she asked.

"Yes, so far," said Treasure.

"Then consider this a great adventure," said Grammy. "Just don't lock yourself in any dark closets with a certain lunch lady."

"Who? Thelma?" Treasure teased.

"You know who I'm talking about," said Grammy. "That poor love-lorn fool. Has he managed to say anything to you?"

"Just that he didn't want me to break my tailbone," said Treasure, simplifying her conversation with Dennis for Grammy's sake.

"Hasn't taken my advice, has he? Does he think that I just dole out pearls of wisdom free of charge? No sir. I demand action!" Grammy fumed.

Treasure didn't know what she was talking about. "Look, Grams, I've got to go. Bonnie's giving me the eye. And we've got more parents to call."

"Well, girl, you rest easy. I've got the situation here under control, and you can tell Dennis that, if you get the chance."

"Will do, Grammy."

"I love you, girl, and so does he."

Treasure pressed "end" and wondered how that could be true. And if so, why did only the old or dying proclaim Dennis's love for her? She shook her head to clear her thoughts. How could she even entertain the idea that he might love her? After all, they broke up three weeks ago—a fact that Grammy had apparently forgotten. And Dennis himself didn't seem inclined to say anything. She just didn't know how he felt any more. Perhaps she was reading too much into that little forehead smooch. Maybe it meant that he thought of her like a little sister, or a goofy younger cousin. He could have kissed her on the lips. All he had to do was aim lower.

"Treasure Blume, if you are going to spend your time making personal calls, go down to the kitchen and help Thelma," Bonnie ordered from across the room, her hand over the receiver.

Treasure decided not to argue. She was about to wander back down the hall to the kitchen when she heard the whir of an engine out the front door. Aussie and Dawn heard it too. Together, they pushed their way through the door and stood huddled in the semi-darkness.

A four-wheeler, complete with a snowplow on the front, a trailer on back, and chains on the tires roared its way across the lawn toward them. Three flexible flyer sleds, with three kids on each, streamed behind it like ribbons. Treasure couldn't make out the identities of the kids. They wore colorful tuques pulled down over their eyes and striped mufflers up to their noses. But it didn't take long to identify the driver. Dennis Cameron took off his goggles and shook his hair like a dog. He shut down the machine and ran back to the kids.

"Everybody okay?" he asked.

"That was awesome!" shouted one kid. "Can we do it again?" yelled another.

Dennis smiled. "Nope. Start hauling in supplies."

Dawn and Aussie hopped into action, helping the kids to unload the trailer.

"Well, you've got my ride, but where's my hubby?" asked Dawn.

"He'll be here in just a minute," said Dennis. "By the time I got there, he and the bus driver were already working on getting the bus out of the ditch. They dug out the rear wheels, then Don got up in the driver seat and started twisting the wheel and popping the clutch. The next thing I knew, he had the bus back on the road. Then he flipped a U-turn with that monster. It was amazing how he manhandled that thing. So anyway, he told me to drive this up, and that he'd be right behind me. Look, there he is," said Dennis pointing at the horizon.

Treasure, Dawn, and Aussie followed his finger. They yelled like cheerleaders as Don pulled the bus up to the parking lot. He opened the doors, and kids started filing out, followed by the bus driver. Dawn and Aussie channeled them through the front door. Treasure scanned faces, but only recognized one. Octavio climbed out of the bus and gave her a high five. "Isn't this the coolest thing that's ever happened?" he said, grinning as he walked by, hauling three frozen ducks by the feet. The enthusiasm on his spider-monkey face was enough to bolster Treasure. And she needed it. A few of the other kids were crying. She stepped forward and wrapped them in hugs.

"Don't cry. You're safe now. And it's warm in the school, and we're going to have a sleepover," she said, mustering all her enthusiasm. One little pigtailed girl refused to be comforted. Treasure picked her up. She clung to Treasure's neck sobbing. "But we fell right off the road," she snuffled against Treasure's neck.

Don Robbins jumped down from his seat and came over to them. He patted the little girl's head. "Don't cry, princess. Didn't I push that old bus right back on the road? You don't need to worry."

Then he stuck out his hand. "You must be Treasure Blume. Dawn speaks highly of you," he said smiling.

Treasure had a hard time responding. For one thing, she had three crying first-graders howling against her knees. For another, Don's appearance threw her off. She'd been expecting Dawn's husband to be as big and brawny as she was. But Don Robbins only reached up to Treasure's shoulder. He had bright red hair, which stuck out in a fringe under his green trucker's hat, and a giant mustache. For a moment, Treasure wondered if she was talking to the real-life model for Yosemite Sam.

Treasure put the little girl on one hip and took his hand. "Pleasure to meet you," she said, as Dawn bowled out of the school and right into her little husband's arms.

"I'm better than a mailman, aren't I? Neither snow nor rain nor gloom of night can keep me away," he said, squeezing his wife. His arms spanned about halfway around Dawn's bulk.

"You're better than Santa Claus," said Dawn, before she planted a kiss right below his mustache. Treasure wondered how anything that bristly could possibly feel (or taste) good.

Don gave them both an "awe shucks" look before speaking. "It was all luck that I made it back up the hill. It's a skating rink down there." He looked over to where Dennis had parked the four-wheeler. "Did we get that unloaded?" he asked Dawn.

"Yes, sir, and I saw my snow hat and muffler wrapped around one of the sled boys. So thanks for that," said Dawn. "What did you find us for dinner?"

Don took off his hat and scratched his head. "Well, we didn't have much. I brought that brace of ducks I shot last week, and the rest of the Thanksgiving turkey. "

"I'm sure Dennis and Thelma will turn it into something wonderful," said Treasure, shifting the little girl's weight.

"You brought your ducks?" said Dawn, incredulously. "I thought you were saving those for a special occasion."

"Well now, a snowstorm in Vegas?" said Don. "That's pretty special."

· · · · · · · · · · · · · · · · · · ·

Bonnie had the kids all sitting in rows in the lunchroom. She stood in front of them, lecturing. "Despite the unusual circumstances, all school rules will still be in force tonight," she said. "You may not leave this room. You may not run. You may not talk. All your parents have been contacted. We will eat and then go to bed," she said.

"You've got to be kidding me!" bellowed Octavio, jumping up from his seat. Treasure's little pigtail girl started to wail again. "I want my mommy," she cried. A few of the others joined in. Treasure pursed her lips. Beside her, Dawn growled like a bulldog. She and Treasure exchanged a glance, and in that one glance, they staged a coup. Bonnie would be deposed without her even knowing it.

Dawn grabbed Aussie, "Go to the front desk and page your mother with an urgent message. Just make something up."

"Got it," said Aussie, sprinting.

Treasure stopped to comfort crying students as Dawn edged her way up to the front.

"Now, if you have questions, or need to use the restroom, you may raise your hands," said Bonnie, straightening her glasses. Several hands went up.

Just then, Aussie's voice crackled over the PA system. "Bonnie Baumgartner, there is a matter at the front desk that needs your attention," she said, manufacturing as much urgency as she could in her voice.

Bonnie couldn't resist the call of duty, not even for fun-squelching. "What now?" she asked, feigning exasperation as she hustled up the aisle.

Treasure winked at Dawn, and Dawn slid into position at the front.

"You can just forget everything Ms. Baumgartner said. We're going to have some fun," Dawn said. She turned toward Treasure and tossed her the keys to her classroom closet. "Miss Treasure, would you please walk back into my room and grab my kickballs, and anything else we need out of my closet?"

Treasure nodded and motioned to Octavio to follow her. Together they flew to Dawn's room where they grabbed four balls, a roll of tape, three jump ropes, and all the candy they could find in Dawn's stash: M&M's, Reese's Pieces, and chocolate-covered pretzels. Treasure stuck the candy in a bag, and then they jogged back to the cafeteria.

Dawn had already had the students clear away the tables and chairs. "Hey, Mrs. Robbins," said Octavio, throwing a ball at Dawn. "Think fast."

Dawn caught the ball without blinking. "Let's start off with eating candy. Who would like to help Miss Treasure pass out treats?"

Every hand went in the air. Treasure selected six helpers and supervised the doling out of sugar, which the kids scarfed immediately. Everyone's mood seemed to brighten as they ate.

Dawn clapped her hands to regain the students' attention. "Okay, kids, tonight we're hosting the biggest, baddest Four Square tournament in the city of Las Vegas. Are you ready?" she barked. A bunch of the older boys jumped up and started moving tables. Don grabbed Treasure's masking tape and started marking out courts.

"But I don't like Four Square," wailed Miss Pigtails. She put her head down on her arms.

"Do you like jump rope?" Treasure asked. "I just need two spinners and we can start jumping."

The little girl raised her head from the crook of her elbow. "Can I turn with you?" she asked. Treasure offered her the end of one of the jump ropes. She grabbed it and hopped up.

Within ten minutes, Dawn and Treasure had every kid involved in either jump rope or Four Square. The cacophony of thumping balls, whirring ropes, and laughing greeted Aussie when she came back into the lunchroom.

She sidled up to Treasure and whispered in her ear. "I told her that she needed to alert Uncle Bob about our situation. She's got him on the phone, talking his ear off about emergency procedures. It should keep her busy for a while."

"Great," said Treasure, turning the rope. She glanced around the room to discover the location of the other grown-ups. The bus driver was refereeing a heated Four Square match between four sixth-grade boys.

Dawn was walking toward jump rope central. "I've got Don taking a group down to the bathrooms," she said. "This should entertain them until dinner, I hope."

"That's what I was just going to check on," said Treasure, handing her end of the rope to Aussie mid-twirl.

Aussie took the rope without breaking rhythm. "Be careful around Dennis. Don't do anything stupid," she hissed at Treasure. "Remember that my mom is here. And if I'm on the jump rope crew, I won't be able to protect you."

Treasure smiled at her sadly. "There's nothing to protect. We broke up."

Aussie dropped the rope, making the jumper squeal. "This is a do-over," yelled the third-grader. "It's her fault I messed up," she said, pointing at Aussie.

"My bad," said Aussie, starting to twirl again. "When did you break up?" she asked Treasure.

"About three weeks ago," said Treasure, suddenly tired. Neither of them remembered that Dawn was standing right next to them, and Dawn could not remain quiet any longer.

She grabbed Treasure by the shoulder. "You," she said, her eyebrows shooting off her head. "You and Dennis Cameron! Together?" She lowered her voice.

Treasure smiled again and started walking away. "Not anymore," she said, pushing on the door to the kitchen.

Dawn and Aussie looked at each other openmouthed but for different reasons.

"Now we're doing hot peppers," one of the little girls said to Aussie. Aussie shut her mouth and started spinning the rope faster.

When Treasure looked in the kitchen, she saw Thelma rolling out dough, her arms covered in flour. Dennis was adjusting the heat on two steaming pots on the stove.

"Do you need any help?" she asked, stepping inside the door.

Thelma looked up. "Ask the mad scientist," she said, making a face.

Dennis looked at Treasure and smiled. He felt the stress fade back a little bit. She was as comforting to him as homemade pie. "I think I've got it under control," he said as he lifted a lid on one of the pans.

"What are you up to?" Treasure asked, coming closer to him.

"Some wild idea that I don't approve of," said Thelma, pounding the dough with her fists.

Dennis shook off her comment and turned back to Treasure. With his eyes, he pleaded for her to believe in him. "I'm making turducken," he said.

"Turducken?" asked Treasure.

"It's a chicken stuffed in a duck stuffed in a turkey," said Thelma, starting to pat her dough into roll shapes.

"It's reverse deconstructed turducken," said Dennis. "See, we don't have enough of any one of our ingredients to make a full meal for the kids. But we have a lot of chicken, a couple of ducks, and a little bit of leftover turkey. So I'm going to put turkey inside the duck, then put the duck inside the chicken breast."

Treasure cocked her head. "Wouldn't that be chiduckey then, rather than turducken?"

Dennis stifled a laugh. "I may have to copyright that. I'll brown each ingredient individually, then roll it together, then flour it, then panfry it. We'll serve it with the carrots I'm glazing and sweet potato fries. "

"Soup," said Thelma. "I wanted to make soup. But I got overruled," she said, slapping her rolls into a pan.

Treasure had to make a choice. Sure the kids might eat (and recognize) soup better than chiduckey, but one look at Dennis and her mangled heart started to thump wildly. In that moment, she knew that she would personally eat every bite of chiduckey that he made. She would lick every plate clean.

"This man is an Iron Chef," said Treasure. "And today, this is his kitchen stadium."

With those words, Treasure Blume chased doubt out of Dennis's mind. He loved this woman. He loved her, loved her, loved her. The strength of his emotion nearly overpowered him. "You could peel the yams," he said, forgetting for a minute that he had just done that.

"Already cooking," said Thelma, shoving her rolls into a hot oven.

"Then I'll do whatever else you need," Treasure said, lifting her face toward Dennis.

Dennis knew she was offering more than just her cooking skills. He closed the gap between them in two strides. "Then just forgive me. I was an idiot. I don't ever want to be without you again," he said. "I don't care what anyone else thinks."

And with that, he wrapped his arms around her and whispered three words in her ear, the three words that both Grammy Blume and his mother had claimed that he felt. But somehow, hearing it from him, Treasure could finally believe it. She answered back with the same words.

Thelma kept cooking. She took out one pan of rolls and put in another. She kept her eyes on her own station, but a blush crept up her cheeks. "Must be the heat," she muttered. She finally looked over in their direction, just before Treasure's lips connected with Dennis's. "I'd turn down those carrots if I were you. Otherwise, they'll boil over."

. . . .

After the championship game of Four Square, Dennis, Thelma, and Treasure served dinner.

Don raved over the chiduckey. "My compliments to the chef. Why, I'm proud to have donated my ducks to this. I'd order this at a restaurant," he said, wiping the gravy off his mustache. Several kids asked for seconds. Treasure didn't hear one complaint.

"This just proves that everything tastes good fried," Thelma assessed, nudging Dennis with her shoulder when the two of them finally sat down to eat.

"Seriously, you've got to add this to the menu," said Dawn, carving up her last bite. "It beats rib-e-ques hands down." Then she turned to the students. "Let's hear it for tonight's chef, Mr. Dennis Cameron!" she shouted. The kids clapped and yelled.

Dennis stood up and bowed. "I owe it all to my lovely assistants," he said, indicating Thelma and Treasure. And if he only looked at Treasure when he talked, Thelma decided that he didn't mean to slight her. It was the way things were with people in love.

At 9:30, Treasure, Dawn, and Aussie were trying to settle the kids down for the night. It was not an easy job. To start off, Treasure organized a game for them, complete with a map and clues, that led them through the bathroom, then over to the library to pick out a couple of bedtime stories, and finally over to Dawn and Don's pile of blankets. Once everyone had gone potty, picked a book, and selected a blanket, Dawn turned the lights down and started reading a story up at the front. The kids still couldn't calm down. One little boy punched everyone around him until Aussie got him to play tic-tac-toe with her. Another kept running in dizzy circles until Treasure captured him. And most of the kids seemed near tears, missing their mommies, their own beds, and their toothbrushes. Treasure soothed, patted, and comforted as best she could. She looked for Dennis but only caught glimpses. Once he blew her a kiss as he patrolled the halls with Don for stragglers. But they had to be careful. Bonnie still manned the office up front. A few intrepid parents had braved the storm in search of their kids, and Bonnie was reuniting the groups. But the storm was growing worse. The last parent through the doors had decided to stay at the school rather than brave the roads again.

It took over an hour and four bedtime stories before anyone started to drift off. In the quiet, Treasure picked her way among the children, stopping here and there to rearrange blankets. Octavio had snuggled down like an owl in a burrow. She gave him a soft pat on his bushy head and then stole out of the cafeteria. She headed back toward Operation Headquarters, where Bonnie was checking the weather on her computer. She had retreated there after she discovered that she had been deposed as despot. In fact she seemed relieved.

"Everyone secure?" asked Bonnie as Treasure rounded the corner into the office. "And you have the first watch, right?"

"Yes. I just wish I was Albus Dumbledore and could wave a wand and have pillows and sleeping bags magically appear," said Treasure.

"Who?" asked Bonnie, with a blank stare.

"You know. Dumbledore. From *Harry Potter?*"

Bonnie humphed. "I don't read fiction. It's a waste."

"See, I think the world would be a waste without fiction," said Treasure, her eyes full of light. "When I was a teenager, fiction is what kept me going. The real world was too harsh and nasty."

"Well, if you don't learn to deal with harsh and nasty as a teenager, you won't be prepared," announced Bonnie decisively. She scrolled down the page. "They say they'll be able to reopen our road sometime tomorrow morning," she said.

"Sometimes I think I was too prepared for the real world. I can hardly believe it when something good happens to me," said Treasure, thinking of Dennis.

The lights bounced off Bonnie's glasses.

Treasure remembered who she was talking to. "I just hope my cat's all right," she said, trying to fill time and prevent Bonnie from hunting down the reason that she seemed so happy.

"You have a cat?" asked Bonnie, picking up her mug from the desk and examining it.

"Yes," said Treasure. "I've had Howls for three years now. I hope he's okay."

Bonnie turned her mug around so that Treasure could see the front. It had a picture of Bonnie hugging a hairless alien cat. "This is Dinka," she said, pointing at the cat. "I've had him for almost ten years. He's one of my studs."

Treasure was clearly expected to comment on Dinka. "He has such expressive eyes," she said.

Bonnie nodded, turning the mug around so she could look at Dinka. "You know, that's what the judges say about him every time. And he has great confirmation and perfectly spaced ears. Not to mention how well behaved he is. You couldn't find a more obedient Sphynx in the world."

Treasure was amazed to hear Bonnie's voice cloud with emotion as she spoke about Dinka. "How long have you been breeding cats?" she asked politely.

Bonnie paused for a minute and set down her mug. She turned back to the screen. "Since my husband left me. And that was when Aussie was a baby. After he left, it was something we did together, raising and training those cats. We'd go to a show every weekend. Aussie became one of the top junior handlers in Clark County. I thought she could go national, and I pushed her hard. But then she hit puberty, and it was like she just became a different person."

Well, now Treasure understood Aussie's animosity toward cats. She decided to sidestep. "You know, Aussie is a tremendous girl," Treasure said. "She's been so good through all this. She jumped rope with the kids, teaching them how to double Dutch. And then later, when one of the little boys started crying, Aussie let him use her phone to call home and talk with his mom. Then she held him on her lap until he went to sleep. I don't know many teenagers that would have done that."

"The biggest problem I ever had with Dinka was ear mites," said Bonnie. "But with Aussie, it's been ditching school, and shoplifting, and pothead boyfriends, and navel piercings." She shook her head and said stiffly, "I'm glad you think well of her. I just don't know what to do with her anymore."

"I think you just have to love her," said Treasure, who, as of tonight, thought that love was the answer to every problem.

"Now that's some sort of romantic notion. And I am not a romantic."

"Neither am I," said Treasure. "But I think it would go a long way with Aussie."

"When she started to go wild, no one told me. I was just so in the dark. If I had known what was happening in the beginning, I might have . . ." Bonnie's words trailed off into silence.

"Might have what?" Treasure prompted.

"I don't know. Been able to stop her, to put her on a better course."

For the first time, Treasure thought about Bonnie as a person rather than a demon, someone who loved her daughter and her cats and wanted the best for them but was unable to make that happen. With a start, she suddenly saw herself in the person before her—someone who had substituted cats for people because people were too unpredictable, someone who had given up on the idea of love and its power to transform everything. She felt a rush of gratitude for Grammy and her goat lectures, for Dennis and his declaration tonight, for all the people in her life who kept pushing her toward people, telling her not to give up.

And she wouldn't give up. She thought about Liwayway and how even Dawn doubted she'd ever find her again. In that moment, Treasure Blume made a decision. She squared her shoulders. She knew what she had to do. Quickly, she explained Liwayway's absences to Bonnie, and her fears that the family had wound up in worse circumstances because of Treasure's interference.

Bonnie looked in Treasure's eyes, and for the first time, Treasure could see a glimpse of the real Bonnie buried deep down in: the one who wished she could have helped her daughter before trouble pitched its tent on her lawn. She opened a file and dug out several papers. "Normally,

I'd say you should alert the authorities, but in this case, I think the best you can do is contact someone at the homeless shelter. I have a friend who works there, and she might be a good first contact. I have some info here on helping them get into temporary housing. Let me give you her number," she said, scanning through the papers.

"Right," said Treasure, exhaling loudly.

Bonnie tapped Treasure's hand with one finger. "She's a lucky girl to have you looking out for her," she said.

As Treasure bent over the papers, Bonnie considered her for a moment. She still didn't agree with her outrageous teaching methods. But tonight made her reconsider her opinion of Treasure Blume. She had stayed when Lucinda had bailed. And after all, someone who loved cats couldn't be all bad.

. . . .

Snowplows had the road to the school open the next morning by 5:00 a.m. Thelma took off just after. Parents started arriving at 5:30. At 6:00, a local TV crew had dropped by to interview students and teachers about the ordeal, and Bonnie became the public face of Elbert Edwards Elementary School. Dawn and Don slipped out after the last parents showed up. By 7:30, only Bonnie, Aussie, Treasure, and Dennis were left. Bonnie was on the phone, doing a radio interview, so she didn't notice Dennis sneak his arm around Treasure as they walked out to the parking lot. Aussie witnessed it and blocked her mom's view, just in case she happened to glance up.

It was the first time that Dennis and Treasure had been alone together. Treasure was exhausted. Several of the kids had woken up in the night. The heat had gone off around two and the outside chill began to seep through the building. Treasure had spent hours holding the kids, listening to them talk, and singing them lullabies. But oddly, as she stood squinting at the rising sun, she didn't feel tired. Instead, she felt light, like she might drift up toward the sky if Dennis didn't hold on to her.

Dennis looked at Treasure and marveled at how lucky he was to have her back in his life. He'd watched her all night as she tended and comforted, and he'd never thought she was more beautiful, not even when she danced with the Steppers or ate dinner in Liwayway's hut. She didn't complain or declare that she needed a break (as both Dawn and Bonnie had done). Instead she turned a potentially frightening episode into a memorable, exciting party for every kid there. He was a little in awe of her.

"You know, the kids really loved it when you did that treasure hunt with them, you know with the map and the clues. Did you have that planned, or did you just come up with it?" he asked, wanting to stretch this moment out as long as he could.

Treasure shrugged. The snowflakes kept getting caught in her eyelashes. "I just threw it together."

Dennis looked sideways at her. "Pretty ironic, don't you think, for a girl named Treasure?"

Treasure rolled her eyes and began to recite, as if she were recording a message for an answering machine. "For the three hundredth time in my life, I would like to point out that I did not select my own name. Please forward all complaints or declarations of irony to my parents. Really, in my family, I'm lucky I didn't end up as Utahna or Hardworker or Agapanthus, or something like that."

Dennis couldn't help himself. He kissed her. Hard.

All thoughts of the Blume family naming traditions scattered out of Treasure's head. When they broke apart, the cold air stung her lungs, whipping away any words she might have said.

Dennis took a step back, so that he could look at her. "I like your name. It rings true. You wouldn't be you without it. Because of you, I've found hidden treasures everywhere."

As he spoke, she came to the realization that he had just kissed her for the first time since they broke up. She wanted to dissolve, the way Jell-O does in warm water, but she didn't dare. He could still walk away. She drew a jagged breath, afraid to show him how his words thrilled her, from her cockles to her ankles. If she kept it light, he might stay here in this moment. If she got all serious, he might run again. So she reacted to the corniness of his last line. "Is that from a fortune cookie?" she teased.

Dennis laughed. "It's possible. You know how I love New Fong's." He paused and twined his fingers in hers. "Let me ask you something. Do we have to carry on the crazy naming thing with our own kids? Can't we just name them something like Judy or Dana?"

"First of all, we can't name anyone Judy, because then her name would be Judy Blume. And second . . . Wait! What did you just say?

That we'll be having kids of our own? Does that mean . . . ?" Treasure felt dizzy. This conversation was happening too fast for her to keep up. Twenty-four hours before, she wasn't even part of his present, let alone his future. Could this man that she loved really be suggesting what he seemed to be suggesting?

"First of all, when we get married, you take my last name, not vice versa, so it would be Judy Cameron, not Judy Blume. Who is Judy Blume?" Dennis asked, wiping a snowflake off Treasure's nose.

"She wrote *Tales of a Fourth Grade Nothing*, and *Superfudge*. If you were an elementary school teacher, you'd know," said Treasure, deciding not to take him seriously.

"My mistake. And second, yes, I said have kids, get married, the full meal deal."

"The full meal deal?"

"A protein, two sides, and a dairy product. You'd know that if you were a lunch lady," said Dennis, cupping her face in his hands.

Treasure looked into Dennis's bright blue eyes. The wind whipped around them. "You want to have kids with me?" she asked breathlessly.

Dennis laughed. "Yes. I want to marry you and raise children with you. We do live in Las Vegas. I say, let's roll those genetic dice."

Treasure couldn't wrap her head around what was happening. Was she really standing in a Vegas Winter Wonderland? Was Dennis Cameron really proposing to her and talking about having children?

"But my curse . . ." she said slowly.

"You mean gift," said Dennis, kissing each of her fingers individually.

"Our kids could inherit it," Treasure said, struggling to think clearly.

Dennis Cameron laughed and looked into her eyes. He could see the soft petals of the golden inner ring. "Then they'll be blessed," he said. "Just like their mother."

Treasure couldn't answer. She hugged Dennis tightly. They looked out on the perfect, clean, dazzling blanket of white that had transformed the barrenness of their city. Then together, they got in Dennis's car and pulled out, leaving fresh tracks.

Acknowledgments

THIS BOOK IS THE PRODUCT OF YEARS OF TEARS AND LAUGHTER. LIKE Treasure, I have my own supporting cast of characters who helped me and encouraged me. They made this book a reality. I can't thank each of you enough.

To my friend, Debbie Harrison, for editing the book, and encouraging me to keep going even when I was ready to give up.

To my sister Anne, for inspiring me with all of your horrible first date stories.

To my sister Elaine, for giving the Lunch Daddy his soul, and for accompanying me on many ugly sweater quests. We write at midnight!

To my father, Philip, for tirelessly reading my first draft, for surrounding me with words and books, and for exemplifying kindness in all that you do.

To my mother, Cheryl—who is both an outstanding writer and an inspiring teacher. You taught me everything I know. I would never have been able to do either without your example.

To my daughters, Sela and Sasha, for reminding me of the joys and pains of elementary school, and bringing sunshine into the grayest of days.

To my husband, Griffin, for believing in me, and for making dinner all the nights that I was writing. No one has done more to bring Treasure Blume to life than you (except me). I love you.

Discussion Questions

1. Grammy Blume believes in the family gift passed down from her ancestor, but Treasure's mother doesn't. Is the gift real or imagined?

2. In what way is Treasure's curse a gift? Have you ever had something in your life that you thought was a curse, but turned out to be a gift?

3. Grammy tells Treasure that she is "old at heart." What does it mean to be "old at heart"? How do the ideas of youth and aging play in this book?

4. Dennis decides that it is more important to take a job at the school cafeteria in order to be near Micaela and his mother than to pursue his dreams of becoming a well-known chef. Have you ever had to sacrifice a dream?

5. Every time Treasure reaches out to someone, she knows that she will initially be rejected. And yet, she still reaches out. How hard is it to reach out to others?

6. Why does Dennis struggle with the idea that everyone hates Treasure? Thelma tells him that it doesn't matter what anyone else thinks. Does Dennis believe her? How much do other people's opinions affect you?

7. As a teenager, Aussie experiences the full measure of Treasure's gift, but she eventually becomes her friend. Why does Aussie decide to

help Treasure? How are they able to build a friendship, despite Treasure's gift?

8. How is Dennis's mother able to overcome Treasure's gift when she first meets her? How does Dennis feel that meeting went?

9. Treasure's passion is teaching, Grammy's passion is dancing, and Dennis's passion is cooking. What is your medium of self-expression? What activity makes you feel most alive?

10. Grammy Blume talks to Dennis about how Treasure worked a "resurrection" on her, forcing her out of her chair and into the world. Have you ever experienced a "resurrection" moment?

11. When Grammy starts training for the competitive gift wrapping tournament, she practices by gift wrapping everyday items like socks, canned food, and even Howls. How does seeing everyday items wrapped as gifts affect Treasure? How does Grammy's new hobby help Treasure to heal from her break-up with Dennis?

12. Why does Dennis decide that he can handle the challenges of Treasure's gift? How does spending the night in a snowstorm at an elementary school prompt Dennis to propose? What do you think will happen next?

About the Author

Photo by Kelli West

LISA RUMSEY HARRIS GREW UP WRITING STORIES AND RIDING HORSES in Southeastern Idaho. She received a bachelor's and master's degree in English from Brigham Young University, where she now teaches writing classes. She lives in Orem, Utah, with her ancient Siamese cat, her husband (who cooks nearly as well as Dennis) and her two adorable daughters. When Lisa began writing this book, her oldest daughter was in first grade. Her youngest daughter finished first grade this year. As a writer, Lisa writes short stories, essays, and even cowboy poetry. She won the Brookie and D. K. Brown Memorial Fiction contest with her short story, "Topless in Elko." In 2005, her short story "The Resurrection of the Bobcat" won a Moonstone Award in the same contest. Her essay "Honor in the Ordinary" won the Heather Campbell Essay contest in 2006, and was published in *Segullah*.